GREEN

BY SHAREEKA ELLIOTT

Green
By Shareeka Elliott

ISBN: 979-8-9852060-0-5
Copyright 2021 @ Dynamic Image Publications, LLC

Manufactured in the United States of America

First and foremost, I am grateful to God that I have this gift. I'm both humbled and excited to share it with others for Your glory.

To Mommy, thank you for everything. You are truly the best and I won't let you forget it.

To Aalisha and Melissa, you're my reason each and every time.

To Janaya Middleton, thank you for being a consultant at the beginning of my rewrite. Your advice went far. I love you!

Thanks are also in order for Jacqueline Fuentes-Santana for consulting as well. Te quiero!

I'd be remiss if I didn't mention Lisa Harvey in the dedication of my very first book. My first beta reader and cowriter. My first friend beyond the boundaries of New York City. I've already told you this a million times and I'll tell you this again. You are a gift. Thank you for always speaking life and encouragement as well as bearing your gentle critique when you thought it best. I appreciate you.

To the Dynamic Image team, the friendship and sisterhood I share with you cannot be measured in value. I love you all and pray our journey continues.

To Christian Cashelle, there aren't enough people like you in the world. Your vision and your obedience to the call is the very reason I'm able to see this dream of mine through. I'm thankful everyday that you tapped me to be a part of your team. I'm with you until the wheels fall off. Prayfully they don't.

To all of my family, near and far! This one's for you!

This dedication also goes out to everyone and anyone who can identify with Christian Adams. I pray like Ms. Adams that you persevere through the pain and learn that it is okay to let go, heal, and enjoy happiness anew. I hope that the story both enlightens and enthralls you. I hope that most of all, it changes you for the better.

Chapter
One

It'd been a calm morning despite the constant blaring of horns from car to car driving into downtown Atlanta. The air was light, belying a humid day to come. The skies were blue with nary a cloud in the sky. Christian Adams enjoyed the backdrop of the perfect canvas the sky made as she tapped her freshly painted nails on her dashboard. The calm allowed her mind to focus as she contemplated her moves for the day.

Pushing into the beginning of the summer quarter, things were going well. She couldn't complain about the progress of several new accounts her company garnered from different corporate bodies. A couple of Hawks players were having preliminary meetings with some of her staff as well. She wondered if she needed to give her Controller and best friend, Sharin, some time off to prepare for her wedding but thought better of it. She needed her and hoped that she could manage the stress of both the business and her upcoming nuptials.

If not, that would force Christian to either temporarily take it over herself or she'd have to hire someone to take over in Sharin's stead. Sharin was the best- and only-Controller she's ever had and her department ran excellently. As far as Christian was concerned, her friend had a place to work with her until she decided to resign or retire. She didn't want to upset any other employee from having the taste of being a Partner and losing it in a matter of months with only a pat on the back.

Stuck on Peachtree Street, she grinned, thinking it got no better than days like the one she was having although it hadn't started yet. Sure, she was a little stressed at having to get through the many meetings scheduled but it was just a regular day in the life. Christian remembered praying for the days when she ran her own business as well as her own life. From the moment she'd realized freedom from her parent's household she promised herself she'd make the best of it, even on her worst days. So far, she couldn't complain.

Before long the traffic gave way, allowing her to drive further into the city and towards the building that she and her team owned outright. She drove up to it, smiling as the name *Adam's Accounting* came into view. She almost sped up, excitement to get through her working day bubbling up in her, until she saw the growing crowd in front of her place of business.

"What the hell?"

Christian slowed to a halt behind a WAGA-TV van and felt her face harden as she took in the scene before her. A slim, delicate white woman recited her story as a group of people took candid shots of the building and an entire crew huddled around the woman as she relayed a story of possible embezzlement.

Hearing the words made Christian's body go into a state of shock as she tried to piece together what was going on. Before anything made much sense, more vans pulled up to her work place except some of the people that hopped out of the vans came with less equipment and bodies than their FOX News' competitor. The accusations and rumblings in the crowd disturbed her so badly that she hopped out of her red Cadillac ATS coupe, strutting purposely through the crowd. What she thought had been a boss move on her part had been the worst mistake she'd made to date.

The newscasters ran to her as fast as they'd made her.

"Ms. Adams, is it true that you're a part of an embezzlement ring?"

"Ms. Adams, is it true that you've stolen over ten million dollars from King Tires' enterprises?"

"Mr. King has stated that he's suing you for damages, would you like to respond, Ms. Adams?"

"Ms. Adams, how can you steal money from the people who've made this establishment what it is?"

The questions came rapid fire from every direction and the normally stalwart woman found herself, for the first time in her life, as a deer caught in the headlights. She felt the heat of the cameras sear into her red skin tone, pinking her flesh. As the questions made themselves clearer in her brain, Christian felt herself shaking even more, totally caught off guard by the scene that was occurring. Even with that much happening, she realized a bevy of microphones were pointed in her direction, the rabid newscasters awaiting her response to their many inquiries.

"I have no knowledge of any embezzlement transpiring in my company. I believe you have it all wrong."

"Evander King is preparing to sue you for fifteen million dollars stolen. Are you really going to deny you and your company's involvement in the matter?"

Christian looked to her left from where the voice came from and saw a black newscaster and found herself boiling inside. It was always the sisters who were more willing to tear down the character of other sisters before white people even started. That alone reddened her tone even more. Christian opened her mouth to respond when she felt herself being pulled backward and a swarm of men rushed ahead of her, motioning the media heads away.

"You shouldn't even have spoken with them that long."

Christopher Langley's voice grated in her ear. Christian was so grateful she wanted to give him a raise. She bit down on her lip before making the pronouncement however, wondering how he'd gotten to her as fast as he had.

"How'd you-"

"A thank you would be nice," Christopher quipped, a smirk in his voice as he motioned for Christian to enter the building past his other personnel.

Christian turned around as she watched her head of security double back and head outside into the fray to oversee the fracas happening right outside of her building. She shuddered, the memory of the questions finally taking root into her mind and making her queasy at the same time.

"Embezzlement? What the-"

"Christian! Move!"

She was knocked outside of her reverie by Christopher once more. Hearing the sharp command made her come to herself and smart at his tone. Considering the situation, she sucked it up and went upstairs. Christian did pay him to keep her and her building safe. With that much sorted out in her brain, she walked past the security checkpoint and deeper into the building.

At the elevators she started to tremble, still lost as to why her company was being framed and was trying to be hopeful that it was a joke at the end of the day. The charges that were hurled at her in the front of the building were devastating and the rumors alone could hurt her business. The acknowledgement of that much bought on a low grade headache. She breathed in and out, trying to calm her nerves as the bell dinged to the top floor.

She was greeted by Tiffany Hart, who stood up from her desk as soon as Christian entered the foyer of her office floor. Normally, the sight of the marble floors and floor-to-ceiling windows on either side would brighten her day but at the moment Christian found it hard to concentrate.

"Brown called," Tiffany announced. "I have conference room B set up. The Partners are waiting for you downstairs."

"Send a call to give me ten minutes. I'll be there shortly."

Christian walked through the double doors of her sprawling office and closed them. When she heard the click of the doors, she started to pace back and forth, recapturing the moment.

"Embezzlement ring? How is that even possible?"

Christian stalked back and forth and left and right, taking deep breaths every time the scene before her business started to overwhelm her again. None of it made sense and that much was upsetting her even more as precious minutes ticked by. She would've paced for fifteen minutes had she not caught the look on her face in her window's reflection. The horror she saw stopped her short. A mental check brought her back to her senses.

"Christian, stop it," she reprimanded. "Worrying isn't going to change this. Go in there, face your staff, and ask them what the hell is going on."

Still, she took deep breaths until her heart was as calm as she could get it. She went to grab for her Louis Vuitton Neverfull and forgot she'd left it in her car when she hopped out without thinking. Dread sunk in momentarily thinking she couldn't yet face an angry crowd if they were still outside of her establishment.

Christian stepped out of her office, facing Tiffany again.

"Tiff, see to it that Christopher grabs my bag from my car and locks the door. I'm heading to the conference room now."

"Got'cha. What about these calls coming in?"

"Hold them off. I'll get to them at some point in the day."

"Evander King has been calling non-stop."

Christian had been walking towards the elevator again when Tiffany made the statement. The sentence halted her as she remembered the name that was being thrown around outside.

"Tell Mr. King that he can come in tomorrow morning and speak to me

3

personally. Otherwise, I'm not available to speak with him right now."

Tiffany nodded her head silently, thankful to be armed with a response to give the man. Christian read her secretary's relief and sighed, already seeing that the man was giving her a hard time. She was surprised he hadn't shown up to the office yet to raise a ruckus.

Stepping onto the elevator, Christian silently prayed that a quick solution would be found to the problem.

Her prayer went unanswered.

Chapter
Two

It hadn't taken long for the police to show up and present an arrest warrant to Christopher as they stormed through the building. The forensics team Lieutenant demanded to be led to the wing where Jupiter Classon and Jamie Phillips were. Hearing the name of his young niece rang wrong to Christopher and he'd been vocal about the fact that they had their facts wrong. His niece was building her career and was only a junior accountant. She was a recent graduate of Clark Atlanta and he'd gotten her the job through much begging and pleading to Christian and then Sharin. She complained day in and out about her job and about her boss, Jupiter.

Those were his thoughts in the midst of the lieutenant threatening to arrest him. When the threat reached his brain, he cursed lowly but turned to lead the team to where they needed to go.

Christian had actually been the easier person to convince. It was Sharin who was particularly hard to get through to. She was a very meticulous Partner, working tirelessly to make sure her team provided excellence. Although she was an heiress, she worked like she had something to prove. More often than not it was a silent understanding that Sharin ran a tight ship. The Small Businesses wing was Christian's pride and joy and Sharin would have it no different.

Not that the other wings were slackers. Christopher just had an easier relationship with Sharin than the other Partners. What he thought would be an easy way in for his niece to gain job experience and then advance on to a Big 4 firm if she so chose was done in love. At the very moment he was leading the policemen to her demise, his stomach turned on him in more ways than one. If he hadn't had any idea what Christian was going through, he had a full bird's eye view in that moment.

As far as Jupiter, he wasn't shocked about her involvement but still disappointed.

Christopher led the small band to the office wing and took in the look on his niece's face when she in turn saw the police approaching. He read the shock, then read the terror, and then the acceptance. His heart broke as one of the woman officers laid a hand on her shoulder, gently forcing her to stand to her feet. His heart broke further as her rights were read to her and the silent tears came when Jamie made eye contact with him. Christioher read her shame and turned his face away. Her sobs were heard as she was led outside of the office. It was enough for him to turn to Jupiter whose face read contempt for the fact that she was caught.

"You bitch!" he felt himself screaming, as a male officer started to escort her away from her desk. "*You* pulled my baby into this! This is *your* fault!"

Jupiter smirked as she was led away. "No, this is all *her* fault."

Jupiter's head nodded toward Sharin who rushed into the scene, looking distraught. Her gaze turned to Christopher's even as she watched her senior accountant get pushed out of the room. Both Sharin and Christopher stepped outside of the room to watch the twosome be escorted out of the building.

"She's right, you know. This shit *is* your fault. You knew this broad was no good and you haven't thought once to put her on suspension *or* fire her."

Sharin sighed, turning her face to her normally logical friend. She wanted to lash back at him but thought the better of it. It was already heavy on her mind that the forensics team might come after her next. She was certain there might be penalty from Christian except she hadn't not once caught any discrepancies in the books for King's Tires. Jupiter rarely, if ever, made a mistake and she was by far the best on her team of senior accountants. Sharin knew of the fact that she wanted to make Partner. She also shrugged off those concerns because as much as they bothered her, she couldn't very well fire the woman over her personal ambitions. Jealousy and envy were barely any basis to fire the woman on. Especially if up to the point they were standing in, she'd always made her look good.

"Christopher, there was no reason for me to ever put her on suspension. And to fire her? All that would do is bring about a court war that we didn't need."

"Oh, so keep her around, knowing she was a piece of shit?"

"Like I *stated before* Christopher, we had no real reason. Her believing that she would have made a better Partner than me was hardly a reason. For me to fire her based on her personal beliefs would have been inane and stupid. She was the best. The very best and before this moment I didn't have a real issue with her. So stop while you're ahead."

Sharin's tone had gotten tighter the more she bore her case to Christopher. The latter eyed Sharin and all the vitriol he wanted to spew was in his eyes. It was enough for Sharin's back to go ramrod stiff as she marched to the office door that bared her namesake. The slamming of the door was the exclamation point that let Christopher know that she was thoroughly pissed off. Of course, that mattered to him none as his niece was being hauled off to prison because of her actions.

Picking up the small signage on Jupiter's desk that bared her name on it, he tossed it to the floor in utter disgust. Without another word, he stalked out of the room. Despite his own duress, Christopher had to make sure the rest of the building was secured. He had to live with the fact that his niece's face would play on repeat on every channel for days to come.

As soon as Christian stepped into the conference room, her anger and ire came back full force as Jasmine was the first one she saw.

Jasmine Brown was a lawyer who represented many big names in Atlanta.

She doubled as a public relations expert whose life's work was spinning a bad story into a fairy tale. She was surprised when she'd gotten the call from Christian's assistant. She'd done some light PR work with them in the past but highly doubted the accounting maven would ever need her help to dig her out of a bad space. Christian Adams and her company's name were the epitome of squeaky clean.

"What the hell is going on?!" Christian yelled, pacing back and forth. "I need answers and I need them immediately!"

"Christian, you have to calm down first. I'm not about to start relaying anything to you while you're in this mood."

"I don't understand what other mood there could be right now with news vans outside of my place of business and a bunch of people accusing us of embezzlement!"

"If you'll have a seat, Ms. Adams, I'll tell you."

Christian took a deep breath and sat at the head of the long oak wooden table. Her Partners, Sharin Reynolds, Monica James, and Sonya Powers sat on opposing sides from one another. Jasmine watched Christian, reading her mood. When she was satisfied that Christian was calm enough, she continued.

"So, long story short, somebody's been siphoning monies from King's Tires for upwards two years. Between him and a couple other accounts you have here, you have yourself an embezzlement ring operating under your nose."

"Girl, what?" Christian said. "How is this possible?"

"Easily. The senior accountant pockets monies from the client. The senior accountant hands over their amended statements to the junior accountant to compile any and all financial statements for the billing cycle. Sharin checks in on the clients, trusting that her team has everything running smoothly. Everything balances out on paper so she's none the wiser as she checks everything off. So far, a total of more than fifteen million has been stolen from Evander King. He wants to see you and this company disbarred from my understanding of his lawyer."

Christian began reconsidering what she thought of her friend being the best Partner she had. It was Sharin's job to oversee that every account came back balanced and correct.

"How did you miss any of this?" Christian asked, turning a hard eye to her friend who's face reddened as she looked down. Christian noted that Sharin already took on the blame for the mess that occurred outside. Still, it didn't make her feel any better.

"I don't know, Christian. To my eyes everything was on the up and up."

"Of course, it was," Christian thought. *"Since you've been engaged you more than likely weren't paying close attention the way you should have. Now we have a mess..."*

Christian took in her best friend, dissatisfied with the look of scorn on her face. Christian knew that it was unrealistic for Sharin to catch every instance of fraud. Still, Christian felt as if Sharin was much more thorough of an accountant than to just glean over their accounts and put her stamp of approval on everything. It suddenly made her decision that much more final.

"Christian, you can't ask her that question though," Sonya said. "If you're asking her that, you have to ask us that as well. You need to understand-"

"-you're right and I intend for every single body in this place to get questioned."

"Christian," Jasmine intercepted. "You have to calm down. It's not as bad as it seems. The worst part is that you might need a public relations spin on everything once it's all said and done but this whole mess can be fixed. That's what I'm here for."

Christian sighed. She was suddenly tired and it wasn't yet eleven o'clock in the morning.

"This is bullshit. I don't run my company like this. It's been excellence from day one. Now I have a whole fucking circus outside of my space and not one person knows what the fuck is going on?"

"Jupiter Classon and Jamie Phillips were arrested on my floor this morning," Sharin added. "Atlanta Police Forensics has also bagged the work computers that belong to them."

Christian cursed out loud. "And you're just now telling me?! This is worse than I could have imagined. So, they're the ones stealing from this man?!"

"That's the allegation. Jupiter was in charge of his account and was taking care of his books. Jamie was the one filing the statements under Jupiter's direction."

Christian swore again, tapping her fingers against the wooden table they were all seated at. Sharin moved to speak again but the CEO lifted her hand to cut her off.

"Evander King has been calling to set up a meeting. I'm unsure if making one with him was in our best interests."

"It's not, not without a lawyer present," Monica answered. "I highly doubt that man is trying to reason with us right now."

"Well, I had Tiffany extend the invitation. I'll make sure to have him on record if he says anything slick. More than likely we'll have to pay him, period. I'm just really stressed about the press this is getting."

"This is business, Christian," Sonya said. "These things happen all the time. It just doesn't happen to us."

"It shouldn't have," Christian grated through her teeth. "I hired each and every head here based on knowing you all personally and the high standard of excellence you've demonstrated thus far. All this showed me is that I have an unreliable staff and a Partner that's been lazy up to this point."

Sharin threw her long-time friend and boss a side eye. Between herself and Christopher, she'd already been blaming herself for the mishap. However, to hear her friend place blame on her so openly and brazenly made her back go ramrod stiff again.

"Christian. You've known me for years and you know that I put every bit of blood, sweat, and tears into this company and into your vision. You know that I wouldn't steal or undercut or allow anybody else to do so. Once you finally calm down and look at the books, you'll realize the level of theft we're dealing with. I would *never* have caught that."

Sharin's tone had been passionate and full of heat. She stared into her best friend's eyes as Christian stared back, just as passionately. The two came to a truce in that moment silently as Christian turned away, having to accept her friend's statement. All that she said was fundamentally true. The problem was; however, somebody had stolen under the name of her company and had therefore stolen their good name with it.

"Let's not get too upset. This isn't irreparable damage," Jasmine said, again. "Let's put our energies into fixing this mess. At this point what's done is done and the system is going to handle those responsible how they see fit. As for this business, let's get it back to the once shiny reputation that it's known for."

The more that Jasmine rambled on, the more that Christian felt her shoulders sag. In the ten years since Adams Accounting had been erected, never had there been a question of honor and integrity. Her heart almost couldn't take the fact that her company was already on the news and that she'll more than likely make the evening news looking like a less than capable leader. It was enough to make her vomit.

"Are you even sure we can pull this off?" was Christian's next question.

Monica raised her hand silently.

"We're still courting new accounts and a lot of those deals are starting to funnel through, so all isn't lost. Plus, we have to take into account that we have to pay King back, no matter which way this swings. Ten or fifteen million isn't much in the grand scheme of things, but I think we need to put our energies into clean-up rather than acting like it never happened. If it's not that serious of a problem as Jasmine is inferring, we just need to get some PR work done and push forward."

"Understood," Christian said, standing to her feet. She looked around at every face at the rounded table and for the first time in a long time, felt unsure of herself. She wanted to offer words of reassurance but presently, there were none to offer. "Dismissed...Sharin, let's walk to my office."

Sharin rose a brow but got her thoughts together before picking up her things and following her best friend and Chief Executive Officer out of the door. The rest of the Partners watched the twosome but didn't feel confident of whatever the outcome of the meeting would be. However it went, they hoped that Christian still kept in mind that this was also her best friend and didn't deal with her too harshly.

Chapter
Three

"You're *suspending* me? Christian, what the-"

"Hear me out. I've been thinking about it for a while anyway."

Sharin had been drinking her favorite apple-cinnamon tea to calm her nerves. She knew whatever Christian was going to tell her wouldn't be easy for her to bear. If she thought back over the past couple of weeks, she wouldn't be surprised either. Things had gotten a little tense but Sharin didn't pay much mind to things as she was simply busy. She put her energies into the accounts; double and triple checking what was put before her. If she wasn't making sure every penny was accounted for, she was stressing about her impending wedding. About six months ago she'd gotten engaged to her boyfriend, Maddox Lennox, and the wedding planning was more stressful than she wanted to admit. She was perilously close to throwing it all away and marrying her fiance at the courts, especially with the current events at hand.

"I've been doing that bad of a job and you haven't told me up until this point?" Sharin questioned. "Why would you even wait to have this conversation, Christian?"

Christian swallowed. The meeting from earlier had cemented her decision but it was hard to even answer her friend. Up until this moment there'd been no real reason to question her.

"Honestly, I was wondering if you planning the wedding was adding strain to your position or not. Nothing came up so I was going to leave it alone until it was time for your vacation but as of now, I'm not sure what to think of you if I'm brutally honest."

"Christian, you need to calm down before you call yourself throwing me out on my ass as if I'm a first-year. When I tell you I would've *never* caught those mistakes? I mean, *never*. Up until now we haven't had an issue in this place, but people aren't always honest. They lie, they steal, and if they can get away with things, they will. King only figured out he'd been stolen from because he had an outside auditor."

"I understand what you're saying. Still, until things get cleared up and until you finish getting married, I don't need you at the helm right now."

Sharin raised a brow. "So who's going to take my place?"

"I had Classon in mind until this whole mess. Now the only place I'd like to see Ms. Classon is behind bars and stripped of her certification. I'm sorry you couldn't have fired her before."

Sharin was sure her face was set in stone just listening to her friend spout her nonsense. It'd been a long time since she'd seen Christian Adams afraid but somehow, she knew that's what this was. It was the only reason she hadn't taken things a level higher. If her boss felt she should take the time off to get married, then so be it. She'd take the time off, she'd get married, and afterward she'd happily bang her husband in Mauritius as planned. Maybe if she were extra petty, she'd come back pregnant and hope that Christian sent her along her merry way again to raise her child.

Those responses were brimming on the tip of her tongue but instead she shook her head in disbelief.

"As your colleague, I'm pissed and as your friend, I can't help to say I'm *fucking hurt.* I've been busting my ass for the past couple of months, putting this office before my own wedding planning more than half the time and you would call me lazy and incompetent in front of everybody like I just sit on my ass and scratch it all day. For all that I should've been pissing the time away on theknot.com and FaceTiming my man some sexy shit while I'm on the clock."

"Sharin. Let's not get emotional though," Christian said. "I get you're upset and you have every right but-"

"No, Christian! It's bullshit and you know it. *I'm* going to go clear my desk out and *you're* going to calm down. Once you do, you know my favorite wine to get."

Sharin stood up gracefully and stepped out of her friend's grand office. She sighed, passing by Tiffany's desk without a word edgewise to the woman. She missed the smirk that crossed the secretary's features as she heard the last couple of words Sharin said before she made her dramatic exit.

Tiffany sighed and continued typing up all the reports that had to reach Christian's desk. Silently, she prayed that they all got it together. The easiest time for any company to implode was when it was going through internal struggles. Though the group of women that ran Adams' Accounting were dynamic, they didn't come without their own brand of drama.

"Get it together y'all."

"So, we just kickin' niggas to the curb, now?"

Sharin chuckled mirthlessly as she spared Monica James a glance. Monica had a look of disappointment on her face although at first glance she sounded amused.

Monica ran accounts for the few celebrities that patronized Adams'. It was on a fateful day years ago when Christian and Sharin met her in detention for an isolated incident back in high school. The younger Monica had been going through growing pains, having to adjust to a school that she would've never chosen to go to for herself. That'd been the case for Sharin and Christian back then who shared a common bond of hatred for Pace Academy. However, while Christian flourished, Monica took every chance to buck back at every teacher or student that dared get in her way. Meeting Christian and Sharin gave her a reason to actually like going to school as she felt she'd found her tribe. To this present day, Monica was grateful to have met them.

"Girl, I guess. I understand everything looks shaky, but I'm very pissed off at how she handled that. I'm doing my best to practice patience…but it's like *bitch, for real*?"

Monica sighed, shifting her body from one side to the other as she sat on Sharin's desk. She fixed the black sheath dress she'd decided to wear that day, wishing she'd gone for pants. Later on that evening, she had a date with her boyfriend, Reginald, so she wanted something that could easily shift from day to night.

"You want me to talk to her?" Monica asked. "Somebody has to run in there and tell her to calm her nerves."

"No. I'm taking my leave gracefully and I'm not going to cause any more waves than I have already. She has to sit down and look over the books and judge for herself. Besides, the one thing I've noticed was that I do need to finish up plans for the wedding, so I'll get a jump on that. I haven't seen my man before evening the past couple of days so I'm going to enjoy my time. Sometimes we ignore ourselves for the bigger picture and perhaps I do need the time off to gather my bearings or something. I've been working non-stop and missed $15 million dollars off of our books."

"Sharin...stop it," Monica said, sternly. "You weren't going to see all that doctoring. Whoever played with those numbers did that at the same high level that they know you work at. That's first and foremost. Second, we both know Christian's scared. This whole situation is scary for all of us. Right now, we're all hoping this doesn't end us or mar our reputation horribly. It's already bad enough I have to put the fear of God in a lot of these bookkeepers and they still have Similac on their breath from all of this. Putting emotion aside, just stick to your guns and enjoy your leave but don't get too comfortable. You'll have to come back at some point."

Monica looked down at her friend who'd been frantically putting things away in her bag for the past ten minutes. Sharin had been resting on her knees, packing away incessantly but slowed down and sat on her leather chair. She took a couple of breaths and then opened her eyes to stare at her friend dead on and nodded in acceptance of everything she'd said.

"You always know what to say," Sharin said, smiling softly. "Now I have to calm down further and only take what I need to take."

"I see. You're packing up like you and Christian broke up."

"In all of ten plus years, this is our second disagreement."

Monica laughed. "We've had several. That's a fact of life with us."

"That's a fact of life with *you*. We don't argue either, though."

"You're so damn zen. I know this shit rocked you. You're normally so calm, I don't get it."

The truth was, Sharin Reynolds was always a calm individual. Something about her was so regal, even in situations where her anger would've been justified. Monica loved being around her growing up because Sharin's calm generally soothed her ravaged mind. In the reverse, Monica's daredevil ways provoked Sharin to do things she normally wouldn't. Like Christian, Monica brought color to her world. She loved them both deeply.

Sharin methodically pulled out the files that needed to be handed over to her temporary successor and packed up her own work computer to surrender it to Christian. She also went through her desk again, stripping it of any personal effects. The picture of her and Maddox, her name plate, her desk planner, and more she placed into her Louis Vuitton Neverfull.

"So...I'm going to go home and screw my fiancé now," Sharin announced once she'd finished packing. Sharin delivered the announcement with such a straight face that Monica howled and slapped her friend's shoulder.

"Stop! You were so graceful and now you're leaving here on a petty note."

"I'm not on the clock now. Walk me out."

Monica sighed but slid off of Sharin's desk and walked over to her door. Opening it, she bowed as if to motion, *after you*. It caused Sharin to laugh as well.

The twosome walked towards the elevators amicably and rode the double gold-plated doors back to the first floor. Upon stepping out, Christopher appeared before them.

"I'll take it from here, Ms. James."

"Huh?" Monica blinked.

"I'm escorting Ms. Reynolds to her car. Reporters are still camping out, so we're covering y'all until things blow over."

Sharin edged a look at Christopher, unsure of how she felt about him from earlier in the day. She almost wanted to risk walking to her car by herself but decided against the notion. Sighing, she turned to hug Monica and told her she'd meet up with her later. She turned her face towards Christopher and with a neutral expression, motioned for him to lead the way. When he gave a sad one in return, Sharin's heart almost broke. She suddenly felt compassion for him, understanding that he just witnessed his niece get escorted out of the building by police.

"I'd like to apologize for earlier, Sharin."

Sharin looked up at the head of security and blew out a sigh that was unladylike in nature. Still, it eased her nerves.

"Don't worry about it, Chris. It couldn't have been easy watching your niece get escorted out like that. If I knew better...this wouldn't have been an issue."

"Don't put the blame on your shoulders...I was angry and afraid. I don't know how deep my baby girl is involved and the thought of failing as someone who raised her is...I can't find the words, Sharin."

Sharin sighed. "I can assure you, whatever the charges are, I'll seek to have them lightened. We both know that Jupiter did most of the dirt. Also...your baby girl is grown now. You need to understand that while you raised her, she went along with the mess, too. Don't beat yourself up."

Christopher nodded as they approached Sharin's car. Without words, he opened the door and took her hand, helping her to slide in.

"You're right. I just knew something was off about that woman. I'm sorry that you couldn't have gotten rid of her."

"I am, too. More than likely I'll have to get grilled by the police at some point and Christian suspended me so I might be out of a job if things don't pan out well."

Christopher nodded his head solemnly. He knew that while Sharin didn't have to work a day in her life, she immensely enjoyed the day-to-day hustle and bustle of her job. She helped Christian to erect Adams' Accounting and it was as much her pride and joy as it was Christian's. Hearing the sadness and fear in her voice broke his heart. He was even more abased that he'd uttered the words he had to her earlier in the day.

"I know it looks bad but y'all will pull through. I'm sure of it."

Sharin eyed the head of security and stopped herself from rolling her own eyes at his brand of positivity. Considering all he'd been through in his life however, Sharin normally admired the stalwart man for always seeing things on the brighter side of life. It had taught her to do the same when she'd been a dedicated pessimist.

Christopher Langley was Atlanta to his core. He stood at six three with brown skin. His dark brown eyes could harden on you in a moment's notice, showcasing that he wasn't the lamb he generally put himself out there to be. Christian met him while she was interviewing for head of security and his name was put into the hat by Tiffany who'd beat Sharin to the punch years ago and introduced herself at the club.

To the very day, Sharin remembered the elbow jab Tiffany sent her to the gut when they'd both laid eyes on him. Until she'd met Maddox, Sharin remembered being upset with Tiffany for the longest time. However, getting to know him, Sharin knew she and Christopher weren't a good fit. They were better off as friends.

Not that he wasn't dreamy all the same.

"I'm sure, Christopher. It doesn't stop me from being stressed about it all the same. Give my best to Tiffany. I didn't stop by her desk on the way out."

"Will do."

As Christopher mentioned, there were people waiting nearby with a microphone ready to interview anybody who saw fit to come out. Sharin bristled but kept her head held high as she was escorted to her Black S-Class Benz.

"You'd think they'd be gone by now. The police haven't shooed them away yet?"

"They're working for theirs like we're working for ours. Unfortunately, their job is to be grimy. It might be war in a little while, though. They can't camp out here all day."

"Right!" Sharin said. "You'd think we were the celebrities...except we are handling some celebrity cash. I don't know how this is going to affect our future endeavors."

"Today is important, Ms. Reynolds," Christopher replied, swiping his forehead. "There's no use worrying about tomorrow."

"You're on point today, Chris," Sharin threw back, just as they reached her car.

"I try. Anyway, give my best to Maddox when you see him."

Sharin laughed. "I think tonight I'll do my best to give him my best at this point. Like you said, today, right?"

"Today," Christopher laughed. "Get home safely, Ms. Reynolds."

"Thank you, Christopher."

And with that, the head-of-security watched Sharin drive away. He sighed, hoping that the little bit of laughter they shared would at least start to heal their spirits.

Chapter
Four

Hours later, Monica stepped outside of Adams' Accounting, flanked by both Christian and Sonya. She could feel the stress reverberating from them. Monica sighed, the thought of telling Christian off eating her up inside. She didn't agree with how she handled things with Sharin but also didn't want to get into a fight over her friend's judgement. She also understood as well as Sharin had that Christian was under a lot of stress from the day's events. Pictures of her surfaced in the newsfeeds and under a couple of well-known financier blog sites. The news story did its due diligence to make her friend look totally incompetent and lost. That was enough to send anybody over the deep end.

"Ladies, I know it looks bad right now but we're going to get this cleaned up as quickly as we can."

Sonya looked over at Christian and decided she admired her for putting on a brave face. She had a neutral mind on her suspending Sharin. The emotional part of her wondered why she'd been so quick to undercut her best friend. The logical part of her surmised that sending Sharin out of the door for a couple of days afforded Christian a better mind to go through the books without emotion clouding her judgement. It also might clear Sharin of having anything to do with the doctoring of said books.

Might. All of it was sketchy and like she'd mentioned to Christian earlier, all of the Partners were essentially suspects. The process would be grueling but worth it to figure out who would set out to mar their good name.

"I'm not worried at all," she replied. "I don't care if it takes longer, we need to figure out who went out of their way."

"I prefer quickly," Christian said. "This fracas is threatening to make us lose money. They're already dragging my name everywhere like I didn't build on it for years."

"We," Monica chided softly, laying a hand on her friend's shoulder. "All of us, Cash."

Christian glanced at Monica and her expression softened. She nodded in acquiesce to the gentle correction.

"You're right. That's exactly the thing though. We put our lives into this place and that's what insults me the most. I look at all of it as me. Y'all, these bookkeepers, even Sharin. Especially Sharin. I know y'all are pissed."

"I am," Monica said. "However, that's between y'all. I think once you calm down..."

"...I'm calmer now. I still stand by my decision. I need everything on the up and up and I'm unsure how to feel about her right now. She essentially makes a lot of decisions for my company and if I can't depend on her now..."

"Just go over the books, Christian," Monica said. "She wasn't going to catch those mistakes. Ever. I honestly believe the only reason shit hit the fan now was because the person underneath all of this mess wanted to be caught. That woman has been there for you more than herself and the least you can do is put that at the forefront of your mind before you embarrass and then toss her out."

"You just told me it was between us, Nik," Christian said, laughing a little bit. "Now you're coming for my head."

"Because you're *wrong*," Monica replied, shifting her stance a little bit. "However, I'm leaving it at that. I wasn't supposed to say that much."

Christian sighed, heavily with no retort to offer. The conversation they were having was all but forgotten as Reginald Brooks pulled up to the building in his pearl white Bentley Continental GT. Christian inwardly rolled her eyes at the man's presence and almost caught herself rolling them outwardly at Monica's reaction to the man. She grunted as if she would jump him right then and there.

Christian didn't have a true personal problem with Reginald minus the fact that he came off privileged in her mind's eye. He was the son of investment banker Reginald Brooks, the First who was wildly renowned in Georgia and in the finance world elsewhere.

Reginald stood at six five. He was a strong tower with an athlete's build but was shockingly graceful in his movements. It always boggled the much smaller Monica's mind how fluidly he could move. The man never had a clumsy moment. His finesse was something that Monica enjoyed tremendously.

"Ladies, I bid you adieu."

Sonya chuckled as Monica walked slowly and deliberately towards Reginald whose smile spread as if he'd won the lottery. Ray Charles could sense the tension between them and they both were unapologetic about those who witnessed it.

"Goodnight, girl."

Sonya laughed, even as Reginald acknowledged them with a nod. He helped Monica in his car politely, but Christian knew if they hadn't been there, he would've tried to devour their friend whole in front of their business.

"Ms. Adams. Ms. Powers."

Both turned at Christopher's beckoning.

"I'm about to lock down the entire building. You two need me to escort you or y'all good?"

"We're good. Just watching this bozo get in the car," Sonya replied. "I'm blowing this joint. I'll see you in the morning, boss lady."

Christian laughed at Sonya and waved. She looked up at Christopher and sighed as Sonya walked off.

"Well, she was good. I don't know if I am."

Christopher felt his heart break reading the hurt in Christian's voice. Without another word, he walked her to her car.

"You need anything else at all, Ms. Adams?"

"Nah, Chris. You went above and beyond, today. I can't thank you enough."

"Just thank me by getting home safe, Ms. Adams."

He opened her car door much the same way he had Sharin's and watched Christian get in much the same way her friend had. He wasn't sure if his heart could take the sadness that seemed to loom over each of the women.

"Will do. I'll see you in the morning. Do you think you can have it open by seven?"

"Yes, ma'am," he replied. "I'm going to have the building partially staffed as well. I'll personally be there by nine, but the front will most definitely be covered if nothing else."

Christian nodded. "Thanks again. I'll see you."

Christopher watched Christian drive away and thought back over his day as it stood. He'd gotten the tag from one of his guards that watches everything from the security war room. It was no more than thirty seconds later when he ran towards the front. He missed catching Christian come out of her car but did his best to snatch her away from the spotlight. It was a personal failure on his part that he hadn't made it to her fast enough. He hadn't considered that her desperation to know what was happening was stronger than his will to keep her out of harm's way.

As he patrolled with his men during that day, Christopher witnessed the ladies deal with the new events in varying emotions of despair. Christian swung the pendulum. One moment she was the picture of strength. The next, he could tell she just wanted to curl up in a ball and weep.

He simply saw the fracas as a time for the team to be tested. It was always easy to reconcile to strength when things went well. The true testament came when war came knocking on the door.

Christopher just hoped they were able to raise up the same standard that was raised against them.

"Your friend needs to be properly fucked."

Monica slid a glance over at her boyfriend with a playful smirk and questioned what made him make his announcement. Reginald chuckled in response as he twined his right hand with her left and caressed it lightly while he drove.

"Just watching her while you walked to me. I could tell she wants to spit every time she sees me and you together."

Monica sighed. "Reginald, we just had probably the worst day in all the years we've been running Adams'. If she's giving you any kind of side eye, I don't even hold it against her today. You do have a history of being an asshole to her."

"I do. Still. It's all over her aura. There's no way she's getting worked over the way she's acting. Besides, it's you and Shay's fault. How can y'all allow y'all friend to walk around uptight and not set her up?"

"We're grown women and Christian knows exactly how to get laid. Besides, you know it's different for a woman than a man. If that's her pleasure, she definitely has to go about it differently. She's the face of a multi-million-dollar establishment. She's a known symbol. People might not know me or Shay or Sonya, but they know Christian and she can't just be out here offering ass to any and everybody. Besides, the last time me and Shay tried she cursed us out."

Reginald was caught up in Monica's reasoning. When she reached the end of her argument, he found himself laughing with no abandon. His laughter was cut short when Monica added,

"That was five years ago."

Reginald sobered up, seeing that the subject bothered his woman. He liked to bother Christian as she often seemed to take herself too seriously but always backed off where Monica was concerned. Anybody knowing the friends knew that their friendship ran deep. As it was, he was shocked Monica hadn't told him to leave her friend alone.

They pulled up to Nikolai's Roof and were approached by the host. After confirming their reservation, Reginald took her smaller hand in his own and led her as he was being led to their booth.

After making sure his beloved was seated, he sat across from her with a smile. Monica smiled back softly, reaching across the table again to grab his hand and gloried in the feel of his fingers caressing hers.

"Will there be anything to start with?"

They were broken out of their spell long enough for Reginald to order for both of them. The waitress nodded and disappeared as quickly as she had appeared. Monica giggled.

"What if I wanted something else?"

Reginald smirked, "Forgive me, love. It's been awhile since I got to look into those pretty eyes of yours, so I got ahead of myself."

Monica smiled in acceptance. "Since you put it that way, I'll let it go."

Both knew Monica didn't want a different order of wine, but flirting was a thing with them. It was also true that they hadn't seen each other in a couple of days. Monica had missed him as much as he'd missed her. Even more so she was touched that Reginald had dropped everything and came rushing to pick her up after work. He normally worked longer hours depending on the day but she had needed his ear. The emotions she had experienced during the day had put her on edge and although she only got to give Christian a tiny portion of her mind, it made her feel leaps and bounds better.

Once they received their wine and ordered their first course, Reginald looked into her eyes and nodded.

"Tell me what's wrong, love."

Monica breathed in and out, running a tired hand down her face. It was the first time she'd shown an outward expression of her emotions all day. Reginald suddenly wished they were alone. He wanted to pull her into his arms and give her the silent comfort that she needed.

"Baby..."

And then she unloaded the events of the day. She detailed how they started getting phone calls and emails out of the blue. She walked him through the meeting that she pulled together at a moment's notice of getting a lot of the emails and calling her Partners. She sighed over seeing Sharin brokenhearted when Christian accused her of working less than her best. She divulged her fears over what damage Evander King might do to the company over the missing monies.

"It's like I hope he has mercy on us but at the same time, fifteen million dollars of his money is missing. As it is we have to restore that, but it hasn't come at a worse time. We were starting to court celebrities and a couple of new basketball players were starting to have conversations about doing business with us. It's looking really bad right now. Monica sighed. I'm still pissed Christian would suspend Sharin."

Reginald laughed and Monica started to see red. Before the steam could come out of her ears Reginald swallowed his laughter but the smirk hadn't left his face.

"Baby. Christian already meant to put her on ice. This...fracas...just presented a good enough reason to do it."

"Explain."

"Your friend is getting married. She's walking around with hearts in her eyes. She's the epitome of love right now. Christian has been single for however many years and seems to scoff at any kind of expression of love outside of y'all and Adams'. You really *think* she wants to see that shit on a regular basis?"

"That shouldn't have any bearing on her job." Monica's eyes furrowed. "Why would she..."

"Oh, you think your friend is impervious to envy? You really think your friend doesn't *want* love?"

"No and no but not enough to-"

"-you love your friends beyond reproach and that's why you have the shocked look on your face when shit happens. Take a closer look and see things for what they are. It's like how my family promises you're the wrong choice for me but I know you, Monica, inside and out. I know you and I love you and I see that their heads are so far up they ass that they don't see or *care* that I'm happy with you. I love my family but they're elitist. I see them very clearly and it's about time you did the same."

"Leave my friend alone, Reggie," Monica warned. "She has her reasons."

"She might. Still. Most choices people make aren't one dimensional. She's a single woman. She's been driven by nothing but this company for years. She might love Sharin like a sister but even sisters have their shit. Don't worry about it though, love. That'll blow over. In the end, as much as Christian can be an asshole, she loves y'all. Somehow it'll come together."

"You act like you know so much."

"A little about a lot. However, I might need to know what it'll take to get you out of that dress later."

Monica smiled at him salaciously. "Maybe two more glasses of wine. Maybe one."

Reginald smirked and raised up his hand to signal the waitress as she walked towards their section. Without missing a beat, she approached their table.

"Are you ready to order, sir?"

Reginald held Monica's eyes captive as he requested every other course along with their subsequent wine pairings. Monica found herself crossing her legs as she watched her man take total control of the situation. Suddenly, everything at the job didn't matter. Christian's issues or non-issues withered into nothingness. The longer she stared into her beloved's eyes, the more nothing mattered except the fact that she found herself lost in him. The air fizzled and popped with their electricity and she found that it lit her up with new life. She always felt there was nothing she couldn't do as long as they were together.

"I almost want to cancel this dinner but you're going to need to eat."

Oh yes, Monica thought, *this was exactly what the doctor ordered.* She wasn't sure if he needed her as much as she needed him however, she needed every moment. She needed the dance to stretch her torn mind. She needed the flirting to rewire her ragged body. Every bit of preparation he was taking before he devoured her the way she knew he would devour every dish, she needed it.

Sometimes, a woman just wanted to be reminded that apart from everything else going on, she was still desired and loved. It warmed her heart to know that Reginald provided every reassurance.

Sharin sang softly to the sounds of Jhene Aiko, allowing the soft timbres and harmonies to calm her ravaged mind. The day replayed in her mind over and over and she had to stop herself from getting pissed off and throwing one of her expensive vases at a wall in her house.

Since she had all the time in the world, she decided to run a bath. She poured a mixture of lavender and sandalwood essential oils in the bath and added a wealth of bubbles into the mix. Stepping out of the bathroom she picked up her iPhone and sent the music to her Bose speakers. Once she sat the volume on low, she padded to her bed and pulled out her latest read. She held the book to her like a child would hold close a favorite teddy bear and walked back to the bathroom.

The cool tones of the master bath calmed her. Ten minutes later she turned off her bath water and after stripping down, leaving her clothes scattered, she stepped in. Placing her book on the side ledge she lowered herself in, melting even as the warm-almost hot-water enveloped around her. She laid her head on the bath pillow and again let the smooth, velvety sounds of the LA singer pull her away from the present.

Thirty minutes had gone by when the water started to cool. Sharin went through the motions of emptying her bath water halfway and adding more water to warm it again. Once she had, she repeated her actions from earlier, not ready to walk away from the soothing moment.

Another thirty minutes passed by when Maddox walked in, spying his fiancée with her head still in a book. With a sideways grin, he walked up to the tub, leaning in and effectively popping the bubble she'd encased herself in. He chuckled a little bit when she jumped but wondered how she didn't hear him approach at all.

"Evenin' baby."

His voice was like silk and his lips even silkier when he'd pressed them against her lips. She sighed and then looked up at him.

The memory of the day came rushing back at her full force and it was all she could do to not sob while she watched him strip. Maddox caught the expression on her face and found his own face creasing into worry over his beloved.

"What's wrong?" he questioned, as Sharin shook her head furiously.

"I'm not ready to talk."

"I mean, is it me? I don't remember doing anything lately, baby."

"It's not you at all."

Maddox took in his woman, warring between his lusts and his worry. When he'd walked into the bathroom and saw her engrossed in her book, all he'd thought about in that moment was pulling her attention from the book to him. He loved how she could dedicate so much focus and attention on something whether she was reading or working. He always found her a joy to watch whenever she bought her work home with her which wasn't often. When they first started dating seriously it was a rule that he'd established between them that work doesn't follow them home. If they both fell into the trap it was easy for them to miss each other in the chaos of their jobs.

Maddox Lennox was a realtor in Georgia who was making a name of himself daily in his line of work. It'd taken him years to reach the point of his career where he felt as if he were finally on fire. His name was reaching places he'd never dreamed it would and as the icing on the cake it seemed like Sharin walked into his life at the right time. Rather, she fell onto his lap at the right time.

One isolated meeting after another led them to an engagement. Sharin fought him at every turn in the beginning until she surrendered to his love. Since then, it'd been blissful. His successes were funding his bank account better than he could've dreamed and with only better to come, it only made sense that he proposed.

The only problem it seemed was that once Sharin accepted his proposal, her working life began to suffer.

Sharin took in her fiancé as he walked towards her, his milk chocolate skin glowing against the soft lights of the candles she set around the bathtub. She moved forward as he motioned to move in behind her. Once she was encased in his arms she sighed, melting lavishly against him. The action caused him to groan and kiss the side of her neck.

"Talk to me, baby," he said. "That look on your face isn't one I'm used to seeing."

Sharin sighed. "Let me enjoy this for a couple of minutes more."

Maddox sighed in kind and pulled her in closer. Enjoying her closeness in a way he didn't know he needed, he kissed along her neck again and caressed her face with his own. They sat in a peaceful quiet until the water had gone cold again. Sighing, Sharin finally stood up, emptying the tub. Maddox chuckled and motioned for his woman to follow him to the shower.

Once they were fully showered, Maddox backed off as Sharin went about going through her womanly routines. He decided to cook dinner, noting that she still wanted some time alone.

When he finished about an hour later, Maddox called for Sharin who had just walked into the dining room. He grinned at her silk grey housecoat and matching fluffy slippers. She grinned upon seeing him and watched her take a seat at their dining table.

"You're so bougie," he said, chuckling, in turn making her roll her eyes.

"Am not."

Maddox ignored her as he plated her dish. Sharin smiled when he returned from the kitchen with both of their plates in hand. She smiled harder when she saw the puff pastry salmon that was his specialty. It was light, yet comforting and it was obvious that she needed both. Besides, she was going to ruin the light meal with ice cream later on. Those were her thoughts until Maddox returned with a bottle of Sauvignon Blanc.

"Trying to get me drunk, fiancé? You know wine does one of two things to me. Or both." Sharin said, giggling.

"I'm looking for the first option. Hoping you get politely turnt up," he said, grinning. "Let's eat."

So, they had. While eating it'd been quiet. Soon as Sharin had reached her second glass in the middle of polite conversation, she'd said:

"Christian suspended me."

Maddox looked from his own glass to his woman's eyes and saw how despondent she was. His own face furrowed, the turn of events throwing him off.

"What the fu-"

"-Maddox."

"I'm just trying to understand. Why?"

Sharin took a deep breath and still, she reached for her wine. She methodically took a sip and then edged a look at Maddox again. Seeing the concern and quiet anger resting in his eyes bolstered her.

"Evander King's personal auditor caught some discrepancies in his books. Fifteen million dollars' worth. He's suing for damages. The press showed up at Adams' today and pretty much ran the story as if nothing else pressing is happening in Atlanta."

Sharin thought of the panicked look on Christian's face and her anger towards her softened. Still, she couldn't help the anger she felt toward her best friend for firing first and asking questions later. It wasn't unlike her form, however. There were times Christian often spoke before she understood the consequences of her words. Sharin felt in all of their years as friends that she'd handle things with a little bit more finesse.

"So, in response, she suspends *you*?"

Sharin nodded. "I missed a lot of things in the books so that falls on me. I should've figured out that someone was stealing about six months ago. I believe the person was stealing for years. Monica feels like I was never going to see those mistakes and a part of me feels the same way. Still, I'm unsure that I was paying attention well enough."

"Baby, I don't know who's more dedicated to their job. In the beginning I had to strong arm you away from the computer in order to get a proper date with you."

"I also wanted work to be the excuse I pushed you away," Sharin answered. "It didn't work out."

"Exactly. I was just thinking she's been a little shaky since I proposed."

"No, she hasn't," Sharin rolled her eyes. "I don't need that to be the reasoning behind her reactions."

"Shay, baby look at me." Sharin quietly looked up at Maddox, dark browns meeting light browns and she sighed. "You don't think your friend is a bit envious?"

"No," Sharin answered. "My love life isn't the reason that I'm suspended from my position. My overall performance and perhaps her upset with the situation is. Don't do that, Maddox."

"I'm not doing anything but stating a truth you won't look at. Y'all were fine for the longest time. Anything you wanted, you got without resistance from this woman, at least while we're dating. As soon as I get on bended knee, suddenly your workload is getting heavy. Suddenly your hours are getting longer. You're looking at your friend as if she's a god and above human emotion and I wouldn't say it if I didn't see the shit, Sharin."

Sharin shrugged. "Be that as it may, we're still getting married. My best friend is genuinely happy about that fact and her suspending me is definitely not because of our upcoming nuptials! You and Reggie need to stop with that bullshit about her needing a man!"

"It's not bullshit, baby. You just don't want to see the truth for what it is. Whatever is it egging at your friend, she's definitely taking it out on you. This fracas just provided a more solid reason for her to do it."

"Either way, I'm definitely out of work for the interim. Whatever her reason, I'm sick over it and don't even want to look at her right now."

And just like that she was sad all over again. Maddox quietly sighed and stood up from his chair, walking over to hers. He pulled her out of her seat and into his arms, closing them around her waist. Sharin moved to bury her head in his chest but he intercepted with a finger to her chin. She lifted her head to look into his eyes.

"This isn't permanent."

Hope shined into her eyes. "It's not?"

"No. You needed the time off anyway. I missed your face the past couple of days."

Sharin laughed and leaned up to kiss Maddox softly. Pulling away, she reached for his hand and led him up the stairs to their master bedroom. Once there, she slowly lifted up the white t-shirt Maddox wore as she leaned up to kiss him again.

"Thanks for taking care of me, baby," she whispered. "I appreciate you."

Their master bedroom was their retreat. The neutral beige tones added both warmth and calm to their psyche and was the reason they'd agreed on the colorway. Neither wanted the same grays and whites and neutrals they'd seen in a lot of homes.

The king-sized bed was always the center of the show for whatever reason. Napping, relaxation, alternate exercise such as the one Sharin's mind was focused on when she heard the plea in her man's tone.

She wasn't sure of Christian's motives anymore but knew one thing. Sometimes things happened and you had to roll with the punches. She'd said a lot of things to Monica out of spite while she'd been packing but the fact of the matter was, she hadn't been planning her wedding as much as she could have.

Adams' had been getting ready to receive a lot of clientele so she was gearing up for the influx of work that her department would have to oversee. She had a lot of corrections to make. Sharin hadn't expressed as much to Maddox but she had also missed him as well. Work did take its toll most days, but her solution had been to ask Christian for more support.

Jupiter had been excellent but as the work was becoming too much and there was no immediate raise, the only other solution was to hire-or promote-more bodies.

Every avenue should've been taken to ensure excellence but that was neither here nor there. If her best friend felt she should take some down time, she would. If she needed her back, then she'd be back.

Maddox was stripping without more of her assistance and instead had taken pleasure in opening up her housecoat to reveal the simple but sexy matching grey nightie underneath. He returned his affections once he'd gotten her fully unclothed and began to explore her with more purpose.

"I appreciate you too, baby. I'm about to appreciate you some more."

For the next several hours, he took his time doing just that.

Sharin turned in for the night but Sonya was just getting revved up. In the midst of her own round with her man, she was currently begging for release. Jerell, her boyfriend of more than a few years, was teasing her as he often did before he got around to devouring her whole. Panting and heavy breathing was the background music that surrounded them until Sonya's soft, desperate cries pushed Jerell over the edge and he'd climbed on top of her.

An hour of their love making passed and then two when the phone rang. Jerell froze, knowing the ringtone to be for Christian Adams. He looked down at Sonya whose glazed eyes looked back at his own.

"What you stopping for? I'll get that later."

Jerell smirked and decided to finish off strong when he caught the haughty look in his girlfriend's eyes. He went from a steady to a frenzied pace, reminding her who was running the show. When she succumbed to pleasure, he released inside her with a hard grunt as well. He laid inside, catching his breath and without much preamble he pulled away from her. Sonya stretched out as he'd done so and padded to the bathroom to freshen up before she went to bed.

Jerell's mind floated away, already back in the past by the time Sonya started her shower. He was already picturing Christian Adams walking in his direction for the first time as his girlfriend. He grinned, thinking of times' past when it'd been hard to conquer her at every turn. It'd taken weeks to get her number. It'd taken weeks for them to get together. It'd taken almost as long to finally get her into bed. When he had however, she fully surrendered, and her surrender was intoxicating to him.

Christian had been an amazing girlfriend to him and he even toyed with the idea of marrying her but hadn't lingered on the thought too long. He hadn't been ready, and he wasn't sure that she was it for him. Jerell has been a year older so when it was time to graduate from Clark Atlanta, it was then he decided it was best for him and Christian to part ways. He'd been accepted to Harvard's Law School and a long-distance relationship wasn't in his best interest. He could still remember the way her eyes teared up when he first told her he was done.

It'd been almost gratifying to watch her cry and pound on his chest. It made him feel like another man couldn't take his place in her life. Years later as she was still single, he was very certain his hold over her was strong. He was pleased with that much. What she didn't know was that if she came back to him, he'd leave Sonya. Until then he'd punish her daily by being with her friend. While he was truly fond of Sonya, she was merely entertainment until Christian stopped being stubborn and came back to him.

Sonya came out of the shower, interrupting his reverie. Jerell watched her naked form as she moved around, gathering clothing to sleep in. He licked his lips as she did so, unabashedly taking her in and enjoying her from her caramel skin to her rounded eyes. Everything about her was small and compact but she'd been just as obstinate as Christian when they'd first met. Taking her down enthralled him but not as much as when it'd been his former love. She wasn't a bad consolation prize, however. He could live with her if he had to.

When Sonya was finished freshening up, she joined Jerell in the bed. She snuggled against him and the action caused him to smirk.

"I thought you were calling her back?" He questioned, as she kissed his chest.

"Morning is soon enough. Today exhausted me."

Without another word edgewise, Sonya was sound asleep. Jerell waited twenty minutes and moved out of the bed. Moving towards the dresser, he snatched Sonya's iPhone 7 up and dialed back Christian's number.

She answered on the first ring.

"Sonya? I'm glad you called back."

Jerell smirked. "Nah, this is her man. The one who's over here handling her while you're over there trying to interrupt our shit." Radio silence was the response and it caused him to chuckle. "You think I don't know you, Christian? You're still on me and we both know it. Stop calling my woman after hours because you had your shot and you blew it. If this happens again, we'll have a problem."

The silence was shorter this time before Christian sighed heavily. "Jerell, from my heart to yours…go to hell."

He wanted to chuckle with glee, having gotten under her skin. He almost responded with an equally barbed insult but hadn't had the chance. The call disconnected while he was busy taking joy from his ex's pain.

Satisfied with that much, he tossed Sonya's phone on the dresser and lazily strolled back into bed with her. He checked to see that she was still sleeping. Satisfied that she was, he pulled her into his frame and drifted into the sweet dreams he didn't deserve.

Chapter
Five

"My company is going through a crisis and this fuck nigga thinks I still want **his** ass?!"

Christian felt her hands shaking and was ready to hurl the bottle of Riesling she had in her hand. She thought better of it, instead deigning to take a hard swallow. The semi-sweet wine worked its magic to take the edge off of her nerves, but she had wished it was something stronger. She wanted the liquor to carry her away into dreams and erase the day away from existence.

It had been about ten years since she'd last spoken to Jerell Williams directly. He'd been a reminder to her that men served as nothing but a costly distraction. Everything from their courtship all the way to their break-up had put her through an emotional rollercoaster she would never again go through, especially with him. She'd given her heart to him freely and since then, she's hid her heart under a heavily guarded lock and key. Her business was the only thing that she toiled and worried over and up until recently, it hadn't betrayed her.

"Thanks for that much, Shay."

The thought was bitter and she was ashamed seconds after it passed her mind. Her best friend was more loyal than most and if she were honest with herself, she grappled with the idea that her best friend in the world was about to get married. For years they'd been on the same wavelength. Both of them suffered broken hearts and had turned their energies towards the business. Sharin was the one who came up with the ideology in high school. Christian had adopted her thought process in college and perfected it. Her mindset was so perfectly shifted that by the time Jerell tried to make a comeback at Harvard, his presence meant absolutely nothing to her.

However, it had angered her greatly when he started dating Sonya not long after she befriended her. Christian never divulged the fact that she and Jerell dated two years ago and Jerell never seemed to share that information either. Christian decided to let sleeping dogs lie since as far as she was concerned, Jerell Williams was dead to her. If the subject ever came up she'd simply inform Sonya that their courtship was of no consequence and that she had nothing to worry about.

Jerrell's haughty tone and inappropriate announcement did nothing but put Christian into a state of sadness. It was very true that besides a fling or two when the need to mate came on strong, she'd been alone. Christian vowed not to let another man enter her heart and sitting on the chaise lounge in her room she wondered where that had gotten her.

For years, her business was on a high. Once it'd gotten off the ground and she received business, it was almost predictable to predict the highs and the lows. She was proud to say she ran a prosperous business that was becoming one of the best places to work. There'd been much to celebrate in the past ten years since the company's erection.

Still, she came home to an empty house. It was a beautiful penthouse apartment at the end of the city, and she'd celebrated hard when she first purchased the apartment. As of the past couple of years however, she wondered the purpose of such grand surroundings if there were no one to share it with.

Sure, there'd been the get togethers with friends or the twice a year visits from her parents. Past that, Christian found that her place was beginning to feel empty and even at times sterile to her. It was on her mind for a couple of months that maybe she needed to downsize her home. Deep inside of her being, however, she knew she was starting to yearn for a partner of her own.

It was on nights like this that were very few and far between that it would've been nice to unload.

Christian walked past her living room, opening the door to her sprawling balcony. She took in the city line of Atlanta, remembering when she first viewed the apartment. She couldn't wait to pour a bottle of wine and look out at the city line. There'd been many times when she'd done just that, the feeling of accomplishment satisfying her on most nights. Normally the view would center her and remind her subtly of her goals and dreams. On this night however, the view didn't satisfy her or bring her calm. All it did was make her yearn for a partner to share the view with.

It was sitting on her mind heavily that there'd been absent a partner to share her wins with. There was no one waiting for her to pull her into their arms while she worried over her losses. Nobody that she could support and vice versa. She didn't voice her hurt often and as time passed on, she realized she wasn't too sure how. Being vulnerable wasn't something she was good at and when her vulnerable moments showed themselves, she was always thrown off when they did. The biggest part of her fears to seek companionship came with the knowledge that vulnerability with a partner is inevitable. She wasn't sure if she could be vulnerable with a partner ever again.

Christian's thoughts were a tornado inside of her while she calmly sipped at her wine. Each swallow of the sweet imbibement took along with it the tears that wanted to well up from the pit of her stomach. She forced the saltiness to a dark corner and let it quell there for the time being. Staring out into the city line, Jerrell took center stage in her thoughts as the college romance replayed in her mind. Once the present moment reminded her of the vain man she'd dated, she sighed heavily.

Christian wished Jerell knew how dead her love was for him. It'd taken a couple of wild college parties and another handful of bitter tears, but she'd gotten over him. Once she had, she couldn't even bother wanting to make him jealous with another person. The emphasis on getting over him was getting back to herself. She had felt lost when they'd first broken up and almost without an identity when he had coldly left without a backwards glance.

There'd been at least two days of crying non-stop until Sharin showed up at her door after a bad argument they'd had over him.

She never forgot how Sharin had showed up with a quart of her favorite ice cream and the twosome spent an evening binge watching Sex in the City. They'd bashed men the entire time, but it was all healing to Christian's heart. The laughter and the camaraderie above all were healing balms that she'd always love Sharin for. Her best friend had come in the clutch to remind her that she was Christian Adams with and definitely without Jerell Williams. Once she turned her focus back to her, she was unstoppable and Jerell was dead to her.

The realization that she didn't love him anymore was freeing. However, the past twenty minutes after their quick tete a tete only showed her that while her love for him was dead, the trauma that he'd wrecked was alive and living. Christian faced the truth that while her focus on her business put her ahead, her fear of love left her far behind anyone else that she knew.

Those thoughts trailed alongside the crippling fear that Adams' Accounting was nearing the end of an era. They followed her in the long shower she took. They followed her while she straightened and wrapped her hair for the day ahead. One by one they all disappeared for later perusal in the back of her mind. The only thought that was left behind was that she wished there was someone to lay her burdens on.

The last thought that finally set the quiet tears free as she laid down to sleep was that there might not be a soul out there for her. With a heavy sigh, she laid down in the middle of her king-sized bed. Her quiet tears said all the prayers she didn't know how to verbalize. Her quiet sighs begged God that her fears wouldn't come true.

Paparazzi and newscasters had been planted outside Adams' Accounting since three in the morning. The first sign of drama was almost eight hours later. The talking heads couldn't be anymore thankful when Evander King's Bentley pulled up in front of the bricked establishment. When the man himself stepped out of the backseat of the classic car, the newscasters wasted no time in trying to breach his space. That was until his bodyguards appeared before them like smoke, daring them to test him that morning.

Evander sucked his teeth lightly, trying not to let his disgust show in front of the world. To him, the whole situation was a private matter and he wasn't huge on the media trying to use his name for fodder. It was already bad enough that he had to punish a sister for misusing his money. He was disappointed at the very least that he entrusted his monies to a team of women and they would allow an embezzlement ring to take place under their nose.

He wasn't sure whether he felt compassion or utter distaste for Christian Adams. Evander had spent hours watching the same news clip over and over trying to decipher whether he felt like the woman had stolen his money or not.

He memorized every eye blink. He committed to memory the way her face flushed with either embarrassment or terror. The way her eyes widened was the part that pushed him over the edge to believe the woman had no clue what was going on. Still, he was so angry that he could grind her bones into dust. Fifteen million dollars was a drop in the bucket to him but the fact that someone would steal his money for the longest time to fund their lifestyle was beyond him.

There were many changes he went through in the past few years since his father's death. The organization that his father ran wasn't the same that Evander wanted to run. He'd put in too much time to build an honorable organization to have someone steal from under his nose. The anger he felt almost overtook him when he thought about it.

Evander never met Christian Adams in person as his financial advisor had recommended the team to him. Since he trusted his advisor, it was a no-brainer to entrust his money there.

Adams' Accounting had shiny marble floors that sounded at almost every click of the heel when you stepped through the foyer. The walls were a beautiful sheen of muted grey. The lights were bright but not offensive to anyone who walked through. The showstoppers were the shiny golden elevators that added a kind of panache to the space. Seeing his reflection through the doors as he pressed for the top floor, he smirked. Whoever decorated the space went for understated elegance. A person could almost forget that they worked there.

The doorbell dinged and Evander stepped inside. Once the elevator reached the tenth floor, he stepped out, his eyes landing on the secretary's desk that sat on the opposite end of the hall. Evander walked over, looking down at the lady who looked up at him with a raised brow. He was two seconds off of asking if she'd forgotten her manners when she straightened up.

"Good morning. Mr. King, I presume?"

Evander smirked and nodded in response. The brown skinned lady smiled politely and motioned for him to take a seat. He turned and saw a row of two brown, blocked leather chairs adjacent her desk. Evander bristled inside but took a seat. The more he sat around the more his energy swirled within him. He was already on edge and the more he had to wait, the more displeased he became.

"Ms. Adams will see you shortly. She had an overseas phone call and it's running a little long," the secretary explained. "Would you like any coffee or tea, Mr. King?"

"No, thank you," he answered. "Just make sure your boss meets with me at her first convenience."

The secretary's eyes widened at his tone but she said nothing in response, and he thought her the wiser for it. In his mind, Christian Adams should have already been at his office begging for every bit of mercy he had. The fact that he had to come to the lady's home court was beyond words to him. He wondered if she even had an understanding of the importance of money as it stood in the world or if she were one of those ladies who had nothing else better to do than to start a business with their rich father's money. Not that he was against it, but he had better respect for a person who had to fight for theirs. Granted he had his father's money, but his situation was different than most. Buddy King didn't just give anything to anybody.

He made you fight for it.

"Ms. Adams will see you now."

The secretary knocked him out of his reverie, but the words put a smile on his face. Standing tall, he followed behind the pretty secretary, thinking he might've asked the woman out had he not been so obstinate in cursing her superior out in every way that he could.

All of those thoughts ceased however, when he had laid eyes on the boss.

Christian Adams was a vision at five feet five inches. The peach suit that she wore emanated power and authority but didn't drown out her femininity and he'd felt it in waves. Evander looked down at her as she thanked him for his patience and reached out to shake his hand. He shook it, hoping he didn't come across at dumb founded. The woman that stood before him didn't at all look like the lost doe-eyed woman whose face he had on repeat for hours the night before.

Her auburn hair was swept away from her face. The bangs framed her rounded face just right and the rest of her lengths were pulled away. Her makeup was visible, yet it wasn't too much. Her eyes were a beautiful light brown. Evander found himself trying to catch his breath as the lady walked back around to her seat after she offered him the one in front of her desk. She sat behind it and as he watched her do so, he found himself very impressed.

That angered him even more.

"May I offer you coffee? Tea? Water, perhaps?"

"Don't worry yourself. This won't take long," he answered, pulling himself out of his trance. "I thank you for your hospitality but none of that is going to get my money back. I'm beyond pissed that you would allow someone to take money that doesn't belong to them and then on top of that, you haven't even reached out to me to figure out a way to make amends. I'm pissed because I'm someone who supports Black women and it's looking like I should've just gone with the usual means of letting someone else handle my funds."

Christian's eyes rose as she regarded him. She reached for her own water. Evander figured she wanted to wet her throat for all of the garbage she was ready to feed him. He hoped that she understood that he wasn't going to fall for anything except him getting his monies back.

"First of all, Mr. King let me formally apologize for having kept you waiting while I endeavor to run my business, which most of it yesterday had been dedicated wholly into finding out who was the person within my company responsible for stealing your funds. I've just gotten wind that two of the women responsible were arrested and there's no doubt they will be charged heftily for their crimes.

However, as I'm the head of this company I take full responsibility for everything that goes on here. I can only give you my word that I am not the one who stole from you and you have my word that every cent will be returned to your accounts. I do profusely apologize for the attention this whole fracas drew to your business. Adams' is looking into every possible solution to ensure this doesn't happen as my position is to earn money, not steal it-"

"-I pray you use *every* possible solution. You and this establishment will pay dearly if I don't see every red cent back."

Christian's face furrowed but it was the only indication that anything he had said upset her. Evander found himself calmer now that she was starting to show her fangs.

"As I've said before, your money will be returned to you. I would rather not drag this out in court and instead pay you back posthaste, plus any damages your lawyers feel righteous to pay back to you. I will also remind you, Mr. King, that this isn't a drug sale gone wrong in the streets, but this *is* a corporate body, and I will not take on any threats to myself or my company lightly. We can either do this politely or we can do this otherwise. Despite what you believe, this is an honest company, and I will do everything I can to restore the funds that were stolen."

Christian arose, signaling the end of their meeting and Evander found himself disappointed. He'd been enjoying their back and forth. It hadn't gone on long enough.

"So noted, Ms. Adams. Please accept my sincerest apologies but do understand my duress. I'm running my own company and it's not a good day when your personal accountant tells you someone's been stealing from you."

Evander responded to her while she moved to see him to her door. He watched her backside move, almost unabashedly and had to stop himself from licking his lips. Christian was a perfectly formed coke bottle and he'd wanted nothing more than to fit his arms around her small waist and kiss away every bad word he'd hurled at her. The way that she responded in kind however, turned him on in the worst way. He berated himself for reacting to her as if he were a high school boy not in control of his urges.

"I do understand, Mr. King," she said. "I'll update you on any and all developments that arise, personally."

Evander reached into his pocket and pulled out a business card. Pressing it into her hand, he marveled at her softness even as he looked into her eyes.

"See to it that you do, Ms. Adams or I will escalate this matter further."

He turned on his heel and walked away as smoothly as he'd walked in.
—

Tiffany watched Evander walk into the wide, golden elevator and smirked as her office phone rang. She couldn't bother to hide the smirk when her boss ordered her to set up conference room B for a meeting.

"So, we're just going to ignore the fact that the finest thing on two legs just walked out of your office with a smile on his face?"

"I didn't notice anything past the fact that he's a 15-million-dollar liability to my business right now, Tiffany. Make sure to tell them I need them all there, immediately."

The laughter was still in Tiffany's voice when she answered that she'd do so. Tiffany sent an inter-office message to the Partners relaying Christian's message and then went to prepare the space for them. She also set up her own space so that she could take down the minutes from the meeting. She almost wished that she had popcorn because she knew it was going to be a good episode. Evander King walked in furious but had walked out placated. He didn't want anybody to know his feathers were smoother, but they indeed were. She wanted to ask Christian what magic she worked but knew better than to ask. Her boss was so prudish sometimes it made her look like a whore. The funny part of it all was that Tiffany was the virgin of the group.

Whatever the exchange had been, Tiffany could tell that Christian didn't have anything to worry about.

—

Christian sat through the meeting she pulled together, listening to her Partners' thoughts and findings at the point they were at. Her mind bounced in different directions and it was all she could do not to berate herself for her own thoughts.

She gave a report on the meeting with Evander King and she prayed she wasn't blushing crimson as she'd done so. Tiffany wasn't totally off when she snidely questioned her earlier as the man walked out. It had taken everything in her to ignore the fact that he was walking sex with his lithe form filling out whichever expensive suit he'd worn. Christian had no clue what brand he chose to wear for the day, only that she wished they'd met under less extenuating circumstances.

"Calm down, Christian. He's just a man," she chided inwardly. *"He's just a man."*

Dragging her mind from Evander, although he was the center of the conversation, Christian turned towards Monica.

"What do you have for me, Em?"

Monica cleared her throat. "I've decided interviewing over seventy-five percent of the staff wasn't necessary as that would pretty much cost unnecessary overhead and man hours. We already know it might be one or both of them involved."

"I think the interviewing should stretch out to coworkers they also work with closely and also bookkeepers in the department," Sonya added. "Something of this caliber couldn't have been kept secret."

"I'm unsure about that line of thinking," Christian interrupted. "This operation has been going on for more than six months and whoever's behind it was able to funnel a whole fifteen mil, so I think the person has the discipline to keep their mouth shut."

"There's also the fact that the person was able to pull one over Sharin," Monica added, shrugging her shoulders when Christian spared her a glance.

"So noted, Ms. James," was her response. "Sharin Reynolds is still on suspension until further notice."

The meeting pushed forward, Sonya pushing for Christian to have security look back over the past couple of months and note any patterns in the twosome's days leading up to the big break. Christian agreed, although hearing Sonya's voice did nothing but drag her back to the moment she had with Jerell the night before. The thought of him did nothing but turn her stomach inside out and it made her wonder for the first time in years what kind of man did the things that Jerell Williams did.

It was true that she responded to her heartbreak as if it were a fresh wound at times. The insecurities placed in her by her last relationship didn't sit well but she owned that more often than not. Christian was a woman well aware of herself and she knew ever since they'd dated, she hadn't been the same afterward. Most of her movements were from a survival standpoint but she had no clue how to heal and let everything go to have a healthy relationship with another person. What had upset her the most was that Jerell actually went out of his way to hurt her and to her recollection, she'd done absolutely nothing wrong.

Christian recalled the chase that she'd given him. She'd been taught from young to not just let a man have his way with her but to work for her. She hadn't realized he was only chasing her for the thrill until it was far too late. He had already packed up ship by the time he announced that he was leaving for Harvard in the fall and that he'd be doing so as a single man. It tore her apart that it hadn't even been six months beyond the gifting of her virginity to him that he'd do such a thing. He left her without a backwards glance only to try to get back with her when she, Monica, and Sharin arrived at Harvard themselves the next year.

The lowest thing she felt Jerell had ever done was date Sonya. She never knew how to approach him about it, so she never had. It was always interesting to her that out of all the women vying for his attention back then, he'd decide to date the one girl that she befriended outside of the circle of friends she already had. She had enjoyed Sonya's intelligence and quick wit. The couple of classes they had together cemented a friendship that Christian hoped stood as strong as the rest of her friendships.

Now that Jerell was walking around picking up calls that didn't belong to him, she wasn't so sure.

"So, to recap, we're going to keep an eye on Jamie and Jupiter. Plus, we're going to interview close friends and allies?"

Monica's question threw her out of her reverie. Christian hadn't wanted to waste time and had agreed on Monica's thoughts about wasted energies and money; however, she wanted to cover all bases, so Sonya's thoughts were sound. With a huge sigh, she nodded and then gave her verbal consent. There was a sadness in Monica's eyes, but she nodded. Christian knew her friend didn't enjoy the process she was undertaking; however, she was the only person she could trust to push information out of everybody. Monica was a person who got results. That'd been the case ever since they were in high school and it was a trait about her that Christian both loved and hated. Monica scaled back on many of her bad habits over the years and while she was grateful, she needed Monica to utilize the fear that she was good at pulling out of people.

The fact of the matter was that repaying Evander King for damages wasn't her biggest problem. Somebody had not only set out to steal but had marred the integrity of her business and it left her and the rest of her team feeling stripped bare. It was a hard thing to come back from, but Christian Adams' was a fighter if she was nothing else. In this fight she'd use whatever was at her disposal to reclaim the innocence of her company and of her people. The thought put new fire in her heart as she edged a look to every person in her team.

"Listen. I get that this isn't easy, but we didn't sign up for easy when we chose to start this business. We deal with misogynistic men on a daily basis. We deal with the media and their foolish comments because we're women dominating in a generally male dominated field. Celebrities and the elite are knocking on our doors for our services and we've been on an upscale for years. Let's prove our mettle and show the men out there we can roll with the punches just as easily and *gracefully* as they can. Dismissed."

Christian stood and walked out of the room with her head held high. Monica watched her friend and had to admit being inspired by her strength. She'd been rearing to walk out with renewed strength when Sonya tapped her on the shoulder.

"Hey. I'm heading out to lunch. Come out with me."

Monica raised a brow at the request, ready to deny it when her stomach growled loud enough for all those left to hear. Tiffany chuckled on the way out, forcing an embarrassed smile on her face. She shrugged and questioned Sonya if she were paying. When Sonya nodded in the positive, Monica rose her brow again but accepted the invitation.

"Give me ten minutes and I'll be downstairs."

"Cool, you pick the place. I'll be out front."

Sonya walked out of the conference room, her heels clicking the sound of her departure and it left Monica feeling slightly uneasy. Still, she shrugged off her bad feelings and decided to get ready for her impromptu lunch with her colleague. She hoped nothing untoward was about to come up. Hopefully, lunch was the only thing on the menu when they decided to sit down to eat.

Chapter
Six

"Is Christian screwing Jerell?"

Monica James couldn't quite call herself an elegant woman so when the question was posed out of the blue, she wasn't surprised that she spat out the wine she was daintily sipping as well. She coughed lightly as she dabbed at her mouth, truly shocked and unprepared for the question. The more the question marinated in her mind, the more the coughing turned into laughter. The laughter overtook her so much that Sonya's earlier concern turned into irritation at her friend's display.

"Monica..."

"Girl, bye. Christian probably isn't even screwing herself." Monica waved at her eyes as she attempted to calm down.

"I'm serious, Monica."

"I'm serious, Sonya."

Monica took a couple minutes more to stop laughing and when she had, she looked Sonya in her eyes to realize the question was indeed something she wanted to know. It was puzzling that after ten years of being with Jerell this question would come up because as far as Monica was concerned, Jerell Williams was pretty much dead to Christian. She barely acknowledged the man and unfortunately any other after their split. That much Monica did know.

"Sonya, you've been with Jerell for like ten years?"

Sonya nodded. "So imagine what I'm thinking when Jerell gets out of our bed to call Christian to pretty much tell her she's had her chance and that she needs to stop trying to interrupt our night."

Monica raised a shocked eyebrow and yet she shook her head at the absurdity of it. She took another bite of the lunch portion steak she was plowing through and then glanced at Sonya again. Sighing, she decided telling the truth of the situation was the best cause of action. She hoped Christian didn't get upset with her after the fact however, something had to be said to clear her friend's name. Jerell Williams was obviously trying to make a problem for whatever backwards reason he had.

A man like Jerell had many.

"Sonya, Jerell and Christian dated way before you met. He broke up with her before he went to Harvard. They'd been together for almost two years and he decided that he should be single when he left. Naturally, this broke her heart."

"Oh?"

"Yeah," Monica said. "I don't mean to say this to offend you, but I don't

39

understand this questioning or thought process that anything's going on based on a couple of words he had with Christian."

"Obviously she never got over him. Why would he call her at all to make such a statement?"

Monica sighed heavily, ashamed that she let her vices get her in uncomfortable situations to this day. It was already in her spirit that she knew Sonya was up to no good with the invitation of lunch and knew she should've declined the outing. Now her steak and potatoes weren't as enjoyable as it should've been due to the content of the conversation. The conversation itself was draining her mind more than the food was.

"Sonya...have you not even for a second wondered why *your* man picked up *your* phone to *call back* your boss?

Sonya rose a brow but didn't have an answer to offer her. Monica stared back at her pointedly, awaiting an answer. Thirty tense seconds passed and the only sound that could be heard was Monica chewing and swallowing.

"Okay, let's list the facts and you'll deal accordingly, okay? Jerell and Christian dated briefly. I will say that this was Christian's principal relationship since going to college. To know Christian is to know that she had a strict upbringing so that meant no boys. I don't believe she could even mention a boy so when she gets from under her parents' roof and goes to college, she meets Jerell. Jerell is about a year older so he gets accepted into Harvard. He feels like he wants to be a whore for the time-being, so he tells Christian he doesn't want to be distracted while he studies-national fuckboy line-and pretty much walks away cold-"

"-What's the point of this..."

Monica lifted a finger. "I'm not done. We all put our bids in for graduate school. Ironically, all of us together got accepted to Harvard. Sharin didn't make Yale. I didn't make Princeton, Christian somehow made all three so Harvard it was."

"Oh, so y'all couldn't bear to be-"

"-Still talking. So, we go to Harvard. Christian met you first if I'm correct. Before y'all met, Jerell was doing his best trying to shatter Sharin's reputation and get back with Christian in the same breath. Sharin never and I mean *never* liked Jerell and after he left Christian, I understood why. I don't know how he is with you but from the little I can remember he chased her. He showed up with flowers. He bought gifts on her birthday. He wooed her in a way that most women want to be wooed by a man. They were pretty close I think...but most of the relationship had been about him. She got so wrapped up in it that when he left it was like...he left a shadow at first. Shay and I did what we could, and it did go a long way. She just never let anybody back in since."

Monica took a break to sip on her glass of wine. She raised a finger once more to signal to Sonya that she was still talking. Once she finished about three swallows, she continued.

"Back to you. Christian and you were friends. Jerell was still trying to get back with Christian who actively refused him at every turn. He suddenly pops up with you at a party we're at to show you off. We're all shocked. The conversation did happen where I did mention that Christian should tell you. She always seemed so put off of doing so and her decision was to act as if Jerell didn't exist. Which she had, for about ten years."

"So why did neither you nor Sharin say anything?" Sonya questioned. "I'm unsure of where my trust stands with either one of you at this point."

"I can understand those feelings but honestly, it's not that deep," Monica answered. "I'm indifferent to him. Sharin doesn't like him. Christian equates him to Voldemort."

Sonya would've laughed if she weren't confused as it were. She wondered if Monica was even telling the truth or covering for her friend and boss.

"I didn't say anything because that wasn't my story to tell. I'm only saying something now because I believe it's high time you check your man on a number of violations. There was no reason for him to call Christian nor touch your phone. Do you have the free reign to just pick him up whenever's clever?"

Sonya bit her lip because she felt she didn't have to answer that question. Though her arguments on the situation made sense, it still put her in a bad place as far as trusting her Partners. She worked alongside these women to forward the vision of one of the best friends she ever had. It had been an honor to work alongside Christian Adams and to be a part of a team of strong Black women who were becoming a force to be reckoned with in the finance industry.

"I'm just saying. So, I can personally vouch that Christian isn't checking for Jerell at all."

"No, you can't. I don't believe anybody can vouch for her at all," Sonya responded. "I'm pretty much convinced that something is totally off and I'm not about to take any bullshit lying down. I don't give a shit if she is my boss."

Monica sighed as she raised her hand, signaling the waiter to bring over the check. Sonya raised a brow at the action.

"I told you I'd pay."

"I know but that's not necessary. You only did that to draw me into this conversation and while I didn't know what it was about before it was had, I know now that it was for some bullshit. I love you, Sonya. We all do. I just hope you smarten up."

"Smarten up? Our boss may or may not be fucking my boyfriend and you want me to play it cool?"

"You know some people have to come to work after burying their mother? Some women still have to show up to a school play after their husbands beat the breaks off of them. Some people even, Heaven forbid, have to run a business even in the mire of the outside world calling them a thief. We still have to figure out who siphoned money from the company in a timely manner. What I'm trying to say is feel how you feel but we still have business to attend to. This conversation went on too long. If you have any further issues between Christian and Jerell, you need to consult with them. Don't ever dangle food in my face for some bullshit ever again, Sonya Powers. I'm a grown ass woman. Ask me what you need to ask me or don't ask me at all."

Monica hadn't realized how angry she'd gotten until she went into her tirade. When the waiter appeared, she requested separate checks.

Sonya stared at her as she'd done so, wondering where this fierce loyalty to Christian Adams stemmed from. She wanted to ask her but decided against it as she already seemed to have upset Monica enough.

Still, the temptation to ask her laid on her shoulder like a monkey. Its unopposable thumbs dug into her shoulder, literally egging her on but she bit her tongue. It was obvious that Monica was on Christian's side in the whole ordeal.

Once her mind cleared up however, Sonya decided she understood Monica's position. When she apologized for it, Monica graciously accepted. On the way back to the job, Sonya logicized that she wasn't against any of the others about Jerell, but she couldn't get over how Christian never made mention of their liaison not one time in ten years. She might not have dated Jerell at all but that would've been back then. Now, Jerell was definitely her man and as much as she loved her job, Christian stopped being her boss when that line was crossed.

It was her hope that her job wouldn't be lost in the process, however. Sonya did love her job and every perk that came with it. Adams' Accounting paid her a generous salary. Holiday bonuses were a fact of life and it did fund the lifestyle she'd always wanted to live from her high school days. Christian wasn't a very hard boss although she demanded excellence from every Partner. It was half the reason she wasn't as emotional about Sharin's suspension as Monica was. As it were, Sharin was definitely lucky Christian hadn't terminated her completely for her long oversight. Still, as much as she loved her job, Sonya would give it away if she felt she were being a long-term pawn.

That just wasn't how she did business.

Two days later, Sharin woke up with a renewed sense of being. Stretching, she smiled slightly to realize her fiancé had taken off for the day, so she had the house to herself. Turning on her side she glanced at the clock and groaned. She'd forgotten the last time she woke up at eleven o'clock let alone one in the afternoon. The guilt started to trickle in and then shrugged it off as quickly as it piled on. If Christian hadn't suspended her, she'd have already been at work and through at least thirty accounts by then. Lunch would've been her main priority but as she was temporarily banned from working, she decided she would take on the day as she saw fit.

First, she laid back and whispered her salutations to God. Fifteen minutes later found her praying in a way she hadn't in about six month's time. Before she'd known it, tears cascaded down her eyes as she vented about Christian. Her other worries and fears carried her to the shower where her tears mixed in with the water as she laid down her burdens. For the first time since she'd walked out of Christian's office, she could say she felt peace in what happened.

Endowed in another silk robe, she padded downstairs to cook a light breakfast for herself that consisted of bacon, eggs, and home fries. She cut up her own potatoes into small cubes and seasoned them with garlic and onion powder. Adding chives at the end, she felt accomplished as she sat down to dine. Lifting up a finger, she doubled back to the kitchen and poured herself a mimosa and grinned cheekily as she settled in the living room with a book. Putting on some smooth jazz in the background, she ate her food and engrossed herself in the life of Michelle Obama, falling in love more with the former first lady as she read on.

Her excitement couldn't be contained when she first introduced Barack into the story and she might've jumped up and down in excitement when the doorbell rang. Sucking her teeth soundly, she stood up and walked the length of the living room and through the dining room to get to the door. Upon opening it Sharin was greeted by her cousin, Chastity.

Chastity McCain stood at five feet seven to Sharin's five feet two. Many times, during their childhood, Chastity was good for using her height to instill fear into Sharin. She did many other things to make her life a living hell whenever she could as well. There were many things Sharin was still getting over. Both of their families were born into privilege. Their grandfather left each of his daughters a sizable trust fund upon his death but Sharin's mother, Mona, received much more of his estate than her younger sister, Mila. Mila had always been bitter towards her for that and pretty much condoned whatever evil her daughter would do to Sharin. Sharin in turn would always implore her mother to do something about it but Mona never would, in turn imploring her daughter to make it all stop herself.

Sharin had always loathed her cousin but there'd always been a hurt layered in her feelings. At the heart of all of the drama she didn't understand why Chastity went out of her way to make her life hell. Chastity's life wasn't much different. They'd both been to the best schools and were afforded the best opportunities. They were around top tier people and had their pick of men. Sharin shied away from men because of a long-term prank that Chastity pulled on her in high school. Even afterward, she'd been stuck in her life of singularity that she didn't trust another man until Maddox.

"Baby cousin! How are you?"

Sharin raised a brow. "What are you here for, Chastity?"

"Oh, so you're not going to invite me in?"

"You didn't even have my address in the first place," Sharin crossed her arms. "So no, you're not invited in."

Chastity giggled and Sharin was left wondering what was so funny. She took her cousin in, with her clear, smooth chocolate skin and light brown eyes. Chastity was shaped naturally the way many women risked their lives under the knife for. Her waist was cinched in at a whopping twenty-two inches and her backside pronounced its presence at thirty-six inches. Her double D breasts jutted out whatever she chose to wear, which at the present moment had been a pink wrap dress. She wore a matching pink brim hat to ward off the sun's rays as it was a whopping 90 degrees in Atlanta. Sharin had always felt inferior growing up because of her slender frame. It was another thing Chastity made her feel insecure about.

"Me and Momma just found out about you and Maddox's wedding. I wanted to know why we weren't invited."

It'd been a year before at another industry party where Sharin and Christian were drawing in clients. Maddox had been there in support but the whole night he was running away from Chastity who'd been there just because of the men in attendance. Sharin noted her cousin's apparent attention on Maddox but it wasn't revealed until later on that night that she had tried to get with him with the full knowledge that he and Sharin were together. Sharin had never approached her cousin about it, feigning peace but told her mother in no uncertain terms that both her aunt and Chastity weren't invited to her wedding. She would've only been invited in the first place because she was family.

"You weren't invited because you tried to screw my fiancé, Chastity. Why would you think you'd be invited afterward? You're lucky I didn't try to kill you."

"Kill me? You'd kill your cousin over a piece of dick that doesn't even want you?"

"I'm not for the childish games, Chastity. Get off my doorstep and don't come back. I'll have you arrested."

"You? Have me *arrested*? Oh, so little Sharin is grown now so she can tell me where to go!" Chastity laughed, obnoxiously. "I see Ms. Adams Apple finally rubbed off on you. That's cute."

"Chastity...what are you hoping to achieve?"

"Achieve? I'm just here to prove to you that you're nothing as I've always told you. All this running around with a bitch you're so loyal to and you're at home, twiddling your thumbs instead of giving up this stupid notion of working and going back home. You're just a pretty face, Sharin. You're meant to be a socialite and nothing more."

"How did you know that I was suspended?" Sharin questioned, raising a brow. "I haven't told anyone."

Chastity made a show out of covering her mouth, but a chuckle slipped out. Sharin's face turned red and her fists started to ball up. The whole scene only made her cousin glory more in her display.

"Oh, you thought it was so top secret that you were suspended? It's all over the blogs and the updates that keep happening. You think those people you pay will keep their mouths shut if a newscaster paid them top dollar to talk? You're basically a suspect for all that money y'all been stealing but I don't get why you'd need to steal...when you're an heiress."

Sharin crossed her arms and leaned against her door. She stared at her cousin, still not understanding why she'd want to kick her while she was down. None of it was making sense.

"Either way, none of it is your concern. Get off my porch, Chastity," Sharin said, slamming the door hard.

Sharin walked back into her house, sadness cloaking her being all over again. By the time she walked back into her living room, anxiety had joined the party. Instead of returning to her book and breakfast, she found herself on her iMac, searching through all of the blogs. She'd typed in her name on Google, waiting to see a bunch of stories confirming what her cousin reported to her still, nothing came back that confirmed her as a suspect. Her hand was shaky by the time she picked up her phone to call Christian. Her friend picked up on the second ring.

"Shay? You alright?"

"Did anyone leak to the press that I got suspended?"

"What? No. Your suspension is only office gossip fodder at best. Only the Partners know about it. Why?"

Sharin sighed deeply and told Christian that Chastity was at her house. Relaying the story made her vibrate with anger all over again.

"Shay, you have to calm down...listen, we need to talk. Let's meet at Glenn's later on tonight."

"I don't even want to look at you either, Christian if I'm honest," Sharin snapped. "This wouldn't have happened if-"

"Shay!" Christian cut her off, "Just meet me tonight. We definitely need to talk."

Sharin rolled her eyes, "Yeah. I'll meet you at like nine."

"Cool. And relax!"

"You relax," Sharin mumbled. "I'll call you when I'm on the way."

Sharin was shocked to hear Christian chuckle lightly before she hung up. She rolled her eyes and again laid on the couch. Before she knew it, she was praying again. Her prayers incited more tears and before she'd known it, sleep had surrounded her and peace consoled her.

SkyLounge was the premiere rooftop lounge in Atlanta. It sat above Glenn Hotel in the midst of the city, affording views of the neighboring buildings and a magnificent skyline. Christian loved to come during her off-time but hadn't done so in months. She normally conducted a lot of business meet-ups and fundraisers in the space when it was available but reserving the space never came without a fight. Glenn's also drew in celebrity clientele that got first dibs more often than not.

The ambience was sexy and it was definitely the place to see or be seen in the Atlanta night scene.

She and Monica sat at their reserved table, preparing to snack on appetizers as they waited for Sharin to arrive. Christian groaned inwardly to see Monica so giddy.

"Stop it," Christian said. "She's still on ice."

"I don't get why," Monica shrugged. "You've seen the books. She was never going to catch those discrepancies."

"I know. But she called earlier sounding frantic and if we're both thinking the same thing...I have to keep her suspended. I have a bad feeling it's about to get worse before it gets better."

Monica's right eyebrow raised daintily, "So what's the hunch?"

"That my cousin has something to do with it."

Both women looked up to see Sharin standing before them in a red faux wrap dress. The spaghetti straps sat on her broad shoulders and the gold chain belt cinched her in. Sharin's hair was curled loosely, giving the appearance that she wasn't trying. Her makeup had been light with only her eyebrows shaped and her lipstick painted a soft nude. The look on her face hadn't been friendly but she never failed at naturally giving off a sex appeal that drew in men and the occasional woman. It was one of the things Christian loved about her friend. This was her best friend whose loyalty traveled leaps and bounds for her. The reminder made her ashamed of her treatment of her. Her voice was sheepish when she greeted her.

"Hey, sis."

Sharin rolled her eyes and took the seat adjacent to Monica. Looking into Christian's eyes, she rolled hers again.

"I'm not sorry that I suspended you. I'm sorry about why."

Their waiter, a tan colored Indian man, appeared questioning if they were ready to order. Monica and Christian both replied that they weren't. Sharin ordered a glass of Merlot as she started to pick around from the appetizers already laid out on the table. The waiter nodded and rotated to his next table, allowing Sharin to turn her attention back to her best friend once more.

"Enlighten me, Christian," Sharin said. "Matter of fact, that's not the issue here. The issue is how you tried to make me look like I was less than capable of a job I've been doing for years. A job that damn near made me lose the one man I actually love. I need to understand Christian, why you'd actually climb on top of a high horse and talk to and about me like…girl, I think you treated shit better."

Christian released a sigh, suddenly feeling tired. She owed her friend the explanation, but she surely didn't want to give it.

"The thought process was that you can't plan your wedding and work at the same time. The real reason is I know I'm losing my best friend to a man after we painstakingly fought to ward them off."

Sharin's eyes immediately filled up with tears. "You're an *asshole*. How does that work when we work with each other every day?"

Christian sucked her teeth. "You're playing coy but let's be real, Shay. Marriage is a big deal. Maddox isn't just your boyfriend anymore. Anything can come from this. A move, a baby, you deciding that being rich for real is what you'd like to do while he works…it can go either way."

"First off, I've been with you from the beginning…or you've been with me. I don't know anymore. I just remember one day my cousin was giving me hell and the next we're building the blueprint for Adams' during recess. We were a unit…the three of us and I dedicated my life to proving my loyalty as well as showing my family I was more than an heiress. The charmed life has its upsides, but I was happy building something that had *my* name on it. You're crazy to think that after all this time, I'd just pick up and leave."

"It's a logical thought process."

The defense came in softly and while Sharin might've believed her days before, she now saw her friend in the same light her fiancé painted her in. It broke her heart that she'd lash out in the way that she had but understanding caused her to soften and not hold it against her. She loved her best friend more than most of her family and in most cases, considered her as such. While it was true that most of the dynamic between them would change, Sharin had no plans to just disappear as if her life's work hadn't been Adams' as well.

"No, it's not. Sometimes you're under the assumption that you built that place all by yourself and it's the opposite. We're all angry, confused, and fearful about what happened. At the very least however, I deserved better."

"You're right," Christian conceded. "And I'm sorry."

Silence fell between the threesome whilst they sipped their separate imbibements. The view enjoyed them more than they enjoyed it as the music started to pick up and a bigger crowd started to form on the dance floor. The waiter came and returned with Sharin's glass and disappeared once more, seeing none of them were ready as yet. Sharin sipped daintily, enjoying the ambience when Monica interrupted breezily.

"So, I'm just chopped liver, huh?"

Christian chuckled, "Don't start, Nik."

Monica giggled and threw back her thick tresses that threatened to cover half of her face. She leaned back and watched her two best friends reconcile. Inwardly she rolled her eyes, however. Reginald had been right, but it didn't alter her thought process on her friend. Most people wouldn't admit their mistakes and apologize for it. All in all, she just hoped Christian faced her own issues with the same fire that she took on everything else. At some point she was going to have to admit to herself that she needed help as far as her own issues went. They ran deeper than Sharin getting married to Maddox, that was for certain.

"I'm just making sure. If you don't try to fuck me over because I'm getting married, I'm gonna get jealous."

"I'm sure I'll be over myself by then."

Christian paused to take a sip of the Riesling she ordered and looked at her friend.

"I wasn't right for that. I wasn't right for how I treated you and I'm sorry. You're still suspended though."

Sharin smirked. "I accept your apology...and I understand."

"That I'm not shit or that you're still suspended."

"Both," Sharin said. "But I love you...you do need to work on your abandonment issues though."

"I don't have any," Christian said. "I had a bad moment and I'm over it."

Monica motioned to raise a finger and reversed the action when Sharin bumped her lightly with her leg.

"Okay, Christian," Sharin said. "So now that I'm finished crying, I'm hungry."

"I personally want to dance so I'm hitting the floor," Monica said. "Order for me, Shay. You know what I like."

With a flirty wink, Monica jumped up and walked on the dance floor. She found Jasmine and the twosome danced to the live band that played their rendition of Whitney Houston's infamous, *I Wanna Dance with Somebody* in the background. Christian turned to Sharin and sighed.

"I'm tired, Shay."

Sharin took in her friend and sighed at the dogged tiredness she could see all over her. She wanted to give her a hug and reassure her that everything would be fine but tamped down against the emotion. Unfortunately, those were the breaks when it came to leadership. It was a role Christian took on with all the gusto of a seasoned Olympian. Sharin was confident that Christian would find her stride at some point. To coddle her would be blasphemous.

"Talk to me," Sharin replied instead.

"We looked over the books. Everything was balanced. Everything looked right and correct. You wouldn't have questioned them. I wouldn't have questioned them."

Sharin nodded as she picked up her Merlot and sipped again.

"Also, Jerell picked up Sonya's phone three nights ago to tell me to stop interrupting their time and that I had my chance."

Sharin choked, "Excuse me?"

"Girl. I'm beyond undone."

"What would give him the audacity?"

Christian shrugged. "I haven't talked to him in ten years, Shay! He happily inserted himself in my life the best way he knew how when I did my best to shut him out. Who told him to date Sonya? Not a soul!"

Sharin sighed. "He needs his ass whipped."

"He needs more than that," Christian mumbled. "The worst part of it was…it hit home that he left me. He left me broken-hearted to pick up the pieces but it's like, in a sadistic way he has to keep reminding me that I'm alone and I don't get it."

"No, he just wants to reinforce his presence back into your life because you won't let him back in. All this is, honestly, is his childish way to get your attention. The sad part is he'd leave Sonya even though they had ten years together. All of it just to satisfy his own ego."

"To make it all better, Monica just told me that Sonya asked her about it all earlier. So now, my ex-boyfriend is an asshole and now Sonya might make more of it than what it is."

Sharin sighed hard, picking up her Merlot once more. She sipped slowly and shrugged as she set the glass down. "I don't know, sis. Maybe it's good that it's all coming out. She needs to dump his ass, too."

"It'd make my life easier. If I could get him and Mr. King out of my life for good, that'd work just fine."

"So, what's the plan with him?"

"Settle, since it's still our fault," Christian said, rolling her eyes hard. "I didn't tell you how he came for me the other day."

"Well sis…the man is out of more than a few million."

Christian giggled at Sharin's dry response. Christian relayed the details, pausing only when the waiter came back around. Sharin finally ordered the vegetable Bolognese and Christian requested another glass of the Riesling she was sipping on earlier. Once he left again, Christian continued.

"So, after all that I tell him I'll contact him personally should anything else come up. He hands me his business card and tells me to do so."

Sharin smirked as her friend told the story. Tiffany mentioned that the man was handsome and she wondered if her friend was truly bothered by his words or if there was something more to the tale. Christian didn't waste words about anyone if they weren't important.

"Well, again sis, more than a few million. It's not like we're rolling in Bill Gates' money out here. Every cent we make, we treasure."

"I know, but damn. He went on and on and on and I'm like ugh, I'm sorry, shut up!"

Sharin laughed and shook her head at her friend. "You're just not used to being in the position of someone telling you about yourself," she pointed out. "He's just moving the way you would in the same position."

"Still…" Christian laughed. "I know you're right, but still…"

She then sighed wistfully, staring out into the dancefloor. Monica and Jasmine were having a good time dancing with each other and mingling with the different characters that they would bump into. Some of the men flocked around them and it wasn't surprising. Their energy was very effervescent separately so together it was a double whammy for any man in the vicinity.

The wine was starting to take its sedative effect on her but Christian still wished she'd ordered a stronger drink. She wished for the stresses of the day to wear all the way away. The local news was dragging her name into the mud and that alone was hurting her heart in a way that she felt nobody could understand.

Adams' was an honorable business. It was black-owned and female-operated. She wasn't against hiring a capable man but at press time, the top slots were only for her girls. She also wasn't against hiring outside of her race as she had quite a few people who weren't Black or female working under her. She set out to find people who were capable enough to do the job to a high standard on a daily basis. Christian went well beyond the call of being a great boss and an even more great leader. One thing about her was that she didn't demand of her staff more than what she demanded of herself.

To see her business threatened was more than she could handle or bear. She put her all into it, her very namesake. That someone could be so rotten as to-

"Christian," Sharin broke into her thoughts. "Calm down. It's okay."

"No, it's not, Shay. Somebody really went out of their way to tear us down and I'm livid," she confessed. "I don't know entirely what's what and it's a sickening feeling. That's like going to sleep one way and waking up another. I promise I'm going to figure out who did this. I'm definitely going to make them pay."

Sharin smirked. "I know you will. Still, you're out here. Might as well have fun."

Christian nodded solemnly, her gaze drifting back into the dance floor. That was when a familiar face stuck out in the crowd to her and suddenly, her heart started to race. Her hands started to get clammy and she cursed inwardly. There was actually no reason why she should react the way that she was.

There was no reason why she should be tripping over herself because Evander King was walking in the direction of the booth they were seated in.

He was dressed comfortably but still suitably for the setting. A crisp white button down with two buttons open fit him as if the tailor studied his physique well. Black slacks that were neither too tight or too loose sat just right. They moved with him easily as he strolled leisurely toward their table.

"Evenin' Ms. Adams."

Christian discreetly swallowed as she returned a wan smile to his more bright one. It was all over his aura that he meant to throw her off after their first meeting. He strolled as if he knew she'd be waiting for him there. She inadvertently crossed her legs and wondered if she'd become a horny teenager around him. The last thing she wanted to do was turn into a mindless heap whenever he came into sight. It wasn't in her character to ever fall apart.

"I'm surprised that you're out here considering that you promised to be sweating over who's stealing my ends."

Christian's smile spread. "I check in with you when I'm at work. Off the clock is still my life, Mr. King. Enjoy your evening because I'll definitely be enjoying mine."

Evander's grin turned softer, making Christian's heart rate speed up more. It felt familiar.

"Actually, I was hoping to spend part of my evening dancing with you."

Although the music was pounding on the rooftop, Christian felt a deafening silence come to her ears after hearing his response. Did her client just try to make a move on her or was she losing her mind?

"I wouldn't mind under other circumstances. It just seems inappropriate to dance with you after you threatened me not even 24 hours ago."

"Well, like you mentioned, you are off the clock. And I think I'd like to admire you in the dress you picked to enjoy the evening in."

"Maybe I will. I think however, I'm still smarting from some of your chauvinist remarks earlier today. I think I'll pass."

Evander rose a brow. "I never put you down as a woman."

"You didn't have to. You were way too obvious," Christian rambled. "I didn't even get upset because I knew you were upset about the money-rightfully so-I just needed to set you straight. I'm still a human being; woman or not. I still demand respect."

Sharin watched as the chemistry between them bubbled over like a glass of the driest champagne. She only came out knowing that Christian wanted to make amends. It was a bonus to unwind from the stresses of both the job and wedding planning. Truth be told, the longer she sat and witnessed the back and forth between her friend and Evander King she found herself adding everything up. The sum of every part made Sharin slightly nervous realizing he was the gentleman that was demanding repayment from Adams'.

Sharin took him in, defensiveness entering her psyche. It wasn't that he was an ugly man. The opposite was true. He was probably a good man just showing interest in her friend, but memories of Christian's ex infiltrated her mind. She'd forgotten the last time her friend looked at a man with unbridled interest.

"Excuse me miss. Is it okay if I spend some time with your friend?"

Sharin's thoughts were interrupted as Evander suddenly included her in the conversation. It stunned her for a quick second as she offered a polite smile. She took one more sip of her wine as she caught Christian's eyes. They begged for her to stay but Sharin couldn't help but exact a little bit of revenge on her friend for her earlier stunt. Besides, it wouldn't hurt for her to have alone time with an interested suitor for once.

With a smile she replied, "Sure. I actually ordered a nice entree but I suddenly have no appetite. Enjoy it for me."

Evander's smile was again boyish as he thanked her. Sharin announced that she would join Jasmine and Monica on the dance floor and then made her exit. She giggled lowly, feeling Christian's eyes on her back like daggers.

Revenge hadn't tasted that good to her, ever.

Chapter
Seven

Christian was surprised by a number of things as she sat across from her unlikely date. They sat in silence, seizing each other up quietly as they ate. Christian rolled her eyes inwardly at Sharin, preparing to curse her out at the first opportunity. The last thing she wanted to do was share a meal with a 15-million-dollar liability, even if he was the finest man she'd laid eyes on in quite some time. She hadn't wanted to, even if his voice sounded dreamy to her ears. The last thing she wanted to do was share the moment with a man who all but pulled a gun out to her head not even a whole day ago.

She was trying to figure out his angle.

"I have no angle, so stop looking at me like that."

Caught off guard once more, Christian blushed and decided to keep eating. Sharin had annoyed her earlier by ordering the meal but it was suddenly her saving grace.

"Are you sure you don't?"

Evander looked across from him, taking in Christian's every feature and decided his earlier reactions to her wasn't just him having a moment. He admired the way she stood in the face of him airing her out for what he felt like was her brushing him off in the face of his money being stolen. He had only come to heckle her a little bit more because he hadn't been prepared to see her at Glenn's. He'd been fantasizing about her being home, burning her eyes out over a screen and tracking down his missing money. Again, Christian shocked him by her flippant dismissal of him.

Naturally, he accepted the challenge.

"If you want my honesty, frankly, you're gorgeous…I wanted to show you just how gorgeous I found you this morning. I know I'm being brash but it's the only thing I can tell you right now."

His admission was like a gut punch and rendered her speechless. Thankfully the food was still there, and she ate slowly and methodically so she was able to digest all he was saying to her. As she turned over his thoughts in her own mind, she came to the conclusion that his honesty turned her on. She'd be lying to herself if she said she hadn't felt the same way. She had never met Evander King in person the whole time his accounts were in her firm and wondered why his namesake hadn't traveled all the way up to the top? She had to assume his own people dealt with the money aspects of his business and not the man himself.

"I couldn't tell," Christian answered, coolly. "You were busy trying to burn me for my incompetence in running my company."

"Come on, you know that's all in a professional arena. I can't help it if what my mind was thinking inwardly was opposite to my feelings on my business. I can't help that you're so damn fine that every man in here wishes they were in my position. Especially that man that's sitting at the bar acting like he hasn't been watching us the whole time."

Christian raised an eyebrow and looked over in the direction that Evander angled his head. There, Jerrell sat at the bar trying to look inconspicuous and failing miserably. He bobbed his head to the music while sipping on whatever drink he had in his hand. Seeing him made Christian sighed heavily as she turned her face back to Evander.

"So, is he someone I should worry about?"

Christian regarded Evander with a questionable glance, furrowed eyes, and all. It made him chuckle lightly.

"Is he my competition?"

The question forced laughter out of Christian, who picked up her wine glass and sipped again. When she put it down she giggled once more.

"Excuse me for that. No, he is in no wise any man's competition. He's a mistake I made long ago and that's where that ends."

"It looks to me as if he's the one who's made the mistake and not you."

Evander's intense gaze on her made her want to shift around but she sat still. Shaking her foot somewhat, she sighed at the bombardment of emotions attacking her. It'd been a long time since she laid eyes on Jerrell Washington and seeing his face did her no good.

"Honestly, it doesn't matter at this point. It'd be all the same if I never saw him again."

Evander nodded his head, understanding her sentiments and continued to eat the meal that Sharin chose for herself. He noted that it was delicious.

"This is good. You know this is my first time here?" Evander questioned, causing Christian to gasp in shock.

"That's surprising. Since this place has been open just about all of Atlanta's been here. We do a lot of business here."

Evander explained that it was a friend of his who referred him to the place when they bumped into each other earlier. His friend, Terry, worked with the police force and often did security there on his off nights or when he needed the extra money. It'd been sometime since they'd seen each other and the move was to come to Glenn's and blow off some steam. Again, Evander was shocked that the night was going differently than what he had in mind.

Turning his face into the crowd, Evander eyed his friend Terry dancing with one of Christian's friends. He noted that she was a beautiful woman and it made him chuckle. Terry was never one to turn down the company of a beautiful woman and this night was no different than the many others he'd hung out with his friend.

"Well, I like it. Maybe we should come back for a second date."

Christian choked on air at the casual way he slid in the statement.

"Second date? What happened to the first?"

Evander smirked, "We're already here. We ate. I'm assuming we're going to dance because why not? I planned to see you to your door safely. That would've been after footing the bill."

"You're not footing the bill."

Evander deadpanned her. "Stop it. This isn't a Destiny's Child video. I'm aware that you run a multi-million dollar company. I know you're more than able to foot the bill, but this shouldn't even be a discussion. You're letting me foot the bill."

She lifted up her hands in mock-surrender, realizing her error in that moment. Christian could almost feel Sharin's disapproving gaze on her for the misstep.

She was out of practice.

"Well, excuse me. If it makes you happy, be my guest."

"I hope to be more than your guest sometime soon, Ms. Adams."

Despite herself, Christian smiled. It wasn't every day that the smoothest man she'd met in a long time was almost falling over himself-in a smooth way-to get to know her. The unfortunate part in all of it was that Jerrell's presence marred it all for her. It wasn't only in his physical presence but also in her mind. She wouldn't go as far as her heart because that part of her was cold to him for the longest. He served as a lesson to her that all men wanted to do was steal the very essence of a woman and disappear after they'd won their prize.

The last person she should have been thinking of was Jerrell, not when this masterpiece of a man sat before her giving her every bit of his attention. She blamed it on the last word conversation they ever had.

"No. This is her man. The one that's been fucking her while you were busy calling trying to interrupt our shit."

She wondered what his thoughts were standing next to the bar. Catching herself wondering it led to shame. She pushed shame and Jerrell aside for two moments and looked Evander in his eyes, still smiling.

"I'd think I'd like that, too. But for now, my girls and I have to get home."

Evander nodded. "So are we good for a second date?"

"You mean the first date?"

"Whatever you want to call it, Ms. Adams. It can be whatever you like as long as I can see you again…outside of your office."

Christian grinned wryly, almost forgetting the conditions they met under in the first place. It was enough for her to open her mouth and cancel the next date before it even began. Still, looking up into his face again dispelled her concerns. His dark bedroom eyes pierced her round ones and Christian shuddered inside.

Evander pulled out his phone and handed it to her, watching her as she entered her phone number. When he saw her phone ring inside of her purse, he smiled down at her.

"I hope you pick up quicker than you did for me at the office," He quipped, making her flush red again.

"If you hope for me to pick up at all you'll stop while you're ahead."

Evander smirked, wanting so badly to put his arms around her and kiss the snide remarks off of her lips. He wondered who she thought she was fooling but it wasn't him. He thought he'd been alone in his attraction to her but saw with clear eyes that she wanted him as well. Perhaps she wasn't into fooling him more than she just didn't want things to progress too fast. He understood that the woman called the shots and he merely was hoping to get a foothold into her life.

Evander King understood that Christian Adams was the boss in her world and in this dance they started to dance, she was the boss as well. He might make the advances but knew if she weren't pleased, all dealings between them would cease. So, for the interim, he'd think wisely before he poked more fun at her.

Still, watching her light face turn red amused him. It did something to him to know that she was as affected by him as he was of her. Knowing that was a balm to his mind.

"Text me when you get home, Ms. Adams. Matter of fact, let me make sure you make it."

When Christian looked up at him questionably, he lifted up his phone to show her he opened up the Uber app. Her eyes widened.

"No, it's okay, really."

"Let me do this, really," Evander looked into her eyes, and because she saw the plea in them, she softened.

Christian motioned to her girlfriends to gather around when Evander told her to and he put the addresses for each one. When he had finished and the rest of the ladies thanked him graciously, Evander lifted up Christian's hand and laid a chaste kiss there.

"You'll text me?" he questioned. "Just let me know you made it."

Christian swallowed lightly and nodded to him. Still blushing, she walked out of Glenn's to catch up with her girls.

Terry appeared next to Evander as he watched Christian walk out of the door.

"So, you do know that's the woman responsible for losing your bread, right?"

"Yeah, I know."

"And…you just paid for her and her friends to get home?"

Evander nodded. "Yes. What point are you making, Terry?"

"I mean…I never knew you to be so generous. Back in the good old days-"

"-I like her, Terry. We already settled the money issues…everything that happens after she gets me back my bread has nothing to do with me, except I want to know who exactly was responsible for taking it. Depending on how I feel, I might have them lined up but of course, that's off the record…"

Terry smirked at the point that Evander didn't even have to mention. As long as his friend covered up his tracks, he couldn't bring him in. Also, he wouldn't pursue any lead that pointed in his direction.

"…either way, I'm not that pressed to find out right now. All I know is, she wasn't responsible and that's enough for me."

Terry shrugged his shoulders but said not another word to his friend. If he believed that Christian Adams wasn't directly responsible, then he would go by his word. He knew the forensics team was salivating at the chance to dig into the funds and make an arrest. He thought that it was sad however, because the gleefulness was only present because the Adams' Accounting team was comprised of Black women. The team would have moved at a regular pace had they been anything but that. He wasn't a man to condone wrongdoing as he believed strongly in right and wrong. However, he found it shameful who the country chooses to jump faster for in the name of justice. It was a sin and a shame and until things changed it was a fact of life.

"Either way, be careful man. Don't get fucked out of your money, bruh. I don't care how fine she is."

Evander rose an eye at him but chuckled. He knew his friend meant well, so he didn't bother to get annoyed by his warning. If there was one thing he wouldn't do, it was let someone get over on him. They couldn't, even if they were the finest thing he'd seen in all of his life.

That just wasn't how he did business.

"Christian, I don't know what you did to that man but I'm okay with it."

Christian smirked as Jasmine luxuriated in the back row of the Suburban they all were currently riding home in.

"I didn't do anything to that man. Besides, I don't know why you're hype over a Suburban. It's not like it's UberBlack."

Sharin smirked. "So you're going to dismiss the fact that he paid for you and all your homegirls to reach home safely? All four of us?"

"You know Christian, Shay. I don't know why she's so damn mean when first of all, she knows she likes him," Jasmine interjected. "I haven't seen her blush at somebody like that in years."

Christian wanted badly to reject what her friends were saying but knew she was at a disadvantage because that's all she'd done. Blush and toss back witty comebacks when she could but overall, who was she kidding? In her mind's eye all she could see was his tall stature, his beautiful dark eyes, and full lips beckoning for her own and it was all she could do not to melt in the presence of her girlfriends.

"He's still a fifteen-million-dollar liability so why should I not be excited?" Christian weakly questioned.

"Hold up," Monica cut in. "What do you mean, fifteen million? I know that wasn't-"

Christian nodded silently and Monica cackled and shook her head in disbelief. Sharin grinned quietly beside her friend. Jasmine questioned what they were talking about as she was slightly lost.

"That was Evander King, Jasmine," Sharin revealed with a smile in her voice.

"Is that so, Ms. Adams? You better see what's up with that man and stop playing! He might have a change of heart!"

"That man does NOT have a change of heart and even if he did, we messed up and we're bound by this license to make it right. I don't give a damn if I have his baby tomorrow, we have to pay him back."

"I mean, I get that. But it never hurts to try," Monica said, giggling. "That's still fifteen million, okay?"

"That's enough, y'all," Christian pressed, rolling her eyes. "Y'all need to stop policing my pussy. I'm a grown ass woman."

The Uber slowed down to Jasmine's residence and as he did, she chuckled a little bit at her friend's rising annoyance. Still, stalwart leader or other, Jasmine saw to the heart of her friend and decided somebody needed to tell her about herself.

"Yeah, you're a grown ass woman, Christian. That we can agree with. I just don't get how you're so grown but still letting ghosts haunt you?"

Jasmine held her friend's gaze as she got up to shuffle out of the SUV. Christian was rendered silent but again turned red at the line of questioning. She swallowed the bitter anger that swelled up in her throat to fight back because the question was valid. Especially as she struggled to separate Evander from Jerrell. It hadn't been lost on her the level at which Evander was trying to come from. It reminded her of how hard Jerrell had gone for her in the beginning. She had given chase and made the chase worth his while until she'd finally fallen. Once she had, it seemed like he was the victor and had been for several years since.

"That's something you need to think about, girl. Tell Mr. King thanks though, I'll catch y'all later!"

And Jasmine Brown was sashaying into her own abode. Christian rolled her eyes hard but turned to Sharin and then Monica.

"Do I look like I entertain ghosts?"

Monica smirked and turned her head to the window. She decided she wasn't going to entertain Christian's absurdity for the rest of the night. As Sharin was her principal best friend, she'd leave that to her. As far as she was concerned, Christian wore her out emotionally for the rest of the week.

"Christian, there hasn't been another man since Jerrell in college more than ten years ago. I'm happy you didn't go back to him but I'm also sad that you haven't let anybody in since. I don't like to judge because it took a lot for Maddox to get in…but I was much younger and I shut down from my cousin's games in high school. It's like Jasmine said, we're grown now. When does Jerrell stop being a reason?"

Christian was rendered silent again, knowing that her friends were right. However, the fear was so much some days that only work fulfilled her. The numbers never lied-until recently-and the numbers never gave preference. The thing about accounting that she loved so much was that the numbers always equaled out. The statements always balanced out and there was nothing more or nothing less than the truth. When the truth was set before you, an informed decision can be made on what to do next. The accounting principles were reliable. Men on the other hand? They were about as reliable as a bowl of ice cream left outside on a hot, summer day.

The Uber driver took the highway to get them home faster and Christian was elated because she was suddenly tired. The week had caught up to her and instead of it closing on a happy note, all she found herself being was exhausted.

Her business' integrity was in question. Evander King wanted his money back and apparently her. Sharin was getting married. She looked over at her long-time best friend and wanted to tell her that none of this was what she bargained for when she left for college. Life was supposed to have swung differently. It was supposed to have kept going in the straight line that she had meticulously planned out.

Except in all honesty, it had gone the way she hoped. They'd all met in high school. They'd all excelled and were accepted into a major HBCU. Afterward, they all were accepted into Harvard. They'd all gotten their Masters and then, with multiple donors, investments and gifts, they endeavored to open up Adams'. The last couple of years were definitely feathers in Christian's cap so honestly, she couldn't complain. The issue was truly that she wanted the past couple of months back. She wanted the same level of honesty that put Adam's on the map.

Again, Evander pierced her thoughts and she sucked her teeth quietly. Why did he even have to come into her life and for what reason did he need to be there? Christian felt herself start to vibrate and inwardly told herself to stop the madness concerning him. She would pay him back, continue the investigation, and do her best to usher the man out of her office and life. The order in which it happened didn't matter much.

"Christian. You're thinking too loud. It's not that serious."

Monica lazily replied to her friend's silent duress.

"You never take anything seriously, Em."

"Because it's not. We pay the man back. You date him. Figure out if you like him or not. If you do, great! If you don't, move on. Run your show how you've always done. But for Heaven's sake and my sanity, let go of the past!"

The driver pulled up to Monica's abode. She air-kissed both of her friends and made her exit with a flourish that made the remaining ladies laugh in her wake. She grinned, just a little bit.

Christian sighed. "Shay, you know what the hard part is in all of this?"

Sharin raised a brow in response, egging her friend on silently.

"I realize that all of my safeguards were to keep away men that were like Jerrell but...all my life has become...is Jerrell Washington. The finest man on two legs wants to get with me and I'm afraid because again, Jerrell Washington."

Sharin sighed and pulled her friend in for a hug. Christian sighed into her friend's embrace, not knowing that she needed it. The action caused her eyes to water up unexpectedly and before she knew it, tears streamed down her face. It was almost overwhelming the pain that was being released from her being at the realization that she may have failed to totally move on from the hurt and betrayal of her college sweetheart.

Sharin pulled away after a couple of minutes and stared at her friend as she wiped her face of the last remaining tears.

"I'm sorry," she garbled. "I don't know what's wrong with me."

"You're human," Sharin sighed. "That's it, that's all."

Christian wiped her face, sighing once more. It'd been a truly stressful couple of days. She prayed that the hell she walked into would come to a sure end.

A week later, Christian sat in McGinnis and Rowe's Law Office, sighing inwardly as she read the terms and conditions of repayment for all monies owed to King's Tires LLC. She sat on one end with her lawyer and assistant, and on the other end of the table was Evander with his own set of lawyers from the same firm. Christian shuddered as Taylor McGinnis quoted the terms of her company's repayment.

"Our client is asking for payments of 5.3 million thrice to recover all monies lost. He is graciously waiving the lawyer's fee of 800,000 dollars plus based on your good faith to start payment today. Should the body of Adams' Accounting be late in repayment or at any point renege on the same, we will add interest to your payments."

Evander watched Christian as the terms and conditions were cited to her. He had to admit being again impressed with how she adorned herself. Christian had arrived prior to him so he wasn't able to see what the bottom half of her looked like but the silky, white blouse she was currently wearing made him wait in excitement for the rest. He berated himself lightly for the thought but hadn't dwelt in guilt for too long.

He wasn't sure what it was about her that drew him in. He was trying to understand why he was so placated by the fact that she was paying him back all monies and damages. Normally, he was ready to cut to the quick whoever was responsible for stealing from him. Back in his street days, the penalty was death. There was no back and forth. There was no pleading. The street life was very unforgiving and even as he lived it, he hated it.

Evander inwardly sighed. His father had taught him how to deal out street justice, yet he could hear Christian's voice, planting her own edict.

"This is not a drug sale gone wrong in the streets, Mr. King."

Which, she was absolutely right. There were moments where although he abhorred it, he missed the street life. Handling certain matters in a classier setting was more often than not unpalatable to Evander. It was a new situation having to deal with things corporately versus how he would have liked to. Having researched the women responsible for mishandling his money, he still had the taste for revenge but wanted the whole story first before he made his move.

"Each payment shall be made before five PM, eastern standard time, to be considered on-time."

Evander came back to the conversation in time to see Christian nod dutifully. Her assistant, Tiffany, wrote everything down, her face frowned up in concentration. He looked on at her and realized the reason he was placated.

Still, he knew overall, he was saddened that he had to meet the lady in the circumstance he had. Still, would he have met her otherwise?

He wasn't sure. Evander was known in Atlanta, mostly because of his father. He had the king-pin ties to his father but that was a reputation he sought to change. He didn't want the legacy of his family to be doused in the sins of his parents. He often wondered why his mother wouldn't leave but had to come to terms with the fact that while he lived, Buddy pulled all of the strings. There wasn't one detail out of life that missed his notice. He had planned to run the Atlanta drug scene forever. That wasn't in Evander's plans by a long shot. In his mind, there was much more out there.

His endeavors pulled him into money laundering. The capital that he had "washed" started King's Tires, LLC. Evander wanted a college education and entrepreneurship. Buddy had only supported his entrepreneurial pursuits so as long as they sold his brand of drugs all over the city. Evander had never thought he'd be happy for the day his father died but pure joy filled him. He was free.

Still, there were moments when the residue of his sire infiltrated his thought processes. Sometimes, the thrill of power seduced him and so, for the interim, Jupiter Classon and Jamie Phillips stayed on the back of his mind.

It took an outlaw spirit to be comfortable with taking money that wasn't their own. It was a spirit that Evander felt someone needed to bring to heel in these women. Thievery was something that disgusted him. It was something he couldn't tolerate. Even in his darker days, stealing wasn't in his system. As dishonorable as it was, every drug transaction was honorable. The goods were exchanged with the cash. None was stolen without paying the price for it.

"*If you'll steal, you'll kill*" was a phrase his grandmother used to run into the ground before she passed on. Evander had kept that near his heart. He wasn't in the business of stealing but he would definitely kill for what was his.

"If all parties are satisfied with the terms and agreements?"

McGinnis looked to his client, who nodded somberly. He then looked to the opposing side. Christian nodded in much the same manner.

Papers were signed and before long, all parties were filing out of the office. Evander hung back, allowing Christian to walk through before him. Taking her in he decided he was pleased with the black pencil skirt she'd donned to attend the meeting. Her outfit was a simple study of black and white but her red pumps broke the monotony of the outfit. If he'd been alone, he was certain he would have licked his lips.

"Ms. Adams," He called out. "A moment of your time?"

Christian slowed down, turning to take in Evander King and felt her heart start to speed up. She cursed herself as it all happened, wondering why she would react to this man as if she'd never seen one before. Her feelings were again mixed as she took in his likeness and had to admit to herself that most men weren't made like Evander King.

He stood at six feet, two inches. His dark skin shone a smooth clarity. Evander wore a light brown suit jacket with a blue shirt. His pants were chocolate, a beautiful contrast and compliment to the jacket. Evander stopped within an inch of her space and she knew he was waiting for Tiffany to take the hint and wait for her in the front of the office. She wasn't sure if she was pleased with that fact or not.

"Was there anything else missing that we needed to talk about?" Christian questioned. "The terms and conditions were made clear. Thank you for being *gracious* enough to not charge lawyer fees."

Evander smirked. "You really think I pulled you aside to talk about money? We squared that away."

"It's not squared away until our final payment is made to you, Mr. King," Christian said, shifting on one foot. "If the money isn't what's on your mind, then what is?"

"It's a beautiful day. You're here and I'm here. Let me take you out to lunch."

Christian gawked. "I…I have things to do. I don't have time for lunch."

"I don't see why not?"

"I have to prep for office meetings. I have to meet with my Public Relations rep. I have to figure out a way to set up systems for new ways to combat fraud so I don't have to deal with-" Christian motioned between him and her. "-this again. Not to mention, payment is due to you by five today so there's that."

"You have a capable team and a secretary able to handle that," Evander shrugged. "Take a break. Like I said, the day is beautiful. You look beautiful. Allow me an hour."

Despite herself, Christian smiled. She wondered if she was blushing as well. She'd forgotten the last time a man seemed to want to spend his every moment with her. When Jerrell threatened to cross her mind, she pushed him out before the thought could take a foothold.

"You should smile more, Ms. Adams. You glow."

"I'm smiling at your persistence. What's in it for you?"

"If I told you right now, you'd run away and I'd probably never get to see your pretty face again."

Christian wanted to ask but decided against the notion. He was more than likely right.

They walked companionably towards the front. For a moment the prior meeting was all but forgotten.

"So, you'll ride with me?"

"No, I'll meet you there."

"Why go through those motions when I can drive you?" Evander paused, looking into her eyes. "Am I that detestable, Ms. Adams?"

Christian gazed at him, shame starting to cloak over her being. She sighed, also hearing Sharin disapprove of her movements again. Her friend always preached about letting a man go through each and every motion. Monica would also berate her for making things harder than they had to be.

If it works, great if it doesn't, move on.

Monica's advice was the push she needed to apologize.

"No, I barely know you to think so. Since you want to change my first impression of you so badly, I'll ride with you."

Evander smirked. "Nah. I just see you're trying to keep me out when I

62

barely made any moves to get in. Relax though, Ms. Adams. I don't bite."

Christian smirked but noted the seriousness in his eyes. She wanted to ask him what made him think she was going to play games long enough for her to find out. She wanted to ask him what made him so sure they'd even have interest in each other after this supposed lunch date. She wanted to ask quite a few questions but filed them away for later. She tried to simplify things as best as she could. He was a man showing interest in her. He wanted to take her out for lunch. She was hungry and it wouldn't hurt to refuel on his dime. Besides, for all she knew this would be their first and last date. She wouldn't have to worry about him ever again, save for a professional area.

However, by the way Evander had led her out of the door and to his car, it seemed he was thinking otherwise. It was enough to make her shudder in fear.

Still, she was along for the ride.

Chapter
Eight

Christian requested Pappadeux's and Evander found himself quite intrigued by her selection. He'd heard of the place but had yet to frequent it since its opening in Georgia a few years ago. He was used to finer dining and had a place in mind for his impromptu date but when she requested the seafood eatery, he couldn't help but to indulge her this time. Since she'd given him some pushback earlier, he was shocked that she was showing enthusiasm in the present moment.

Evander pulled his stone-grey Mercedes S-Class Benz into the parking lot and smirked as he felt Christian's excitement, palpable as she did a shimmy next to him in the seat. He rose an eye at the sparkle he saw in hers as she unbuckled her seatbelt, giggles filling his ears.

"I would have taken you for a Miller House kind of woman," Evander said. "And yet you're dancing in your seat for…"

"After today, you might, too," Christian said. "I'm excited because I haven't been in a while and it just hit me. It's not fine dining but it is delicious."

Evander smirked, stepping out of his side and walking to Christian's. He opened up the door when he got to her side and reached in. Smiling inside, he marveled at the warmth and softness of her hand when it fit into his. He watched as she put one leg out after the other and stood gracefully with his assistance. He shut the door and took her hand gently again, taking her direction to the entrance of the place.

They'd been greeted happily by the host, a young woman who had trouble hiding her appreciation for Evander. Still, she was respectful as she led them to the bar. Christian might've felt a pinch of jealousy except that looking at Evander again, she couldn't hold it against the woman. Christian pulled her thoughts away from their sordid visions as she took a glance at his hands. She hadn't realized how massive they were until he took hold of her hand earlier on and then again as he helped her into the stool. She blushed, unsure of why she was still acting as if she had zero experience with men.

"Hello, my name is Jeraya and I'm happy to serve you today! May I start you off with any drinks?"

A shapely, medium toned woman appeared before them as they got settled. She blinked twice, taking Evander in as well and Christian smirked, enjoying the way women responded to him. She wasn't sure why save for the fact that it made her feel less conscious of the way she responded to him herself.

"Riesling, please?" Christian requested, effectively pulling the lady out of her spell.

"Yes, I'll get that right away. For you, sir?"

"Water is fine," Evander said. "Also, we'll start with the jumbo lump crab cakes."

Jeraya answered him with a smile and then disappeared to fulfill their order. Christian blushed lightly, realizing she hadn't even touched the menu placed before her. She hadn't even noted when the woman had slid them on the counter. She filtered around in her mind when she'd gotten so far off track that she missed a tiny detail.

"You were so busy looking at her looking at me," Evander supplied, his voice tinged with amusement.

"I didn't ask-"

"-No, but I knew you were lost in the sauce, so I caught you up," he grinned. "It's okay to say you like me, Ms. Adams. I'm growing quite fond of you, myself."

"Fond, huh? You threatened me over a week ago and now…"

"I'm grateful that we even met," Evander grinned. "I'm grateful you gave me the time of day after my slip-up."

Christian smirked, holding her tongue when Jeraya returned with their drink order. She reached for her Riesling and sipped slowly, grateful for the interruption. Evander mirrored her, wondering if she knew he meant every word that he said. Although she was calmer than when he first met her, he could tell that she was still very much entertaining him with her guards up. He wondered momentarily about what damage her ex-boyfriend had done. Wondered if at any point it made sense for him to pursue the woman in front of him at all.

His worries were laid to rest when the crab cakes arrived and her smile at the offering spread. He smirked as she helped herself, delighting in the fact that he was bringing a smile to her face, however inadvert. He wasn't sure why she pleased him just by existing but something about Christian Adams turned him on.

"So, tell me about yourself, Mr. King," Christian said. "I should apologize for not knowing much about you beforehand."

"I accept your apology, Ms. Adams. You'll be getting to know me better soon anyway, so I'm not up in arms about that."

"That so?"

"That's the plan." Evander's smile spread. "But all that aside…I'm the product of rich parents. I attended Morehouse and got a business degree. I opened up King Tires afterwards and KT has been my life's work ever since."

"Tires, though? I thought that was interesting." Christian looked at him, raising a brow. "What is it about a tire that you like so much?"

"Not so much the tire but the fact that it gives momentum to get you to point A to point B. Summer tires, winter tires. People wear them out and need more. I was born and raised rich, Ms. Adams. I have to pay the bills for myself somehow."

"You got cut off?"

Evander smirked. "Nah. I took over my father's holdings when he passed.

So, everything runs in my name and although I have some…street awareness, I'm mostly spoiled by my creature comforts."

Christian smiled, satisfied with his answer.

"So, about yourself?" Evander questioned. "Who are you, pretty lady? What gets you going?"

Christian smiled, despite herself. "The numbers. It's always the numbers." Evander rolled his eyes and it forced laughter from her. "I'm serious! But if you must know my business…"

They were interrupted again by Jeraya who appeared calmer than when she first approached the couple. Christian smiled at her this time around and ordered the blackened catfish with red beans and rice. Evander decided on the half chicken meal and immediately turned back into Christian as Jeraya collected their menus. Christian was pleased to note that he hadn't noticed when the bartender had done so.

"So, about your business…" he grinned. "Educate me."

"I love painting. It's…like a healthy outlet for me," She explained. "I love going to paint and sips and going through the process of painting a picture. It soothes me in a way."

"The painting or the drinking?"

Christian smirked. "Both have their place but seriously, I love to paint. It was the only other thing I did well in school other than math."

"English wasn't your thing?"

"I'll read a good book-even *the* Good Book-but you won't catch me writing a novel or anything," Christian answered. "But quiet as it's kept, I do keep up with a couple of hobbies outside of my job. I…just love numbers most of all."

Evander nodded but kept his gaze steady on her.

"May I ask where your mind is at?"

"Getting you naked."

Evander enjoyed the way her face flushed, although he knew it was partly from the wine she was drinking. Still, seeing her eyelids get heavy at his boldness turned him on as well. It was a good feeling for the second time knowing that he wasn't alone in his attraction. It was definitely mutual. He could appreciate the fact that she was fighting it, based on any number of reasons she had.

"I hope you don't believe you're getting me naked any time soon."

"Of course not, Ms. Adams. I'm still trying to get to know you, but I won't deny that something about you…anyway. Excuse me for being so brash."

"Hm. It appears that you wanted to talk about sex over seafood, Mr. King. I don't enjoy the thought of being simplified to a pair of legs for your entertainment."

Evander smirked at her emphasis on his name to indicate that they weren't even on a first name basis yet. Catching the reproval, his grin spread wider.

"I haven't known you that long but the impression that I get is that anyone that can break down your wholeness to just a pair of legs is an idiot. I assure you that I am not one." Evander held her gaze after his declaration and Christian wondered that she didn't melt at the intense gaze in his eyes. Clearing her throat, she reached for her wine once more, taking a dainty sip. She looked back at him again, wondering at the rollercoaster ride of emotions that swirled within her. "I'd like the permission to pursue you romantically, Ms. Adams," Evander announced, breaking her train of thought. "I don't know what it is about you but something about you has me wanting to know more."

Christian blinked and set her wine back down. Biting her lip, she again looked at Evander from under her eyelids, wondering at his angle. She wasn't even sure why she was contemplating things, considering he hadn't asked for her hand in marriage. She thought of her ex, who painstakingly pursued her but again, pushed him out of her head space. She wasn't sure why it touched her that this man would even ask for the permission to…court her. It was much different than what she was used to and threw her completely off.

"Permission to pursue?"

Evander smirked. "Has a man never asked that of you? I'm embarrassed at the standard of men these days. I'm surprised they're not all falling at your feet."

"I'm not. I don't…quite put out the signal that I want to be bothered with romance. You're a surprise, Evander."

He smiled at the sound of his name on her lips. He wasn't even sure she noticed that she slipped into the personal arena with him that easily and he didn't plan to point it out either. The thought that he surprised her into a place of comfort put him over the moon.

"Am I? I could say the same about you, Christian." His voice dropped lower. "Do I have your permission, beautiful?"

Christian felt herself floating even as she fought within to pull herself out of the cloud. Still, with his eyes pinned on hers the answer was clear as the blue skies she floated in.

"You have my permission."

Evander lifted her hand once again, softly kissing it. Christian hadn't bothered to hide her smile at the action. She hadn't bothered to berate herself at the notion that she'd just started a romance in the midst of drama at her job. She hadn't bothered to wonder why she would do the opposite of what she meant to do concerning Evander King. She hadn't bothered about any of it for the first time since she laid eyes on him earlier in the afternoon.

It would either be a wonderful time or it would end horribly. Still, any movement forward was better than none. Her friends were right. It was high time to move on and allow herself to be happy. Besides, even if things didn't work out, she wouldn't be too up in arms.

If nothing else, Evander King definitely was a bona-fide upgrade.

Chapter
Nine

Chastity's face turned up at the sight of Atlanta's Pretrial Corrections Facility. She sucked her teeth as her driver opened up her door and reached in to pull her out. When she was on sure footing, she snatched her hand away from the man without saying thank you. She missed his snarl as he walked back to his side of the car.

"I'll call you in about an hour. Don't drive too far."

Without deigning her with a response, the driver settled back into the car and drove off. Chastity turned without another thought and walked through the doors of the facility and up to the front desk. A heavy-set white woman looked up from a random YouTube video as Chastity approached.

It'd taken nearly thirty seconds after for the woman to greet her.

"Afternoon, ma'am," she said.

"Good Afternoon. I'm here for a visit."

The woman processed Chastity through, calling another female officer to scan her body for any prohibited items. Chastity huffed and puffed her way through the process, already annoyed that she deigned to waste her time in the building. It was clearly beneath her and felt as if her presence upgraded the place. Still, going through the rigamarole of a visit was annoying her. Jupiter was foolish to get caught in the first place.

Another officer, this time a man, escorted her to the visitor's area. She thanked him none too graciously for doing his job. Chastity also missed his snarl when she lowered herself to sit in front of the window. Her smile spread just in time for a policeman to escort Jupiter out.

Jupiter Classon was beautiful. She had milk chocolate skin and slanted eyes, giving a hint to her mixed heritage. She was also twice as smart as she was beautiful. The fact that she worked for Sharin was the draw for Chastity, however she never thought it would be easy to rope the woman into her schemes being that most people that knew Sharin loved her. They were also twice as loyal. So, seeing that she obviously dropped the ball with this woman worked out for Chastity in spades.

It hadn't taken long for the women to become fast friends, mostly because both of them hated Sharin Reynolds to no end. While Chastity felt Sharin didn't deserve the wealth that she was born into, Jupiter felt she didn't deserve her position as Partner. Both could definitely live without Christian Adams, but were ambivalent to her. The twosome forged a friendship after a particularly bitter day for Jupiter. That was when she'd met Chastity by chance at a bar, drinking down her bitterness mixed in a Long Island Iced Tea. It took every bit of courage Chastity had to approach Jupiter that day. She had only wanted to politely tell the woman to pull herself together in the establishment since she was coming across as sloppy, but things took a turn once she'd sat next to her.

It hadn't taken long for Jupiter to share the fact that her boss dumped a ton of work on her before disappearing for a meeting earlier in the day.

"She gets to look pretty and run around all day while I do her dirty work. Sharin Reynolds deserves nothing."

That one sentence stopped Chastity in her tracks and every bit of disdain she held for the woman turned on its head. A sick curiosity took its place and on that same afternoon a plan to take her cousin off her high horse was born. Countless hours had gone into a years' long operation. Siphoning money from one of their biggest clients had been no easy task. Jupiter had a stable relationship with Kings' Tires and actually enjoyed working with them. She was unsure of why Chastity chose that company to steal from but all in all if it made Sharin look bad, she was all for it.

However, sitting on the other side of plexiglass hadn't been in her plans. She'd taken the escort from the building with grace and a sick satisfaction knowing Sharin would take the brunt of punishment from Christian. She wondered if Sharin was suspended yet and the thought filled her with glee. Still, the victory was plenty hollow at this point. It wasn't as if Christian would elevate her to Partner level now.

At the present moment, all that was left was divvying up the funds. She wondered why Chastity sat on the other side of the plexiglass with a smirk on her face instead of informing her that her lawyer would be around to bail her out shortly.

"How are you, Jupiter?" Chastity's cooed. "I didn't think I'd ever have to say this, but orange is *not* your color."

"Technically, it is but I'm pretty sure the cut isn't it. Cut to the chase though, Chastity. When do I get out of here? We need to…" Jupiter slowed down and took a deep breath, knowing she had to choose her words carefully. Before she could find an appropriate word however, Chastity rose a brow.

"Get out? Why are you rushing this?" she questioned. "You do know who Evander King is, right? Being on the outside isn't the safest place for you at the moment."

"Wait, what? You had me…girl, make it make sense because it's not making any," Jupiter demanded. "I held up my end of the bargain. The bucket is filled up nicely. My next move is to get lost. Why are you now telling me about who this man is?"

"Because I don't want you to get hurt, darling. Why else?"

"How safe am I, really? Me and the girl got locked up. You paid her nothing to keep quiet. You already know she's afraid and it won't take much for cops to get her to squeal."

"Oh, I already have her taken care of," Chastity shrugged. "She values her life more than anything else. Even her precious uncle. She knows the payment for disloyalty."

Jupiter looked away from Chastity, for the first time since knowing her feeling uncomfortable. Jamie caught onto the discrepancies as she was the one creating all the statements based off of Jupiter's work. Generally, she might not have seen them except Jamie saw all the real numbers that Jupiter kept on her laptop screen. Unperturbed, she confronted Jupiter. Jupiter had threatened Jamie's job and forbade her to say a word and even to go as far as to forget everything she saw.

Still, she didn't know that Chastity had confronted Jamie. She wasn't sure that it'd been necessary. She was yet a young woman who was getting her feet wet in the accounting world. Jupiter knew that her plans were to move on to a Big 4 company. Though she liked working for Adams', staying there hadn't been in her plans.

"Disloyalty? Chastity, you threatened that young girl?"

Chastity shrugged. "Don't tell me you're getting cold feet, now?"

"Obviously not if I'm in a fucking jail cell. Off that, the question is if you even have a lawyer willing to go to bat for me? I'm pretty much out of a job now so compensation is paramount at this point. You know what we agreed on so…don't *play* with me, Chastity."

Jupiter's heart started pounding as she took in the expression on her accomplice's face. Her forehead started to sweat as Chastity's brow rose and she regarded her with a look of disdain.

"What agreement? We made that agreement on the terms that you delivered without getting caught. Now that you're caught, love, I don't know what to tell you. I don't plan on going to jail with you or revealing *my* involvement. Besides, when was this about the money? We both agreed to make Sharin look bad and we succeeded." Chastity leaned closer into the plexiglass so that she can look Jupiter in the eye. She almost laughed with glee as a tear started sliding down the woman's face. "It's all thanks to *you*, love."

Jupiter swallowed the sob that threatened to let loose. "I'll air out everything if you don't do what you promised, Chastity McCain. We'll either have it all together or nothing in prison. Pick wisely."

"Sis…get real. Even if you aired me out, I'm not staying in jail. I don't *do* jail. If you were smart, you wouldn't be doing jail either. Such a waste for a pretty woman like you."

Jupiter's vision tinged with red and without thought she spat viciously at the glass. Chastity jumped and shivered as laughter started to rise from her accomplice's throat.

"We'll see how true that is, *bitch*. Somehow, someway I'll pay you back for this. If it's the *last* thing I do."

Chastity stood up, shrugging carelessly.

"You have to catch me, first."

A delighted giggle escaped her as she rose, gathering her Chanel bag with her and turning on her heel gracefully. More giggles escaped as Jupiter flung vicious curse words at her back. Chastity shook off Jupiter's empty promises, knowing there was absolutely no way the lady could drag her to jail. All of the evidence would point to her. Even Jamie could get out of jail as she was only the party filing the documents. She hadn't created them. Jamie could barely claim to know Evander King at all. She was the one Chastity was more worried about. With the right pushing and prodding her story could be spun into the accidental third party. A confession from her could mean less time for her and even a slap on the wrist for her involvement. If she did however start naming names, Chastity could end up in jail for serious time. Even her father's lawyers couldn't do much to keep her out of that kind of trouble.

The thought made her stomach turn for the first time since it all happened. It also steeled her resolve. As long as Jamie Phillips kept her mouth shut and did her time, there'd be no issue. If even a peep escaped, Chastity would have her disposed of. That was the promise she made to the young woman and in Chastity's mind, if she wanted to lose her life that badly, then she'd be all the happier to assist her.

--

Sharin swallowed nervously as she was escorted to the interrogation room at the precinct. Detectives Houston and Garcia entered the room and sat across from Sharin, both with neutral faces. Sharin prayed her face was neutral because the memory of Elijah hit her like a ton of bricks. She wasn't sure what her every emotion was, but they weren't all flowery.

Elijah Garcia was a gentleman she met in her junior year of high school. Chastity had planted a ruse in which he dated her cousin with the promise that he got to meet Chastity's father to interview for an internship. The plan had been going well except that Elijah hadn't been prepared to fall for Sharin Reynolds. The plan was only supposed to go on for six months and in the mix of it he was supposed to have ruined her reputation but, in the end, he turned against Chastity. He'd fallen for her cousin and as far as he was concerned, it made no sense to ruin her for kicks. Chastity, however, wouldn't let sleeping dogs lie and decided to reveal the truth to her cousin. Brokenhearted, Sharin chose to never date again.

Maddox had somehow broken through her guard but by then, she had to face the fact that she hid behind her pain. She'd given Maddox an honest try and was happy that she had. It was wonderful when a person challenged your way of thinking and showed you that there was a better way. Sharin couldn't wait to marry him and start a new journey with him as his wife.

Still, looking at Elijah, she was triggered. She'd known that he joined the force but the chances that he'd be the one interviewing her were slim. It caught her off guard and forced her to remember their brief history with bitterness.

"It's nice to see you, Bella. You're looking beautiful, as always."

"Respectfully, don't call me that, thank you," Sharin smiled, thinly, crossing her hands on top of the table.

"I apologize," he smiled. "I couldn't resist."

Detective Houston coughed, politely intruding on the conversation and bringing it back to the main event.

"Ms. Reynolds, I just would like to ask you a few routine questions. We thank you for your cooperation in coming to the station."

Detective Houston stood, walking over to a recorder. "Just to let you know, this interview will be recorded. If we require further questioning, we will be back in touch. Do we have an understanding?"

"Yes," Sharin answered, tightening her grip. "We do."

"Good. Now I'm to believe that you are a Partner at Adams' Accounting?"

"Yes. I run the Small Businesses Division."

"That's quite a feat. The business is run by all Black women, correct?"

"That it is. We're proud of our accomplishments."

"So, here's the thing, Ms. Reynolds. I also understand that you're an heiress. Why work?"

"Why waste an excellent education just twiddling my thumbs and looking pretty? I pride myself on my smarts more than the resources that I was born into."

"So, there was no discord with your family to be cut off?" Elijah jumped in. "No reason why you'd embezzle to the tune of 15 million?"

Sharin chuckled. "No. If I wanted to quit tomorrow and live lavishly, either by means of my family or my *fiancé*, I could."

Sharin eyed Elijah when she answered him. The chill that went through his body made him grit his teeth. The fact that she would throw in his face that she was getting married caused him to ball his fist.

"So how did it escape your notice that 15 million dollars was being siphoned from a company that entrusted their service to you? Are you sure you didn't need the 15 million to support your husband?"

Sharin's eyes narrowed. "That's foolish, Detective. My husband nets millions a year selling luxury real estate. He's gearing up to become a broker as well. Trust when I say I've chosen *well*."

Sharin took a deep breath in and out, realizing that she was in the middle of a pissing match. Turning toward the other detective, she eyed her and continued to speak.

"It escaped my notice because my senior accountant reports the numbers to me and not the other way around. I make checks to make sure the books are balanced. My accountant was the very best I've ever had and the need to check the books wasn't paramount especially as the head of my department, my focus is on building relationships with our company. I'm the one who has to go out and find clientele whenever I can. My accountants under me are the ones who handle transactions for these businesses."

Sharin thought of Jupiter and felt her body shake again. If she could've wrung her neck in that very moment, she would have. She agonized over the fact that Jupiter was so perfect an employee that besides her cockiness, there was no apparent reason to fire her. She was the star of her department. She came to work on time. She daily completed the tasks that were required of her. Jupiter was a fan favorite. She wouldn't have gone against a promotion for her or a raise if at all possible, but the fact of the matter was, her overall attitude had been the barrier.

"So I'm to believe that you have not a clue that monies were being siphoned from this small business?" Elijah butted in. "Do you believe us to be stupid?"

"If you're from the accounting forensics team, you know generally how an accounting company works. You also know that my being blind to this mishap is *not* out of the realm of possibility! I would *not* have allowed anyone working under me to steal from right under my nose and risk *my* reputation and the reputation of this company. I am beyond livid that it's happened and for my integrity to be in question even now makes me angry."

"Angry? Or guilty, Ms. Reynolds?"

The question was so pointed and calmly delivered that Sharin almost missed the audacity of his question. She'd asked him the same question years ago before she turned around and walked out of his life for good.

Sharin wasn't sure if her heart sped up or slowed down. She stared into Elijah's hazel-green eyes, tears running down her face unchecked. Before she could stop herself, she opened up her mouth and spat, "Fuck you, Elijah."

"Okay, let's settle down."

Detective Houston walked over to the recorder and shut it off. She then thanked Sharin for her time and escorted her out of the room. When she was taken out of the room, Elijah kicked at the chair, sending it flying across the room. He'd taken a few deep breaths to calm himself down. He shook his head at himself, wondering why the look of the woman who'd just left had wrecked him in every way.

The memory of her invaded his mind as if it all happened yesterday. His shame cloaked him like a thick blanket, causing him to sweat. He could still see her pretty face, twisted into consternation and the tears that fell unchecked that he couldn't erase.

He was still so deep into memories that he hadn't heard his partner walk back in until she slammed a hand on the desk.

"Hey!" she screamed. "Wake the *fuck* up, Garcia!"

Elijah blinked and shook his head, waving his partner off. Houston jumped in front of him when he tried to walk past and she pierced him with a look of disappointment, staying him from moving any further.

"Listen. I don't know what the *fuck* that was about, but you should have told me you had a personal gripe with this woman. I'm unsure that I can report that she's in the clear because you were so emotional. That was a whole lover's quarrel."

"It was not, Nadja. Mind your business."

"This investigation and your conduct *is* my business. If we're going to be partners, you need to keep it a buck with me. I can safely assume she was telling the truth but your emotionalism in this interview could threaten that. So, tell me now, Garcia, should I be asking to sit you down for this investigation and what's left of it?"

"No, Houston. I'm good."

"Well, I hope to fuck you're good, Garcia. Whatever is killing you softly about this woman, put it to bed. She made sure to let you know, however you fucked up, that you have no chance. Let's put these loose ends away and move on."

Houston turned around and before she walked away, turned back around.

"That goes for this investigation as well."

Without another word, she turned around and left Elijah to stew.

"Sis, I almost lost it."

Christian looked on at her friend as she sipped slowly on her Merlot. Sharin was still visibly shaking but her face appeared calm. She placed down the glass and put both hands on the table. Christian watched her take even breaths in and out and waited for her to divulge her thoughts.

"Girl, what happened?"

"Elijah was one of the investigating officers."

Christian's eyes widened, not having heard his name in more than ten years' time. Christian winced, both intrigued and appalled that Sharin was going through any emotional changes regarding Elijah Garcia.

"This *nigga* couldn't interview me and go about his day. He had to take shots at me. Shots at the fact that I work. Shots at Maddox. This *nigga* had the nerve to ask me if I was stealing to support Maddox. I'm not the best detective in the world, sis, but *shit*."

Christian giggled. "The irony in this whole setup is glorious and I want to cry laughing."

"My discomfort shouldn't be funny to you, Christian."

"I mean...I can't help but to see that this dude really shook you up and that you still have feelings for him."

Sharin looked up at Christian and opened and closed her mouth. She then grabbed her wine again, sipping slowly. She methodically placed the glass back down and then looked up at her friend, her face full on red.

"You'd be one to fucking talk, Christian."

"Listen. I'm not without my shit. Still, I'm slightly surprised but I shouldn't be. I got all my best moves from you. And y'all are surprised when I have trouble dating when you were the blueprint. Now you're sitting here looking crazy."

Sharin shrugged. "I'm embarrassed. The back and forth was like a lover's spat. I have to admit to feeling good that I could shove his face in the fact that I moved on. I'm not a superficial person-you know this-but it felt fucking good to tell him that Maddox could basically buy him and the rest of Atlanta if he wanted to. I'm glad he broke my heart. I could do better than a detective."

Christian smiled sadly. "Baby, if he was with you, he might have been the Chief of Police by now. That's probably what's got him upset. He knew every day that he lost the best thing to happen to him. And I know you don't truly love him, bestie...but you have to let that whole thing go. You can't fall apart every time you see him. Hopefully you won't have to see him again."

Sharin sighed. "I don't want Maddox to think..."

"I highly doubt that. Chastity did a number on you, love. Honestly, both of you although he had a part in it."

Sharin shook her head, breathing out heavily when a waitress approached their table. They both made their orders and then waited a beat before she disappeared. Christian giggled a little bit.

"So…you shoved it in the man's face that you're engaged, Shay?"

"I did and I was proud of myself. He tried to flirt when I walked in, sis! Like bygones were bygones. I know I need to work on that but right now? Screw him." Sharin sighed. "I…I'm still pretty hurt by that day. I loved him as much as I could understand. He was my friend and then became my boyfriend. I was ready to introduce him to my family. I was ready to start talking about colleges and how we were going to make it work…I lost twice when I lost him, but the punch line was that Chastity didn't give one damn that she orchestrated the whole thing and then picked the moment she had to tell me that it was all a ruse."

A tear slid down her face and Christian felt her heartbreak.

"I did nothing to this woman to deserve any of that. And worse, to know she has a hand in this whole mess with Adams' makes me sick."

Christian sighed. "You can't worry about that. We know who's directly responsible. We're presently paying back Evander. What's done is done…just time to move forward at this point."

"She's still a burden and if there's any way to take action against her, I'm going to take it. I've endured enough trauma from her to last the rest of my- Evander? Oh."

Christian looked up at rose a brow, "What?"

"We're on a first name basis with the client now?" Sharin giggled, "Let me know, sis!" Sharin watched her friend flush and it forced a smile to spread on her face. "Oh, word?"

Christian shook her head, waving her off. "No, don't start with me, Shay!"

"I mean-I would calm down if you told me something."

Christian smirked, shrugging her shoulders. "Not much is going on. We hung out after the meeting with his lawyers. He's…asked for the permission to pursue me romantically."

"*Permission to pursue*? Oh, okay!" Sharin laughed. "I'm loving this!"

Christian blushed deeper. "I don't know why I tell you anything."

"Because, we're besties! You were wrong for not even telling me before now. I forgive you of course, so don't beg."

Christian rolled her eyes, grateful when the waitress returned with their food. Still, she looked up at her friend with a half-smile.

"I…am well out of my depth with this."

"Don't be. It's not as hard as you think it is," Sharin sighed. "I might have to realize the part I played in how you closed off from everybody. I was the one filling your head with a lot of things based on my trauma."

"Well, you did okay. You and Maddox are in love. You're engaged."

Sharin smiled sadly. "It doesn't stop me from needing therapy. If I hadn't seen Elijah earlier, I wouldn't have known that I had that issue still eating at me. It wouldn't hurt for you to get some either."

"I don't do therapy."

"Okay Ms. Out-of-your-Depth."

Christian rolled her eyes again. "I am fine."

"So, Jerrell can walk in at any time and it'd be of no consequence?"

Christian was silent, deigning to dig into her food instead. Sharin smirked, deciding not to push the issue onto her friend. She realized that she needed therapy and that was enough. Her mental health had been taking hits since the entire fracas started and she would address those issues.

Chastity McCain and Elijah Garcia were not going to take over her life. Subliminally, they'd already done that long enough. Almost losing Maddox was enough pain and fear to last her a lifetime.

"Anyway, I'm giving this a shot. I think that's a good first step. Jerrell Washington is not enough of a reason for me to sign up for therapy sessions."

Sharin bit her lip, moments away from telling her that her abandonment issues were enough of a reason. Still in all, she'd be patient with her friend. Someone had to be.

"I'm happy to see you make strides," Sharin grinned. "Tell me about how it happened."

Christian started to blush again but gave her the entire story. Sharin listened happily and dutifully, thankful that out of the chaos, it seemed that the buds of something new was springing to life.

Jasmine Brown walked through Adams' with her head held high and her mind full of purpose. She'd been up more than half the night putting together a reformation strategy and was both nervous and excited to share with the CEO. On one end she was hoping that her hard work wouldn't go in vain. On the other, she was fully prepared to tell Christian that if she didn't like what she had to offer in terms of getting the good name of the company back, she was prepared to walk out of the door and not stress herself over Adams' again.

Christian and Jasmine met later on in life after they figured out that they grew up in the same neighborhood. Their friendship was fostered in graduate school where Jasmine had been studying for the bar. Her path ran adjacent to her friend but not until Christian was close to graduation did the two meet by chance at a paint and sip. Christian liked Jasmine's quick wit and hold-no-bars speech. She wasn't afraid to tell Christian about herself, but she also knew that Jasmine's honesty came from a place of love and wanting to see people win.

Jasmine stepped into the second elevator bank, moving through its gilded doors, taking a steadying breath as she pressed the button for the top floor. She would have worked Christian's case for free but the fact that it came across as messy in the media excited her. When other high-profile people saw her in the mix of helping the accounting whiz get her groove back, she knew the money would come rolling in as well as the good press. Jasmine lived a good, full life and although she wasn't doing too badly as far as her finances, it still didn't hurt to add more money to the equation.

"Besides," she thought. "I haven't been to Bali yet. That needs to happen this summer."

Jasmine stepped off the elevator, a serene look on her face when she laid eyes on Tiffany at her desk. Her grin turned into a smirk, seeing as the secretary was doing nothing but flirting with her boyfriend shamelessly.

"I'm just sayin' what you gon' do about that?"

Jasmine shook her head and thought of letting the conversation play out for her amusement. When Tiffany's face flushed however, she quickly changed her mind. The last thing she wanted to do was be an unwitting third wheel. With that much in mind, Jasmine rapped the front of her desk lightly with her fist. Tiffany jumped out of her stupor and stared at Jasmine as if she appeared by magic.

"Excuse me, bae," Tiffany said. "Good morning, Ms. Brown. I didn't realize…" Tiffany took a moment to search for her appointment on her monitor. Jasmine rose a brow, swallowing a chuckle. "…that it definitely is eleven… hold on bae, I'll call you back."

Tiffany paged Christian and within moments, Christian was opening her office door and waving Jasmine in. She chuckled as she walked by Tiffany who was clearly trying to hide the fact that she was giggling on the phone with Christopher. She heard Tiffany lightly mumble for Jasmine to mind her business and she wondered to herself whether she would check her on the way out of the door or not. It was highly unprofessional for the young lady to be on the phone as she was in front of a CEO's office door. Even if Christian allowed the lady to have personal phone calls, she needed to know when to schedule them.

"Good Morning, Ms. Adams," Jasmine said, taking a seat in front of Christian's desk. "How are you, these days?"

Christian sighed, heavily. "I could be better, but I could be worse. That's how I've been looking at it these days."

"Well, we're going to get you to best." Jasmine grinned, forcing a smile to come to Christian. "I've put together a whole program that I think you and the firm should follow for six months' time. There are some items I need you and your team to implement immediately. I'm pretty sure some things have been touched on already, but each Partner should pull together team meetings and direct the staff going forward on how they're to deal with media personnel. They might not hang out in the front of the building anymore but if they can track down some of your employees, even down to the bookkeepers, they will."

Christian nodded. "Yeah, I didn't think that far ahead."

"Yeah, we need to treat Adams' like Vegas right now. I'm going to give you a copy of an NDA agreement. Read over it. If I have to change around some words or whatever to frame the business, I will. Still, everybody signs this. Working or not." Jasmine edged a look up at Christian. "Is Sharin still suspended?"

"Pending her police interview. I wanted her to be cleared by the police before I reinstated her position. She might still decide to fall back in the throes of planning her wedding."

Jasmine nodded. "Have a copy delivered to her. I would also suggest that she takes some time away from her home for a time. She's a high-profile

Chapter

Ten

Sonya felt her hand tremble as she touched the doorknob of her home. She wasn't sure if she wanted to walk in or not and face the truth on the other side. She wasn't sure if she wanted to look at Jerrell Washington in the face and demand answers for the questions swirling around in her mind. Sharin crossed her mind and it was all she could do not to curse savagely and turn back around and go at it again with her friend and colleague.

Flashback

"I just want to know. You knew Christian dated Jerrell years ago. Why have you never said anything?"

Sharin leaned against the entryway of her kitchen, her eyes turning cold in seconds flat. If Sonya hadn't been a longtime friend, she was certain that she'd escort her out of her house without another word edgewise. She didn't understand women who flitted from one party to the other as far as personal issues went.

"Sonya...I don't have much to say in the way of Christian and Jerrell's prior relationship. If I had my way, they would have never dated."

"But they did and everybody knew about it except me. Then my man is talking to Christian as if she's chasing him in the present tense and I want to know why."

Sharin felt her back go ramrod straight. Normally, she would fight her friend's battles to the very death. However, Sharin had had enough. She had enough of the past few weeks. Between Adams', her best friend, her ex-boyfriend from many moons ago, and her job hanging in the balance pending a police investigation, she couldn't very well add Sonya to the list as well.

"I think you want to watch your tone in my house, Sonya. We're not getting emotional over Jerrell Washington."

"So, you can dictate when I can and cannot get emotional?"

"When you take a tone with me that denotes that you'll beat my ass in my abode, yes. Since we're taking it to this level however, I'll serve you notice that I could care less about Jerrell. I already know you've had this conversation with Monica and I will double down on what she said. They dated. They broke up. He started talking to you. It was mostly because he noticed that you and Christian became friends. He wanted to spite her. My recommendation was for her to ignore him. It was also to speak to you about it. She refused. We've been all working together for quite some time now."

"What does that matter when-"

"Because Sonya, there's never been a time when Christian went out of her way to get back with Jerrell. Christian is not entirely a discreet woman. I love my best friend, but facts are facts. If she had deigned to get back with him, especially years ago...he would have left you high and dry as if you didn't exist. You are dating a textbook narcissist and you need to manage that instead of demanding answers from me."

"I still deserved an explanation."

Sonya's left hand sat on her corresponding hip. Her right one waved in a small circle, further driving her point. Sharin crossed her arms in response.

"You do. Still, not from me. I already have much on my plate, Sonya. I should be preparing dinner for when Maddox-"

Keys could be heard jingling on the other side. Sharin looked over to see the door open and both women stopped short when Maddox stepped inside. Sonya watched him take in Sharin as his eyes filled up with excitement upon seeing her.

It was like slow motion. Maddox closed the door and walked over to Sharin, pulling her into his arms and slowly kissing her. A moan escaped when Sonya turned her head away.

"Love, stop being rude! We have company."

Maddox pulled away and had the grace to look embarrassed when he finally noticed Sonya standing across from them. Sonya giggled weakly but waved him off.

"Sharin...I'll see myself out. Talk to you later, girl."

End of Flashback

Sonya sighed, sadness cloaking her. She opened the door to her apartment and was grateful when she found Jerrell wasn't home. Still, she wondered to herself.

In all of the ten years that they'd been together, she wasn't certain that her man ever looked at her with a burning passion. She slowly realized that Jerrell never looked at her in such a way that everybody else disappeared in his eyesight. She couldn't recall, even in their early dating days, that there was much more than the rush of the chase. Their relationship became increasingly serious, but she wasn't sure whether there was true chemistry.

Christian's name barely ever came up between them. The most she could remember was that they were acquaintances, according to Jerrell. She felt her face frown as she finally stood up, trekking to the kitchen to grab a glass of wine. She sighed, realizing she should have taken Sharin up on her offer before jumping on her.

Sonya poured the Cabernet Sauvignon, sighing before she took a healthy gulp. Her mind still ran, unsure of why everyone got defensive when she asked a simple question. She didn't understand Sharin's anger although she never truly hid her dislike of Jerrell. She just never paraded it in her face, which she could respect. Maddox wasn't quite her cup of tea either.

Still, seeing the love and recognition fill in his eyes when he saw Sharin rocked her. Another two sips of her wine were ingested when she heard the click of the door. Sonya eyed Jerrell as he walked in, a smirk on his face upon seeing her drinking.

"You ready for me? What's taking you so long to get undressed?"

"Why did you never tell me you and Christian dated?"

His smirk fell and Sonya slowly placed her wine down on the living room table. She crossed her shoulders and leaned back into the seat, looking into her man's eyes.

"How did you find out?" was his question. "That was on a need-to-know."

"Jerrell what the fuck do you mean, need-to-know? We've been dating for ten years. I was none the wiser until you picked up *my* phone and called *my* boss, telling her that she had her chance. So let me know, how deeply does this thing run between you and Christian? I'm told you dated her in college and then you dumped her. Let me know now, Jerrell. Should I be packing your shit up to go?"

Jerrell rose a brow as he placed his briefcase down next to him. Sonya watched him expectantly.

"There's no need for all of that, bae. You know I love you. Christian was... fun. She was just something to do when we were at Clark years ago. I broke up with her because I didn't see her in my future. You know me, bae and you know your team. Christian always been sore about our breakup from what I hear. She hasn't dated since. I wish her well, but I just wanted her to know she shouldn't be calling you knowing we were probably busy. She's bitter and needs to get over herself."

"We're in the middle of a crisis, Jerrell. I'm unsure her calling had something to do with you and me. Unless there's something you're also leaving out."

"No. I want nothing to do with Christian and you're looking crazy trying to press me about it. You know we've been together for ten years so why you tight about it now?"

"Because she's my friend, Jerrell *and* she's my fucking boss! How would I look, knowing you may or may not be still fucking my boss while I'm out working in the same fucking building? And you're bold enough to call her phone?! Let's see your phone!"

"Sonya, stop this shit."

Jerrell shrugged off his suit jacket, shaking his head as he walked past her and into their bedroom. Sonya huffed, rising to her feet and following him. She skipped-stepped until she was in front of him, effectively blocking him from walking into their bathroom. Jerrell's brows furrowed as Sonya crossed her arms and cocked her hip.

"Let's see. If you're not calling her...if you're not having a whole emotional affair with her just let me know."

"I'm a grown ass man-"

"-Let's see it! If it's all good, I'll have nothing else to say about it."

Jerrell smirked and leaned in, taking her lips with his. Sonya moaned, trying to pull away but found herself buried into his chest when he caged her in. He kissed her thoroughly, his hand reaching up to grab her tresses. He gripped lightly, growling as he pulled away and looked into her eyes.

"Ten plus years…" Jerrell ground out. "Ten plus years and you're making an issue now…take this shit off."

Sonya reached up, unbuttoning the dress she was currently wearing. She'd done it without question. It was like an out of body experience. Jerrell leaned in, kissing every part of her naked body while he himself was still clothed. He kneeled down and ate until she overflowed. Tears sprang from her eyes as he pulled away and she watched him strip. He nodded over to the bed, pulling at his erection. He licked his lips as Sonya did as she was told. To add extra spice, she spread her legs for him willingly.

Crawling on top of her, he slid in, pushing her legs back and wasting no time in thrusting. Sonya was overwhelmed with tears springing in her eyes. She looked into Jerrell's eyes, unsure of if he was even looking at her at all.

"Ten plus years…there's been no one else. Ten fucking years."

He kept thrusting, giving no quarter. Sonya felt herself release again. More tears. More orgasms. Still, Jerrell kept repeating himself. Nothing about the moment felt like love. Nothing about the moment felt like reassurance. Nothing about it felt redemptive.

"Stop this shit," He paused. "I don't want to hear about it again."

Sonya felt her tears release more, pushing Jerrell off of her. She balled up into a corner of the bed and cried.

She thought Jerrell would comfort her. She thought her man for ten years plus would kiss away the tears. She thought the man who claimed to be with her would reassure her of every fear.

All Jerrell had done was step into their master bathroom. She wept softly as she heard the shower run. She was still weeping when he dressed up without another word and retreated from their home.

That was the moment Christian Adams ceased from being Sonya's friend in her mind.

It had taken no time for Christian to return home. Once she parked her car, she turned to the arrangement of flowers on the passenger side. She grinned widely as she picked it up and hugged it lightly to her chest. Her Neverfull followed as she maneuvered her way out of the door. Closing the door, she mindlessly hummed an Isley Brothers' tune she remembered her parents overplaying in her youth. Her off-tone humming led her and the clicking of her heels was the background as she walked toward the parking lot elevator entrance. She smiled softly, smelling the bouquet arrangement as she remembered the man behind the roses.

Rewind

Jasmine had just finished giving her some final instructions when Tiffany paged her, alerting her to Evander's arrival. Christian's brows furrowed, not remembering the twosome having a standing appointment. That was when Tiffany pressed that she wanted to go ahead and squeeze him in. When Jasmine assured her that they were done for the day, Christian opened the door to let him in.

Evander King stood on the other side with a bouquet of light pink roses. The display caused Christian to flush against her will and it caused her to automatically turn around to see Jasmine standing next to her with her arms crossed and a smirk on her face.

When Evander noticed Jasmine standing next to Christian his smile spread, having the grace to be embarrassed. "I apologize, Ms. Adams. I didn't realize you were working..."

"You're fine," Christian managed. "Jasmine and I were just wrapping up-"

"I do request an audience with you, Mr. King, so if you don't mind sparing me some moments of your time in the near future?"

Evander turned his attention to Jasmine and shifted the bouquet of roses to receive the business card that she offered him. He rose a brow, unsure of what was happening entirely but decided to go with the flow.

"I know your focus isn't all here but just stay with me. Have your people contact me...I won't take up too much of your time."

"So, we can talk here and now," Evander said. "We're all here and I assume this is a business meeting?"

"If Ms. Adams doesn't mind?"

Christian was both excited and affronted. While she knew what Jasmine's play was, she was looking forward to receiving the roses that were in hand of her suitor. The thought made her smile at both of them. She nodded her head, smiling again as Evander presented her with the flowers. Christian thanked him with a smile and laid the arrangement on her desk. The threesome sat at Christian's boardroom table.

"Okay, Mr. King. Long story short, we're running a campaign to restore Adams' good name. I understand that all is not well as far as your business relationship-"

"There's no issue on my end, so long as all the monies are recovered to Kings'. So far, we're already one payment in as Adams' has shown good faith. I don't disbelieve that Adams' will pay the rest."

The fuzzy feelings threatened to leave as Evander kept talking. It made her stomach turn and left a bad taste in her mouth at how much money was being lost in the process. There was also still the issue of the shareholders who might be worried about the rate of return on their investment into Adams'. Their payment would definitely be affected for the short term unless business didn't become affected as much. Suddenly, Jasmine's thought process made all the more sense. If Evander publicly forgave the company for the mishap, more than likely every other business wouldn't be so quick to recant their business, plus outside businesses and people might be impressed by the bounce back.

"I stand corrected. I wanted to request that you be a part of the campaign."

"I wouldn't mind except that I don't understand what impact my presence would bring to such a campaign. I was the party that was affected in all of this."

"If I may speak frankly, Mr. King, as you've said, you are being repaid plus

you are on a first name basis with my client. I'll step outside formality for a few moments to add that from where I'm seated you've gained quite more than you lost out of this situation. If you have the time to wine and dine my friend, then you have the time to assist in building back her glowing reputation."

"I'm not against helping Ms. Brown, I just want clarity on the how," Evander pressed, a brow raised, "Like I mentioned, I don't see what part I play."

"You're a well-known face in Georgia and you've done business with Adams' for quite some time. If you give the word, people will forgive and even do business with Adams' again without reservation. I'm not asking you to lie or conflate the truth but just to more or less give your stamp of approval on the business as it stands."

Evander was quiet, edging a look at Christian. She found herself looking back at him, unsure of what was on his mind as his expression was neutral. He turned back to Jasmine, the same look on his face.

"What do you need exactly?"

"No more than a video or two of you explaining your experience," Jasmine said. "Your presence at a hearing or two might be required but I'd let you know in advance. Just make yourself available if at all possible, Mr. King. I won't be in the way as far as your life, but you might find that I work organically anyway. If you're around, I'll leverage your presence. If not, we'll work it out."

Evander nodded. "When you explain it like that…"

Jasmine's smile spread. "Thank you in advance."

Evander chuckled. "How'd you know that I would agree?"

Jasmine stood, again grabbing her purse with a grin of her own. She walked over toward the door with a chuckle. She wouldn't tell him that everything about him illustrated that he'd go with her wishes for Christian's sake, but it wasn't hard to notice. She wondered if her friend saw it as well.

"Oh, just a hunch, Mr. King. You two enjoy the rest of the day."

And like that, Jasmine Brown had disappeared. Evander looked at Christian once more and smiled. Christian smiled back.

"Thank you for your assistance, Mr. King. Adams' is appreciative of your gracious effort during this time."

Evander gazed back at her, his eyes full of mirth. He stood, rounding the table to walk to where Christian sat and picked up her hand, softly kissing the top of it.

"Adams' is appreciative but how does the boss feel?"

"I'm touched," Christian said, without thinking. "I didn't expect you to go along with what was proposed."

Evander grinned. "Because the CEO has such quality customer service?"

Christian snatched her hand away, pouting cutely. Evander grinned. "What was your previous business, Mr. King?"

"Oh, I'm Mr. King, now? I thought I made such strides in gaining your favor, Christian?"

"You're getting on my nerves now so you might have lost a couple of points."

Christian stood, walking back towards her desk. Once she eyed the bouquet that still sat there however, she softened. She turned to look at Evander, her bad mood all but forgotten.

"Thank you for the flowers, Evander."

He smiled, walking up to her. He took her hand again, while looking in her eyes.

"I was meaning to ask you out on a date. How does Friday night at eight sound?" he questioned, lightly rubbing the top of her hand.

"It sounds perfect," she smiled. "How should I be dressed?"

"Cocktail attire would be appropriate. Sexy underwear in case-"

"In case of what, Mr. King?" Christian's eyebrow rose, regarding him but a smirk was on her face. Evander wasn't sure whether she was daring him to test her limits so all he could do was offer a smile as innocently as he could to make up for his boldness.

"In case you're feeling generous later on?"

"Spoiler alert, not yet," Christian said. "What you can do is walk me to my car since I'm done for the day."

Evander smiled and walked towards her door, opening it. He watched as Christian walked past him and swallowed the groan that threatened to tear from his throat. If Tiffany hadn't been present, he would have let it go freely.

They walked out companionably. Evander complimented the outfit that she chose to wear for the day. Christian thanked him, having enjoyed her ensemble herself. She'd worn a blue satin sleeveless blouse and paired it with a darker blue pencil skirt. Her curves were on display, but she still maintained the professional air that she was going for. The matching jacket had been in the car just in case she became cold in the office, but she found she didn't need it. Her black heels weren't too exciting, but they got the job done.

Evander had gone for the casual route, having worn a pair of khakis and a white polo shirt. He wore brown loafers, ever looking the part. Christian had a fleeting thought of what it might feel like to lift his shirt over his head and stopped herself. Still, she turned away from him momentarily to gather herself.

"Am I fourteen or what?" she berated, biting the inside of her cheek. "I need to stop."

Evander took her roses as they reached her door and stood by as she unlocked her door. Once she'd done so, he helped her inside. He gave Christian the roses back and he watched as she laid them in the passenger seat with care. He marveled at the reverent way she'd done so and wondered about the woman who sat in front of him. It was nothing for him to buy flowers, but it was also nothing for the woman to receive them. He wondered about the woman who was cherishing the arrangement as if he'd gifted her diamonds. He found it adorable.

"Drive safely. Text me when you get home, okay?"

Christian looked up at him with furrowed brows, ready to berate him for the request until she noted the care in his eyes. She softened, nodding her head in acquiescence. He was only being a gentleman and not trying to be overbearing. She wondered why she was ready to be defensive but filed the question away for *later.*

"*I will.*"

End of Flashback

Christian entered her abode, going through her ritual. Her shoes were kicked off. Her bag was tossed on her couch. The only care she had was for putting her roses in a crystal vase that she never thought she would use. Once she placed the bunch on her living room table, the next order of business was placing her keys on the console. She made a stop in the kitchen and poured her favored Riesling in a wine glass and took the first sip as if dying of thirst. She took a few more before she remembered Evander's request and padded back to the living room to retrieve her phone.

She texted him, waiting for his reply when another text came into her phone. An unknown message filed itself away separately and Christian rose a brow, clicking on the tab. The message preview alerted her to knowing that it was Jerrell. She rose a brow, confused as to why he would text her.

Money, it's Jerrell. We need to talk…

Christian felt her face turn red again as she went through the motions to block his number and his message. Right after she was done, Evander replied:

I'm glad that you're safe. I'll see you on Friday.

Christian smiled, getting ready to text him back when he called. She giggled and answered the phone.

"You had to call, too?"

Evander chuckled, "I got your message but wanted to certify that you were really safe. Also, I wanted to hear your voice."

"I see. Are you satisfied now, Evander?"

"I'm placated for now. I'll be satisfied when I see your pretty face again, Christian. I won't hold you for too long, however. I know you just got home and want to relax."

"Also, I'm starting to get tipsy," Christian said. "Which might lead to a conversation I'll hate myself for later."

Evander laughed again. "Maybe I should stay around for a little longer and see what you might tell me by accident."

His voice deepened and the sound and texture fell over her, warming her from the inside out. She giggled but swallowed the words she wanted to reply with. As painful as it was, she was sticking to her guns. She wasn't giving more than she had to. Pursuit meant pursuit, nothing more and nothing less.

She'd missed this part of the dating game. It was at that moment she realized it.

"Hm. I don't think that's wise. I'll see you Friday night?"

"You will, beautiful. Have a good evening."

"You too, handsome."

Christian floated on air the rest of the evening. The sweet promise of the date tickled her pink. The torture of waiting two more nights egged at her but the excitement filled her. She hadn't thought to become terrified yet and wouldn't as long as she was drinking.

What had floated in her mind was Jasmine's suggestion for her to tread carefully while they were dating. She hoped that Evander chose a discreet place for them to dine. She understood Jasmine's point about everything looking flaky in the long run, so she didn't want to jeopardize the restoration of Adams' reputation based on carelessness on her end. It was easy to blame someone else but to have to swallow pain because of an easily avoidable mistake would be too much.

Still, she drank, washing the worries of the day away. There was no point to worry about the past as it was gone. There was also no point in worrying about the future. It hadn't happened yet. Also, she was moving on and doubling down on her actions.

It was a change that she was beginning to welcome, even hesitantly, with open arms.

The next morning, Christian settled back into her office. She was getting ready to pick up her phone and page Tiffany to run through her schedule. Just as she did that, Tiffany opened the door with a slight look of panic on her face.

"What's wrong?"

"You have an unscheduled visitor," Tiffany said. "I don't know what to do with him. He insists on seeing you."

"Hm," Christian said. "Let's get him out of the way, then."

Tiffany nodded, motioning for the mystery man to walk in. When Jerrell stepped into the office, Christian saw red taint her vision but swallowed deliberately. Tiffany made to disappear, but Christian halted her, motioning for her to stay. Jerrell turned as he saw Tiffany closing the door and his eyebrows furrowed together.

"This isn't a meeting-"

"You've come to my office without so much as a call to make an appointment, so you take what you get. The last time I spoke with you, our conversation was hostile. I will not have another one with you in my place of work without a witness. So, whatever you have to say, say it."

Jerrell was at a loss of words. Christian took him in totally for the first time in over ten years. She wondered to herself what had it been about him that made her lose air when he approached her at first.

She took in his frame. Jerrell stood at six feet two inches. His form was lithe and he didn't look half bad in a suit. Christian idly remembered that he was charismatic. When they first started dating, she turned into jelly for him. She had loved him desperately. She remembered the feeling of walking on air until he showed up in her dorm room that fateful evening. She remembered the calm way in which he'd broken her heart. She wasn't sure a month had gone by since he'd taken her virginity. The thought of it bought a cold feeling into her chest. That feeling expanded the more she looked at him and annoyance creeped in when she found that he was only staring at her, dumbly.

"Since you have nothing to say, let's not waste time or mince words. I'm going to make one thing clear to you, Jerrell. If you see my name come up on Sonya's phone, ignore it. Act like you didn't see it. The same way I've been ignoring you for years. The same way I've been acknowledging you as *dead*. Do that when you see me. I haven't said a word to you in the longest and I've done all that I can to show you just what I think of you. Do not come to my office again or you'll suffer the consequences. Have a nice life."

Jerrell opened his mouth and then closed it. He opened it up again, ready to counter but was overtaken by Christian.

"I *said*, have a nice life."

Another knock resounded on the door. Tiffany opened the door and Christopher stepped in. Jerrell sucked his teeth, turning to leave.

"You can front for all these people if you want to, Christian. You're not over me and you'll *never* get over me. You might as well just get over yourself and come back. You know where it's at when you-"

"-Alright, brother," Christopher cut in. "Let's go."

Jerrell eyed Christopher, ready to give him some words but decided against it. Christopher looked back at him, nodding as he saw Jerrell weigh out his options mentally. He didn't take kindly to Christian feeling unsafe as it was and it went double for Tiffany. His girlfriend sounded alarmed when she sent him the text to escort the gentleman off the premises and it wasn't hard to see why when he entered the room. Hearing his parting shot was enough to make Christopher roll his eyes but professionalism always reigned.

Jerrell exited first and the door closed behind Christopher. Tiffany turned her attention to Christian and was alarmed when she saw tears falling down Christian's face.

"Oh…no…" Tiffany said, rushing over to her.

Christian raised her hand up, stopping Tiffany in her tracks. "I'm fine. I'm good." She said, "Just give me two minutes and I'll be right back with you."

Tiffany nodded and then stepped outside. As she settled back into her desk, the elevator doors dinged and Evander stepped out, holding two bags. She smelled the coffee emanating from one of the bags and her heart melted and sped up at the same time.

"Good morning," He said, approaching her. "I know I didn't schedule time but is it possible that Ms. Adams is free?"

"Ahh-" Tiffany said. "Let me check with her."

Tiffany paged Christian, alerting her that Evander was waiting outside. To her surprise, Christian told her to let him in. With her eyebrows raised in surprise, she set the phone down and with a smile motioned for him to walk in. Evander smiled at her pleasantly and walked by.

When he walked in and caught sight of Christian, he smiled, holding up the bags.

"I bought breakfast. Thought you might want coffee before you-"

Christian's eyes were tear filled and without thought he'd placed the bags on the table and rounded her desk. He reached for her and was surprised when she allowed him to pull her up in his arms. He held onto her, rocking her gently back and forth and shocked again when he felt her body vibrate against him.

Evander felt bewildered and knew the only thing on his mind was figuring out what to do about what ailed her. For the moment, all he could do was hold her in her arms and let her cry. He'd wondered what vulnerability looked like on her, but this wasn't the way he'd wished to find out. His mind had been on another track whenever he thought about tearing down her walls.

Five minutes had passed when Christian came back to herself, looking up into Evander's eyes.

"I...I'm sorry."

Evander tilted her face up, his own frowned in consternation and questioned her what was wrong.

"I haven't been gone that long so you shouldn't be crying," he said, wiping traces of her tears away.

When the meaning of his words dawned on her, she giggled and attempted to push him away. Still, he held on, laughing with her.

"I...I don't really want to talk about it right now. I'm sorry for that. It's been a long day already and it's still morning. What brings you in, Mr. King?"

"I wanted to start my day with you," he answered, grinning. "I figured you wouldn't mind a light breakfast before you started your day. Plus, I was wondering about Ms. Brown and my role in all of this...rebranding you're doing."

Christian smiled, softly. "Not so much rebranding as in rebuilding the trust that my current clients have in me. There's a lot of rumors I need to put to rest about the whole mishap. Jasmine just sees you as being an instrumental part in the success of that. One mistake shouldn't cost me my whole business, should it?"

Her tone had softened and in turn, so did Evander. He realized that she was appealing to him and the picture she'd painted while she did so in his arms was beautiful. He leaned in, kissing her lips softly. Christian felt her eyes shut as he took another kiss, softly nuzzling her lips with his own as he'd done so. She returned the affection once more before looking up in his eyes.

"No, it shouldn't." Evander leaned in once more, giving her one more last, lingering kiss before he pulled away with a hard swallow. Christian blinked at the action as she watched him step away from her. Catching her duress, he smirked. "You make me want to take things too far. It's not you at all, beautiful."

Christian felt her shoulders sag in relief and decided to sit back down in her own chair. Evander had busied himself with unloading the bag of goodies he bought.

She watched him as he'd done so and smiled softly. Christian couldn't remember the last time a man went out of his way to show that he wanted her in his life. She wanted to compare him with Jerrell but this time she forced herself not to draw up the comparison. She took him in as he was. She watched him pick up the coffee cups and load them in her microwave. She watched as he served her and then himself. The picture he made while doing so was striking.

He sat before her on the other side of her desk, clearing her documents without asking. It made her chuckle, but she didn't stop him.

"I don't have much time, Evander. I have to prep and then hold a staff meeting in an hour."

Evander smirked. "You need to block off your entire morning, if you ask me."

"I didn't."

"You should. I don't know what happened but you're in no real condition to give staff meetings. I understand you're the CEO; the end and beginning of Adams' but there's no point in running things if you can't even run yourself."

"Evan-"

"-There's no point in running some shit if you're unable to pass the baton every now and again. You have a very capable team, Christian. You had a rough moment and you need to unwind. I'm aware that I can't tell you how to run your business. Still. I see all over you that you need a break. At some point, you should take it. That's all I'm saying."

Christian looked into his eyes furtively as she processed his words. Then, she nodded in acquiescence.

"You're right. At this moment as I have all the directives from Jasmine, I can't block off the morning, but I might take off early in the afternoon. Is that a worthy balance for you, Mr. King?"

"If it's good for you, then it's great for me, Ms. Adams," he smiled. "Still, all I'm trying to get across is to prioritize yourself. The business can't run if you can't."

Christian smiled at him, deciding that his advice was sound. "Maybe I oughta keep you around, Mr. King."

Evander grinned, licking his lips as he took in Christian's smile. He ached to reach across and caress her face but held back. His kissing her was in the moment but he wanted to pace himself and at the same time, make her comfortable with him. He knew that the object of his affections built up walls around herself. He intended to take his time knocking them all down. Still, he didn't want to rush the process. There'd be enough time for him to touch her in every way possible when the time was right. That was his conviction when he answered her back.

"That of course, is entirely up to you, Ms. Adams. Still, I hope you do."

The twosome enjoyed a relaxing breakfast afterwards.

Two nights later, Christian agonized over her outfit choices for her upcoming date with Evander. Both Sharin and Monica bemusedly looked on as Christian held up her two choices in front of them, going back and forth.

"I like this one, but I feel like it'd be too sexy, no?"

Christian's first choice was a rust colored, satin midi number. It had spaghetti straps and was simple yet sexy.

"The other dress...isn't?" Sharin deadpanned. "It's identical to the first one, save for it's red. Make me understand what you're saying, Christian."

"Besides, you got ass. Flaunt it. No point in wasting that beautiful figure in a potato sack. You are trying to get laid, aren't you?"

"Not tonight, Nik," Christian shot back, rolling her eyes. "It's the first date."

"I mean…I gave Reginald some well before the first date, so you know that means *nothing* to me. If a man wants you, he wants you."

"No, Monica, you're just nuts," Sharin said. "Christian has to go based on her own speed. I prefer yesterday, however."

Christian, rolling her eyes, turned to her two friends, wondering how they were friends at all. She walked over to her phone, snatched it up and fumed as she saw the twin smirks on their faces.

"Stop policing my pussy," she spat. "Just because you two are hoes don't mean I have to be."

"You're absolutely right, sis. Still, I just don't see anything wrong with appearing sexy. It's not going to kill you. Maybe him, but not you. I'm just saying not to worry about it. With that being said, I'll talk to you later."

Monica cackled as Sharin disappeared.

"First off, I'm not a hoe, m'kay? I'm just sexually free and not consenting to the bonds of patriarchal constructs. If it feels good, I go with it."

"That still doesn't tell me which dress I should be wearing."

"Since you're still afraid to bust it wide open, I think you should go with the brown. The red one is going to be too much for both of you."

Christian held up the rust colored one, deciding she would go with Monica's advice. Turning to the phone again, she smirked. "Sometimes, you're good for something."

"I know a little about a lot. Either way, relax! It's just a date. Enjoy it. Do your makeup, blast some music. Enjoy you! If it goes well, enjoy him! If you're not ready…enjoy yourself!"

"Monica!"

"I'm just saying," Monica cackled. "That man is fine and you're lying if you tell me he doesn't inspire something to throb."

Christian flushed but said nothing. She thanked Monica for her help and clicked off, laughing to herself at how off the cuff Monica could be. Still, the rest of her advice was sound, so she put on a 90s R&B playlist that she hadn't played in some months and started to get ready. Left, right, or otherwise, she'd count it all as experience. She highly doubted that with Evander that it would be anything but good, however.

Still, she was slightly nervous. Her record with men wasn't the greatest. However, she wanted to keep pushing forward. Something about Evander scared her yet exhilarated her. In her mind, she'd be foolish to not at least give it a try.

Her two best friends had found love. Recklessly and cautiously, they'd stumbled around until they'd fallen into submission to the call of love. Christian wondered if it were her turn. She hoped that finally, it was.

Janet Jackson was her background singer as she decided to run her shower and prepare for her date. She'd done a stand-up job of keeping men away thus far. Perhaps Evander could show her why her efforts hadn't been in vain.

Chapter
Eleven

Evander merged onto the highway, trying his best not to glance at Christian every two seconds. In his mind, he still replayed over and over when she stepped out of her apartment building, her strut confident and her smile beguiling. It was enough to make him swallow hard before he approached her to greet her for the evening. It'd taken every bit of his control not to drag her into his arms and kiss her thoroughly as he'd been aching to since the day before in her office.

He wondered idly if she even knew her own allure. He was amazed at how she can both carry both dominance and submissiveness like a practiced swordsman. Every move she made was subtle but cut into him deliciously.

They hadn't even been talking about anything of note. The soft jazz played between them, filling in the comfortable silence. Evander reached over and picked up her hand, without taking his eyes off the road. His awareness that Christian was taking him in kicked up and he struggled not to return her attention.

"How was your day?" he questioned. "I hope it went well."

"It wasn't bad. I finally went over the new protocols as far as our dealings with the media with the apartment heads. I personally ran through them with Sharin's department. I have to figure out when I'm reinstating her…"

"You suspended your Partner?" Evander questioned. "That's a bit rash, isn't it?"

"It was. One of my lesser decisions in hindsight," Christian sighed. "That's behind us, now. Still, I'll have to grovel at her feet or whatever nonsense she told me before I kicked her out."

"She was head over the department that messed up my funds?" Evander questioned. "I can't see any other reason you would…"

"The thought process was to suspend her pending anything that came up in the investigation. So far, she's been cleared as a suspect as she had no clue the books were being mismanaged. Jupiter Classon…"

Christian risked a look in his direction, unsure that she wanted to delve into the goings on of what happened. She turned away, unsure she wanted to spoil their personal time with business dealings. Still, they had a business relationship and she owed it to him to be truthful, no matter what came of their personal relationship as it stood.

"You don't have to talk about it, beautiful. I don't want a nasty taste in my mouth and you don't seem like you want one either. I understand what you're trying to say for the most part."

Christian smiled softly, as he squeezed her hand gently in reassurance. "Overall, it was a good day. I'm hoping for a good night to cap off the week."

A smile ghosted Evander's mouth. He absentmindedly rubbed the top of her hand with his thumb as he found the exit he was searching for.

Christian took him in, appreciating the picture he made while driving. Summertime in Atlanta meant that he didn't wear a blazer on this particular evening, but she enjoyed watching his frame in the navy-blue polo shirt that he wore. It was speckled with small white dots that added more than took away from the design. When she saw him earlier on, she noted he wore matching navy-blue pants that were solid in color. His black shoes were just the right dose of casual and formal melded together.

She also couldn't get the way his eyes lit up when he saw her. His excitement emboldened her and comforted her at the same time. It embarrassed her slightly that she hadn't wanted to be a disappointing sight but his reaction to her made her feel less anxious about the evening.

"What's on your agenda tonight?" Christian asked, breaking the silence again.

"Is this a date or a meeting?"

Evander turned to look at Christian, meaning to joke with her but was taken again as he glanced at her face. He turned once more, smirking at himself and how he responded to her and suddenly the words that his friend said weeks ago made perfect sense. It wasn't hard to notice that Christian was beautiful. At first, his concern seemed foolish to him, but the more Evander found himself falling for her, the more the concern made sense. Women were definitely able to tear down empires so what made the one sitting next to him any different?

Evander pushed the wayward thoughts aside, knowing exactly what set her apart from many women. It was the honor she adorned herself with. It was also the power she wielded better than most he knew. In his eyes she was a perfect complement to him and he was without shame in admitting that he had to have her.

"I apologize. I'm just excited," Christian confessed, breaking into his thoughts.

Evander blinked as he pulled up to the restaurant in question, momentarily forgetting what they were talking about. When he had remembered, he chuckled, slowing down as they neared the entrance.

"I was playing with you, love," he said, grinning. "Don't take me seriously…too seriously."

Christian smiled as he caressed her chin with his fingers. Pulling away, he stepped out as the valet neared the car. He walked on to the passenger side and opened the door, reaching in for Christian's hand. She stepped out deliberately, placing a foot after the other and grinning as she stood upright, making eye contact with Evander again.

"Shall we?"

The twosome walked through the doors of Bacchanalia. Christian followed Evander's lead, relaxing bit by bit as someone else took on the reigns. She had to admit that it was very nice not to have to think of every detail for once. Evander handled the conversation as far as their reservation and she thought such a simple detail was sexy. She was used to having to deal with those details whenever she and the girls went out on business lunches.

Bacchanalia was one of Atlanta's fine dining giants from the early nineties. They were held in great regard by the general populace and food critics alike. It had been on Christian's list of places to dine but she hadn't the chance since she started working. The surroundings made her feel better about not having visited until the present moment. The air wasn't truly romantic, but it was a nice space to explore with someone.

It hadn't been long until the twosome was escorted to a restricted area. Behind the door was a table set for two, complete with candlelight and dinnerware already set up. Christian gasped in pleasure, looking up at Evander whose smile was spreading.

"Private dining?" she questioned. "Who do you think you are?"

Evander led her in as the doors closed behind them. She smiled as he led her to the table, with his hand pressed lightly to the small of her back.

"I'm the man very intent on sweeping you off of your feet," he said, pulling her chair back.

Christian moved to stand in front of the seat and sat down when he pushed the seat inward. He walked to the other side, seating himself and looking into her eyes.

"For once, you don't have an objection, Ms. Adams?"

Christian smirked, flushing with pleasure as she reached for the glass that contained water. She took a sip and set the glass down, a smile still on her face.

"I don't. Not yet. I'm just surprised at all the pomp and circumstance around the first date."

"Well, I am in pursuit of you. I haven't hidden that fact," Evander shrugged. "I just simply go for what I want. Who I want. This is just me showing you how I treat the lady in my life. Also, I was warned that I should tread lightly with you in the mix of the scandal as it progresses and wanes."

Christian smirked. "So Jasmine got to you, too?"

Evander nodded. "She did. I've agreed as I want to be a help and not a hindrance to you. Especially as you always get my money to me on time. As a businesswoman, I hold high regard for you. As a woman, I want to spoil you. So, this was my solution to do both."

Christian smiled, despite herself. "I appreciate that, Evander."

His smile spread again. "I'm glad."

A waiter approached the table from the exit dedicated to the room. The telltale sounds of the kitchen sounded as the doors opened but died down once they closed. That'd been the only indication that the man walked into the room. He approached Evander and Christian, introducing himself. Brighton read out loud the course offerings for the night, turning to Christian first.

Evander watched as Christian smiled softly, reciting her choices and making small conversation with the waiter. He wondered that he was slightly envious that she smiled at the man at all but pushed the feelings to the side as silly. It was beautiful that she was polite and engaging.

It hadn't taken time for them to come to an agreement over their choices before the waiter disappeared quietly.

"I must say, you look lovely this evening, Ms. Adams. I can't keep my eyes off of you."

Christian blushed, pleasure filling her to the brim. "Thank you. You look handsome as well. I like the shirt."

Evander grinned as the waiter returned with Christian's drink order. He was surprised to see that it was a red, instead of her usual white. He chuckled slightly as Christian toasted him.

"I know you're shocked. Have to mix it up, sometimes."

"I've scheduled a paint and sip after this," Evander smirked. "So pace yourself, love."

She lightened up, despite his smug delivery.

"You're going all the right ways for it to be a perfect night. Are you for real?"

"Very real, Christian. I plan to spoil the shit out of you and you're going to be asking me what took me so long to get to you."

"Hmm. I doubt that but we'll see. I'll have fun watching you try to fulfill that promise."

"I love a challenge, baby. I deliver each and every time so be prepared to ask me. Either way, I'm fully prepared to apologize for the delay."

"Are you?"

"I am."

Christian held his gaze as he'd responded and felt the warmth spread from her chest to the rest of her body. She wasn't sure what it was about Evander that got her engines going but they definitely ran where he was concerned. She found herself biting her lip, noting that in the moment, he was undeniably sexy. His dark brown eyes pierced her light ones. His full lips were upturned in a smirk, but she knew he spoke his words in all seriousness. Still, she took him in unabashedly with a smirk of her own, enjoying how dark and smooth his skin was. His full lips parted again as if he were ready to double down on his statement when Brighton appeared again with the first course.

"Enjoy."

Brighton urged them to call for him if they needed anything and then disappeared. Christian smiled as she looked down at the perfectly plated dish in front of her. Before she dug in, she looked back up to catch Evander gazing at her, still.

"Yes, Evander?"

He smirked. "I was just thinking of the gentleman telling me to *enjoy*. All I can think of is I will. I'm going to enjoy the food and you."

"You're so mannish."

"I have my moments. You haven't seen anything yet."

Christian bit her lip and decided to dig into her food. She didn't have a comeback that was adequate enough. Besides, she couldn't quite hide behind her farce any longer. It went without saying that she was excited to see what more he had to offer her. She was excited to see if for once, a man could hold up his promise. She was starting to see that with Evander, life would be anything but boring.

She hoped against hope that he would deliver.

Chapter
Twelve

Christian drove up into the first parking space that she saw and thanked the heavens that it was close to the entrance of the event space. She took two deep breaths, forcing the stress to leave her body, even as she picked up Sharin's bridal gift.

Sharin's cousin, Linda, had taken the liberty as her maid of honor to put together the event. Southern Exchange Whitehall Ballroom was housed in a building rich and ripe with history, many years before the company took over the space.

In her opinion, the soiree was way too extravagant, even for her best friend but perhaps the celebration was more about the people who were happy to see Sharin becoming engaged to Maddox Lennox. He was indeed quite the catch and with the climate being what it was in Georgia, as well as everywhere else in the United States, an eligible Black man who still desired to be with a Black woman was rare. Double points if he were well established and rich.

A win for one was a win for all. At the very least, a crowd of two hundred and fifty or less. Even if Sharin's impending nuptials weren't the reason for such an event, not many people were able to turn down a party for any reason. Christian found that she wasn't quite in the mood to be around so many people, with the scandal still alive and well. Still, her best friend was celebrating her engagement and it was a happy time. She would be remiss if she wiggled her way out of what was undoubtedly one of the best moments of her friend's life.

So, with a deep sigh, she secured the Tiffany blue box that held Sharin's gift and opened her car door. She swung her heeled feet over to the side and stepped out, taking in Atlanta's gorgeous blue skies. The sun warmed her face and she sighed, slamming the door before it could pink her flesh too much.

Christian hoped the orange wrap dress she chose to wear for the day was sufficient. She walked easily, knowing that there was no way the event space would be packed by the time she got there. She decided to make a smooth exit once more people started to show up.

When she stepped through the building's double doors, she was thankful for the signs that pointed her to the room she was to walk to. She smiled softly at the beautiful picture of her friend on each poster. She was already impressed with the amount of work that Linda had put in. Seconds later, shame fell on her. Months ago, Sharin had asked Christian to be her maid of honor and she declined. She suddenly wished with all her being that she could turn back the clock but the past was in the past. Linda was definitely more equipped to give

Sharin the grand parties and had much more patience to deal with Sharin as she progressed further and further into planning her wedding. Christian knew at the moment that she lacked every bit of patience that her cousin had in abundance. So, it was all's well that ends well. Still, Christian questioned herself why.

"Because I did feel like she was abandoning me. I wasn't about to very well help her move on without me..."

The truth hit her like a ton of bricks when she acknowledged it. She took a moment at the door to wipe her eyes as they started to leak.

"Maybe I do need counseling...nah, I'm good."

Taking two more moments to steel herself against every bit of energy behind the door, she pushed through them. Christian gasped at the scene before her. There were round tables littered around the space on opposite ends. The decorations were a study of neutral colors with pops of pinks and peach. Each table's centerpiece had pearls flowing out of clear vases. Out of the vases were ostrich feathers of either white, peach, or pink. Sharin had a table in the front for herself and the bridal party.

Christian watched her best friend smile widely as other women regarded her happily. It seemed although Sharin didn't take the socialite path her mother intended for her to take; she was still highly respected in their world. It was a breath of fresh air for Christian to see it, as she was used to the dog-eat-dog competitiveness of the accounting world.

"Christian!"

Linda was seen stalking toward her, all smiles. Linda Reynolds was a beautiful picture with skin the color of brandy. She was Sharin's favorite cousin, but she only saw her once in a blue moon growing up. Linda's family lived in Portugal for years before Linda came back into the states for her college years. They reunited during those years but Linda opted to attend Spelman instead of Clark Atlanta. They took different avenues for their lives but overall still loved each other.

Linda had been excited when Sharin asked her to be her maid of honor, albeit surprised. Still, she loved Sharin recklessly and took on the task with all the seriousness of a trained assassin.

"I'm so happy to see you!" Linda said, kissing her lightly on the cheek. "You look beautiful."

Chrisitan flushed, unprepared for the compliment but thanked her graciously. "It's good to see you, Linda. How've you been?"

"Well. I can't complain. Just waiting to get married like this one here." She rolled her eyes for effect. "I'm good though. You good? I...I've been hearing the news nonstop."

"I'm maintaining, sis. Thanks for asking."

"Well, don't be discouraged. Everything is only for a season and this too, shall pass...let me take this from you and get you seated. You're right next to Sharin."

Christian giggled. "That so? I thought that was your reserved seat."

They walked through the crowd, slowing down every now and again to address guests that recognized Christian. She smiled as best as she could, since so many were asking the same question that Linda had. Still, she could tell some of the women were being disingenuous. She was pretty sure that it had more to do with Sharin's suspension than anything else. She held back from rolling her eyes at the thought but understood the concern. They were close to the front when Linda interrupted her thoughts.

"Don't pay them any mind. Most of them don't understand the perils of running the show. They only have to look pretty and spend their man's hard-earned money."

Christian giggled. "Maybe I ought to follow their lead."

"Maybe…but it's not your time yet. You'll know when you're ready to call it quits. It's also going around that you may or may not be seeing a certain Atlantan bachelor yourself."

"Who's been saying that?" Christian asked. "Jasmine will kill me if-"

"Oh, no. It's not on the rumor mill. Between me and Shay," Linda winked. "I just wanted to startle you a little bit."

Christian laughed helplessly. "So you're just being nosey."

"Oh girl, I couldn't help but to ask you because I'm invested in this going far."

"So, you're going to keep my friend hidden the whole time, Lin? You didn't even tell me she was here!"

Sharin floated over towards them, causing Christian to smile fully as she took her best friend in. Sharin wore a white, flowy dress with side splits stopping at her mid-thigh in the front. She wore a braided gold belt at the waist. On her feet were golden sandaled heels that boosted her height about the same as Christian. Sharin wore her hair in a butterfly braid with assorted gold adornments placed throughout the braid. Her makeup was light but it was obvious that whether she wore makeup or not, on this day, she glowed.

She walked over to Sharin, pulling her in for a hug.

"Look at you, looking like someone's fiancée!" she squealed. "You look beautiful, bestie."

Sharin's smile was bright as she thanked her friend. She also found herself blinking back tears because she felt in her friend's energy that it was the first time she truly accepted her engagement to Maddox. She wasn't sure what change brought about her attitude change, but she was grateful for it.

Linda snapped candid photographs of them while they giggled and enjoyed each other's company. In about two minutes' time, the twosome was sitting down and talking about various things. Neither realized the time had passed until it was about an hour later. The food was being dispersed and when Sharin realized it, she blushed lightly.

"I've been ignoring everybody for an hour like I don't see you every day."

Christian laughed. "Honestly, it's your party. They should be coming up to you. Everybody's gossiping with each other."

"That's true. I'm shocked the crew hasn't shown up yet."

"Let's find them and curse them out," Christian said. "Also, I haven't seen Linda since she sat me down with you."

"You won't see her much since she's running the show. I have to do something special for her when this is all said and done."

Christian smiled softly. "Let me know. I'll help if you need it."

Sharin and Christian walked hand-in-hand to the table that had all their workmates together. Monica eyed them approaching first and hopped up to greet them both. Her long arms pulled them both in.

"My girls! I love you!"

Christian laughed, seeing that Monica was way ahead of her in the race of tipsiness. She was slightly envious that she was still sober and told her as much.

"That's because Sharin's a bad host," Monica pulled her in for another hug. "You look beautiful, Shay."

"Thanks, Em," She giggled. "Even though you insulted me. I'm the guest of honor and Linda is the host."

"Forgive me, doll. You know I'm a train wreck when I've had a few. Bring on the stripper, let's get this party going though!"

Jasmine's laughter could be heard as she approached the trio. She'd been waiting for her moment to congratulate Sharin and decided she had to take it or Monica would keep running the conversation.

"That's for the bachelorette party, Monica. I see you rehearsing already for it."

"I rehearse on a regular," she winked. "I'll move out of the way. I see you're ready for your moment, big time."

"You know me so well," Jasmine winked back. "I won't be long."

Jasmine hugged Sharin lightly. "Congratulations, again. I hope you're staying well?"

"I am," Sharin answered. "Much as I can."

"I know this isn't quite the time and place to bring up business, but I just want to remind you to stay safe since you're high-profile. I'm chilling now because security in this place is pretty good but afterward please stay as low as you can. I also hope you and Christian worked out y'all shit during that hour y'all were giggling."

Jasmine eyed Christian who shrugged her shoulders.

"We're okay," Sharin answered. "I'm not pressing her to come back to work or anything if that's what you mean."

"I don't doubt you'll be restored to your position since you've been cleared. That being said, Christian needs to take the time to run over some things with you *when* she restores your position and you're back to work. I'm not going over any of them now because we're celebrating your pending nuptials, but I just wanted to stress your safety again."

"Yes, Mom," Sharin smirked. "I'll be fine, Jasmine. Linda has security in places we don't even know about. Maddox has someone, against my better judgement, keeping watch over the house since Chastity's visit sometime ago. I'm being driven everywhere and it's a pain but I try not to complain much."

"Good. I don't care about your discomfort as long as you're safe," Jasmine grinned. "Christian, take our picture and make sure you get our good side."

"Some niggas are so bossy," Christian said, taking the phone Jasmine thrust in her face. "I don't know why I take the treatment."

"The pot calling the kettle back," Jasmine retorted. "Congratulations again, Shay."

Sharin laughed, despite herself. "Thank you kindly."

Christian snapped a few poses, fully enjoying herself in ways she hadn't known she would. Once Jasmine moved out of the way, Sharin made to walk in Christian's direction again when Sonya cut in between them. Christian felt the coldness as she air-kissed Sharin, making small talk with her. She stood off to the side, for the first-time in years feeling awkward. She wanted to add herself into the conversation but everything about Sonya's energy stopped her from doing so.

Christian took her in and wondered why Sonya was even dressed in a pants suit as if it were a work affair. The color of her outfit was black and her hair was pulled back severely in a bun. She wasn't dressed for a celebration. Christian didn't consider herself a spiritualist, but she couldn't help but to think her friend chose her outfit for a reason, down to the color.

She thought hard about pulling Sonya aside, as the conversation with Sharin grew longer and longer. It wasn't envy that stirred her actions, but she knew that Sonya wasn't happy with her. Whether she was trying to hide it or not, Sonya was starting to make the atmosphere uncomfortable for everyone involved. Christian didn't deny her wrong-doing and wasn't upset with Sonya for her anger but didn't understand why she was being childish.

Christian opened her mouth, ready to interrupt but stopped herself just as she was going to ask Sonya to speak with her privately. She didn't want to bring strife and anger to her best friend's celebration. Not when the issue of Jerrell wasn't worth the trouble. It was becoming obvious that Sonya had an issue with her and it didn't seem wise to push it as she knew she was in the wrong. In her mind, when Sonya was ready to address it, she would. Until then, she wouldn't be the one to start the conversation. If she would just dump Jerrell it would make life for all involved much easier.

If only life were that easy.

Christian was shocked out of her reverie as Sharin touched her on the arm. Thrown off, she looked around for Sonya and realized she was gone. She looked at Sharin, a confused look on her face. Sharin sighed, concern etched on her face.

"She got a phone call and told me she was leaving," She shrugged. "You two haven't spoken yet?"

Christian shook her head.

"Well, I'll leave it alone, then."

Christian nodded. "Definitely. It's your day and you shouldn't be worried about my drama. When she's ready to grow up, we can hash it out."

"Good. I'm ready to get drunk now," Sharin said. "Monica is way ahead of me and it's my party."

Christian giggled. "You still have gifts to open."

"I might need to be inebriated for some of those gifts. The boxes look rather small on the display."

Christian glanced at the display and giggled at the bevy of gifts, though most of them were small. Glancing back at Sharin she held up two fingers.

"Maybe this many?"

"Deal."

The twosome giggled as they walked back to the front of the space, both deciding not to let Sonya's obvious childishness ruin the day for them. If she were content to be miserable over a man who she still went home to night after night, it was her prerogative.

Life still went on.

Christian smiled ear to ear as she took in the beautiful blue skies. The clouds clumped together beautifully into assorted shapes and blankets. It was a rare moment that put her into worship as she thought to herself of a God who can knit the universe together. One who kept many secrets and the few that He bestowed upon the world was enough to wow for many millennia. It made her think of the fact that miracles happened every day. She wondered at the fact that she was seated on a private charter jet with the object of her affection sitting across from her, conducting business of his own.

She took him in covertly as he sat across from her in his own seat with a table propped in front of him. He was on the phone, closing a business deal with another company that she never heard of. Still, the look of concentration was on his face, his fresh line up and the dark suit that he wore was a triple threat of sexiness that begged to be noticed. Christian picked up her wine glass and sipped, again being grateful for miracles.

Evander was opposite of her, wondering about his good fortune that Christian sat across from him, looking as delectable as the dessert he'd eaten the night prior. A light, fluffy cheesecake had been his portion but as he'd eaten it, he thought of nothing but the headstrong CEO that he ached to undo over and over again.

It was in his thoughts that he wanted to fly her with him to Phuket but realized the timing was terrible, especially as they both couldn't be away from Atlanta for too long. Miami was the consolation prize, although it was a popular destination. Evander knew however, that he could make it a memorable experience for her.

Evander smiled softly to himself as the phone call with his business partner wrapped up. He watched Christian looking out the window and adored the way she was taken in by the clouds. It'd been sometime since he'd done so himself as most times during travel work had to be done in the mix.

"You wake me up at almost two in the morning and demand for me to pack a weekender just for me to be ignored for maybe two hours straight."

Evander grinned as he ended his call. Looking up at Christian's unamused face, he beckoned her with his hands. With a smirk she stood, walking to him, stopping just short of him. His smirk grew deeper as he reached out and pulled her into his lap. He leaned up to meet her lips and kissed her softly. His arm wound around her waist. He was pleased to see her smile.

"Are you placated, love?" he questioned. "Or do you require more?"

Christian leaned in, returning his affections. "More. Always more."

Evander's answering smile was the last thing she remembered seeing for the remaining hour of the flight.

Once they landed, the day seemed to go by in a blur, but Christian kept up. They checked into 1Hotel South Beach, only having seen the space for all of ten minutes. Once they were freshened up and ready for their time together, their first stop was the beach. Christian and Evander played in the waves for some time before retreating back upstairs. A nap had been in order since they'd flown from Atlanta at about five that morning. Noon time saw Christian back in her very own bedroom, surprised that Evander went through the length but was impressed that he didn't just assume they'd be sharing a room. She thought it very classy of him and swooned at the thought.

She'd just finished taking a lovely shower in the en suite bathroom and decided to just sleep in the satin nightgown that she packed. She slipped it on, thankful for the softness against her body and found herself at a loss. She wondered to herself when was the last time she took a moment for herself. It'd been sometime since she slowed down and took a few moments to slow down and just…be.

Christian exhaled as she laid down on the king-sized bed and let the white noise of the ocean lull her away to peace.

"I…I can get used to this…"

She drifted off into peace.

The evening saw her again at dinner with Evander at Watr, the hotel's rooftop restaurant. Christian enjoyed the vibe as she and Evander talked on and on about random childhood memories.

"My parents were strict," she said, sighing. "That's where I get a lot of my rigidness from. I had to be up at a certain time, washed up by a certain time… my father wanted me to always be able to recite a story to him out of the paper during dinner time. Well…report it rather."

"I'm sorry about that. What made him do that?"

"He was persistent with me always being in the know. I switched it up on him one year and started buying the Wall Street Journal. I could stomach things better if math was involved. I used to read a lot about the scandals that happened in these companies. Now I wonder if I manifested my own ruin."

Evander chuckled. "Nah. Long as there's businesses, there's corruption. Thankfully you were able to spot it before it got too out of hand."

"That was blind luck. I have to reinstate my Partner but I'm unsure of when…or if she even wants to come back."

"Well…leave that worry for another time. We're getting to know each other right now," Evander grinned. "Much as I find your Partner adorable, I'm getting to know the Boss."

Christian blushed. "I did derail the topic. But yeah, Pop said no boyfriends and Ma went with it. She had mercy on me for senior prom, but I didn't even want a date by then. I was just ready to graduate and head out to college. They promised me that my life was my own after I graduated high school."

"That's a huge shift though and so early…they pretty much controlled every aspect and then just set you free? How'd you manage?"

Christian shrugged. "Like a boss, I think. I was good until…Jerrell."

Evander noted the sadness that came into her eyes and wondered if he should ask about the gentleman or not. He let the temptation pass however and was glad when her eyes cleared up.

"I was good though. Shay, Nik-Sharin, Monica-we were pretty solid. We came up in high school together and we carried ourselves through to the end. We were a unit the whole time. I mean I did have rough days where I adjusted because my parents weren't easily accessible but after the first six months, I was good. I knew I couldn't move back in with them, that was for sure."

Evander laughed, enjoying the candor of his date. It was the freest she'd ever been with him and he had to admit to enjoying her thoroughly. Her maxi dress was a beautiful study of white with spring flowers scattered amongst them. He wasn't sure if they were peonies or hydrangeas but he didn't too much care. On her feet were gold, flat sandals. Her toes were painted white as well as her manicured hands. His thoughts threatened to travel south as she was talking but he halted them.

Her face scrunched up as her phone vibrated. He'd been ready to make a joke about her rudeness when her face flushed red. She looked from Evander back to her phone.

"Is everything okay?" he questioned. "Is there an emergency?"

Christian shook her head with her face furrowed. "No, no emergency. I got a really mean message and I'm both angry and embarrassed."

Without prompting, Christian showed Evander.

You might have everybody else fooled Christian but it's obvious you need to come off the truth about you and Jerrell and do it quickly.

"This Jerrell character seems to be more trouble than he's worth…" Evander mumbled. "What's this about?"

Christian sighed. "You remember the guy from the bar a few weeks ago?"

Evander nodded. "I take it that's Jerrell."

"I'm going to be completely open about this…I'm unsure how you'll feel about me after this but…"

"If you're going to be completely open I'm going to keep an open mind," Evander said. "I'm listening."

Christian smiled wanly before she took a sip of the wine that was next to her. Evander smiled softly, briefly remembering the first time they met.

"I dated Jerrell during my sophomore year at Clark. He chased after me. I never had a boyfriend, but I was taught not to make it easy for a man-"

"-Much like you're doing to me right now."

Christian giggled. "Stop before I lose my nerve." Evander motioned for her to continue. "When he got accepted to Harvard Law, he came and told me about it. He also broke up with me in the same moment…

Evander felt his face furrow but kept quiet.

"He basically told me that he couldn't be distracted while he was pursuing his Masters. I was heartbroken. I never had someone just coldly cut me off. I used to wonder what I'd done wrong because it wasn't coming together for me. Long story short though, Sharin was left to help me pick up the pieces after he graduated. We partied hard and I pretty much learned from her to harden my heart against men. From that point forward, it was all business. No men."

Evander nodded. Christian took another sip of wine.

"When it was time to apply for graduate schools, it was a toss up. Sharin didn't make Yale. Monica didn't make Princeton. I made all three…so Harvard it was."

"Impressive. You never thought about going it alone?"

Christian shrugged. "We were a unit. Separating hadn't been in our plans. So, we go to Harvard…and we meet Sonya. Sonya was brilliant then and still now. We became fast friends when I defended her in a low-level law class against some incel who thought they were smarter. Jerrell noticed we'd become friends and decided he would date her. That's after he tried to get back with me several times.

"So, you told ole buddy to keep it moving? Good."

Christian smirked. "Thank you. So…he dated her to spite me but something about her must've worked for him. They've been together since. The only issue was…I hadn't clued her in. I didn't think it a huge detail to add in. I didn't have to see him that often. Sonya was a person who kept her affairs private and Jerrell wasn't shouting from the rooftops that they were dating. Years had gone by and they moved in together, even after we graduated. We'd been busy building up Adams', so it was all the same to me. Adams' was my focus so really, he was the last thing on my mind."

"So…how did she find out? It's obvious that you weren't the one to tell her."

"I wouldn't have. I didn't want to lose her as a friend or a Partner. Again, Sonya is brilliant. I'd be remiss if I didn't stress that part."

Evander was impressed about the stress that she put into uplifting her fellow Partner. Most leaders weren't good with stressing how important other people were to their success. It was easy for Evander to note that Christian valued those who were a part of her company. He respected it.

"Anyway, I called her phone on the night that the news broke. I wanted a sounding board because Sonya's a good listener and she's ambivalent to my emotionalism. However, Jerrell picks up the phone and tells me some pretty heinous shit. She heard it."

Evander winced and decided to reach for his own glass of wine. He took a sip, wondering at the kind of man Jerrell was.

"So, this woman would have been blissfully unaware if homeboy didn't pick up the phone just to whet his ego? That's what you're telling me?"

"Yes." Christian said. "I…can't fault her for her anger. She has the right to be upset. Still, she's talking to everyone but me about it and now she's sending me nasty text messages. It's too much on top of this scandal going on and it just makes me want to break."

"She should be taking him up to task, not you," Evander said, simply. "If she's known you for this long, it has to be obvious that you don't have eyes for the man anymore."

"You're so sure about that?" Christian raised a brow. "How so?"

"Well…you're with me. I woke you up at two in the morning with no notice and demanded for you to pack a bag. You answered me with no questions asked except if I were out of my mind. But we're here now in Miami and enjoying each other's company. If you wanted the man back after all this time, I highly doubt I would have a chance."

Christian blushed. "You're so sure of yourself, huh, Evander?"

"I'm very sure of myself," Evander said. "I'm very sure in the now. Right now, you're sitting right here with me. I don't much care about your past…I just wanna be in your present."

"My present?"

"Yes, love. In short, I'm asking for you to be my woman. I know this hasn't been too long of a courtship but…it doesn't take long for me to know when I've found a real winner."

"After everything I told you, you still find me to be a winner?"

"You're a perfect complement to me," Evander answered. "There's no person in this world that's perfect but I'm convinced you're perfect for me. I think we're fine complements to each other. I say we find out."

Christian smiled, despite herself and felt her cheeks warm as Evander lifted up her right hand, kissing it gently.

"Shall we?"

Christian bit her lip, looking into Evander's dark eyes and wondered that she was even in the position she was in. A quick flashback entered her mind, Jerrell's face momentarily hitting her psyche. She blinked, shaking the image away from her. Focusing in on Evander again, she sighed and nodded. It would have been a shame to leave the gentleman hanging, as he put his best foot forward in providing everything she wanted or needed. It'd be a waste to turn him down. Christian was determined to prove that she could take steps forward to her own happiness.

"We shall," She smiled. "We'll see if your hypothesis is correct."

His answering smile was wide. It made Christian smile as well, overcome by his happiness at her acceptance. She didn't remember that same excitement from Jerrell. The night and day difference was astounding. She remembered her former beau walking around as if he conquered Mount Everest but not being excited that she would give her approval of being his girlfriend.

"Let's get some champagne and celebrate."

"I'm already a little tipsy, love," Christian said. "Unless you have an aim for this evening."

"Oh, I don't need to get you drunk for that. Besides, I'm slightly ahead of schedule anyway. I didn't want to assume…"

Christian smiled. "I noticed."

"I'm not used to my lady turning down imbibements, so I have to say I'm slightly surprised. What would you like to do next?"

Christian looked at her boyfriend and grinned.

"I think I'd like to turn in for the night and figure out something fun to do after breakfast in the morning."

Evander nodded, standing up. Reaching out for her, Christian laid her hand in his. She smiled, standing up to meet him.

"Let's turn in, old lady."

Christian laughed. "It's been some time since I've gone to bed relaxed. I'd like to take advantage of that tonight."

Evander grinned, thinking she hung with him pretty well considering he wrecked her sleep that very morning. He'd woken at around one, suddenly craving a different pace and could think of nothing but just picking up and leaving. Christian was also in the middle of his thoughts when he made the arrangements to fly to Miami. So, he called until she answered and made the demand that she pack a weekend bag and fly out with him.

When he did pull up to her place of residence, he was surprised when she walked out looking put together, albeit slightly sleepy. Still, she pulled him down by his collar and laid a fat one on him. It left him aching for more.

All things considered, the trip turned out much better than he expected it to. He was surprised, considering how defensive Christian had been when they'd met. Still, it was beautiful that despite her misgivings, she was giving him a try. He didn't know what miracle transpired but he was thankful. The woman walking side by side with him was now his and in his mind, he'd do whatever he had to do to keep her.

Including letting her in on some harsh truths.

The thought alone almost caused him to sigh but he stopped himself short. It didn't make sense to worry about an impending moment. He could only hope that she was as gracious with him as he'd been with her. Of course, he couldn't blame her if she walked away from him after he told her his truths. He just hoped overall that everything worked out.

So far, so good.

Chapter
Thirteen

"I just want to know, is it in our best interest to keep donating money to this if you're having scandals every five minutes?"

Christian gritted her teeth, swallowing the vitriol she had sitting on her tongue. She took the moment to breathe in and out and remembered the tips that Jasmine gave her prior to the meeting.

"Do not clapback at these people. You were smiling when you took their money and you have to keep smiling and reassure them that they made the right choice, Christian. If I saw you looking crazy on television I'd ask your ass the same thing."

"Granted," Christian thought. *"Still, nobody told her to be extra."*

Adams' Accounting Firm had investors who assisted with the erection and continuing business of Adams. Christian was grateful for their patronage and knew that to have to facilitate a meeting with them would be rough. Still, she wasn't sure how she felt as far as being talked down to.

"I might come off as arrogant when I say this, but I don't see why not? This scandal-rather this slip-up-is the only one we've endured since Adams' has opened. The suspects have been taken into custody and all monies have been returned to Evander King. At the present time we are only one payment away from settling the score. As far as business-"

"-You cannot tell me it's business as usual when you're a walking pariah within Atlanta, Ms. Adams. You might have shied away from the news outlets and the blogs, but many are talking about pulling out and-"

"The only thing that talks is money, Mrs. Hall. I can assure you that. Unfortunately, Adams' was the answer to many journalists' prayers as I have become a news cycle. People say what they want all day, but the fact of the matter is, there is no better firm in the state of Georgia of this size and capacity. I will not act like this is a shallow matter nor do I take the situation lightly. Yes, my reputation has been tarnished but the main concern here *is* your monies."

Mrs. Hall moved to speak again but was settled by the hand of another woman present. Christian inwardly thanked Mrs. Persons for stepping in silently.

"Adams' is still making the necessary monies to sustain the business and we are still profiting overall. I will deliver payment to you as scheduled with no interruption. I do assure you that as the head of this company I personally take responsibility for the fracas that has occurred. Myself and my team are making the necessary adjustments to make sure nothing of this magnitude ever happens again."

Jasmine stood off to the corner, fighting to swallow the smile that threatened to break out. Each and every bit of the coaching she gave Christian was paying off and watching the group of investors eat out of her hand was magical.

"I hope so, Ms. Adams. It was my hope to continue to watch greatness unfold with you being a Black woman running a Black-owned establishment. I do promise, however, should this happen again-you looking crazy on public television like you don't know any better-I will pull my support of this place. You made us all look bad that day, whether you were guilty or not."

Mrs. Hall stood, gazing at Christian with eyes filled with venom. Christian swallowed the poison she wanted to fight back with and pretended that her rebuttal was sweet. In the back of her mind however, she was thinking of a way to replace Mrs. Hall.

"Your concerns are duly noted, Mrs. Hall," Christian answered. "If there aren't any other questions or concerns…"

The meeting came to a close as all ten investors exited, all but Mrs. Hall shaking her hand. Christian and Jasmine walked towards her office. They passed Christopher along the way, who was overseeing the safe passage and exit of the investors from the building. They nodded as they passed by each other and Christian stopped at the elevator. Jasmine allowed her smile to stretch as she tapped Christian's arm.

"I'm proud of you," she said. "That went well."

The elevator dinged and the twosome stepped in. Christian waited a beat before the elevator closed.

"I'm going to end our business relationship with Mrs. Hall, though."

"You should. I was surprised you hadn't checked her. I know I told you not to, but that parting shot was disgusting."

"Right. All of that grandstanding like people forgot that Mr. Hall got around and she was just standing around crying as well. The nerve. All money ain't good money and while I get that she'd be concerned about the return of investment, I don't have to keep taking that every quarter."

"Noted. Other things of note however…you are glowing, Red."

Christian smirked, Evander flashing in her mind. "I don't kiss and tell."

"You might as well. Everybody that knows you sees you walking a little different. Smiling and shit."

Christian giggled as the elevator doors opened again on her floor. They stepped out to see Monica at Tiffany's desk, laughing at whatever was being said in conversation.

Monica turned around and smiled wide.

"Well, well, well. I see you survived the Lion's Den."

Christian smirked. "I did…barely. What's up? Something going on?"

"Nah, it's lunch time," Monica said. "I wondered if you wanted to catch lunch outside."

Christian looked over at Jasmine, silently questioning if they were done for the day.

"Well…I was going to do a debrief of the meeting but overall, we're good.

We already spoke on actions that need to be taken. I'll be back tomorrow morning so if there's anything that needs to be addressed, we'll address it."

Christian nodded and smirked as Jasmine bid everyone but Tiffany a good day. Tiffany raised a brow, noticing that she was slighted.

"Good day to you, too, Ms. Brown."

Jasmine turned, regarding her with a nod as she pressed the elevator button. Tiffany turned to Christian with a raised brow.

"You're really going to let her treat me like that?" Tiffany questioned.

"Considering she's a huge part of the reason you still have a job, yes."

"She's out of line-"

"Tiff, let's not do this right now. If you're feeling slighted about how she addressed you, think about how you present when she and others come here to meet with me. I'm very lenient with you, knowing what I know, so let's play nice, okay?"

Tiffany was humbled into silence and Monica clapped her hands together, stepping into the awkward silence that was created by the conversation.

"So! I'll meet you downstairs?"

Christian turned her attention away from Tiffany to smile softly.

"Sure. Matter of fact, call an Uber to take us. No use in losing our spots outside for the hour."

Monica nodded and walked away. As she pressed the elevator button, Christian turned back to Tiffany, who's aura was full of attitude.

"My thing is, Ms. Adams, if my performance was lacking, I should have known by now."

"Your performance isn't awful. There are just some things that need to be addressed. I'm out to lunch though. I'm pretty sure I won't be back in so take off when you're ready. I'll see you tomorrow morning."

Tiffany nodded and watched Christian walk into her office. She wondered to herself just how deeply Jasmine's influence with Christian ran and if she would have to check the woman herself. One thing she wouldn't tolerate was disrespect. She felt like Jasmine was underhanded and controlling. In her mind, people with a level of power always abused it and hated when someone of lower status didn't kowtow to them.

In her mind, Tiffany wasn't the one or the two and Jasmine Brown would figure that out quick, fast, and in a hurry.

Tiffany rolled her eyes, thinking of the way Christian checked her in front of Monica. If she were able to have a full-on fight about the way she was being addressed, she would. Some people let power go straight to their heads and needed humble pie in her opinion. Some days she adored Christian but other days she wondered what possessed her to even work for her. Not when she was just as smart and just as capable of running a business. In her mind, the way that she ran out to eat every few days whether it be with Evander, Monica, Sharin, or whoever else fancied her, it was a wonder that work got done most days.

Then again, that was what being at the top of the food chain afforded a person.

Tiffany shook her head, texting Christopher about the whole debacle. He replied, saying that he'd take them out to dinner later on and not to let people worry her. She rolled her eyes at her generally positive boyfriend and slid her phone in her pocket.

She decided to leave for the day but a ding from her phone alerted her to Christopher's next text. It was a Cashapp notification for five hundred dollars and a note that told her to have an impromptu spa day and grab a dress for their date later on tonight. Further instructions gave her an idea of what kind of dress she should be looking to wear. It was uncharacteristic for her boyfriend, but she squealed, almost immediately getting over her misgivings about Christian and company in that instant. She had a wonderful partner and promised not to ever taken him for granted.

"You might have everybody else fooled Christian but it's obvious you need to come off the truth about you and Jerrell and do it quickly. Quickly?"

Christian shrugged, pulling her phone away from Monica's face as she started to giggle again. She moved some of her tresses out of her face and went to work slicing the steak that sat in front of her. As she worked, she giggled some more, thinking of the absurdity of the message.

"She wants you to do something quickly that she hasn't been willing to do for years but now you need to come up off of some truth…quickly? The audacity."

"I'm befuddled as to why she would wait until she knew I was away to send that. I thought she was more mature than that."

"Some women can't handle getting dick, girl. Even the smartest women become grade-A idiots over some good dick. My only issue is she pressed everybody but her man about the shit-"

"We don't know that, Em."

"We might not but it's a healthy guess."

Christian sighed, shoveling a healthy portion of garlic mashed potatoes in her mouth. She chewed thoughtfully, enjoying the flavors but Sonya at the forefront of her mind threatened to sour the experience. Swallowing, she sighed.

"I just wished she'd come to me first. All of this drama over Jerrell is exhausting. I didn't tell you he showed up at the office the other day right?"

Monica raised a brow. "Did he?"

"Yes. Girl, I had to tell Christopher that he's on the banned list after that. At the very least, he only gets an escort to Sonya's office and that's it. He pressed Tiffany to speak to me. So I gave him his marching orders."

"Letting him visit Sonya was still generous. I say change the orders back. He rarely, if ever, visited Sonya. I've seen Maddox up here more often."

Maddox Lennox rarely visited Adams' himself as he was busy trying to sell the state of Georgia to anyone who was interested in buying. Being that Jerrell was a lawyer, it was assumed that his job should've kept him busy. It appeared, however, that he had time to cause problems.

"He left me, Monica. I don't know what might've happened in the future had we stayed together but he left me. I'm no angel but I deserve better than how she's acting."

"You do."

"You damn right I do. I pay y'all better than Georgia says I should be paying you. Give you each a whole department. I give damn near every holiday off, including the ones that have nothing to do with us. We've been friends for a long time now and the way she's acting has me…disappointed."

"A lot of that shit is petty mind games," Monica said, shrugging. "I don't respect it at all. I suggest you don't give your time to it either."

"At some point…"

"When it's time to address her, do so. Otherwise, it's hearsay that has nothing to do with you. You're trying to get Adams' right. She's caught up in losing her man instead of respecting herself and again-that has nothing to do with you."

Christian reflected for a minute. She did contemplate pulling Sonya aside and getting the whole mishap dealt with and out of the way. Surely, she understood that Jerrell Washington was the least of her worries.

"Still, if she understood there wouldn't be any strife."

She sighed again, continuing to eat in silence. Monica chuckled a little bit, interrupting the deep dive Christian took into her thoughts.

"What's funny?"

"Thinking about Tiffany." Christian rolled her eyes. "She really doesn't like Jasmine."

"There's no real reason unless I missed something," Christian said. "Jasmine did mention to me that she doesn't present well when people visit the office. It wasn't something I was pressed about but it makes sense. She's the first person people see and essentially my eyes and ears. She can't be at her best if she's pissing away the time flirting with Christopher all day. I let it go for a while but I realize she's starting to feel like we're equals and the truth is, we're not. I try not to be a hardass but…"

"It's coming to that," Monica said. "I have no problem getting my people in line. It's like you said, you pay well. If you pay well there shouldn't be any issues. Especially if all she has to do is sit and be cute for eight hours a day."

"Yeah. I told her we'd talk. I also thought the way she spoke to Jasmine was out of line as well. I know I'm going to hear an earful from both sides."

"You will but as far as Tiffany, she's either going to tighten up or work elsewhere. You need to stop hiring your friends."

"How can you say that when you directly benefited from our friendship?"

"I'm the least of your worries, that's why. Plus, I know how to carry myself accordingly. Sharin does as well. Sonya was someone you should have avoided based off of her liaison with Jerrell. Now look at us."

"Us? I'm the only one suffering here."

"You and the rest of us. I had to hear her crying. Sharin had to hear her crying as well. She showed up to Sharin's bridal shower looking the epitome of death."

Christian giggled. "Point made. Still, I can't fire her now."

"You can, actually. Besides, it might be time for us to part ways with her. All she's done for the duration of this scandal was worry about whether you're still screwing him. What good has she been, Christian?"

"She's been good all these years. Versus my best friend who had two whole criminals working under her leadership."

"Really? That's what you're going with?"

Christian paused, taking in the expression on Monica's face. She sighed. "You're right, that was low to say. I'm sure if Sharin knew about it, it would've been nipped in the bud. Still, Sonya's been with us for a long time. I can't just let her go."

"Even if it meant to the detriment of the business?" Monica questioned. "I'm not suggesting you fire her now. Not even next week but it's something to consider. Her behavior is directly influenced by Jerrell being a narcissist and doing his best to keep every bit of attention on him. We already have enough on our hands without him trying to showboat as per usual."

Christian thought over her friend's words.

"Plus! Think of your mental health overall. Seeing this man walk up to the office had to be traumatizing to some extent."

Christian thought about the way she fell apart when Jerrell left that day. It was true that she didn't have any feelings of love left behind for him however, it was also true that he stirred up negative feelings in her all the same. She shook her head, dusting off Monica's wisdom like a gnat flying in her face in the summer heat. Monica shrugged.

"I think you'd do well to see a therapist, Christian."

"I don't do therapy."

"Why? You think you can pray away your anger and bitterness towards this man? Sis, you almost pushed away your best friend because she decided to stop being toxic and get married," Monica said, shrugging. "I mean…it's only a suggestion and you don't have to marry a therapist."

"I did not-"

"-Did too."

Christian felt her face turning red and Monica's smirk deepened. The former rolled her eyes and Monica shrugged.

"Look. Someone has to tell your crazy ass that you're crazy. But the thing about this life is sis, we're all crazy. Take a number and get in line. You dealt with heavy heartbreak and instead of addressing it in a healthy manner, you built a business. That business kept you warm until you realized that it's indeed fallible. Sometimes what worked in that past can't work anymore. It's obvious you and Mr. King are seeing each other…what happens when he tells you he has to go away on business? You're going to staple the man's shoes into the ground so he can't leave?"

Christian giggled. "I might. Ain't no leaving me."

"That's not healthy though," Monica giggled. "It's just a suggestion though. Something to consider. Ultimately, you're the boss."

Christian smirked. "As always, Nik, you're a worthy advisor and a loyal friend."

"I do my best," Monica said. "So go on a gush about this man. You've been looking happy lately."

Rolling her eyes, Christian grinned. "All of you are so nosey. I said I don't kiss and tell."

"You were gone an entire weekend and came back in on Monday looking like you've been worked out from head to toe. I demand details."

"First off, I have yet to be worked out. Second-"

"-Did you forget how to do it?" Monica said. "X-videos has pretty basic instructions if-"

"No, asshole, I didn't forget how. It just hasn't happened yet. He's a perfect gentleman, which I appreciate."

"*I'd appreciate it if he hurried up and turned your ass out. I need some days off*," Monica thought, picking up her wine glass.

"Okay, okay. So since y'all are waiting for marriage, tell me about the other stuff that I missed."

Christian laughed, pushing aside her reservations about Sonya finally and divulging in her happiness.

As she and Monica parted ways however, she thought of attending therapy as most of her points made sense. Jerrell breaking her heart wasn't enough of a reason for her to attend therapy sessions. She hadn't taken into account the long-term effects of that heartbreak. She also hadn't taken into account that her reaction to Sharin's engagement wasn't normal either. Her emotions had been so long ignored that they were all rising up with a vengeance within her and it wasn't boding for long-term healthy relationships.

She thought of Evander and how much she liked him already. It both excited her and frightened her. There'd been feelings she never thought of before and there were also feelings of doubt. As much as Evander treated her well, she was definitely waiting for the other shoe to drop. Her deeply embedded fear was that he'd up and leave her at some point as well.

Still, she would push forward. It was time for her to figure out healthy ways to advance further in her life and heal from the past.

Maybe therapy would be fruitful.

Chapter
Fourteen

Jamie walked through the prison, en route to the library. She tried as often as she could to frequent the space so she wouldn't lose her mind in her prison cell. The librarian who ran the space was very accommodating and speaking with her on a daily basis was a reprieve from the aching in her heart. She had yet to get a visit from her uncle and it was weighing on her. The look of disappointment had yet to leave her mind's eye ever since she was taken in. Jamie didn't even look at him when she was escorted in for her bail hearing. Her amount had been so high that she heard him curse in the courtroom.

Jamie reached the entrance of the library when she saw Jupiter standing there. She sucked her teeth, wondering if she should turn around and visit later. It appeared that she was looking for her. The last thing she wanted to do was have a conversation with Jupiter and looking at her face made her angry. She felt her body vibrate, the anger wanting an outlet. She felt her heart palpitate as Jupiter looked up and noticed her and she shook her head, walking in the opposite direction.

"Jamie…wait! Stop!"

Jamie's face furrowed and she turned around, taking Jupiter's face in. She swallowed, angry enough to punch her in the face but calmed herself down.

"There is nothing important that you have to say to me," Jamie said. "I was complicit in y'all bullshit and look where it got me. How can I move on with this on my fucking record now? I haven't been working for Adams' for a year yet!" Jupiter was stunned into silence. She opened and closed her mouth. Still, Jamie wasn't placated. "My uncle busted his ass to make sure I got into school. I busted my ass to get that job! You *knew* I wanted to move on from there, now I might not be able to work *anywhere* based on y'all bullshit. You let that rotten bitch get into your brain and I let you get into mine instead of airing all of y'all the fuck out. I pray you're not asking me for a favor. I wouldn't piss on you if you were on fire so leave me alone."

Jupiter sighed, running a hand down her face. Jamie looked at her, unmoved by her tiredness. Even the regret she read in her eyes didn't move her. She scoffed, turning to walk away from her when she heard her name again.

"I wanted to offer my apologies to you. It wasn't supposed to go this way." Jamie paused, turned, ready for another barrage when Jupiter held her hands up. "Just give me a few moments. I know I deserve every word you said but still, give me a few moments."

Jamie swallowed but she crossed her arms. Jupiter took that as her cue.

"I understand your anger, but you still have a better chance of getting out on bail and turning things around for yourself. You can still spin the story to say you were coerced-which you were. It doesn't have to end on a bad note for you. I'm the one who's lost out of all of this and I've accepted that. I just need your help to bring Chastity down for her involvement."

"Why should I be of any help to you at all?" Jamie questioned. "What do I gain?"

"For you to get back at Chastity for threatening your life."

Jamie went quiet. Her hands fell down at her sides, recounting silently the night Chastity visited the office.

Jamie had finished up work for the day. Excitement had been her middle name knowing that Samuel was picking her up. Dinner was the event taking place and while she didn't want to go through the motions of meeting his parents, she knew it was a necessary evil. To her chagrin however, when the limousine pulled up, it was Chastity that sat inside and not Samuel. Her reasoning for the switch-up had been that she wanted to get to know her better. While Jamie hadn't trusted her as far as she could throw her, she hadn't been prepared for the threats that poured from her lips.

"If you feel you have no fear in your heart for me, think again. I don't say this lightly but if you even breathe a word, I will make your life a living hell until you die. Either way you slice it, I will keep good on my word if you mess this up for me at all."

The rest of the ride had been quiet. When the twosome finally saw Samuel back at the estate, there hadn't been a smile on either woman's face. Jamie had toyed around with breaking up with Samuel right then and there but it would have been too obvious a move. Still…her threat loomed. Every move that she made suddenly felt like her last.

Jamie was almost grateful when the police came to take her in. That was until she'd seen her uncle's face, riddled with heartbreak. That was the part that hurt the most. That was why Jupiter's apology meant nothing to her.

"Yeah, she threatened me and my uncle. Threatened pretty much my whole life," Jamie whispered. "I'll never forgive her for that. I don't even understand her angle. That lady talked to me like she hated me for dating her brother."

Jupiter sighed. "It has nothing to do with you and her brother and everything to do with her and Sharin."

"What's Ms. Reynolds to her?" Jamie questioned. "I'm not understanding."

"Sharin is her cousin. We both had a common goal to make her look like the bad guy when this all fell down. Instead, the only person that lost…was me."

"Hm."

Jamie didn't have enough sympathy to dredge up for the young woman. She'd been an awesome accountant and she probably did deserve the role of Partner but the way she went about it from her memory was disgusting. It was on her mind that she felt all Sharin did was come to the office and look pretty. Sharin had, however, secured quite a bit of business for Adams' through her own connections and word of mouth. Most of the clientele came from Sharin and was the prime reason that she had quite a few meetings a week. Though they took the form of lunches or dinners, it was all business.

It was a point that Jupiter didn't understand. Instead of her building a relationship with Sharin, she often talked about her to other coworkers, defaming her from every side that she could. It was a small team so the reports unfortunately made it to Sharin on a regular basis. The only issue was that besides the bad mouthing, Sharin had no other issues with Jupiter. She was her best accountant and anyone that made her look good, she kept around.

"Still, I wanted to let you know, Chastity still seems hung up on whatever she told you. I had no clue she threatened you…it wasn't my intent to make you afraid for your life."

"I know that," Jamie said. "You weren't supposed to know that she talked to me. I'm guessing she left you high and dry after all the dirt you did for her, huh?" Jupiter was silent. Jamie took that as confirmation. "I don't want to lie and say I'm sorry this happened to you. You were a bitch. I hope that you learned your lesson though because I've definitely learned mine. I hope you have a nice life, Jupiter, but don't ever talk to me again."

Jamie finally turned away from her and walked away. Suddenly the need to read vanished.

Two days later, Christopher sat across from his niece, feeling his heart break into tiny pieces as he stared into her eyes through the plexiglass.

"Uncle," she sighed, tears falling at rapid speed. "I'm so sorry."

Christopher sighed, the tiredness falling over his shoulders like a thick blanket. The myriad of emotions threatened to overwhelm him, but he didn't want to put more guilt on his niece's shoulders. He knew when the ordeal happened that none of it was her fault. He understood her part but didn't hold it against her. Not when he understood what kind of person Jupiter was. He could imagine the older woman threatening her job and livelihood. He could imagine quite a few scenarios that led to the choices that she'd made. Still, the only thing he was disappointed in was,

"Why didn't you just come to me?"

Jamie sighed. "It's complicated. It honestly goes deeper than Jupiter, but I can't speak on it."

Her eyes kept watering as she looked into the eyes of her caretaker since her young days. The last person in the world she ever wanted to disappoint was her Uncle Christopher. He'd been there for her when her own parents turned their backs on her.

She came from a drug dependent mother and an absent father. The rest of her father's family passed on taking her in so when she was still in foster care, praying for someone to rescue her, Christopher did. He'd raised her as his own, long after her own mother died. It was her dream to shoot for the stars and make him proud for his sacrifice. He'd given up much of his bachelorhood to see that she had a roof over her head and food in her belly. Then he'd given up even more time to ensure she did well in school and made it into college. She'd graduated with honors and was ripe for the workforce.

So, it was a no brainer for Sharin to bring her on although Christopher begged her. Sharin later on told her she would have hired her in the long run anyway.

The thought of her former boss made her sigh out loud, hating that she betrayed a woman that she admired greatly. Jupiter hated her place of privilege. Jamie loved her in spite of it. Not many people saw fit to shun a life of ease and join the middle class and still, Sharin Reynolds did all the time. She worked at a high level and demanded excellence of her team. Jamie hated that she was a part of any scheme that undermined Sharin as she'd been nothing but gracious to her.

"We'll talk when you get out."

"Uncle, my bail is-"

"Being collected. You won't be in here much longer. It's my promise to get you out of here. I know you fucked up and I don't want to lie to you, I am disappointed. Still, I know this wasn't on you. I just wished you came to me first. I can't imagine why you didn't think that was an option."

Jamie fell silent again, swallowing. She had to push away images of her uncle lying in a hospital bed. She had to push away the thoughts of Chastity's warnings.

"I'll explain when I'm out."

"Alright. How are you holding up?"

"I'm fine. I keep low and stay out of trouble. Jupiter walked up to me a couple of days ago, apologizing."

Christopher sucked his teeth. "Don't bring her name up, please. I hope they bury her ass under the jail."

"They might. Or might not," Jamie giggled. "I told her where to go with her apology."

"Good. Do your best not to talk to her anymore."

"I just need your help to bring Chastity down for her involvement."

Jamie agonized that she couldn't say anything to her uncle about Chastity's involvement but her plea to testify against Chastity loomed in her mind. Although she didn't feel as if she should testify for Jupiter's sake, Jamie felt as if she definitely needed to testify for her own. It was obvious that Chastity was the cancerous one in the situation. There had to come a time when she faced the consequences of her actions. Just like Jupiter had and just like she had.

"I don't plan on it," Jamie answered. "How's the outside?"

"If you mean Adams'? They're doing okay. I'm good. Tiffany's good. I plan to propose to her soon."

Jamie rolled her eyes exaggeratedly, making Christopher laugh. She didn't like Tiffany as far as she could throw her, but she loved her uncle and knew that he deserved his happiness. In her mind, Tiffany was a dramatic, spoiled personality but she matched her uncle's laid-back persona well. If she didn't have to live with the woman another day, it would be too soon. Still, she made her uncle happy, so she didn't have much to say about it.

"I know you don't care for her-"

"I love you, Unc. Congratulations. I'm sure she'll be excited."

"You think so? I'm nervous," Christopher chuckled. "I meant to propose days ago but couldn't bring up the nerve. But it's going to happen soon."

"You'll do fine."

The guard walked up to Jamie, announcing that her time was up. The light heartedness that was between them dropped a few points as the reality was that they were to be separated again.

"Don't worry, baby. I'm going to get you out of here."

"Okay, Uncle. I love you."

Christopher replied the same as the guard nodded to him. Jamie stood up quietly and then followed the guard out but not before turning around to smile at him one last time. He sighed, turning around to leave the premises.

Christian had been in a contented spirit the past few days. She wondered that as busy as the days had been, she didn't fall out from exhaustion but so far everything was returning to normal. Slowly but surely, the news cycle featuring Adams' Accounting was being put to bed. Timid clients were walking through the doors in confidence again, having taken rest in the fact that the company only suffered a slight setback instead of a total wipeout. She had Jasmine largely to thank for the campaign that she put together, as well as her coaching through the storm. She was also grateful for keeping a vigilant eye out for the things in her company that could be improved upon for the near future.

Tiffany had been one of those things and thankfully, when she stepped out of the elevator and walked towards her office, Tiffany was in full on work mode. They'd had quite a bit of an argument when they finally sat down but when Christian pointed out to her how unprofessional she came across, the message was received. Christian was grateful because she was fully prepared to fire Tiffany if worse came to worse. There were way too many people out there that wanted a job and hers paid handsomely. She treated people too well to keep taking flack.

"Good morning, Ms. Adams," Tiffany greeted. "You don't have anything pressing on the schedule today, but Sonya did call up a few moments ago asking if you had a moment to spare."

Christian greeted her secretary and fought against rolling her eyes at the mention of Sonya. Instead, she smiled at Tiffany and instructed her to page Sonya to her office in thirty minutes. Tiffany nodded, getting to sending the message while she walked through the door of her office.

She settled in behind her desk, after sitting her pocketbook in her closet. Booting up her computer, she wondered if she'd stay at work the entire day. Tiffany reminded her that there wasn't anything pressing to do, and she didn't see the point of being in the office all day, just twiddling her thumbs. She briefly thought about Sharin and knew that it was high time they talked about reinstating her back into work.

She grabbed her phone to make the call when a text came in from Evander. Seeing his name come across her screen as *Boyfriend* made her smile.

Let me take you out tonight.

Christian's smile spread when she replied to his message, excitement flowing through her veins. Weeks ago, she might've berated herself for her display, but she was alone. Secondly, she loved the attention that Evander gave her. It'd been a few weeks since their trip, but he went out of his way to show her that he was in her corner and it was all she could do not to fall flat on her face.

Their conversation continued, Christian not having done any semblance of work for the day but getting lost in her boyfriend. When he suggested they meet up for lunch, she sighed, looking at the time. Sonya would be walking through the door in about ten minutes' time and who knew whether she'd feel like eating after speaking to her.

I have to pass for today. Maybe tomorrow?

They'd wrapped their conversation up when Christian mentioned her impending meeting. Evander had sent her a kissy-face emoji and she smiled just when her office phone rang.

"Adams'."

"Sonya is here to see you now."

Christian inwardly groaned. "Send her in."

Sonya walked in, her stride purposeful. Christian wasn't sure whether to greet her or not but decided to lean into her manners to start the conversation off.

"Good morning, Sonya. How are you today?"

Sonya took a seat and pinned her with a gaze that put Christian's back up. The animosity could no longer be hid and it took everything for Christian not to become totally defensive.

"I've been better, Christian," she breathed. "I'm going to cut to the chase."

"Are you now?"

Christian paused to take a sip of her water, gathering her reserves of patience. As far as she was concerned, Sonya was lucky she didn't hop over the table to beat her face in. She was also surprised at the amount of anger that she had toward her friend. Still, she was well aware that she was just as upset over the situation as a whole as she was with the way Sonya was handling it. The moment made her loathe Jerrell more and more because all he had to do was treat her as a person he never met and move on with his life. Christian also took responsibility for her part in the whole fracas. If she had mentioned that she and Jerrell had dated awhile back, none of this would've happened.

Now she had to deal with a personal issue during her work time and all signs pointed to it being an unhappy ending.

"I am. I've sat and thought of it time and again and I have to say, I'm not sorry for how I feel about this situation. It was wrong of you not to have said something in all the years you've known me."

Christian sighed. "I agree. I should have said something but it just…never seemed like the right time. And honestly Sonya, y'all were good from my standpoint. Y'all might've gone ahead and gotten married without you ever knowing."

"Christian, how the hell is that okay? Let's call a spade a spade. If I'd dated this so-called man you're talking to now, how would it make you feel not to have known about it? And you had every chance to tell me. Especially in the beginning."

"You're right," Christian answered. "You're absolutely right. You still went about it wrong."

"What are you talking about? The fact that I questioned everybody? Everybody was complicit with you, Christian! It goes back to the fact that I've been loyal to you for years! What made you think it was okay for you to have dated my man and not say anything?"

It was the '*my man*' for her. In Christian's mind, Jerrell belonged to the streets. He honestly belonged to nobody but himself and it was sickening the amount of loyalty Sonya held for him. Still, as far as Christian was concerned that was her business. What she'd wanted to get across to her friend that her omission was wrong, but she had nothing to worry about. Still, it was stressing her out that the moral of the story wasn't connecting.

"Sonya, Jerrell and I have been over for years. I don't understand why there's so much emotion in this when I don't even have his phone number. I can count on my fingers the times I've seen Jerrell since we've broken up. You and I becoming friends just happened."

"So, you never followed Jerrell to Harvard? For no reason?"

Christian smirked. "I'm sure it was pointed out that if I wanted him back you wouldn't be with him, right? If I truly wanted Jerrell, Sonya, I would've had him. But I had him and he threw me away like I was a piece of trash. He tormented my very best friend and during that time, I all but spat in her face because I loved him. What makes you think I could ever take him back?"

"The fact that you never said shit about it!" Sonya snapped. "Nothing. But I hear my boyfriend pick up the phone to tell you that you've had your chance."

"It sounds to me that you've had the conversation with everyone but who you should've had it with. Why have you yet to speak with your boyfriend on why he picked up a call I made to *you*?! I could see if I was calling his direct line. I could see if I'd been dealing with him for years, but I can't remember exactly the last time I had sex!"

"First of all, the conversation *was* had. Unlike you, I do address my shit. Secondly, what's going on with Mr. Man, now? In your shoes I would've shown him a thing or two by now..."

"Well, sweetheart, you're *not* in my shoes. If you were you'd be deciding when you wanted to show him something instead of wondering why your actual boyfriend isn't worth the fucking ground you walk on."

The conversation was making Christian's stomach turn. The cattiness had shown up, letting her know that it was all a loss. Sonya didn't want to reach a resolution in the conversation but rather wanted to argue for the sake of it. For some reason, Christian felt like she wasn't her true target, but she was just the one who would do. The thought saddened her and angered her all in the same fell swoop. She wanted to get down to the bottom of the situation and hopefully move forward with life. Considering nobody lost anybody in the process, why should there be unnecessary strife?

"You know what Christian? I hope you do end up alone and lonely and that this business goes down. I'm not staying here to watch it go down."

"Is that your way of saying you quit?" Christian said, raising a brow. "You'd really throw away years of friendship and this job over Jerrell?"

"I would. I'd throw it all away and start over. I don't need you. I don't need him."

"This isn't about needing him," Christian said. "This is your fucking job you'd throw away just to prove to me that you're woman and to hear you roar. Over a man you're still fucking! You're still fucking him, Sonya! You talk about me but at least I'm not scared to be alone! That'll *never* be me! I'd rather be alone than to be unhappy!"

"You got me fucked up," Sonya shot back. "I'm not afraid to be alone. But I do know you're not playing me for a fool any longer. I want my unemployment. And, because I've been too damn good of an employee for too many years for your sneaky ass, I demand references to any and every company I apply to."

"Or you'll do what, Sonya? Sue me?" Christian questioned. "You know you can't claim unemployment if you quit."

She couldn't believe she would deign to collect unemployment when her salary was well above what the government would cover until she found a new job. It was all so petty and she didn't understand the motivation. There was no reason under the sun that she could find that made sense for the scene that was unfurling before her.

"Who's going to believe you? You're a *liar*, Christian Adams. That's all you'll ever be. This shit is happening because you lied to someone. Now somebody in your own damn company is lying to you. And the rest of these broads don't want to stand up and tell you the truth, but I will because you don't put fear in my heart. Their lives will go to shit just like yours because they stood behind you and your lies."

"You know what, Sonya? Because you want it so bad, you're fired. Effective immediately. Do not however expect me to speak well to any employer who calls my office. Considering I'm a liar, why would I have anything good to say about you?"

Christian's face had turned red and the sight pleased Sonya greatly. Confident that her job was done, she stood up with a smile as wide as the Grand Canyon on her face.

Christian felt her body trembling, seeing that she was played by a person whose friendship she hadn't wanted to lose. It was in that moment, Christian understood Monica's words perfectly. Being that they made every sense in the world, suddenly, peace overcame her being.

As Sonya walked out of the office without another word, Christian called Tiffany into her office. Tiffany settled in, her facial features coated with concern and Christian waved her off.

"Sonya Powers is fired from Adams', effective immediately. I'm going to put together a severance package that I want you to type up and interoffice mail to HR. I want you to caucus with her former assistant and direct them to cancel any and all meetings that she had on her docket for the month. We have to put together an announcement on the website that reflects the same. You getting this down?"

Tiffany shook her head in the negative but disappeared momentarily to grab a notepad. Everything that Christian had mentioned to her she wrote down and looked up, waiting for her to continue. Christian powered forward.

She'd been working on autopilot as she directed the next few steps for Tiffany to complete. Tiffany felt the sadness come off of her boss in waves but knew better than to poke the bear at the present moment.

"Before you start, do me a favor and page Monica to meet with me in the office. Also note that this information is confidential so if it goes beyond you and Christopher, consider yourself out of a job as well."

Tiffany blinked, unsure of how she felt about the demand but decided to let the threat roll off of her back like water. She nodded, stuck between wanting to defend herself and getting the tasks done that were asked of her.

"The same goes for Sonya's former assistant. Rumors may start to spread. You both are to answer that everything is on a need-to-know basis. I'm only negating Christopher because he's the head of the security team and your romantic partner and I'm not foolish enough to think that piece of information wouldn't be shared. Still, move with discretion. I'm not in the brain space to tolerate any nonsense today. Are we clear?"

"Yes, Ms. Adams."

It was becoming increasingly hard to work for Christian in her mind's eye and she figured perhaps it was time to move on herself. Being berated because of Sonya's defection didn't sit well. Granted, Tiffany knew she had her ways, but she'd always been a good employee to Christian.

"You're dismissed."

Tiffany quietly sighed, walking away out of the office. She settled at her desk, calling first Monica to report to Christian's office and then taking the elevator downstairs to Sonya's floor and hailing her assistant, Addison. Tiffany's heart broke at the confused look on Addison's face. She was currently helping Sonya pack her boxes to vacate the office. The confused look on her face was speaking volumes for her.

"Ms. Adams is instructing you to cancel all of Ms. Powers' meetings."

Addison's face furrowed, "Girl, what is going on?"

"I'll be back to speak with you. I can't really dig in because of privacy reasons. I might have told you now but damn near everybody on the floor is tuned in. Meet me at my desk in about an hour. I have to get started on my tasks for the day."

Addison nodded her head and then returned to the office to help her former boss pack her things. Sonya hadn't been forthcoming either, but she could only assume that she'd been fired. If it was true, it was a sad sight to witness. She wasn't impervious to the way the air had changed with her the past few weeks since the scandal broke.

Addison remembered a gentleman that had passed by the office, that she could only presume was Sonya's boyfriend, but hadn't stopped at Sonya's office. He'd only checked to see if she was available. When she informed him that she wasn't available at the time, he took the elevator upstairs to what was Christian's office. It was a weird sight but nothing she thought was out of the ordinary.

So, when she reported the visitation to her boss, she hadn't expected the emotional response. She watched Sonya's chest heave up and down and the elder woman disappear into her office. She hadn't seen her for the rest of the day. That occurrence had been about two weeks ago.

Whatever had been brewing under the surface probably reached a full-on boil. She was saddened that the woman she'd worked under for a few years was making an exit.

"Addison." Addison turned around to acknowledge Sonya for the very last time. "It was good working with you. Strive to be your best but let nobody-and I mean *nobody*-make you out to be a fool. If you need references, call me."

Addison watched sadly as she walked out of the door.

Hours later saw Tiffany having dinner with Christopher, the latter watching her pout over Christian's swinging moods again. He was saddened, mostly because he respected Christian as his boss. Christian had given him a job way before he had the experience to even run a team, but he also knew he had a part in his girlfriend's laid-back attitude about her job. He didn't have plans to approach Christian about it, mostly because it was her show. She gave him the gift of his own team and the finances to run his department. He was grateful for his girlfriend for plugging him in as the last security team wasn't working up to a standard that made the all-women team feel safe. His presence there gave everyone a sense of comfort in knowing the establishment as well as their lives were taken seriously.

With that much in mind, while he understood her woes, he wasn't too interested in causing a huge issue with the CEO over it. He knew his girlfriend and he understood that Christian had given her a long leash until recently.

"I need to be the boss of my own stuff. I'm not about to sit here being told what to do and what not to do all day while she gets to frolic around and…just be the boss."

"That's what bosses do, baby," he mentioned. "I get that she's being a pain, but I don't know if you're reading the room properly."

Tiffany raised a brow, unsure she liked his tone of voice.

"What are you saying, Christopher?"

"I'm saying bae, you have to understand she's under fire right now. She and homeboy might be cool *now* but there was still a whole bunch of people who made this place a news cycle. You have to look at the fact that the place is run by a group of minorities-double minorities-in fact. She chose you to help her with everyday shit and how can she be so sure that every day shit is being handled if people are showing up and all they see is you blabbing on the phone with me?"

Tiffany was silent. "So, you suddenly on the boat with *her*? Make it make sense, Chris."

"You know I'm not. Don't do that, baby," Christopher said. "All *I'm* saying is, for some time she gave you free reign to do you. It was cool during that time. You don't know who's coming into the office to meet with her. You're their first point of contact. Sometimes their last. Until they walk into the office and deal with her, you represent *her*. She chose you out of a lot of other people to handle her lightwork. I'm sure she's not saying you can't fuck with a nigga while you're at work, but everything is time and place, love.

"Then as far as me, people see me when they have to. I'm able to walk around and be on the phone. How does someone know I'm talking to you on a regular? She's not going to exactly press me about it. She might tell me that my phone calls to you have to slow down but other than that, people don't see me first unless I make myself seen. I have a lot of down time, but I also have men posted on every floor that report to me. I don't have to truly jump until I have to."

Tiffany was quiet, unsure of how she felt about the conversation, but she could understand the logic. Still, she wasn't sure that she could keep dealing with Christian sniping at her when the day wasn't going well. She wasn't sure that she could take blatant disrespect from visitors who thought they didn't have to greet her or wish her a nice day as they left. It was all in the air for her and she wasn't sure how things would go if they kept going in the direction they did.

"All of that to the side...what do you think of me retiring you?"

Tiffany looked up from her plate at the question, with her brow raised again. "Retire me?"

"Yeah. We get a house together and you just stay home and take care of it... and me when I get home," he said, cautiously.

"Like...a kept woman?" Tiffany questioned. "Where is this thought process coming from?"

"It's coming from me being tired of you being my girlfriend."

Forgetting every earlier question that was asked, Tiffany's eyes widened and she felt her face furrowed. She lifted up the hand with the fork, waving it as she talked.

"So, what the hell are you talking about all of this future stuff for if you're trying to break up with me, Christopher?! What was all that time and energy for?!"

Christopher bit his lip to keep from laughing as he remembered their first meeting. It'd been a few years ago at a popular club in Atlanta.

Tiffany and Sharin were together one night and he'd seen them from afar but hadn't thought much about either woman wanting to get to know him. Still, it was a pleasant surprise when he saw them both trying to approach him.

He remembered Sharin faltering a tad and Tiffany making her way to him with all the confidence of a Queen. To this day, the memory made him chuckle, but it was one thing he admired and loved about Tiffany even in the moment. She was willing to fight for their love, even when times weren't the best. It was that quality about her that made him feel like he was never alone in their relationship. In times past, he'd attracted plenty of women with devil-may-care attitudes. While he loved them passionately, they acted as if his efforts were minute in nature. So when he finally left, they suddenly cared and it was all too late.

"Are you really grinning when you're sitting here breaking up with me?!" Tiffany asked. "Why bring me to a restaurant if…"

She was going on and on and while he knew he should be embarrassed, still, his laughter was escaping him, and he couldn't stop. The other thing he loved about Tiffany was that she was never boring.

That was another quality he knew he needed in the woman he wanted to marry. His whole life was an adventure and being bored wasn't a part of his plans. Her voice started to pitch and that was when he decided to take them both out of their misery. He reached into his pocket for the black box that was burning a hole in it for two weeks. He'd tried to propose to her before, but it hadn't seemed right in the mix of all the drama that was happening as of late.

Christopher walked over to Tiffany and sunk down on bended knee. When the scene became clear to her, both of her hands flew up to her mouth. The tears that had threatened to fall in sadness suddenly fell in surprise and delight. They fell even more when Christopher opened the box to present a three stone, princess cut diamond ring set on a white-gold band. There was an accent of baguettes on each side however Tiffany would miss every other detail because of the way she started crying.

Though Christopher had slowed down laughing, his insides were suddenly filled with butterflies. He knew he had to make his move and fast before Tiffany's mind went into a whole other direction. With her imagination and penchant for drama, she was definitely good for it.

"I'm tired of you being my girlfriend, Tiffany, because I'm ready for you to be my wife. That being said, will you marry me?"

A garbled yes was his answer and she found herself laughing, crying, and smiling even as Christopher slid the ring on the appropriate finger. A huge applause could be heard from all the surrounding patrons who had tuned in, mostly thinking that they had a drama on their hands because of the way Tiffany had started going off. The surprise engagement at the end was the plot twist they didn't think they would get.

"I got your ass good, didn't it?" he said, leaning up to kiss her lips. "Getting ready to barbecue your boy in the middle of the restaurant."

"Stop it," she snapped, hitting him on the arm, "You know your opening line was trash!"

"I know but you know I love to see you act up from time to time," he chuckled, raising to his feet. "So future wife, what would you like to do after this?"

"You're going to take me home so I can brag to everybody about my future husband! Please tell me you went to Jared's."

Christopher chuckled. "Actually, I did. Why?"

"That's my new punchline whether you did or not but knowing you did is even sweeter. That commercial cracks me up."

Christopher laughed and continued to finish his meal. Now that he was calming down after the wild joyride that was his fiancée, he could eat in a better mind state.

"You might want to hold off on that. I have a photographer ready to take our pictures when we leave."

"You really hired a photographer?"

Christopher pointed at a gentleman that was sitting at another table, adjacent to the one they were at. Tiffany spied the man with his camera and laughed helplessly, waving at him. He'd been recording the whole thing and having a time himself with not laughing out loud either.

Tiffany eyed Christopher and shook her head, still blown away at the way he'd put together every detail of the night. She could only look at him as he'd laughed with her. He wasn't quite sure what he would do without her humor, nor was she sure what she would do without his mischievousness.

"I love you."

Tiffany smiled at him as well. "I love you, too. Hurry up so we can finish. I gotta call my mama."

While Tiffany and Christopher celebrated across town, Evander and Christian's date had just wrapped up. Christian was laughing at an especially crass joke that her boyfriend delivered and it made her so weak she didn't have the presence of mind to correct him.

Still, with his arm around her waist as they walked side by side, she had to admit that she was getting used to his company and didn't have the same qualms that she had in the beginning of their courtship.

Sonya's defection still riddled her mind however and the foul space it put her in almost made her cancel her evening out with Evander. Though she knew her words were meant to poison her, Christian had to admit that in a way she did believe the parting shot that Sonya gifted her with.

Her position in not telling her anything made her a liar and it was possible that she had deserved the karmic energy being served to her. Still, she wasn't letting Adams' go down without a fight. Adams' Accounting wasn't just her business but she carried a whole community of men and women on her back. It was her job to make certain they stayed employed as no part of the scandal was her fault.

Still, she wondered why she'd let Sonya's words affect her as much as she had?

"You're thinking way too hard, baby."

Christian blinked, looking up at Evander, all but forgetting they were at her front door. She'd checked out of the conversation when Sonya filtered through her mind again. Though she'd told Evander what had happened she didn't want to spoil their night by bringing her up once more. It was more than she could handle. Her defection hurt her more than she realized and the truth was, Christian wasn't sure who to blame in the fracas.

"I know, I apologize, baby," Christian said, leaning up to kiss him on the lips. "But what's up? You're waiting on an invitation?"

Evander smirked, drawing her in for another kiss. She was surprised still when his lips connected to hers, how she could feel the electricity shoot from her head to her toes. She wiggled them in her heels, wondering where the man holding her had been hiding the whole time.

He pulled away, with a questioning gaze in his face. Christian rose a brow to silently ask what was on his mind when he chuckled.

"I thought that's what a gentleman was supposed to do. I wasn't going to very well just march in behind you, love."

Christian licked her lips, despite herself. She reached up, grabbing his tie and gently brought him back down to her face, taking another kiss from him. This time it was suggestive, as she pressed herself against him, winding her left arm around his neck. A groan was heard from Evander as he answered her signal, reaching down to grab a handful of her backside. He squeezed, testing the waters and letting her understand that the waters she was treading were dangerous.

"You've been a gentleman for too long, baby," Christian whispered. "I want you tonight, if you can't tell. I know you want me…"

Evander felt himself start to harden. He swallowed another groan at the look on her face. Another groan slipped out as she leaned up to kiss him softly again, coaxing him.

"You sure, baby? I want you more than you know," he confessed. "So be sure before you let me in."

Christian smirked as she stepped away and opened the door. Following her in, Evander closed the door behind them and took in her living space. He decided that every piece of it was her style.

Christian lived in a two-floor penthouse. He noticed the balcony straight away and could easily see her enjoying the view of the city line while she sipped on her choice of wine. The living area was modern but comfortable. The colors painted in the space were neutral and muted and he wondered if she'd chosen them to calm her down after the most erratic days that she must've had.

Her kitchen was functional and to the point and it made him laugh at how opposite it was to the living room. He pictured that Christian did cook but she wasn't so caught up in the beauty of her kitchen that she didn't enjoy cooking her food. The tall windows that lined every inch of the bottom level was still in line with the woman-in-charge personality that was all her. Evander took in every comparison and contrast in her home as he took a seat at her kitchen bar and thought of the fact that many of those nights she came home alone to it.

Even if she never said it, he knew that he was the first man Christian ever bought into her home, ever. It moved him in its way, knowing that a woman like his woman didn't just bow to any man. It also made him feel worthy to be in her presence and hoped that in return she felt the same way about him.

He thought of the days when he walked back inside of his own house with only his reports and dinner waiting for him courtesy of his housekeeper and chef. Perhaps a football game or a basketball game would have his attention if nothing else for the rest of the night. The thought of having Christian waiting for him in the future warmed him inside. So much so that he'd been daydreaming of the possibility. So deep into the fantasy was he that Evander almost jumped when he heard his name enter his consciousness.

"Hey," Christian said. "Are you there?"

Evander grinned, embarrassment overtaking him as he took Christian in again. She stood in front of him looking slightly concerned.

"Yeah, I'm home," he said, chuckling, "What happened?"

Christian giggled and offered him something to drink again. She found herself enjoying the role of playing hostess to her boyfriend since it was something she hadn't done before. Testing the waters felt more natural to her than she thought it would.

"I'm more interested in taking you out of this dress," he answered, his eyes roving from the top of her to the bottom. "It's cute that you're trying to play hostess though."

"Well…I never played before, babe."

Christian blushed with a helpless shrug. Evander melted, the confirmation of his earlier thoughts endearing her even more to him.

Evander closed the space between them, lifting her off her feet and placing her on the kitchen bar. Walking in between her legs, he claimed her lips again and shuddered as he felt her hands clasp around his neck.

"I'm honored, baby. Still, you're stalling. You were so ready to get me in here and now I'm ready."

Christian found herself giggling as he took her lips again and suddenly, time became nothing as they took theirs. Kisses were exchanged and it reminded Evander that he absolutely loved kissing Christian. If he never went farther than to kiss her on most days, his day was made. There was nothing like a powerful woman yielding to him. The absolute trust that it took for her to do that undid him each and every time. The time was short, but it amazed him how much headway they made, from being the opposition to each other due to an error, to lovers due to fate.

Evander loved her strength and her softness. The very dichotomy of her being was a constant attraction to him and he would have her no other way. He was surprised that another man would think to throw away the very diamond that sat in his arms. He pulled away to look upon her face and like a thunder crack, flashing brightly in his realization, his heart almost stopped.

He loved her. The acceptance was easy and it was teeming to be shared as he picked her up off of the counter to show her as much.

"Let me down!" Christian squealed.

Evander obeyed her wishes against his will but grinned as she took his hand in hers, leading him to the upstairs portion of her house.

The hallway was filled with pictures of herself and friends and he admired the smiles. It was evident that she adored her friends as much as she respected them as equals. He thought briefly of the woman that decided to throw away the gift that was Christian Adams and almost scoffed. Some people didn't know their blessings when they had them. He knew in time the young lady might be back to beg for both her job and the friendship back.

He hoped that Christian denied her both.

They entered her bedroom and he was surprised at how neutral the theme stayed; still, frills and satin reigned in each space. He grinned at the queen-sized bed that stood in the middle of the room and wondered just how much more comfortable she'd be in his king-sized. Still, he filed the thought away for a later moment.

Every earlier thought was washed away at the five by seven photo of them both, taken in Miami during their trip there. It made him smile and glance over at her as she realized what he'd been gazing at.

"I didn't even think you'd keep that, let alone next to your bed," Evander mentioned. "You never cease to amaze me."

"Amaze you? It's not obvious that I'm into you?" Christian blushed. "I had a great time. I liked this picture of us and thought it was nice. I hope we're together long enough to make a photo album of pictures."

The blush rose to her cheeks made Evander lean in to kiss her lips softly at her admission. He was hoping for the same thing himself.

Christian deepened the kiss, while reaching up to push his suit jacket off of him. Her fingers then began undoing each button one at a time while they were still lip locked. The clumsy way she went at it made him smile inside. Her lack of practice endeared him. It also turned him on to know she wanted him as much as he wanted her.

Evander pulled back to turn his woman around, zipping down her dress from the back. The black fabric that had been a barrier between him and her was now a pool at her feet that she stepped out of. Evander licked his lips as Christian turned around to give him a frontwards view of her lingerie. The balconette bra she wore cupped her breasts the way he intended to do and better. He fingered her over and reached back to undo the bra, watching it fall and then looking back up at her breasts. A grin spread at how full and perky they were.

Christian wondered if her whole body was turning red from both exhilaration and embarrassment mixed together. It'd been so long since she'd gotten naked-truly naked-in front of a man that the feeling was foreign to her. Her body shuddered as she felt Evander's large hands cup her breasts and fondle her nipples. She started to moan lightly as he did, loving the sensation that traveled from her breasts to her gut. It was more delicious than she remembered.

Evander leaned in, taking her right breast into his mouth, while still giving attention to the other one. Christian concentrated on not making too much noise although the feeling was starting to get to her. She almost groaned in annoyance when her boyfriend pulled away. She watched him as he got rid of the rest of his clothes and she felt herself shiver in anticipation. She'd seen him mostly in the nude before while they were on the beach, save for the swimming trunks he'd had on. Still she hadn't been prepared when he removed his boxers and the size of his girth was revealed. It took her mind off of her own nakedness and she started to get worried. She hoped she had a condom that could fit him.

"You good, baby?" Evander questioned. "You're not about to run away, are you?"

Christian giggled. "No. I was just hoping I had adequate protection for you."

"Don't trip. I got something."

Christian watched as he furnished a magnum out of his pants pocket and grinned. He sat it on her nightstand and crawled on her bed, lying on his back. He beckoned her to join him and she hesitated and looked from him to the condom.

"I'm not going anywhere near that thing without you wrapping it up. That's non-negotiable." Christian pressed, her voice wavering. She hoped that he went with her wishes, however. She wanted him badly but still wanted to be responsible about her lust.

"Baby, we're not at that part yet. Come here before I change my mind," he said, sitting up and pulling her towards his person. He removed her panties and then guided her up his body until her middle stopped at his face.

When she realized what her man was up to, she gasped at the plan he had in mind. It made her smile as if she won the lottery and then moan raggedly once his tongue started to massage her clitoris. Before she knew it, she was whimpering and gasping whenever Evander hit her spot just right. She reveled in the way he drank from her as if he were dying of thirst. She found herself saying his name over and over as waves of pleasure crashed down on her.

"Baby...I can't..."

Her duress earned her a chuckle from Evander, who lightly slapped her on the backside. He wanted to go for the gold again but decided to table that action for the next time.

"You want to lie down now?"

Christian answered in the positive and another chuckle escaped him. He allowed her to lie backwards, and he rolled on top of her, kissing downwards until he reached her middle again, taking it in. Evander groaned as he spread her open to his face once more and kissed her middle. Licking his lips, he put her legs on his shoulders and started up his ministrations again. He kept his attention on her most sensitive sections, enjoying her soft mewls and the cries that she tried to swallow from. It took a few minutes, but he was pleased to see her grabbing the seats.

"That's right baby, let it go for me again."

He slid a finger inside of her channel and smirked at the groan that bounced back almost immediately. Encouraged by her reaction, he added a second one and began to finger her while he licked her.

It hadn't taken long for Christian to come again. While she worked on coming back to earth, Evander grabbed the condom he had and wrapped up. Christian was smiling from ear to ear as he had. Her glee made Evander laugh momentarily, causing Christian to stop.

"Stop laughing and hurry up!" she snapped. "It's starting to get cold."

Evander did as she bade him, climbing on top of her. He kissed her lips, biting her bottom one, sucking it languorously as he looked into her eyes.

"I hope you like to sweat then, babe. It's about to get hot."

Evander pushed in and Christian sighed out her pleasure. Her eyes slid close and she was glad that he couldn't see her expression. She was pretty sure that she looked crazy but a huge part of her could care less.

"Please take your time, baby," Christian pleaded. "It's been some time since-"

"Shh. I got you. Relax."

And he rocked her gently. Christian relaxed little by little as she got used to him being inside of her. She looked into his eyes as he moved, falling deeper with every stroke that he made. She groaned as he hit her spot each time he slid in and out. Before long, Christian was moving her hips to double both of their pleasure. Still, she kept contact with his eyes, reaching up to caress his face. She melted when he leaned down to kiss her lips softly. She leaned up to kiss him once more and enjoyed the euphoric feelings created in her.

"So beautiful...so mine..."

Christian felt her heart skip a beat as she watched the look come over his face as he said those words. His reverent tone moved her in a way she hadn't been ready for. She had already fallen surrender to him once but didn't think it would happen twice in one night.

"...Yours," she responded back, gasping as he went deeper into her.

The beginnings of her third orgasm began to build up in her. Evander's name was on her lips again as the pressure built. Before she knew it, she was screaming. Evander watched as his woman fell apart beneath him and it sparked his own release. He groaned as he slammed into her hard, feeling the semen fill his condom. He suddenly hoped that he had another pack on him. He was nowhere near finished with his girlfriend.

"You okay, baby?"

Christian nodded. She looked up at him and pointed towards the nightstand.

"Check in there and see if I have another one."

"Oh, so you're ready for round two that quick?"

His smirk was triumphant and it made Christian giggle, seeing through his bravado. She slapped him playfully on the chest, leaning up to nip at his bottom lip.

"Don't make it seem like I'm a fiend for you now. You know you want some more."

Evander pulled out of her slowly and went through the process of discarding and replacing his soiled condom. He almost wanted to do a happy dance when he found another one.

"I just want to hear you say it," he said. "You made me jump through hoops just to get a lil' somethin' shawty."

Christian laughed as he allowed his accent to deepen. More giggles toppled out of her as he settled on top of her again. She leaned up to kiss him.

"I want you, Vann," She said, her tone soft and pleading, "Now give it to me."

Evander licked his lips as he leaned in to kiss her and slid in once more. Christian made him pause and then maneuvered herself on top. She looked down at him and leaned in to kiss him again.

"On second thought, let me give it to you, baby."

Christian tried out a few tricks that she picked up over time and hoped she could still pull them off. Evander's reaction was a sure sign that she could. She rotated her hips just so, making him groan out loud. Cursing the good feelings, all Evander did was hold onto Christian's hips commanding her to slow down when she threatened to make him come again. He never wanted to beat her to the punch line before she made it there.

When the feelings started to overwhelm him again, he pulled her down so they were face-to-face. They tongued each other while they made love to each other. Sweet nothings were exchanged. Raunchy somethings were traded between them. Love stood in between them like a pink elephant. Neither party wanted to be the first to confess.

Evander pulled up Christian's leg so he could go deeper. She moaned as the pressure began to build again, wondering that her body could even reach that summit a fourth time in a row. She heard her man hiss, knowing that she left a mark on his back. She started to throw her hips into the motion again, taking him into the throes of passion with her. His lips swallowed up her moans as he leaned in and kissed her again. Once he'd done that, Christian imploded. Then, he exploded.

He was the first to come back from the precipice they'd reached. When he had, all he could do was gaze upon her. He watched her breathe in and out and swipe at her forehead. He smirked as he watched his handiwork and patted himself mentally on the back. After that, he marveled at how beautiful she was and had pride that this lady tangled up with him was his woman. He had her and intended to keep her. He wondered if she truly knew that.

"What you looking at?"

"You, obviously. I didn't pound your brains out, did I?" Evander winced as he felt a pinch on his arm. He chuckled at his woman's show of sass. "I'm just sayin', baby. You're so damn sexy. Why wouldn't I be?" Christian flushed, shrugging her shoulders. Evander leaned in once more, kissing her softly on the lips. "You're so sexy…so mine."

"I'm not bad I suppose. You got me fair and square, Vann."

A slick smirk came on his face, but the tenderness came alive in his eyes. "And I'm keeping you, Christian."

Christian wouldn't admit it to him then but what he'd told her meant the world to her. Jerrell had never made that promise to her. She remembered the L-word being used. She was sure it was real on his behalf but the way he'd left her had broken her. She didn't want to admit it until that moment, but she had a fear of being abandoned. Evander's constant reminders that he was into her gave her a peace she wasn't used to.

"I think I've graduated to feeling like I can cut the next woman who stares at you too hard."

"You didn't feel that way already? I think I'm hurt."

"You're definitely not. I already know you like female attention."

Evander chuckled lightly. "It's nice to know you're desirable. That means shit compared to what you think of me at this point though."

Quiet settled on them after he made that statement. He watched her, wondering what she thought about that or if she'd even respond. Moments after that thought, she had.

"I think…you're everything I ever wanted. I couldn't ask for better. Matter of fact, what took you so long to get to me?"

She was stroking his face as she made her confession and although he'd guaranteed that she'd pose the question to him, he didn't think she'd be serious when she asked it. Seeing that much, he leaned in and kissed her once and then once more. Pulling back, he played with a loose tendril of her hair as he looked into her eyes again.

"There's no excuse for how long it took me, baby. I apologize but I'm here now."

Christian smiled, kissing him on the chest. She then stretched and mentioned that she wanted to take a shower. She walked into her bathroom and freshened up, her mind replaying the past hour. She was certain that things would be good between them, but things were going better than she expected. She mulled over her thoughts and again, Sonya's biting remarks hit her again.

*"You know what Christian? I hope you do end up alone **and** lonely and that this business goes down. I'm not staying here to watch it go down."*

Tears started to filter down her face, unsure of how one person could flip their loyalties so suddenly. She tried to remember what sex had been like with Jerrell and kept drawing a blank. She couldn't quite remember her other romantic partners either, so she wasn't sure that the sexual comparison was fair, especially in the wake of Evander. Being with Evander made every other man seem non-existent in her world.

Still, she wondered, just how deep was their bond that Sonya was willing to give up her job and distance herself the way she had from her. Christian washed up with those thoughts and they followed her out of the shower, and she quickly washed her face and brushed her teeth. She looked at herself in the mirror, wondering if Sonya's thought process had been valid.

Sure, she'd kept the truth from her for years. Still, she gave Sonya a position that would have taken her more than ten years to get anywhere else. Sometimes longer because she was both Black and a woman. They shared a beautiful friendship and she hadn't wanted to give up her friend just because Jerrell decided to date her. She wondered how Sonya hadn't remembered the good she'd done as her friend.

"Maybe I did deserve it," Christian mumbled to herself. "I could have said something way before it blew up in my face."

It never occurred to her that all she'd done was fall into Jerrell's trap to keep him in her life, even if it were invertedly. He might not have seen her often but every time she looked at Sonya's face, it was a reminder of their prior relationship. Every time a party came around, Jerrell attended one way or the other. Things had been fine as long as he thought Christian wasn't over him but once it seemed that she was, his narcissist ways rose a very ugly head. It never occurred that he never wanted Sonya and that she was just a means to an end. He enjoyed the relationship, but she was only the stand-in until Christian came to her senses.

Which, she never had. So, he took things into his own hands. Once he had, Sonya became completely disposable. Still, ten years with someone was ten years. It was a very evil set up so all in all, could Christian fault her for her upset?

"No, I can't," she thought. *"Still...we were friends. I deserved better than what she gave me. I deserved so much more but..."*

Her defection meant that Jerrell couldn't have a foothold in her life anymore. The mental chain literally snapped when she thought about it. It caused her to breathe more deeply as sadness rushed out and peace took over in its place. It wasn't a total peace, but it was more than she ever had in a long time. Christian grabbed her heart and felt the tears flow down her cheeks. She wiped them away and looked at herself in the mirror. She wiped her face clean and then decided to join her boyfriend again since she'd been away for some time.

She walked back in her room in the nude, smirking when she saw Evander lying on his side, watching her intently as she walked back in. She donned a two-piece satin pajama set and then walked over to turn off the light.

Christian then crawled into her bed, sighing as Evander pulled her in close and kissed her on the forehead. She felt his hands rub her back upwards and downwards in a soothing pattern. She sighed, looking up into his face as he did so as his ministrations made her feel loved. It suddenly occurred to her that she was indeed being loved. The realization made her eyes fill up with tears unexpectedly.

"Sweetheart, what's wrong?" he said, wiping away her tears. "I didn't hurt you, did I?"

"No."

"So, what's wrong?"

"Nothing, Vann. I just got a little emotional. You know how women do every now and again."

"Not my woman," he countered, raising a brow. "She's not a crybaby."

"I am. I just make sure I don't have an audience."

Evander smirked and kissed her forehead. She sighed, his silence making her feel as if she should share what's on her mind. It was obvious that her crying randomly was causing him concern.

"You...just make me happy that's all. Happier than I thought I'd ever be with someone ever again."

"That so? You make me happy, too. Happier than I ever thought I'd ever be with someone at all."

His admission made her smile. She yawned again and then asked Evander to pull back the covers. Christian reached up manually to turn off her lamp and then snuggled back in with her man. She sighed as his heartbeat sounded in her ears. The sound comforted her.

"I love you, Vann," was her last mumbled phrase, before she tumbled off to sleep. Evander felt his heart trip all over itself before he leaned in once more and kissed her on the forehead.

"I love you too, baby. Hopefully next time you tell me when you're wide awake."

Evander tumbled into sleep behind her not long after.

Chapter
Fifteen

Jasmine sipped her coffee, enjoying the balance of creaminess and bitterness that coated her tongue. When she opened her eyes, she giggled as she watched her contact, Terry, staring back at her, amusement shining in his eyes.

"If I knew coffee would bring you out here to see me after so many weeks, I might've asked you sooner."

"I don't feel like being insulted first thing in the morning," Jasmine said, breezily. "I gave *you* my number. You gave me dry text conversation and then faded to black. So, I'm to assume that something else caught your attention or you've been working. Either way, don't put this on me."

Terry chuckled and shrugged. It was true that he loved women. Settling down wasn't in his plans but he definitely saw a relationship with the woman in front of him. He had enjoyed her energies when they met at the SkyLounge weeks ago. He didn't realize she was the same tough-as-nails public relations professional that most of Atlanta had on speed dial. She'd been infectious, laughing and dancing with him with no care in the world. The energy she shared with her other friend left him drunk with sordid desires and he had to admit that when he hadn't met the same woman in her texts, he jumped ship.

Still, she was correct about him not putting his best foot forward. It was obvious her energies were into seeing her friend make it through the wildfire that was her scandal. Also knowing Evander had eyes for the woman that ran the business, he didn't foresee it going any further than it had. Most of the town didn't know that Evander and the Lady Boss were dating but he was wiser than most. Evander wasn't one to go out of his way however, the way he'd seen his friend react to the woman that night had been unsettling. Still, Terry trusted his friend knew what he was getting himself into.

Off-record checks of monies being transferred between businesses let him know that indeed Evander was moving with his logic as much as his heart, so he was comforted by that much. His friend's reaction to the alleged thief had been harrowing. Still, after digging into the case himself he slowly changed his opinion about Christian Adams and the ship she ran. Unfortunately, it just seemed as if she had snakes in the grass that were found by way of whatever auditor Evander hired. She returned what had been stolen and did away with all people responsible for stealing. In Terry's eyes there wasn't much more the woman could do to prove her honor in the situation.

Most of Atlanta had other opinions but opinions were the way of anuses: everybody had one.

"So, I know you didn't want to just enjoy my company," Terry said, moments into Jasmine taking a bite out of her scone, "What's up, pretty lady?"

Jasmine smirked as she picked up her napkin to dab her mouth with. She didn't pretend that their meeting was anything other than business and wondered why he wanted to imply that she did. He was the one who finally called for a coffee date but Jasmine had shut the door on any idea of romance that Terry wanted to instigate. However, she decided that she needed to meet up with him so suggested they meet up after all. It only made sense to her once she remembered he worked for the force. Jasmine wanted someone on the inside to tell her how the investigation was going so she knew where to direct her energies as far as Christian's company.

So far, the clean-up campaign was going better than expected. Christian and her staff were diligent in following any directives they were given. The only person that gave her trouble had been Tiffany, but she was on the smaller end of the scale. She just didn't want her friend to look stupid when high profile accounts came to visit the office. She knew that she paid Tiffany very well and though the woman was good at her job, she took liberties that didn't need to be taken. Thankfully, she noticed a vast improvement since Jasmine brought light to her behavior.

"I wanted to know if they're still looking at Sharin at all as far as the embezzling goes," she said. "Christian is ready to lift the suspension but doesn't want undue stress in the mix of that. We'd rather not see the police at Adams' again if we can help it."

Terry smirked. "No. After she was interviewed, she was cleared. I was surprised though since her ex-boyfriend was the one to interview her. I heard it went pretty bad."

"Either way, I'm glad that's out of the way," Jasmine said. "You hear anything else?"

"They want to cut a deal with the junior accountant. They might let her out early if she rolls on the senior accountant and whoever else had a part in it. So far it's looking good for her to see a release."

Jasmine nodded, taking another sip of the coffee. All of the news was encouraging to her and she knew her client would be pleased at the turn of events. With every rock unturned it put things into a better light as far as Christian and company was concerned.

"That's not bad at all. I hope she takes the bait…I'm pretty sure she was coerced anyway. From what I understand of the young lady she was a recent graduate. That plays a lot into her thought process."

"I agree. I wasn't really looking at her more than the senior accountant. She might need to go ahead and enter witness protection."

"Hm. You think she'll be in danger once she takes the deal? I only see the senior accountant being culpable in this."

"If she were the only party, then yeah. Still, if there's another party in it that we haven't discovered as far as the whole picture then she might not be in the clear before or after she testifies."

Jasmine nodded and made note to bring up to Christian that the young lady might need to have a leave of absence from the job.

"So, that's all I got for you, pretty lady," he said, grinning. "Now that that's out of the way…"

"How'd you know I didn't have any more questions?"

"Because I don't really have any more answers," Terry countered. "There's not much more to tell as far as the investigation. Most of your friends' stories check out. The senior accountant was the one directly doing foul play. Anybody else that was involved is a bonus."

"So, what other business do you think we have, Officer?" Jasmine questioned, throwing a smirk in his direction. "I told you what it was only five minutes ago."

"You saying I lost my shot, then?"

Jasmine nodded, taking another bite of the scone. "I'm not convinced you want anything other than a good time. Plus, you want to make that good time as cheaply as possible. If you hadn't noticed, Terry, I'm not just here for a good time. I work hard. I party harder but still, I work hard. When I want to nut, I have toys for that. I don't need to deal with emotionalism or petty bullshit just to get some dick."

Terry started to feel himself flush with embarrassment. He wasn't sure why because he found he liked her. The way she was lining him up-politely at that-was disheartening to say that least but at the same token, he couldn't be upset with her. Work had been piling up. Plus, he wasn't looking for anything permanent in the space he was in currently.

"So, you're saying all this to say what?"

"If you feel you're deserving of my time, then prove it. As of right now, I have shit to do and I'm not convinced."

Jasmine finished off the last of her scone and picked up her coffee. With a smile that took his breath away, she bid him adieu and he watched her walk out of the Starbucks they were currently seated in. The purposeful strides, the sway of her hips, and the click of her heels did something to him. Her parting words were like a dagger in his heart and very badly, he wanted to pull the knife out. Still, he wasn't sure if he would bleed out proverbially or not. That part annoyed him more than anything else.

Terry finished his coffee and decided to do the same thing that the beauty had before him. He wasn't like his friend. A beautiful face and a pair of legs couldn't move him.

That still put into question what a sharp mind did, however.

Two days later, Sharin sank back into her office chair with a sigh of relief. She'd just finished placing an ad for a new senior accountant but felt the stress of the day building up in her shoulders. It was a different set of pace to what she'd gotten used to and wondered how she would approach Christian with her thought process when the time came.

145

The truth was, she'd been devastated when Christian suspended her and at first she was at a loss of what to do with her time. Most of it had been devoted to Adams'. She was used to waking up early, preparing for her day and then taking off for work. Work entailed double checking the books and flirting with new accounts for the team. She had to admit that it didn't seem like much on the outside but on the inside, it took its toll.

Sharin hadn't known it did until all of her appointments got canceled. She didn't know how freeing it was to wake up first thing in the morning and to take her time enjoying the sunrise. She hadn't known there was joy to be had in cooking a healthy breakfast for herself and her love before he left for work.

Cleaning her house and having the day to command for herself was more freeing than she thought. Getting back into general upkeep of herself and having the time alone to hear her own thoughts was a huge blessing that she hadn't seen coming. Certain things were beginning to take precedence in her life and returning to work was shockingly something she didn't want to do. She was grateful to be back, but she wasn't as happy as she was when she was home. But…perhaps she'd get back into the swing of things.

She was pretty sure being able to enjoy her time with Maddox was high on the list of things that made being home more attractive. Being able to spend time with him in the morning and then greet him when he came home in the evening was beautiful. Plus, being able to have longer date nights than usual had spoiled her. Getting to be around her fiancé was an unintended blessing out of the mess. She was more than ready to get married to him than she had been in the beginning.

Remembering the first few weeks of her forced vacation made her sad. The upheaval of the company had been tough on all involved. Hearing about Sonya's defection hadn't been shocking, but it was saddening. Though she understood her colleague's upset, she wasn't sure that leaving the company over a white lie made sense. At least not the way she had.

With those things on her mind, Sharin opened the door and, poking her head out, ordered her secretary to call Monica to the office. Farrah, her assistant, was all too happy to make the call and Sharin almost giggled when she shut the door. Sharin's suspension meant that she was laid off as well. From what she understood, Farrah had been paid unemployment but was crawling the walls to get back to work. She was happy that her assistant was happy to be back.

In less than ten minutes, Monica was walking through the doors of her friend's office, smirking as she saw the duress on her face.

"Welcome back!" she squealed. "You could look happier to see me."

"I'm very happy to see you. I need your advice."

"You've only been back five minutes and you need me already?"

Sharin giggled, "It's like…I don't know, Nik. I'm happy to be back. I'm just…like a fish out of water."

"I'm sure," Monica said. "You've been out of the game for about a month. You'll adjust."

"I'm…not sure I want to," Sharin shrugged. "I enjoyed the downtime."

Monica raised both brows, "Oh?"

146

"Yeah. I mean, you know I always loved working here, but I got suspended and then I was heartbroken, and then…I wasn't. I got shit done in my personal life. I got to screw my man like I said I would. We've been hanging tough and I actually got to enjoy our house for a while. It's kind of amazing what time down does to put things into perspective."

Monica nodded, understanding her point. "So you're thinking about resigning."

"Yeah, I am," Sharin said, "I just know that if I tell Christian right now, she might lose it."

"Girl," Monica laughed. "You know I can't lie to you. Sonya just up and left over some dick and you pretty much want to leave over the same thing."

"Stop, Nik, it's not the same thing!" Sharin laughed. "It's more like…peace of mind. I've been so happy since I got over my hurt feelings, basically. I almost want to tell her she fucked up when she sat me down."

"Well…I don't know what to advise. I'd hate to see you go. I'm not too sad about Sonya, but you know we been down for the longest now."

Sharin nodded. "I know. I'm unsure if I just need to get my feet wet again or if I truly feel this way."

"I think you might just need another adjustment period," Monica said. "I'm sure that's what your emotions are. Get your feet wet and see how you feel in a few weeks."

Sharin sighed, taking in her friend's thoughts and decided she'd be right.

"After some time if you feel the same way, *then* I'd say something but at least wait until the company's over the scandal fully and Christian's more settled. Sonya just left so it looks pretty bad on paper if you leave, too."

Sharin nodded, taking Monica's thoughts as sound. Still, she wondered if Sonya hadn't left would Christian have even considered bringing her back sooner.

"*She already was,*" Sharin thought. "*I can't think like that…*"

"Also, we have to figure out who's taking over for Sonya. I think Christian's thinking about promoting one of the senior accountants."

"I can see that. She had an excellent team. Besides, we don't want another disgruntled body getting upset and siphoning funds from our clients," Sharin rolled her eyes. "Still, I don't see why not."

"She wants the three of us to vet her choices, together. I think she's looking into Mia."

"Mia Lanston? I think if she can adapt well to the role, it might not be bad. She's a little more personable than Sonya was…" Sharin said. "Though Sonya came with her own charm."

"Oh, you missing the bitch, too?" Monica said, giggling. "Y'all two kill me."

"What? We were friends for years! It's weird how suddenly she left is all," Sharin shrugged. "You're good at detaching-"

"Woah, ho, ho, don't play with me, Ice Queen. I've seen you detach especially well when it suited you."

Sharin blushed, as that much was true. Still, it was more protective than anything else. Monica was just good at detaching herself from situations.

"Mhm! Just because you're retired now doesn't make you a saint."

Sharin balled up a piece of paper and threw it at Monica who laughed, proud of her impromptu joke. Both parties were interrupted by a knock on the door. Farrah poked her head in with a polite smile.

"Ms. Reynolds, Ms. Adams requests you and Ms. James' presence in Conference Room A."

Sharin nodded. "Page her back and tell her to give us five."

Farrah nodded and closed the door back. Sharin eyed Monica and sighed. In turn, Monica laughed.

"You're finally starting to act like an heiress. Work is making your privileged ass sweat now, huh?"

Sharin giggled, "Shut your ass up. Let's go see what Boss Lady wants."

Sharin and Monica beat Christian to the room, catching Tiffany setting up the room with meeting notes, papers, and pens for the two ladies present. When she saw them walking in, she beamed.

"Good morning, ladies, I hope all is well."

Sharin grinned, seeing the aura around Tiffany totally different than what was normal for Christian's snarky assistant. The reason wasn't hard to miss however as the ring on her left hand spoke volumes. Monica had already seen it the day before but waited for Sharin's reaction since she knew she used to have a thing for Christopher. Watching her friend's surprise was so delightful that she abandoned the idea of poking fun at her. The story of how she, Tiffany, and Christopher met never failed to entertain her, but she was grateful that Sharin met Maddox instead. Christopher wasn't a good match for her. She wasn't sure that he and Tiffany were a good match either but so far it seemed, they were working out.

"Congratulations are in order, I see!" Sharin said. "Let me have a look!"

Tiffany grinned proudly as she thrust her hand in Sharin's face. Sharin's face frowned up, demonstrating how impressed she was with the choice. She and Tiffany had gotten engaged in the story, which had each lady doubled over in laughter.

"Yes, girl. I thought I was going to commit a homicide that night because he was really playing!" Tiffany said. "Then he pulled the ring out and..."

Tiffany started to get choked up but swallowed her tears. It wouldn't do to show emotionalism, even if the subject were a happy one. For the interim she was interested in keeping her job, especially after Christopher explained his thought process to her. She was definitely taking his offer to stay home into consideration.

"Well, I'm happy for you, Tiff." Sharin said. "It's been a long time coming."

"I know! It's been a ride, that's for sure."

Christian stepped in the office, calling the meeting to order. She greeted her Partners as she took her seat. Tiffany closed the door behind her and sat in the chair next to Christian. She took down the minutes of the meeting as it progressed, but her quiet, excited energy still filled the room.

"So, first things first. I've already told you both separately but I'm now announcing that Sonya Powers is no longer a Partner at Adams'. She was fired, cited for insubordination and unseemly conduct towards the CEO. Brown suggests if the media questions us about the incident that we are to respond that Sonya resigned her position. Nothing untoward should be said about her in public and be careful about who you share the news with in private. I'm sure you two won't but when the official announcement comes along that's pretty much what we want to get across. She left us at a pretty bad time, so we have to spin the story to favor us."

"What if she gets out of hand in the long run?" Sharin questioned, as she wrote down her own personal notes.

"A cease and desist should cover that problem if she wants to take it there," Monica interjected. "I pray it doesn't come to that but if we must…"

"Sonya is too prideful to say anything that might make her look like a clown in front of the press. That's my assumption. She'll want to start searching for a comparable job as well and she can't look crazy on television if moving on is truly her goal. If, however, she does get out of hand, I'll have Jasmine ready to hit her with the order. Her personal gripes with me shouldn't be a deterrent with business."

The twosome nodded, in agreement.

"Next on the docket…I need a replacement for her. I don't want to rush this, however her spot can't be open for too long. I was toying with the idea of looking outside but if you two think we should promote from within…"

"I think it'd be an excellent opportunity to court the senior accountants that've been here long-term from the various departments. I'd like to see to it that we don't have another occurrence of our dearly departed Jupiter Classon."

Sharin had been the one to raise the point and while Christian agreed, she wasn't sure that she wanted to promote someone based on the fear.

"Jupiter Classon is an isolated incident that had more to do with her jealousy of your position in more than one arena than simply feeling she fit the bill for being Partner. Besides, I'm pretty sure that more news will come out that your family was a part of this fracas, Sharin," Christian said. "Let's not forget about Chastity looking suspect in the mix of it all."

"I haven't forgotten," Sharin pressed. "I'm just putting it out there that we have a few good prospects. I'm pretty sure you were looking at some of them already. I just wanted it clear that I think it's a good idea to look from within before we look outside. It's only the right thing to do."

"True. I just don't want you forcing the issue over the guilt of Ms. Classon. You did nothing wrong and it was all on her."

Sharin nodded.

"I agree with Sharin," Monica said. "But…based on what's fair for our people. We have a few that might fit the bill and probably have been waiting on one of us to leave for a time now."

Christian chuckled. "Have it y'all way. I'm looking at Mia Lanston for it. She's been with Sonya from the inception and she's coming up to the age where she can take over her duties seamlessly. However, I'd like us to further look at any other prospects we have here and if they might fit the bill, I want to explore that. I'm hoping we've made our pick in no less than two weeks so that the pay dates flow seamlessly. Whoever we choose, I'm leaving it up to you to make sure they get comfortable in the role, Monica."

"Why me? Sharin-"

"-Is just getting accustomed to being back," Sharin reminded her, "I don't have time to baby anyone. I still have to replace an accountant and figure out what happens to Jamie."

Sharin then looked at Christian, prompting her for direction. Christian shrugged her shoulders.

"I don't have an issue with restoring her job if that's what you're asking. She might not see a promotion in this place, at least for the first two years of her return. I'm unsure I'd ever be comfortable with her getting any traction based on her history but to be fair I've never worked with her. I believe you had a good rapport with her when she was working there."

"I considered mentoring her in the past. Christopher had mentioned her plans for working for Big 4s in the future. I had hoped to set her up for success in the long run."

Christian briefly thought about it. She didn't remember Jamie well, but she was a lower ranking accountant. For the most part she was Jupiter's assistant. She could understand the coercion coming from Jupiter alone. From what she remembered of Jupiter she wasn't a humble woman, still she got the job done. Christian had been considering her to be a new department head when Adams' expanded. Being that she had to spend the monies to pay back her now-boyfriend's business, the expansion was now on hold. While Adams' was still afloat, the chance to capitalize and make more money was now hindered by the sideshow that Jupiter cooked up.

Sighing, she again looked at Sharin.

"Yeah. I don't think she's a total loss. She'll still be viable to Big 4 companies and having her back with us won't negatively affect our brand. Still, make it clear to her that any more bullshit and I'll personally have her blacklisted from sea to shining sea. She can't walk back into these doors believing that what she'd done was okay. If not for her being Christopher's niece I wouldn't let her back in here."

Sharin nodded. "So noted."

"Is there anything else?" Christian asked. "I believe Brown should be arriving soon. I'm unsure if she wants to meet with us all together or just me."

"I'd like a vacation, effective immediately," Monica said, lifting up her hand to stare at her manicure.

She raised her eyes to look into Christian's and the look on her face forced Christian to laugh, disarming her despite not being amused at all.

"Stop playing with me, Nik." She said, closing the meeting, "Let's get back to work."

"So…I know I already advised this, but you have a man who's willing to move heaven and earth for you. Why is he not being utilized?"

Christian and Jasmine were back in her office, summarizing the week they'd had.

"I didn't want to drag him in if at all possible," Christian answered. "I know you got him to agree but so far we haven't needed him. So why go through the extra mile?"

"Because you pay me for results," Jasmine answered, coolly. "I agree that all is going smoothly, and the cycle is nearing a close but that still doesn't do much for the opinion of the business. You haven't totally lost clients but you're not seeing new ones either. Sonya being terminated on paper doesn't make matters much better in the public eye, either."

Christian sighed, cursing Sonya's name in her mind. Every word that Monica uttered to her concerning Sonya made more and more sense and she berated herself for leaning into her emotions instead of her logic. She promised it would never happen again.

"Anyway, I have the idea to do a mini video series. I figure Evander gives a one minute, maybe two-minute testimonial. You post it to the business' Instagram page. We also post them on your Facebook page. You get your social media people to post and repost, driving the point home in people's head that Adams' is still a viable place for business. They'll post Evander's video the most in tandem with maybe one or two of your long -standing clients who still see the best in the business."

"I like it," Christian said. "I have a few names I can ring up and request."

"Good. Also, a news interview with a local station would help clear your name as well. I've tapped Glenda Smith for it. So, get pretty and-"

"-No."

Jasmine raised a brow, "No? Red, do you know how hard it was to get this woman to pick up her phone? She only picked up because she was told it was me. She only jumped on it-"

"Because she's trying to gain notoriety in her circle by making me look like an incompetent clown. Fuck her. I don't care what you say, Jasmine I'm not doing it."

Christian's face burned as she recalled the first day the scandal broke into the news cycle. Glenda was the Black journalist who pressed her for questions more than anybody else that day. She remembered being affronted that a Black woman was so excited to tear another one down. Christian was always informed that *skin-folk ain't kinfolk*, however, the bloodlust she read in the woman's eyes was despicable. She wasn't going to put herself in the woman's line of fire again.

"Christian. You're doing the interview. You have yet to stand before the people and insist your innocence. In the eyes of the law, of course you're cleared. Sharin has been cleared. Even Jamie will come out unscathed for the most part of her role. You're the face and the name of this establishment however, and in the court of public opinion, you're a piece of shit Black woman trying to make it in a male dominated world."

"Why should I care about public opinion?"

"Because there's no business that talks like word-of-mouth. I have my ear to the street and while educated individuals understand the ins and outs of this situation, the regular joe and even the celebrities that your business thrives off of? It's still not looking good, Christian. Put your big girl panties on and get your shit together."

Christian felt her face redden even more from Jasmine's tone. She opened her mouth, ready to answer her back when Jasmine raised up her hand.

"I don't care if you're offended by what I'm saying. I took on this job because I believe in you and in your mission. I've ruffled feathers here because I want the best of you, and I want excellence to be your receipt in a world that expects less of you because you're a double minority. Of course, don't get it fucked up, the money is right but still. You're my *friend*, Christian, and you're down bad. I can't call myself your friend and not make the best moves on your behalf.

If we don't tackle this head on, all of the work we've put in will be lost. Glenda isn't an ideal interviewer for *you*, but she will put you through your paces. All you have to do is keep your calm and tell the truth. She'll see it and in turn, so will the audience. That counts for more than anything anybody else has to say. Got it?"

Christian ran a hand down her face. Of course, Jasmine was right. Still, it didn't make the truth of it sting less.

"I don't like her," Christian said. "I don't like the idea of helping anyone's career that wants to tear me down."

"You don't have a choice, Red. Besides, it's an even exchange. You never know that you might make a friend out of the whole exercise."

That was the hard part of leadership. You can't always pick and choose your level of hard. Still, for the brand-for the business-she was going to go through with it. Jasmine knew it when she suggested it and Christian knew it although she bucked against it.

"I'm not in the market for friends, either," Christian said, shrugging. "I made all of the ones I'll ever make."

"Hm. I'd trade in Sonya for Glenda any day but that's just me. Get out of your feelings, girl. Everything will be alright."

Christian wanted to desperately believe in that promise, but she wasn't so sure.

Chapter
Sixteen

"I see congratulations are in order."

Jamie approached Chastity, smiling as she took a seat across from her at the restaurant, Bacchanalia. Chastity smirked as she saw the smile didn't reach her eyes, but all the knowledge did was amuse her. She wondered if Jamie thought she had enough backbone to challenge her. Either way if she had, there'd be consequences.

She'd gotten away with stealing fifteen million dollars scot free from every person that ever wronged her mother. As far as she was concerned, her mother was the only righteous person in the world and if she could've had her way, every single person that ever wronged her would pay. Being that her grandfather was dead, she couldn't set her sights on him but so far, Sharin and the King family were the biggest people on the list. She was sure that she'd caused irreparable damage in the noble company that was called Adams' Accounting Firm. The thought made Chastity smile with glee every time she thought about it.

"No congratulations are necessary." Jamie answered, "How have you been, Chastity?"

"I've been well. It looks like you didn't suffer too badly behind bars."

The starter course was ordered. Chastity talked lightly but sarcastically about Jamie's time behind bars. Jamie answered in kind. She wondered within herself how long she would have to endure Chastity's games and when she could find a moment to politely exit without causing too many waves. She again thought she was meeting with her boyfriend when once again, it was Chastity waiting for her when she arrived.

Jamie decided to act unperturbed about seeing her in the place of her boyfriend. They were in public and it wouldn't do for her to act out. She'd simply go along with it all until she was able to walk out.

"What's the point of this meeting, Chastity?"

Chastity had been rearing to say another cutting remark when Jamie cut her off. It hadn't been too long in the conversation when Jamie couldn't figure out a solution. Sitting with the woman made her nervous and she didn't want to be seen in public with her. It was slight paranoia on her part as the media didn't even know her link to the case at all and she was acting as a silent third party. Still, it felt like a slap to all involved that she was even sharing a meal with her at all.

"I've just come to remind you that although you're free from prison, you're still my bitch," Chastity said, breezily. "I'm pretty sure you made a deal to get out to testify and you should know, I will double down on my promise. I'll have you and everybody connected to you killed. You won't get in the way of my plans."

"Nobody's afraid of you and your threats, Chastity McCain," Jamie said. "You're a spoiled brat and it's about time someone put you in your place. Maybe jail will cool your jets."

Jamie delivered her remark with a smile. Chastity smiled back but it wasn't hard to miss the anger in her eyes. The heiress didn't bother to hide it. Jamie's stomach started to turn as she knew the woman meant every word that she said to her, but the fear was more for her uncle than anyone else. Although she and he had the conversation at length about Chastity's involvement, it didn't totally guarantee that he wouldn't be the one to get hurt in the situation. Still, she knew if she had the chance to testify, she would. That was already a given when she was escorted out of Adams' on that fateful day.

"Someone's been in jail for five minutes and thinks they're a hardened criminal?" Chastity said. "We both know you're not so you should quit while you're ahead."

Jamie sighed heavily and stood up. Without another word, she walked out of the restaurant without a backwards glance.

Samuel McCain took in his girlfriend for the first time in weeks since her indictment. She sat next to him on the couch of his apartment seeming as if she wanted no parts of him. He was lost and confused as to what all had been going on around him. He knew his sister wasn't the best of people-matter of fact, he did his best to limit his time with her-still, he didn't know she was capable of the trouble she'd caused. If he had known, he would've done his best to put a stop to it all. At the very least, forbid her to have contact with Jamie again.

He'd said all of that much when Jamie stepped into his space to explain that his sister had drawn her out to the restaurant to threaten her life. Jamie had been in tears and the scene was enough to break his heart and anger him in the same breath.

"Baby, I…"

"You *what*? You're sorry? Of course, you are! You didn't even visit me when I'd been in jail!"

"I couldn't!" he screamed. "I couldn't. You know what kind of family I come from. Being with you now in this apartment is damn near a scandal."

"So why let me in?" she questioned.

"Because this is still my apartment," Samuel shrugged. "Besides, nobody knows where it is except close family."

The McCain's were a huge name in Atlanta as well. They dealt in oil, one of the few Black families in the south to do so. Jamie was always surprised that her and Samuel's paths met because generally, they wouldn't have otherwise. Samuel had visited Sharin a time or two at the office whenever they had family business to discuss and that's when he'd met Jamie. Jamie had been shy at first but soon warmed up to his advances. They'd been dating about a year and Samuel was thinking about advancing their relationship when the news had hit all over the city.

Samuel pulled Jamie into his frame, kissing her forehead. He sighed, taking in her scent and exhaled, joyful to have her in his arms again.

"I love you," he said, kissing the top of her head again. "Don't do me like that."

"Do you like what? I'm being acquitted. I was coerced," she said. "I didn't even see a penny of that money moved into any account I have."

"I'm sure," he said. "I apologize that I didn't come to see you. I'm also glad you're being acquitted so I have the evidence before other women start being pushed into my face to marry."

Jamie winced from the position she was in. She was unsure of why families like her boyfriend's still existed. It was a weird notion to try to marry someone off against their will. It was also weird to further marry them to sweeten a business deal or to further an empire. What happened to love?

"I don't even understand the hatred toward me."

"It's not personal at all. My parents don't hate you. My father is just an opportunist. There was a young lady from a prominent family who would've fit the bill if things hadn't worked out between us."

"Fit the bill, huh?" Jamie said, pulling back. "I'm unsure this will ever work out. Your sister-"

"Half," Samuel interjected. "Half-sister."

"Y'all have the same mother so what difference does that make?" Jamie interjected. "She's basically over here making death threats. Then to top it off, let's say we work out. You decide you want to marry me after all…"

"*After all?*" Samuel questioned, filing the question away for later meditation."…go on." Samuel said, "What are you saying?"

"I'm saying, we get married. Do I have to put up with her as a bane for the rest of my life? I don't think I can handle that. Your sister is evil, Sam. I can't…"

Jamie's voice started to waver and seeing her vulnerable made Samuel distraught and angry. He was also angry at his beloved. Why hadn't she said anything before? That was the question he tossed back to her, releasing her from his arms. He watched her cross her arms over her stomach but stood where he was. She had a right to be upset with him, but he felt he also had the right to be upset with her. Much of the train wreck might have been allayed had she said *something*.

"I wasn't so sure that you'd believe me if I told you. This is still your sister," Jamie shrugged. "Also, she did threaten my life. She also threatened my uncle's life. So…had it only been me I might have said something. But I don't run risks with my uncle's life."

Samuel nodded, understanding her thought process. He'd met Christopher in passing and it was easy to see why he was a likeable man. Jamie's eyes shined like marbles whenever she spoke of him and it was so easy to see that their relationship was definitely more father-daughter than uncle-niece. It was the sweetest thing you could ever witness.

"I'm sorry you felt you couldn't trust me," Samuel said. "I have to admit that I'm hurt about that."

Jamie looked down, shamefaced. Still, she wouldn't take back what she said. She meant what she meant. It didn't make sense to try to allay his feelings when the facts laid before her were simply the facts. She knew that on one level Chastity annoyed him but at the same token, family ties were something she would never test. She knew how she felt about Christopher so she wasn't sure that even if he did something and someone came to tell her that she would be open to believe them at first. Cold hard evidence had to be presented to her first.

"I'm sorry...I'm sorry about it all," Jamie said, sighing. "I think I want to leave now. I need to be alone."

Samuel nodded. He wanted her to stay with him, where he knew she would be safe. Still, if she needed space, then he would give it. It didn't make for a happy ending to ever hold a woman against her will. So, he'd give her a few days and check back in on her.

Until then, he had a bone to pick with his half-sister.

Family dinner had been a few days later at the McCain mansion. The siblings had made nice at the dinner table, not alerting their parents that there was a rift happening in the slightest. Certain topics were broached. Anthony McCain had questioned whether Jamie would be going on trial for her part in the mishap. Samuel had proudly announced that she was let out on bail and would have the charges dropped when she gave testimony of her part of the scandal. Anthony had only nodded in kind, knowing not to press the issue beyond that. Still, he inwardly hoped that things fell apart between his son and Jamie Phillips. She was a delightful girl and he wasn't against her and Samuel's union. It's just that Samuel marrying upward might do well for their family overall. Although the McCain's did well monetarily, more social capital never hurt anyone. Jamie, the nice girl that she was, couldn't provide that for his son.

Chastity was ready to contradict her brother but decided not to. She had the inkling that Jamie tattled on her and the annoyance she was feeling toward the woman was reaching an all-time high. She was ready to reveal that her parents didn't truly like her-especially her mother-but didn't want to default into the normal, basic, evil rich girl patterns. Either way he would find out soon enough.

The McCains retired to their suite after dinner and that left Chastity and Samuel to their devices. Still, instead of Chastity running off like what was her norm, Samuel stopped her before she could walk away.

"You need something, Sammy?"

The nickname irked Samuel to no end, but he looked past it in the moment. Besides, the more important question was,

"Why would you threaten my girlfriend, Chastity?"

Chastity rose an eyebrow. "Father is trying to hook you up with literal old money royalty and you're worried about that dog?"

"Watch your mouth, Chas. I love her and none of that extra shit matters to me. You know that. The issue is why have her look bad in front of the family when all of this shit…stems from you?"

"I don't know what you're talking about," Chastity said, attempting to sidestep him.

Samuel stepped into her space once more. "You know *exactly* what I'm talking about. You siphoned fifteen million dollars from Evander King and *that* shit doesn't make sense. What the fuck are you going to do with that money, Chastity?"

"If I had it'd be none of your fuckin' business what I'd do with it. Ask that lowly *bitch* what she would want with fifteen million dollars, as if that could ever amass the wealth we command."

"We don't command shit, Chastity. Not even your mother commands that shit…not unless Pop dies. Even then-"

Chastity shrugged, "It's still family money. She couldn't even hope to amass that in her lifetime without stealing."

"She didn't steal. She was coerced to give wrong information. For some reason she didn't say a word about it even after having the knowledge. I don't know the other lady but quite a bit of this stinks of your *shit*. This is the last time I'll ever say this to you, Chastity. Leave Jamie alone. You've already done enough damage."

"You haven't begun to see damage, Sammy. That I promise you. I also promise if you breathe a word of this to anybody, you might end up in the same heap as her, brother or not."

Samuel rose a brow, considering her words and chuckled. "You just told me you had nothing to do with it. If you didn't have shit to do with it, why threaten me, too?"

Chastity opened and then closed her mouth. She walked away without another word and Samuel was left without another word to say. He wasn't even sure where to start as far as his sister's part in the whole mess. He knew that his cousin should know but wasn't even sure how to approach the situation from that angle. It was possible that they might start to suspect that they all had a hand in it and the last thing he wanted to do was bring further scandal to his family. Not that he was empathetic towards his stepmother, but his father was definitely not a man who took embarrassment well. It was bad enough that Chastity would already serve him a huge dish of shame when it all came out. One thing that was for sure, he knew that Jamie would testify against her. That was without a doubt.

So, for the interim he'd sit back and watch where the chips fell. He was pretty certain that they would fall in favor of himself and his loved ones. Otherwise, he might have to take matters into his own hands.

Chastity walked into a seedy nightclub deep into the outskirts of Atlanta two nights later. She hated that she stuck out like a sore thumb, but she refused to wear anything but the luxurious designer that she always sported. On this particular night she wore Christian Dior from her headband to her flats.

The scene was dark with only red lights to illuminate the space. She wasn't sure why there was an Amsterdam themed club in the midst of Georgia but considering one of the best hitmen in town patronized the place on a regular basis, the particulars didn't matter. She toyed with the idea of letting sleeping dogs lie as far as Jamie but seeing that she was basically on a tell-all tour these days, she was ready to have her put down.

She'd heard about Neely through a few friends of hers who stepped into dark circles. Out of curiosity she inquired about Neely when his name came up. In confidence, a friend told her that her family had a few people taken out by the young man some time ago when deals went bad. She had never thought she'd ever have to stoop as low as she was about to, but desperate times called for desperate measures. If things went well, she would consider sending the gentleman after her brother next.

Or not. Jamie's death might be enough of a punishment for her half-brother. In her eyes she didn't understand why family didn't bother sticking together. The fact that he hung out with Sharin often burned her up as well.

She'd deal with her on another date.

"You looking for me?"

Chastity turned around and her eyes widened when she took him in. He was huge, almost gargantuan in size. His hands could palm her entire face and still have room to spare. She swallowed, never in her life being afraid of another individual in a genuine way but it seemed this time-this moment-was the first time.

Still, it was a wonder that she took in his face and felt her legs start to shake. His eyes were a beautiful hazel green. His lips were full. He had strong features and his very essence made her want to faint.

Standing before him she wasn't sure whether she wanted to run away or run to him and the very conundrum angered her. Still, she swallowed again and licked her lips, preparing to answer.

"Are you Neely?"

"That'd be right, ma'am," he answered with a smirk. "And you are?"

"I'd rather talk in private, if that's okay with you." Her voice quavered, "Or...or..."

"Or, what?" he said, grinning. "You want to go on the stage and state your contract for me?"

Chastity heard the smirk more than saw it. She forced her legs to stop buckling and straightened herself up.

"Private is fine."

Neely nodded, turning around and walking away, prompting her to follow. She did, catching his hint. In the far corner of the club was a booth. They sat after Neely nodded towards the chair. He slid in on the opposite side, looking very much like he could break the chair. Chastity almost laughed at the sight but thought better of it. Still, she crossed her hands on the table and looked into his eyes. His chuckle threw her off and annoyed her.

"What's funny?" she snapped. "I don't see anything funny here."

"What's funny is that you stick out like a sore thumb and you're really about to sit here and give me a contract. Don't get me wrong, I meet with your kind in here all the time. I just find you very amusing."

"Amusing?" she questioned. "You look like a walking joke and you're the one calling me amusing?"

Neely's left brow rose at the comeback. Still, he laughed again. The richness of his base totally covered her and made her warm inside, until he opened his mouth.

"If you were anyone else, I would have marched you outside and ended you for that," he commented. "As it were, you might only have one chance left before I kill you. I'm not that down bad for money that I'm gonna take no slick talk. You still came to me."

Chastity shrugged. "And you came for me."

Neely smirked. He wasn't sure why he liked her, he only knew that he did. Still, it wouldn't stop him from offing her if he needed to.

"So, what do you need?" he questioned. "Spoiled little rich girls normally don't make enough enemies to have someone killed so entertain me, princess. What did you do?"

Chastity's teeth gritted together under his critical gaze. She found herself at the crossroads of wanting to push his buttons again but not wanting to take his word lightly. So, swallowing her pride she illuminated him on the entire tale, unsure of why she was exposing all to a perfect stranger.

Still, by the end of that conversation, she was giving Neely a signed contract of time, place, and method. Also, half of his payment up front. Chastity had his word that he'd do a job well done but in the event that he didn't, she could keep the other half. Overall, her word that his name would be kept secret was the rule given above all else.

"I don't give a damn how cute you are, princess. If I hear my name come out of your mouth to any type of law enforcement, I'll do you just like you want me to do this mark. Tread carefully."

Chapter
Seventeen

Jamie nervously stepped inside of Adams' for the first time in two months. Her heart was beating so loud she was sure anybody who walked past her could hear her. She wasn't sure whether she would be received well and her stomach joined in on the anxiety party by starting to bubble. She felt her skin flush but still pushed ahead on the elevator to her old floor. She waited patiently and was pleasantly surprised to see Monica walking out when the doors dinged open. The firm's most notorious Partner's smile was big and beautiful as she welcomed her back, pulling her into a hug.

"I'm so happy to see you back!" she said. "Sharin is waiting for you in her office."

"Thank you so much." Jamie said. "I'm nervous."

"Oh, don't be nervous. Life happens. You just push forward and grow from it. That's all you can do. This is coming from someone who's done a lot of dumb shit in their life on purpose."

Monica winked and bid her a good day. Jamie giggled, wishing that she knew the lady a little better to ask her how she overcame it. Watching the older woman walk with an unmatched confidence was still something she was working on. It was obvious to anybody who cared to even glance at her that her nerves were shot.

Still, she would hold her head up high and keep walking. Like she said, learning was the major key.

The elevator took her up to the third floor and once she stepped out it felt like time had stopped. She hadn't been to work in so long that the place felt foreign. What was odd to her was that after a while, the routine she had going on in lock-up had started becoming familiar. She understood exactly why it was hard for people to adapt again once they came out. She'd only been gone for upwards six weeks versus the years most criminals put in.

It made her think about the justice system and how unfair it could be to the people that entered it, most times unwillingly.

Her thoughts led her to the Sharin's office. At the desk she greeted Farrah who smiled at her serenely.

"Good to see you, Ms. Phillips," she grinned. "Ms. Reynolds told me to just send you in."

"Thanks, Farrah. I hope all is well with you?"

"I'm good, girl, you know that," Farrah said. "Let's catch up later on."

Jamie smiled, fully, somewhat comforted by the offer. She accepted it and then walked up to the door. She knocked lightly before pushing her head in.

Jamie almost smiled upon seeing Sharin's face again but felt her color drain out when she laid eyes on Christian. She wanted to run out of the office but knew that wasn't an option. So, biting the side of her lip she entered, closing the door behind her.

"Ms. Adams. Ms. Reynolds," she said. "Good morning."

"Good morning, Ms. Phillips! Good to see you back."

Christian, to her surprise, greeted her first. She'd been in the seat on the left side in front of Sharin's desk. Jamie took the right side, slowly lowering herself and trying to take a deep breath before she hyperventilated.

"Thank you, Ms. Adams," she said. "Uhm…before anything else gets said, I want to apologize to you for my part in the whole scandal. I…it was never my intention to aide anyone in the downfall of the company."

Christian looked into her eyes for a few moments before she nodded.

"I understand that you were under quite a bit of duress, Ms. Phillips. I won't say that I was happy going through the changes that have taken place but that's behind us now. Just give me your word that you'll only put your best foot forward from this point on and I'm over it."

Jamie nodded, profusely before she realized she should speak. "You have my word."

"Good," Christian rose up, turning her attention to Sharin. "So, I'll see you at lunch?"

"Yeah. I might call it a day from there, too."

"You just came back and you're calling early days now, Shay?"

Sharin giggled. "We're slow on business right now. I'm barely getting bites from my end and I've been out and about since I've been back out. I also have to vet the new accountant hopefuls. The juniors are actually foaming at the mouth to be chosen."

Christian smirked. "I don't envy you. I'll see you in a bit."

Christian walked out of the room and once the door clicked, Jamie turned her attention to Sharin, who smiled at her serenely. Jamie started to breathe easier.

"Truly, it is good to see you back. I hope you believe that when people say it."

"Everyone but Ms. Adams, if I'm honest. I didn't even think she knew me."

"Not before this incident, no. Just that you were Christopher's niece and that you were a solid junior accountant. That was until a couple of months ago. Now she knows you pretty well and I'm sorry to say not in a good way."

Jamie lowered her eyes. She didn't need to be flogged by her former boss. She'd had enough time to sit in prison and question why she just didn't alert the proper authorities to what had been going on. It was pretty obvious that the world wasn't truly on her side although it was obvious that she'd been coerced into a situation she hadn't even asked for.

"Again, I apologize for my part. It definitely wasn't my intention to bring harm to you or the company in any way."

"Let's not delve into that again," Sharin smiled, wanly. "We have other business to discuss."

Sharin pulled out a stack of papers and placed it in front of Jamie. She picked them up and gasped.

"Adams' would like to hire you back on a probationary basis. If you agree, your probation will be for a year. You won't be considered for any promotions until you've made two years in based on the situation at hand. You'll have to regain your vacation, sick, and PTO time again as your seniority is at the same as a new employee. Well, you're essentially a new employee all over again. It's understandable if you turn this down but I do implore you not to."

Jamie looked up at Sharin with tears in her eyes. "Are you kidding me? This was more than I hoped for!"

"I take that as a yes. Just fill those out and turn them into HR," Sharin said. "Welcome back."

Jamie smiled. "Thank you for having me back, Ms. Reynolds."

"Good. Now that that's out of the way, I do want you to let you know…"

Jamie turned her attention from the stack of papers to Sharin again. The look on her face had turned serious and put the younger woman's back up.

"Although we understand that what happened to you was indeed coercion, you need to remember that as a CPA, you took an oath to protect people. What happened to Evander King was inexcusable on your part as you had knowledge that he was being robbed before even his own auditors knew. What you allowed to happen each and every time you turned in those reports was letting Mr. King walk around unprotected. He was unprotected by the very bodies sworn to protect his assets and his interests.

I speak for myself and the rest of the Partners when I say that if something like this *ever* happens again, you *will* be stripped of your license and even after that you will be *blacklisted* from every part of the United States if you decide to *ever* move the way you did again. Are we clear on that, Ms. Phillips?"

Sharin's voice had turned cold. Jamie could only nod. She'd been afraid of sitting under the wrath of the CEO, but she would have never pegged Sharin for being a rough customer.

"I need a verbal answer, Jamie."

"Yes, Ms. Reynolds."

"Good. Your starting date is the coming Thursday as that's the new start of the pay period. I'll see you, then."

Jamie nodded, rising up to leave. "Thank you again, Ms. Reynolds. You won't regret me."

"I pray I don't, Jamie."

Christopher walked into his house, kicking his shoes off at the door. He grinned at the aromas of food filling the air and was grateful that his fiancée had deigned to cook for him that night. The fried chicken smelled divine and the vegetables he knew would accompany the chicken wafted in the house as well. He knew Tiffany was happier than usual and he was enjoying every bit of her joy. The past few nights had included him being welcomed back home to dinner being made.

Still, he knew that Tiffany was the kind of woman that desired a working man. Listening to her talk in the beginning had amused him because she claimed that she was an independent woman. Still, he knew the time would come after a while that she would want to be taken care of and he was fine with taking on the role of sole provider. He was used to taking care of family so things wouldn't be much different with his future wife and their own family. While taking care of Jamie had been an honor to him and a privilege, he also yearned for his own legacy to come about. Although he made the choice to become the caretaker and legal guardian for his niece, he was also ready to be married and enjoy Tiffany.

The conversation would have to come around in a small while about Jamie potentially moving out on her own. As much as he would want both women to coexist in the house together, he knew his woman and he knew his niece. It wouldn't happen well. Besides, he was pretty sure that Jamie was being courted by someone. Should things go well he was pretty sure she would need her own space. He wasn't about to tolerate another man coming in and out of his abode to meet up with his surrogate daughter.

Working at Adams afforded her a nice space to live and it was about high time she started to spread her wings. He'd done all he could do and after the scandal that took place in the company, he wondered if she would have made those same decisions had she had more to lose. It was something he often pondered but they still hadn't talked at length about what forced her hand to deal instead of ringing the alarm.

"Hey baby."

Tiffany walked into the living room and leaned in, kissing him square on the lips. Christopher groaned, enjoying the softness of his woman before she pulled away with a smile.

"Wash up, dinner's about ready," she said, stepping away before he could pull her into his arms again. "You want beer or you want lemonade?"

Christopher smirked, thinking that the question was perfect considering his thought process.

"I think I'll take beer, bae," he said. "Kind of ready to kick back and relax."

"Hm. Maybe I'll join you…or actually no, I'll just drink lemonade."

Christopher smirked, knowing why she passed on the beer. He always thought her so cute and always loved the fact that she was so dedicated to her principles. Tiffany was a virgin and was raised in the same vein that sex came after marriage. Christopher hadn't minded her standard, as easy sex had never impressed him anyway. He was one of the rare men who didn't take pleasure in switching his partners up every so often. Also, he didn't want his niece to see him running around in that manner. He wanted to be the very example of a man she should strive to date. He felt a handful of times she bought a guy around he'd done a good job on that.

"Still, where did I go wrong?"

The question loomed over his head as Tiffany returned with his plate and beverage, sitting it at the dining room table. Christopher stood up to join his fiancée as she returned with her own plate. He chuckled as he realized that there were coasters on the table that were never there before.

"When'd you get coasters?" he questioned, chuckling. "You trying to stop me from being a barbarian?"

She shrugged. "Got some extra time to shop at Tarjay yesterday. They were cute and we needed them."

Tiffany looked over at her man, seeing the covert stress all over him. She was confused on why he was upset being that Jamie had been released not too long ago. Not only had she been released but Christian gave the green light for her to work at Adams again. The restrictions were a little stiff but at the same token, it couldn't be challenged that they let her back in without some kind of recourse. She lost their trust when she made her choice and put her entire career in jeopardy.

"Baby…what's wrong?"

Christopher looked up at Tiffany and shook his head, dismissing her concerns. "Nothing's wrong. Why?"

"I can clearly see that you're thinking hard on something. I can only assume it's Jamie."

Christopher stared down at the plate before him, wondering if he should unload or leave it alone. Part of him knew it made no sense to dwell in the situation as everything had come to an appropriate end. Jamie was let out on bail and with the promise of her testimony, the charges against her would be dropped. The police department made the call that she was coerced and making a deal with her put her up ahead. All of the fault, in his eyes, fell on Jupiter anyway and who knew what the woman had threatened her with.

"A little but it's not to dwell on. This whole shit just been stressful that's all. I hate that it happened."

Christopher dug through the food however, feeling better bit by bit as he ate. Tiffany had made a spread of fried chicken, collard greens, macaroni and cheese and cornbread. The meal was sure to warm him up inside and the beer or two he would have afterward would send him on the way to sweet dreams. Making the sudden decision to be present with his woman instead of in the past with his niece made all the sense in the world.

They talked about their future plans while they ate, Christopher staring at his fiancée and falling in love again as he watched the light shine in her eyes. She found herself doing the same as she saw the excitement come back to him as well. She was excited that he wanted to take the steps forward to move into holy matrimony with her. Most days, she was also surprised because of how long they'd dated without one incident that was past indecency. Most women prayed for a man like Christopher and so had she. She just never hoped to find him. The only thing that was wrong with him, in her mind, was Jamie.

"You've been thinking of any honeymoon spots?"

"I'm leaning heavily into the Maldives," Tiffany said. "But my dream spot would be Jade Mountain."

Christopher smirked. "That's everybody's dream destination, bae. You might also need to wait a few years for that one."

"I might but I'll wait. Still, the Maldives would be nice. I'll even take Tulum."

"You got time to figure it out. Don't settle for what you don't want. Long as I can afford it, we in there."

Tiffany smiled and nodded. Again, she thanked God in her heart for the blessing that was her man.

They'd finished dinner and were on the couch together. Christopher had ESPN on, watching sports highlights. Tiffany was cuddled on his chest, scrolling on her phone, deciding which designer bag would be her first purchase. They'd been chilling in perfect harmony when Christopher's phone rang. She shifted a little as he reached for it. Alarm started to rise as he realized he was getting a call from Emory Hospital.

"Christopher Langley?"

"This is he?"

"I'm calling to inform you that your niece, Jamie Phillips, has been admitted."

"Admitted?" he shot up, almost knocking Tiffany over. "What happened?"

"I'm not able to disclose that over the phone, Mr. Langley, as I have to confirm that you are her next of kin, I can tell you that she was critical but stabilized. I do urge you to be there as I'm sure it'll be a comfort to her to see you there..."

The caller furnished the details of the address and directions to the hospital and Christopher hung up with his hands shaking.

"Jamie's in the hospital."

Tiffany's eyes widened, thrown off at the sudden change of events. Still, she got up and wordlessly got ready as Christopher had done the same thing. In no less than five minutes, they were out of his apartment and on the way to Emory Hospital.

Christopher paced back and forth in the waiting area, unsure of how to feel about all that he had heard.

"I'm under the belief that someone attacked your niece. She was found not even ten blocks away from here. She's suffering from multiple stab wounds that have missed vital organs, bruises on her face, and a slice near her throat. I'm pretty sure the attacker meant to kill her but missed and decided not to chance getting caught. She has quite a few bruises on her body. There's no sign of forced entry so we don't believe she's been raped. We want to keep her for a few days to make sure she's fine."

Christopher was saddened but grateful that his niece would live to see another day. There wasn't a greater blessing in that moment. He was angry that anyone would lay a hand on her and the reasoning wasn't adding up for him.

He paced back and forth, still boggled by the turn of events. Evander King wasn't beneath having anyone beat up that had a hand in stealing any money that belonged to him, still it didn't seem like his handiwork. From what he knew and understood of him, he didn't have his marks tortured before they were killed. Christopher mulled over in his mind that the individual wanted his niece tortured for whatever she'd done to upset them. His next thought was Jupiter, but it didn't reek of her brand either. None of it made sense and the more he tried to reason with it the more he got frustrated.

"Sit down, Chris. Pacing isn't going to help her get better either."

Christopher turned to look at his woman, ready to snap but he restrained himself. Taking her advice, he sat in the chair next to her and turned his attention blankly to the television set that aired the news in the far-right corner.

"*None of this shit making sense...*" he thought. "*Who would want to hurt her?*"

"All this girl attracts is trouble..."

Tiffany had mumbled it, but Christopher had picked it up as if she'd said it loudly. Turning to her, his face furrowed as the anger coursed through him even more.

"Why would you say that? Tiffany, you're talking crazy right now?"

Tiffany's back went up. "Am I, Christopher? You had to take on a loan just to get her out. Now that she's out, she's in the hospital? We're supposed to be planning a wedding and now what? You gonna have to pour more money into her just to stay alive? Off of some shit that was *her* fault?!"

"Tiffany, I'm not hearing you right now. Matter of fact, go home."

"You're in no condition to be alone," she spat. "Look at you! Falling apart and acting like you're sending me anywhere! You're out of your mind."

"And you're out of yours for talking about my blood like that. You *know* this shit wasn't her fault, Tiffany!"

Tiffany didn't say another word for their duration in the waiting room. She felt abased minutes after they stopped talking but still couldn't find it in her to apologize. In her mind, Jamie was beginning to be a huge liability. As far as she was concerned, nobody told her to go along with Jupiter's plans. Nobody told her *not* to air out anything that was going on with her knowledge. Closed mouths don't get fed but they also don't get saved, either.

That was her stance and she was sticking to it.

Christian drove up to Evander's house, taking a moment to admire the surroundings. She wondered to herself exactly what one man needed with all the space that he had. Still, she decided that she wasn't upset at it.

Evander's home had to easily be seven bedrooms from what the façade entailed. Christian decided the curb appeal could be a little better, but it wasn't overall bad. It made her grin to see the almost grandiose settings of her boyfriend who she would have taken for an apartment kind of man.

Her phone rang and she smirked as she picked it up, staring for a moment at the picture of Evander that came up whenever he called. Accepting the call, she held her phone to her face, her smirk still in place.

"Are you so overwhelmed you can't figure out where to park Ms. Adams?" Evander's voice purred into her ear.

Christian laughed. "No, just enjoying the scenery. I admit that I'm taken aback at your place of residence."

"I promise the inside isn't as grand. My bed is waiting for you to hop in it."

"Don't tempt me, Mr. King," Christian laughed. "After the day I've had I don't think you want to allude to your bed being the one who scores tonight."

Evander chuckled and directed her to where she should park before hanging up. Christian wasted no time, the sudden yearning to see her man overwhelming her after hearing his voice.

The news of Jamie's hospitalization had reached her and the rest of the Partners. They'd all met with Christopher at the hospital and explored every option they had as far as payment for her surgery. Being that Jamie had just been reinstated at Adams' as a new employee, her health benefits couldn't cover the cost of her stay. The three ladies pooled together money on behalf of Christopher, knowing he'd already spent a pretty penny on Jamie's release. Christian was doing her best to get over Christopher's bloodshot eyes. It was obvious that the assailing of his niece would take him some time to get over. Still, it boggled Christian's mind at who could do such a thing to another human being. Granted, it was obvious that Jamie was going to testify shortly but with Jupiter already being remanded for the crime, who else could want to hurt Jamie?

Though the answer was obvious, Christian hoped against hope that her thought process wasn't correct. Nobody else wanted to explore the possibility but the moment might come when they found they had another head to chop off before it multiplied.

Christian approached the garage door after she stepped out of her car, with her overnight bag in tow. She sighed, the images of the evening still plaguing her. Christopher's tired countenance. The tension between him and Tiffany. Sharin and Monica looking as haunted as she had when they all walked out of the hospital.

"*Just when I think shit is getting better something else pops up.*" That'd been Monica's thoughts as the threesome walked to their respective vehicles.

Christian sighed, pushing the door open and smirking at the drop zone she entered. It might've been true that it wasn't a spectacular spectacle, but she felt the comfort in the space. She remembered Evander telling her that he was raised a certain way and didn't want to change from those standards. Though his house was reading as a bachelor pad of sorts it was also obvious that he was raised with more space than one could want. It was also of note that he was prepared to expand his family when the time came. That warmed Christian's heart to a degree.

She quashed those hopes before her heart dug out the watering pot to nourish them.

"Where are you, already?"

Christian giggled, walking further into the house. She spied Evander in the kitchen, in front of the oven. Her smile spread as she smelled the aromas that escaped once he pulled the sheet pan out and placed it on the oven.

"Ooh la la," she said, grinning. "What are we eating tonight, boyfriend?"

"We're eating a simple meal of salmon, potatoes, and asparagus," he said. "So get freshened up and meet me in the dining room."

"You didn't mention the wine pairing," Christian said, crossing her arms. "I'll give this restaurant a bad review if it doesn't come with reputable wine."

Evander smirked, leaning in to kiss her lips. He nipped lightly at her bottom lip before pulling away.

"I have some Grigio for you," he replied. "Do I pass, secret shopper?"

Christian giggled and then pulled away. Following his directions, she stepped into the half bathroom to freshen up and stopped short of her reflection.

Her skin would pink up because it was a degree too hot or if she walked too fast but neither case was true at that moment. Seeing herself flushed and glowy from the little bit of attention that she received from Evander had surprised her. She knew she was into him, but the revelation was almost overwhelming of just how grand an effect he had on her.

It was obvious to anybody that looked at her that she was in love with him. It was also glaringly obvious to her that she was and the more she thought about it, the more she made peace with the fact. It warmed her heart that she was, for once, in a healthy relationship and that things were going well. It was going almost too well and that thought was the one to cause her heartbeat to race just a little bit.

Pulling herself away from her anxious thoughts, Chritian finished freshening up and then joined her boyfriend at the dining room table. She giggled at his annoyed expression as he watched her enter.

"You love taking your sweet time outside of work. If we were inside of Adams' you'd be trying to move at the speed of light."

Christian smirked, settling into her chair. "Well, I'd been through a lot tonight, so I think that's why I'm moving slow. I'm still trying to process everything."

Christian settled into her seat, reaching for the fork that Evander provided next to her plate and began to eat. She moaned as the flavors hit her palette and looked at her boyfriend with a smile on her face.

"This is nice, babe," she said. "Kind of impressed you can actually do more than boil water."

"Hm. So you're trying to have me butt naked with an apron on from now on?"

"Sounds like your fantasy, baby. I'm good." Evander's smile spread and Christian tore off a piece of asparagus and threw it at him. His chuckles made her laugh in return. "You're so mannish!" she squealed. "I'm not fulfilling that type of fantasy at all."

"Hmm. So, you say. Still, I can enjoy you in quite a few ways, love." Christian blushed at the way she remembered him enjoying her. It'd been a bit of a delay from the last time, so she was elated when he'd invited her over to his house after hours. "So, what happened?"

169

"Christopher's niece was attacked earlier this evening. The hospital's examinations proved that she was definitely attacked and they're looking into investigating who possibly did it. We're all sad…we just welcomed her back to work."

"Welcomed back? Wasn't she a part of the scandal in the first place?" Evander rose a brow. "Why should her job be restored?"

"She was coerced to file the documents. She wasn't the actual person who siphoned your money," Christian answered. Her brow rose as well, unsure of why his mood shifted.

"I guess," he shrugged. "Seems to me everyone involved should be locked up."

"She was coerced, Vann. She stood to gain nothing out of the whole deal except to keep her job and hope it didn't fall apart for her when it did. If she were acting as a willing accomplice, trust me she wouldn't be back. Still, she's on probation for two years' time and exempt from any promotions that arise in Adams' for same. She's been punished enough for her part in it, believe me."

Evander was ready to argue his point but realized he'd be overstepping his boundaries. He knew if he had his way the lady would never see viable employment again but at the same token, he couldn't quite tell his woman what to do as far as her business. Also, he knew it was hardly the woman's first option to go along with the scheme that played out. Being coerced changed the game entirely. The young lady, from what he remembered in his own investigation, definitely didn't seem to be the kind to steal from people.

Evander chewed on his thoughts while he chewed on his food. Looking at Christian as she ate, he finally saw the tiredness around her and felt abased about how he was ready to start an argument. He couldn't imagine what was going through her mind but had to know what she'd witnessed earlier was weighing on her heavily.

"She was poised to testify to everything that happened in exchange for bail," Christian said. "Her uncle spent a pretty penny on her release. The hospital bills from this would've killed him. He planned on getting married next year. This… is a mess."

Christian's plate was hardly touched and watching the forlorn look on her face caused Evander to push back from his table and walk snatch up his phone. Christian looked on at him, curiosity and confusion entering the chat of her mind. It hadn't taken long before the opening notes for one of John Legend's songs flowed through speakers she hadn't taken notice of in his living room earlier.

Evander tossed his phone on the couch and reached out to Christian who looked down at his hand and back up at him.

"Really?" she questioned. "Vann, I-"

"Come on. Dance with me."

Christian laid a hand into his own and allowed herself to be pulled into his arms. The mid tempo beat filled her ears as they swayed back and forth.

"Put everything away for a minute, bae," Evander said, talking through the warmth in his chest. "You've done all you can do. Now put it away."

Christian sighed. It was a hard sell, as Christopher's reddened eyes were still sharp in her mind's eye. Though the team offered to pay for the medical bills incurred and most of Christopher's upset had been lowered as he thanked them, it was still hurting him that someone harmed his niece. Christian wondered if they'd made a misstep in employing her again so soon but was brought back to the present as she felt Evander's hand lay at the small of her back.

"Bae. You've done all you can do," he repeated. "Take it easy."

Christian looked up at Evander, ready to protest when his lips took hers. When he let go, she sighed. Deciding to just take his advice, she laid her head on his chest and allowed the rhythm of the music to be their guide as they did an offbeat two step to the music.

"Hmm. I lost my appetite," Christian whispered, as the song came to a close. "I still want my wine, though."

Evander smirked. "You're such a lush."

Evander leaned in and kissed her lips softly. Pulling back, he swept his woman off of her feet and gloried in her squeal.

"You've never complained before."

"Of course not. You get extra amorous…especially when you drink that red," he grinned. "Still, let me be your Grigio."

Leaning in, he kissed her again, this time slipping her his tongue. Christian moaned into the kiss, loving the sensation it bought.

He pulled away, enjoying the flush in her skin. She bit her lip, not bothering to hide her duress from him.

"Shall we?" he questioned, turning towards the stairs of his home. Christian giggled, leaning up to give an answering kiss of her own.

"We shall."

A few rounds and a shared shower later, the twosome were back at the scene of their passion. The television was on but neither was paying attention. Christian had been the one to first lean back into Evander and kiss him squarely on the mouth. The chuckle came from his chest as he leaned in to return her affections. He pulled back, deciding to sit up and pulled her onto his lap, smirking as she tried to cuddle against his chest.

"Nah, I need you to look me in my eyes. I have a question for you."

"Hm?" She was thrown off as she made to straddle him instead, looking into his dark eyes. Evander reached up to caress her cheek.

"Why haven't you told me you love me yet?" he questioned. "I already know you do and you already know you do."

Christian raised a brow, "How do you know, then?"

Evander smirked. "You told me after the first time we made love…told me you loved me and fell asleep."

Christian giggled, barely remembering the moment but not knowing that it'd been real. "So why haven't you said anything before now?"

"I was wondering how long you were going to hold onto that. So far, it looks like you were going to keep it from me forever."

Christian's brows furrowed as she grabbed the hand that was still caressing her cheek.

"That's not true," she said. "How do you know I wasn't waiting on you to say the same thing? You know my history."

"I do. So imagine my shock when you even utter the words at all."

Christian laughed. "I'm not as hard of a woman as you think."

"I don't think you're a hard woman at all. Guarded, but not hard. In your world you have to be, so I honestly haven't held it against you. I just...I just want you to know you can trust me, baby. I'm not here to hurt you. I'm here to love you."

"Hmph. Not sure you're here to sue me?"

Evander chuckled, pulling her into him by her waist to steal another kiss from her. He bit her bottom lip lightly in response to her sarcasm.

"I was there to sue Adams' Accounting. I wasn't prepared to fall over myself over the boss," he said. "I wasn't prepared at all. I knew once I walked out of that office that I had to have you. Still, baby..."

Christian smirked. "Business is business."

"If you are wondering though, yes, I love you. Yes, I want you. Yes, I need you. I never had qualms about being with women; it was just that nobody ever struck me for the long haul. I was focused on my business. But you came along and now I want to do it all with you."

"What do you mean?"

"Marriage, children, the big house somewhere in Buckhead," he said. "Get some land and build it from the ground up. I want that with you."

"Hm. You looking for me to settle down from my business?"

"Nah. I'm only looking for you to figure out the balance. Other than that..." Evander shrugged. "I'd be wrong to demand for you to stop. I just wanted you to know, bae. This is real for me."

The tears rolled down her face, unchecked. She knew that her heart burst with joy in that moment but what she hadn't known was the tears rolled down her face as if a well burst within her.

Evander was alarmed, not understanding that her tears had been in joy. He reached to wipe her tears with his face painted in concern. Christian reached up to grab his hand, shocked when she felt the tears on her face. They started dropping on her legs and the realization made her giggle.

"I'm not sad, Vann. I'm happy," she said, sighing. "I love you so much." Evander's face softened. "I want to cuddle now."

Evander chuckled but they both shifted so that they were lying on their sides. Christian snuggled closer into his chest and kissed him where his heart beat. Her eyelids grew heavy and she embraced both the comfort of her man and the sounds of the television in the background lulling her away to sleep. A contented sigh left her mouth.

"I love you, Vann."

172

She'd drifted off to sleep again, so she missed the moment when Evander leaned in to kiss her forehead and replied the same to her. Still, her conscious admission gave him peace. He held her in his arms for some time before sleep overtook him as well.

The next morning, Christopher was roused by what his future might smell like on mornings in the weekend. Breakfast wafted around the house, bacon being the most dominant smell that pulled him out of bed. He winced, feeling his hangover come on.

He remembered the bottle of Uncle Nearest that he finished before passing out on his bed and groaned, wondering how he thought that would end his troubles. Still, he stood up and walked slowly to his bedroom door.

Tiffany was a vision in the kitchen as she cooked and Christopher grinned, though part of him was still incensed about her comments from the night before. It bothered him how Tiffany viewed his niece but at the same token understood that the drama was weighing heavily on everybody. Home was spilling into work. Work was spilling into home. They were engaged and not much time had gone by before another hurdle had to be jumped over.

If Christian, Sharin, and Monica hadn't come together with the funds to cover the hospital bill, he would have been in a world of trouble trying to pay for a wedding and a honeymoon. Not to mention, the house fund was looking shaky after he dipped into it to put up for Jamie's bail. The thought of it all threatened to make him reach for the bottle again but a violent roll of his stomach warned him that wasn't a good idea.

Christopher walked over to the entrance of his kitchen, just as Tiffany started pulling bacon slices off of the pan.

"Bae," he said, getting her attention.

Tiffany turned to him, sighing when they locked eyes. She turned back around and kept moving. "I'm just here to cook because I know you've been in here drinking. I'm going home after I'm done."

Christopher sighed, walking up to her as she picked up the bowl to beat the eggs. He turned her to him. "Listen bae, let's talk."

"I don't want to talk right now. I'm not in the mood," she said. "I'm fixing you breakfast. You can eat and *maybe* we'll talk. Maybe not. But right now, you need to wash up and I need to finish."

Christopher sighed, playing it her way. Deciding to shower and freshen up he took his time, as his stomach was begging to be filled with sustenance. On one hand he knew he felt better than he deserved and on the other he wished he could go back to sleep and sleep away the past few months.

Tiffany sighed again as she plated his food. Her appetite had vanished over the state of her fiancé when she looked at him earlier. Never in the whole time they'd been dating had she ever seen Christopher hung over and unkempt. It was shocking and hurtful to see him in pain over the choices that his niece made as a grown woman. In her mind, her choices were affecting their life and it wasn't fair in the least.

In her eyes, she wasn't worth the trouble that Christopher went through.

Tiffany sat his plate on the dining room table, sucking her teeth. Shaking her head, she walked back into the kitchen to pour him a glass of orange juice to round off his meal and decided she would eat later. Not only was the state of her boyfriend hurtful to see, but she knew the words that she said out loud the night before had been heinous. As much as she didn't like the girl, it was obvious that she didn't sign up for a stranger to beat her to within an inch of her life.

Still. In her mind she bought it on herself.

Christopher walked back into the dining area, thirty minutes later looking fresher but still in need of sustenance. He settled in as Tiffany laid his plate in front of him. She turned to walk away when Christopher reached out to grab her hand. She rolled her eyes as she turned around and met her fiance's. Christopher motioned for the chair across from him and waited until she settled in. Once she had, he took a deep breath.

"I didn't appreciate what you said." He started off, "I'm going to start off by saying that. I'm not going to pretend Jamie is innocent. That'd be insulting to you and everybody else that had to go through it the past few months but what I won't tolerate is you speaking bad about her as if she welcomed someone trying to beat her within an inch of her life."

Tiffany started bouncing her leg up and down, the anger starting to peak in her once again. She wondered why it seemed he took everyone else's side except hers. It already annoyed her that he made a case for Christian's attitude towards her as of late. At present he was ignoring her feelings and she wasn't sure she cared for it. She opened her mouth to say something when he raised his hand to silence her response.

"I also get that the incidents are stressful for you. I get it, baby. Still, I raised her. She's like a daughter to me. Up until this point, I didn't have any true issues with her. I believe I raised her well and raised her right. She's a grown woman now and despite what you think she's paid for her mistakes-"

"She damn well is paying for it. Listen, I don't know what you want me to do. You raised her good, cool. She still set out to do stupid shit and she's not the only one paying for it. Christian's been looking stupid for months. The Partners. You've been the most stressed I've seen you, *ever*. I get that she might've been a good girl but now, in my eyes she's an incompetent woman and the sooner you open your eyes and see her for what she is, the better."

Christopher's eyes widened.

"Tiff…"

"No, because if they hadn't stepped in, we wouldn't have a wedding! You would move Heaven and Earth for this girl and leave us straggling and it's not fair! I didn't sign up to play the background, Christopher. You better pray this is the last thing that pops up on the radar as far as her because now at this point, who knows who else's life is endangered because of *her* decisions. If she has paid assassins trying to take her out, then it's deeper than we thought."

Christopher sighed. He didn't want to argue but make peace with his woman. Still, it seemed like she didn't want peace but war. It was all he could do to just get up from the table and seek solitude all over again.

"That's an avenue that has to be explored but it still isn't her fault. It's the fault of whoever set out to hurt her. The sooner you see that, the better. That's like someone breaking into Adams' and they threaten you to open the door to Christian's office-"

"Christopher, how-"

"-and they threaten to kill you. Are you going to tell me you're not going to open that door? Especially if Christian's not on the other side?"

Tiffany fell silent, already knowing the answer to the question. She surely wouldn't sacrifice her life for Christian Adams' nor the body of Adams' Accounting. She had love for her boss and fellow coworkers but knew in her heart what move she would have made. It all made the pieces fall into place as far as Jamie's position.

"Exactly. I still don't know the whole story, but it had to be deeper than her job getting threatened. None of this shit sounds like Jupiter's work. Bad as I don't like the girl, even she has limits. Something's off and we'll get to the bottom of it."

Tiffany sighed, heavily. She understood Jamie better but still harbored resentment towards her.

"Like I said, I get it. I know this is rough, but we'll make it through." Christopher said, "Just bear with me, baby."

Tiffany sighed again.

"Long as you take today off. You're in no condition to go into work. Your team should be able to run the building for a day without you."

Christopher nodded.

"I still have to call Christian and then set up the operation before I settle in again. I'm going to check on Jamie in a little while. You coming?"

Tiffany sighed, "You know I'm coming."

Christopher sighed, with a dopey smile. It was enough to melt Tiffany's heart all over again. It was as if his smile reminded her of what life with him truly was and that the other things were only small inconveniences.

It was almost as if their wedding vows were already challenging her, for better or worse.

Chapter
Eighteen

Two nights later saw Christian getting her makeup done in the living room of her house, trying to will her heart to slow down. She cursed Jasmine in her mind, still not understanding why she let the woman bully her into the position she was currently sitting in.

"You're my friend, Christian and you're down bad. I can't call myself your friend and not make the best moves on your behalf."

She swallowed a sigh and possibly some tears at the remembrance of Jasmine's confession. The truth was, Christian was someone who couldn't be moved unless you touched the heart of her. As far as business she could be cold and exacting but when her heart came to play, she was able to fold. Being that Adams' was both her business and her heart, she was willing to do anything necessary, including more than likely being humiliated by Glenda Smith.

Glenda Smith was a woman who came from the bottom and worked her way up to the journalism world with equal parts education and networking. She landed her job at WAGA-TV and has been the face for the past five years. Her Howard education was something she touted like a rare gem, only second behind the backing of the world-renowned Zeta Phi Beta. Glenda walked around with her head held high and if her first impression hadn't left a bad taste in Christian's mouth, she might've admired the woman.

As it were, her reputation laid in her hands. Christian didn't like the vulnerability it caused in her one bit.

After her makeup was done, she was escorted to the living area. The lighting was being set up by various stagehands and the producer was sharing his notes with Glenda, who's excitement grated at Christian's nerves.

Christian felt like a rock as she settled in, praying inwardly that the interview would be quick and to the point. She was surprised when Glenda offered her a soft smile and motioned for someone to bring them both some tea.

"These lights are bright, aren't they? People always do their best to run from it, but I welcome it. I suggest you do the same, Miss Adams. You look beautiful under them."

"Don't try to flatter me, Miss Smith." Christian said, "We both see I'm sweating."

"You're supposed to. Light emits heat."

She winked and it was all Christian could do not to jump over her coffee table and pummel the woman. Of course, she caught the double entendre that she thought Christian would be too stupid to notice. Still, she knew she needed to keep her eyes on the prize.

There was nothing more important than restoring the good name of her company.

Before she knew it, the producer was counting them down and Glenda sat towards the camera with her camera-ready smile intact. A quick introduction of the interview was made and suddenly, Glenda turned to Christian, still smiling. Christian smiled back but she couldn't keep up the same appearances for long.

"Unless you're in the accounting world, many of Atlanta's residents or the rest of the country wouldn't know Christian Adams' name or of her business-Adams' Accounting-otherwise. Still, a few months ago the accusation that she ran an embezzling ring in her office stopped the press. Adams' started her firm nearly six years ago and enjoyed incredible growth for a start-up. Millions of dollars in funding from crowd sharing and generous donations from old money benefactors of the south keeps Adams' running. So it was a shock to hear that the 32 year old CEO would have to go underground to stretch her wealth…"

Christian admired Glenda's delivery but still wanted to spit at the fact that the scenario was even happening at all. Still she managed to wear a thin lipped smile through the introduction. She wasn't sure that she was emanating power and confidence in that moment but all things considered, a lesser person wouldn't have gone through with the interview at all. She was doing her best to rise up to the challenge but with every breath, the challenge felt like a heavy weight pressed on her chest. It was all she could do to keep from reaching up to rub her chest as Glenda kept talking.

"…many developments have happened since the explosion of the news that's been cycling around and I thought it would be a good idea to catch up with the CEO and check in on how everything is going and to give her the chance to state her case to the nation and more importantly to us the good people of Atlanta. Firstly, Chrsitian, thank you for inviting us into your lovely home."

"It's a pleasure to have you, Glenda."

Christian almost thought she saw a twinkle in her eye at the response and wondered if she wasn't so bad after all. That was until she asked her next question.

"So, Ms. Adams, walk me through it."

"Through it?"

"Yeah. Walk me through the day when it all fell down for you. I will admit to being there that day of course as we caught a tip and so did a few other newscasters."

Christian's smile faltered and she felt herself start to shake. It hadn't been that long ago so it was no shock when the memory reappeared fresh in her mind. It was almost like it happened minutes ago.

"I pulled up to the building with my mind set on starting my day. Then I see a whole gang of news reporters in front of the building. I heard another lady first…but I only heard the words embezzlement ring."

Glenda nodded, her expression turning into a frown.

"So, hearing that pretty much put me up in arms because…an *embezzlement ring*? I'm a girl from the suburbs. I had a pretty strict upbringing, so I barely had time to sneak around to do anything foul so to hear those words was pretty jarring…"

Christian wanted to point out that she remembered Glenda's presence but knew it wasn't the right move. It was tempting to dig in but stopped short of remembering Jasmine's instructions. She wasn't supposed to be emotional toward Glenda at all as she was doing her job. The emotionalism wouldn't gain her brownie points in the long run with the audience so she was better off having pissing contests behind closed doors, if at all.

"…my security came and removed me from the scene but in the next few minutes I had learned that my accountants that were in charge of Evander King's account with us had stolen from him. They've since been locked up. One of them will face trial and the other one will be acquitted for her part in it."

"Acquitted? How so?" Glenda questioned.

"Because she was coerced…technically she didn't steal but she withheld information that would have not made this thing the crap show that it became. Her job was to generate the forms and file them. She was the junior to my senior accountant."

Glenda raised a brow, "That information was new. From the little we know there was two women apart of the heist, but coercion wasn't apart of the story we knew-"

"-Of course, it wasn't. It was a miracle that the arrests made it to the news because for the first few weeks, my name was being dragged through the mud as the principal thief in it all. I have to admit hurt, knowing how gossip mills work that any other time they can find the correct information but in this case they took their time, especially in Atlanta to speak on what was real."

Christian blinked her eyes, surprised when they watered. She berated herself, knowing that it was yet too early to show emotion. However, the action caused Glenda's face to melt into a look of concern. A head nod toward her producer translated to him bringing tissues to Christian when a few tears fell from her eyes. She looked at Glenda and was still shocked when her facial expression hadn't changed.

"I can see this whole thing has been wrecking havoc on your life." Her tone softened, "What's it been like, really?"

Christian sighed, "It's been hell. Unfortunately, in house issues blew up worse than they should have."

"Hm. That does lead us to Jupiter Classon. What motive do you think she had for what she'd done?"

"To this day, I'm very unsure."

"So why keep her around?" Glenda leaned in, "If she were that problematic why would such a body be allowed to stay employed at your business?"

"Because she was one of the best accountants there. Our clients loved her, and frankly, she made us look good."

"Was there any thought of giving the woman a promotion?"

Christian sighed, suddenly wanting to strangle Jupiter all over again. She looked up at Glenda and wondered when she'd gotten comfortable with the woman. Although the twosome were still in the midst of a live interview, it felt like it was them alone. Christian wasn't sure when the energy shifted but it had.

"I did. Like I said, she was one of the best. Her attitude left much to be desired, but it was obvious that she was probably better suited to be a managerial type. I'm unsure though that she would have fit in with myself and the Partners very well based on that much alone. Her respect for Sharin was low being that she's from a different class than us all. Still, without Sharin's help, or any of the Partners Adams' wouldn't be what it is today."

"There were questions about Sharin Reynold's involvement. It was debunked rather quickly."

Christian giggled, "It should have been. Sharin had absolutely no reason to steal."

"None?"

"I've been trying to speak of Sharin as my professional colleague but knowing her as a friend, you'd know exactly why it's ludicrous. Anybody who's anybody and everybody knows that Sharin is an heiress and has no need for the money that was stolen from Kings' Tires. Add to that, her fiancé is a very established successful real estate broker. My friend has no need for money…working at Adams'…building Adams' with me was her motive."

Christian swallowed the ball in her throat and reached for the water that sat at the side of her. Glenda nodded, changing direction with her questioning.

"She was suspended for some weeks however, according to the blogs and other news sources. Why was that done?"

"She had to be cleared. Either I did it or the police did it." Christian sighed,

Glenda nodded, "And she's since been restored."

"Yes. Once the police cleared her of any involvement."

"So back to the other young lady. What happens to her?"

"She'll more than likely do jail time and lose her license. She might practice accounting, but it won't be as a CPA."

Glenda chuckled at the resolute tone in Christian's voice. She wasn't sure why but more and more she liked the woman. She hadn't known much about her either until the fateful day she'd pushed her microphone in front of her face, but she found herself researching her after the fact.

"So, overall, things are slowly calming down," Christian said. "I will say that this was the most embarrassing, emotional thing I've ever been through as a businesswoman and entrepreneur. I run my company under a spirit of excellence and to have to go through the many changes I have over the past few months?"

"I could imagine." Glenda responded, "So, is it possible to ask about the details concerning the truce you and Kings' Tires have come up with?"

"I hate talking about it." Christian laughed, despite the question, "Adams' covered his losses for fifteen million. He generously waived lawyer's fees of almost $700,000 so we're grateful for that."

Glenda nodded, "So what's your takeaway from all that's happened to you? If you were to tell past Christian Adams what she should do to avoid the situation, what would you say?"

"Pay attention to every red flag and pull the weeds out by the root. There's too much talent in the world to put up with someone just because they're great at what they do. You can teach a person a job but at the end of the day? Baby, you can't teach a human being to be civil. If mama or papa didn't instill that in you already, it's a lost cause."

Glenda nodded her head somberly and reached across to shake her hand.

"Christian Adams, it's been a pleasure. I hope to see you rise out of the ashes of this going forward."

"Trust and believe me Glenda, we will."

About three days later saw Christian and Jasmine meeting again at Adams'. Jasmine was all smiles, and it was enough to make Christian giggle at her friend's excitement. While she was a normally fun person to be around, when she was at work, Jasmine was all business and made no bones about it.

"I'm just proud of you, Christian. All professional...listened and didn't come for Glenda's head. The interview doing numbers, girl. You might want to prep your staff for the influx coming back in after this."

"You're sounding hopeful, Jasmine." Christian said, grinning, "It's only been three days and I'm still getting dragged."

"Don't pay attention to that. You're not going to convince everybody, but we just want the majority to spread the news around and understand the basic shit. At the end of the day, we want to drive the point home that Adams' is still reputable."

Christian nodded, "Anything else I should keep an eye out for?"

"This doesn't have much to do with the company at this point but I'm pretty sure there's a third party in this that the police aren't trying to search for...my contact mentioned that Jamie probably should have been put in witness protection, but I hadn't thought..."

Jasmine sighed, the guilt sitting on her shoulders. She didn't see the need when Terry mentioned it at the coffee shop. On the surface it didn't seem like those measures needed to be taken. All suspects were in custody, and it was already a given that Jamie was coerced. If there was a third party involved however, it'd been too soon to welcome her back to work.

"Honestly, that was on us. There is possibly a third party, but we have no proof other than a weird visit to Sharin's house..."

"Wait, what? So, there was a possibility that this woman was in trouble and nobody thought to tell me?" Jasmine gasped, "What the fuck, Christian?"

"I didn't think it serious, myself. Again, no real proof other than speculation."

Jasmine paced back and forth but stopped short and then took a seat again.

"There's nothing we can do about it now." Jasmine said, sighing, "But...I believe if there's a third party in all of this, they need to be bought in. Who do you think it might be?"

Christian sighed, the thought of the woman's name making her nauseous. "Chastity McCain."

"Hm. The McCain family? Oh, Sharin's cousin! Well…shit." Jasmine said, "Yeah, if she's the cause then the police will be hard pressed to make an arrest. She wouldn't stay in for long either."

"Rich privilege biting us in the ass as usual."

"Other than that, Red…I have nothing." Jasmine mentioned, "Your boyfriend's contributions to your social media have helped. This interview put things over the top. Honestly and truly my job here is done. I'll be keeping an eye out every now and again, but the company will keep thriving."

Christian nodded. Evander had come in, good on his word, to shoot one-minute videos delivering his testimony as far as Adams' was concerned. The positive reception on social media surprised Christian but she learned that her man was indeed an important figure in Georgia who's word people ate up like catnip. If she's known the reception would be so great she might've asked him sooner. Still, she was glad things turned out the way they had.

"Also, it wouldn't hurt for you two to go public now." Jasmine mentioned, a smirk in her tone. "It won't add any more undue stress…for the business."

Christian giggled. "It might for me. They might think I gave him some to get out of paying. I've been enjoying the privacy aspect so far though. Just key people know so that's good enough for me."

"Much better that way, too." Jasmine agreed. "Well Red, for the interim I'm going to move on to other clients that need my attention, but I'll be keeping an eye on the progress of Adams' restoration. So far though, I highly doubt you'll see me more than twice a month at this point for the next few months."

"I'm unsure if I'll miss you or not."

"We girls, hit me up to hang girl. You know I'm fun outside my job."

"Definitely." Christian giggled. "I got you. I need to blow off some steam soon, anyway."

Christian's phone rang at that very moment. She looked down, smiling to see Evander's name across her iPhone. Jasmine gave a cheeky grin upon watching her friend's reaction to her boyfriend calling.

"Go on and talk to your lover boy. I'm heading out…it's time to do onboarding with a new client." Jasmine rolled her eyes, "I'll catch up with you."

Christian nodded as Jasmine made her exit. She picked up the call just as it reached the fourth ring.

"Hey baby." Christian answered, warmly, "What's up?"

"How's your day looking? I was thinking I'd scoop you up when you were finished for the day."

"I'll be done in about an hour." Christian said, sighing, "I'm tempted to leave now but I have some things to run by Sharin and Monica."

"Well text me when you're ready for me, baby."

"Okay." Christian said. "Love you."

"You love me, baby?" Evander questioned, laughter in his tone. "Let me find out…"

Christian giggled. "Boy, bye."

Hanging up, she picked up her office phone to page Monica and waited to finish the day off talking shop with her colleague.

Christopher and Jamie walked toward the exit of Emory Hospital after visiting Jamie. She'd been awake and alert when the twosome visited, and it'd been emotional. Tiffany watched as her fiancé unabashed, wept over his niece, undone by the violence that had occurred against her. Although she was still exhausted of Jamie and her overall life, Tiffany's heart softened once she saw how much pain she was in. She understood what Christopher had been trying to get through to her. No matter what her role was in the fracas, nobody asked to be beaten to an inch of their life.

The sadness hung over them both like a cloak when angry yelling filled the lobby as they entered.

"I want to see Jamie Phillips and I want to see her *immediately*! Do you understand ma'am? I'll have this whole hospital left without a dollar and then everyone can thank *you* for it."

"I don't care how much money your family has or who your family is, sir. If your name isn't on a list of approved visitors, you're not going to see the patient. So far it's not."

Both Christopher and Tiffany's ears perked up to hear Jamie's name and took in the scene. They took in the man who towered over the desk, grabbing onto the ends of it with both hands. His body was starting to vibrate. The administrator's body language showed ambivalence, as if she dealt with his type on a regular basis. Christopher wasn't sure whether she was being extra difficult because of his status or not.

Tiffany looked up at Christopher who already made a move to walk over to the front desk where the young man and the administrator were having a stare-off. Christopher laid a hand on the man's shoulder and offered the administrator a smile.

"Actually, you can put his name on the list." Christopher said, "It's no issue at all for him to visit."

The administrator rose a brow.

"And you are?"

"Christopher Ballentyne, Jamie Smith's uncle." He said, "You can confirm with any of your staff if you need to-"

"-ID, please."

Without another word, Christopher dug his identification card out of his pocket and presented it to the lady. Once she nodded, she silently typed and clicked for what seemed like five more minutes. Then she looked up at the twosome standing before her and smiled wanly.

"*Now* you're allowed to see her."

"Good." The unknown man replied, with a tight-lipped smile of his own, "Have a good day, ma'am."

The young man turned to Christopher, opening his mouth to thank him when he held up a hand.

"No thanks necessary. Matter of fact, you're going to thank me by answering a few of my questions. Let's start with your name, sir."

"Samuel McCain."

Christopher's brows furrowed at the last name. As his face furrowed, Samuel nodded.

"Yes, she's my sister."

"Yeah...we need to speak."

Samuel nodded grimly. As much as he didn't want to have the conversation, it was necessary. Samuel already had an idea of who was behind his girlfriend laying in a hospital bed and anyone who could help his cause was deeply appreciated.

"Let's take a ride. I'm going to drop my lady off and we'll chop it up. Cool?"

Tiffany walked up to the twosome just as she heard Christopher's last few words to Samuel and found herself shaking her head.

"You're not dropping me off anywhere." She said, "What business do you have with him?"

Christopher eyed Tiffany and shook his head, indicating that he wouldn't hear any argument she had to make. In his mind, he didn't need to hear any side remarks from his girlfriend about Jamie's judgement. Christopher respected that Jamie didn't like how things had turned out and while they were working through that, he knew he couldn't take any more of her thoughts if she was going to keep complaining about Jamie. It would be too much for him to bear.

He wanted to get to the bottom of things and as he finally had an opening to do so, he was taking it.

"I'm dropping you home and I'll call you later." He said, "Let's go."

Tiffany wanted to argue but decided not to. She watched as the men settled on meeting at Christopher's place and she quietly got in the car with her man and decided that for the interim, she would mind her business. It wasn't like he wouldn't tell her all she needed to know in the long run.

Samuel stepped into Christopher's apartment, taking it in as he never stepped inside in all the time he'd been dating Jamie. Most interactions happened at his private apartment. If ever she visited his family they never stayed past dinner as he didn't want his private life shoved in his parent's face. Chastity and his stepmother were already vocal about not liking Jamie for him and as far as he was concerned, he didn't want that energy around his woman.

Christopher gestured for him to have a seat. Samuel was surprised when Christopher offered him water or anything else to drink but he declined. When

Christopher came from the kitchen with a can of beer and settled in, Samuel had to sympathize with the man. He hadn't been able to see Jamie much during all that happened, and it killed him. For this man to have to witness his loved one going through the pits, it had to have wrecked him.

"So. First off, I'm upset that I'm meeting you under these circumstances. I knew Jamie was seeing someone, but it never came up who."

Samuel nodded. "Yeah. She wasn't ready for us to meet yet. I wasn't sure why and I hadn't pushed it. She speaks of you highly."

Christopher grinned. "I have to assume you're a good dude. But...I have questions."

Samuel nodded. "I might have answers."

"I just want to know first off, why I haven't seen you around much? You're related to Sharin I have to assume..."

"Through marriage but yeah, I grew up with Sharin. My father married Chastity's mother when I was just going into junior high school."

"You've been dating my niece all this time and I haven't run into you."

"To be fair, that was dumb luck. I met her visiting Adams' to hang out with Sharin. She was working in her department and honestly, we bumped into each other when I was on the way out. One thing led to another and it's been about two years now."

"Okay, cool." Christopher said, "That aside...she's been to jail and you only now show up when she's in the hospital. Explain that."

Samuel sighed, heaviness suddenly cloaking his shoulders. Christopher watched, eyes furrowed, awaiting an answer.

"I couldn't actively be around because I come from a high-profile family. There would be questions and scandal if I were to publicly visit. It's bad enough that her name got twisted in with the other lady who actually stole the money."

"You couldn't visit on the low?"

"No." Samuel said, "It's not that I care about my reputation more than her, it's just that with my family, it can become a mess. My father already doesn't approve of her. My stepmother and sister don't make matters any better. I'll be honest with you..."

An awkward pause.

"...you can call me Christopher."

Samuel smiled awkwardly. "I love her. This is the one for me. I don't have any intentions of being with anybody else and down the line I'd like to marry her. My family still thinks I need to marry for the sake of power instead of love, however. It wasn't the choice I wanted to make but I had to stay put until the fire settled down.

"What were they going to do? Shove more women in your face?"

Christopher's tone was incredulous, and it forced Samuel to chuckle dryly.

"Simply put, yes. But not only that, it's a little deeper than that. My father isn't cool with me or my sister looking bad in the public eye."

Christopher nodded, understanding. It was weird to him that a grown man couldn't move without the approval of his family but at the same token, he understood that every family structure isn't the same. The gentleman came from an elite part of town and although everyone does their dirt, it was paramount that that dirt be hidden. It was a different set of rules than the everyday fellow.

"I get it." He said. "How'd you find out she was in the hospital?"

Samuel's eyes cast downward, with a sigh.

"My sister." He said, "She texted me a news link. I opened it up to see a clip about Jamie being assaulted. I rushed down as soon as I saw it."

Christopher watched the young man quietly and wondered to himself if he could've had anything to do with his niece's hospitalization. He believed him when he said he loved her. He could even understand the tight position he was in considering his family. What wasn't making sense was why she was in the hospital at all.

"I'll say it again, Christopher…I never thought in a million ways I'd have to meet you like this. I have some ideas about why she's in the hospital, but they aren't going to sit well."

Christopher rose a brow but waited patiently for him to speak on what was bothering him.

"Jamie mentioned that Chastity blackmailed her. She hasn't come out and said it but I believe she's apart of the scandal that happened at Adams'…"

Christopher looked into his eyes and felt his face harden. "*What*?"

Samuel opened his mouth to explain further when Christopher cut him off.

"So you had an inkling and said *not one word* to someone? Your cousin? *Nobody*?"

"I didn't have cold hard evidence except for Jamie's word and a hunch. Also she didn't want me to step in that. I had asked her why before now she hadn't told me anything and her reason was you."

Christopher was now uncertain whether he wanted to hurt the man or not for obeying his niece's wishes. The fact that this was withheld information that could have change some things around and may have kept Jamie out of the hospital.

Then again, how could one be so sure?

"So basically…Chastity threatened her life and mine? Over some bread?"

"That's my guess. My sister maintains her innocence even after a fight we had. I honestly believe that's what pushed her over the edge. I think she hired someone."

Christopher's blood ran cold at the possibility. There were quite a few contracted killers in the city who did what they had to do. In another life, he knew a few of them. He'd never been one himself but ran in those circles when selling drugs had been his profession.

He wondered which one of those men would take such a contract and why they wouldn't have refused it. It wasn't even about them knowing that Jamie was his family or not but because she was a woman. Normally, such a physical punishment wouldn't be bestowed on a woman. It wasn't adding up but at the same time, no matter the size of the contract price, some niceties went out the window.

"So you don't have cold hard evidence that your sister is behind this?"

"I don't. Just a hunch. I...I know my sister. Still, I can't go to the police about it. Plus there's no pictures of the person responsible for the assault."

Christopher sighed, running a hand down his face. "I need to talk to Christian."

"Christian?"

"Christian Adams. You need to tag your cousin, wherever she is and clue her in. It's time for all the secrecy to be put to an end. My niece can't keep suffering over this."

"Also, I want to cover payment for her hospital stay." Samuel said, "I wasn't sure how her health insurance was set up but-"

"-my bosses covered it already. If you still feel strongly, pay them back. If you feel you need to put up money though, it'd be appreciated if you cover her bail."

Samuel nodded, telling Christopher to send him a receipt for whatever he needed and he'd handle it. Although he hated that the man didn't ring the alarm in the fashion he would've liked, he admired that he would step in for his niece the way he was. Besides, considering that a weight would be taken off his back for he and Tiffany's wedding, all was forgiven on his end.

"I'm heading back to the hospital."

Samuel stood up, awkwardly looking around in the space. Christopher wanted to laugh at how out of place he looked but held back. The situation was not ideal for either of them. He knew Jamie was dating but it would have been nice to meet Samuel in a normal situation. He hoped that they could probably start over but for the moment, justice needed to be served for his niece and for the good people at Adams'.

The afternoon sun was working on closing out the day as Christian settled in Evander's car once more. She was surprised by his choice of ride. Normally it was his Mercedes but instead was a silver LS Lexus. Christian was also surprised by how dressed down he was. It wasn't normal for her to lay eyes upon her boyfriend less than dressed up, but he waited for her in a pair of grey sweats and a white tee shirt. He wasn't any less sexy, but it was a different change of pace.

"Should I change too?" she questioned jokingly, slamming the door.

"Actually, if you don't mind..."

Christian was dressed in one of her power suits and while Evander had wished he could take her out of it himself, he was glad that she bought up the subject. He hadn't known how to approach it otherwise. He was already slightly on edge with what he had planned for her to see. The moment would either make or break their relationship.

"We about to jump somebody?" Christian asked, "I'm *not* that kind of girl you know."

"No but...it would help if you were dressed down, baby." Evander said, "There's no reason for you to pull up to this place with your good clothes on."

Christian nodded but wondered to herself where they were going that she needed to be dressed down.

Still, when Evander stopped in front of her building, she ascended upstairs and chose a baby pink loungewear set. It was the best she could do under the circumstances.

Christian returned downstairs in about twenty minutes, meeting her beloved and in no time, they took off once more.

Christian watched silently as they took the highway and sighed, thinking about all that happened in the past week. News of the upcoming trial starring Jupiter was coming up. She wondered to herself if she would attend or not. She leaned more on the side of not attending, as she never had to look the woman in the face again for his indiscretion against Adams'. Most of the time she did her best not to think about Jupiter as her very name made Christian's blood boil. She didn't understand how the woman couldn't just keep her head down and continue to progress as she had.

Christian's thoughts had swirled around her former accountant, and it'd done nothing but made her angrier as the seconds ticked on. Catching herself, she shook her head and released the troubled woman from her mind. She again focused on the road, reaching over to take Evander's hand. A sigh escaped her lips and her body started to relax again when he received her attentions.

Evander took an exit and Christian observed that they were hearing toward Adair Park and wondered why. Her face creased up with concern as he drove, confidently steering the ride with all the expertise of a hood boy. She watched his eyes sweep the streets from left to right as he drove and felt his energy shift. Questions had bubbled up in her, but she quashed them, astonished yet enthralled by the man she called her own.

Christian was used to the clean-cut version of him that donned an expensive, tailored suit every day and talked with all the confidence of well-trained businessman from the best of schools. She was used to the smoothness in which he walked and chose his words but without his even speaking, she knew she was looking at a different man.

Something about him scraped the bowels of her memory but it wasn't connecting. She'd known this man before, but from where?

Her palms started to sweat and her heartbeat quicker in excitement. Her brows furrowed, wondering when and how she knew the gentleman beside her before when she hadn't remembered him again. She let the thought go, again surmising that she might have been imagining things. That's when like a ton of bricks, the memory hit her.

Flashback

Christian and Sharin had gotten off the wrong stop in Adair Park. Their fear ran at an all-time high, neither girl having ever sojourned through the troubled neighborhood. What was supposed to be an act of rebellion against their parents had gone totally left.

The bus had pulled off however, so there was no turning back.

"Shay…we messed up." Christian whispered, "How are we getting home from here?"

"I don't know, and this is all their faults. If they hadn't treated us like prisoners, we would try to break free every five minutes!"

Christian didn't acknowledge the fact that though they hated how their parents treated them, they were still in the wrong. The thought of punishment from her father was starting to make her queasy so she took deep breaths to settle herself. There had to be a solution to the issue they were facing. Niether of them just couldn't see it.

"Can't we just call Elijah?" Christian asked, looking over at Sharin, "You could get along with him for about twenty minutes, right?"

Sharin glowered at Christian, "I'd rather get punished. I don't want to hear anything he has to say."

Christian sucked her teeth, "But what are we gonna do? We don't know how to make it home."

"Why don't we just ask them over there?"

Sharin tentatively pointed at a group of people sitting at a dilapidated house. Neither of them understood that it was a trap house but that was beside the point. There were men and women straggled amongst the front, having a good time from what the twosome could see.

"I don't know…" Christian said, sighing, "We don't know them."

"True but…"

"You'd rather ask a whole stranger that might murder us than to call Elijah? Are you fucking serious?" Christian hissed.

The twosome started going back and forth so neither had seen the tall boy that was approaching them. When he reached them at the end of the lawn, he coughed lightly making them both jump.

"You two seem to be lost."

Christian took in the boy, wondering why her insides suddenly turned into jelly. His dark eyes bored into hers and it confused her why she felt like she'd give him anything and everything. The thought almost made her quake and for all the wrong reasons. Moments ago, she was concerned for her safety. That doubled in on itself at the look of the boy standing at five eleven in front of her. His presence hung over her like a cloak and forced her to swallow before she said anything.

"How do you know?"

The boy smirked. "Every chick around here we know, shawty…"

Without preamble, he stepped into her space and pulled at a tendril of her hair. He enjoyed the way the light reflected on her amber strands and then looked back into her eyes. His actions caused Christian to blush. Fighting the feeling was futile, even if she'd wanted to. It was also safe to say that she'd forgotten that Sharin was standing next to her, witnessing the interaction. It was a moment that she would tease her for the next few weeks.

"…I would have remembered you if you were around here on a regular basis. Two chicks of your uhm…caliber? Not known around these parts. You would've already been snatched up."

Christian felt a dark shudder go through her body at the twang in his voice. She shifted from foot to foot, unsure if she wanted to run away from him or not. It was all a confusing bunch of emotions she'd never felt before.

"You would've already been mine, shawty. A nigga needs a chick like you in his life."

"You don't even know me…" Christian managed to answer.

"Not yet. What's your name?"

Before catching herself she said, "Christian."

"Pleased to make your acquaintance. They called me Vill."

He finally dropped the strand of hair he was playing with, abandoning images of seeing the girl before him naked.

"Nice to meet you, Vill. If you don't mind we need to get going."

Sharin coughed, popping the bubble that the two had been encased in the entire time. They both had turned to look at her and she gave them both a sheepish smile.

"It's nice that you remember that we have to get home." Sharin smirked, "I was wondering if my suggestion was working after all?"

Christian fought against shoving her middle finger in her arrogant friend's face but decided it wasn't worth the energy. The exchange however made Vill laugh, commenting that they were funny and bought the attention back to him.

"Why don't I give y'all a ride?" he said, grinning, "Y'all can't live that far right?"

Christian and Sharin had reluctantly agreed figuring they were already in deep. They needed all the help they could get even if the man was a stranger.

Sharin's address had surprised Vill, but he didn't mention anything beyond noticing that she came from a prestigious neighborhood. Both were thankful he didn't question why they would hop off of the school bus at the wrong stop. Not that they had anything to hide but their thought process didn't make sense after they went through with their plan. If Vill hadn't stepped in to take them home, they might've been kidnapped, raped or worse. The efforts weren't worth the rewards and it was a game they never played again.

Still, Christian couldn't lie to herself and not say she wasn't elated to be alone with the handsome stranger, as deluded as it sounded. It was pretty much a given that she'd never see him again so every second she cherished.

She watched him covertly in silence wondering what it might've been like to be the girlfriend of a man who was so unlike her in every way. She thought of all the secrets. She thought of the adventure. It was obvious he was a drug dealer with the way he moved. She shook off the dark thoughts, seeing even at her young age that kind of life wasn't for her. It would never work between them.

"So can I get that number, shawty?" he questioned, "I promise I ain't like these other niggas out here. You run with me? Life will be smooth."

Christian chuckled even as her face grew hot again. She was two blocks away from home, away from prying eyes who would call her parents if she were seen with the mysterious stranger. She looked him in the eyes, infatuated with the mischief she read behind them. She wanted to get to know him although something in her felt like she already knew what life would have bene like between them. Sometimes you already know upon the first meeting. She knew through the hard times, they would have shared something special.

"I can't be seen with you. I can't even speak to a boy let alone look one in the eye around my parents. I was lucky you was here to take me close to home."

Vill sighed, "So this is the last time I'll see that pretty face, huh? I hope you fuck up and get lost around me again though, shawty. Then I know for sure it was meant to be."

"I doubt it but thanks anyway."

Christian stepped out of his car without another word, forcing herself to walk ahead and not look back. The singular meeting had ingrained itself into her mind. For days on end she thought of getting lost in Adair Park on her own just to find the stranger that had left that much of an impression on her. Still, she walked away from those fanciful dreams whenever she looked her parents in the eye and recited how school had gone for that day. She knew first and foremost her mission was to graduate high school. After that, college and the promise that her life was her own afterwards.

Before long, the memory of Vill was hidden in her mind. Until now.

End of Flashback

Evander was in her eye view as she sat back and watched as he drove. Everything mirrored the same man from her past. Evander was a few years older but not by much. She kept watching him as he subtly leaned back in his seat, pushing the humble car with one arm, the thug resurfacing bit by bit as he drove on. Chrsitian saw the same consistencies in his face as the younger man he'd been years ago, coming back to life. When it all slid together in her mind, she gasped, her eyes widening as her heart picked up speed.

"Baby, what's wrong?"

Evander had swerved a little to the side to catch the horror on her face. He grew alarmed but turned his face back to the road to avoid an accident.

"Vill?"

She said it on impulse, still stuck in the memory and forcing herself to come back to the present. It shocked her slightly that Evander's eyes widened at the sound of his street name.

"Where'd you know that name from?" he asked, pulling over to the side of the road, "I never told you about that."

"Technically you did." Christian said, nervously giggling, "All this time and it's you…what does that mean, anyway?"

"Short for Villian. That still doesn't answer how you know the name…"

Evander looked into Christian's eyes, puzzled at the sudden mystery.. She looked back at him, her nerves still making her giggle.

"Me and Sharin got lost and you drove us home years ago." She said, "I can't believe I didn't remember you."

Evander sat back, still eyeing Christian as he recalled the memory from years ago. He brought back to his mind that day in late spring when he'd laid eyes on the two girls that had looked so out of place in his normal settings. He took a moment to remember falling on his face as he took Christian in, thinking she was a top shelf woman that should be on his arm. He remembered watching her walk away that day feeling as if he should chase her down the rest of the way but decided against the notion. Her walk had been purposeful and it boggled his mind. He knew that he saw the want in her eyes for him. Never had another woman looked at him like that since. Not until he stormed back into her life without either of them knowing.

Evander thought again about when he asked for her phone number. He remembered not wanting to let her go. Watching her walk away in that moment made him truly look at who he was as a man. Inwardly in that moment he knew he wasn't worthy of Christian.

"I should've remembered your name."

Evander finally broke the silence, a smile stretching his face as he saw the girl in his woman from years ago.

Pulling his seat back, he beckoned for her to get close to him. Christian clumsily climbed onto his lap, barely having a chance to catch her breath when he pulled her face into his again.

"I hadn't forgotten your face for a long time. I was hoping you got lost around my way again."

"I didn't want to walk away from you…it wouldn't have worked out though."

Evander had palmed her backside and taken another kiss, spurred on by the memory himself. It was almost like making up for lost time. It made her kisses taste sweeter than normal. It made her weight in his arms feel better than normal.

"You think so? You're probably right…my life back then wasn't fit for you." He ran a finger down her face, "I'm glad you walked away, no matter how badly I wished you hadn't."

Still, he was amazed that the young girl he wanted for in his youth was the actual woman in his arms. It was enough to call off the trip he wanted to make with her and drive back home. Still, he had his reasons for bringing her and needed to get the hard part over with. After she found out about what his former life entailed, she might not want to deal with him.

"I used to think about you all the time!" Christian squealed, "This is crazy!"

"It is though. You don't know how happy this makes me though. I would've been happy either way. Meeting you taught me I needed to step my game up. I wasn't ready for you, baby. I thought I was back then but I wasn't. My life wasn't right…"

Christian sighed, "I don't need to know about all that, Vann. It's now that counts."

Evander shook his head stubbornly as he held her closer. "I want us to be together in the long run which means you have to know me. I don't know what could happen but if anything does, I don't want you caught off guard about the shit, feel me?"

It was then her stomach started to twist up in knots. Just who had her boyfriend been in his past life? Also, was it something she seriously had to know? She felt her eyebrows furrow and decided to work her way back to the passenger side. The fear in her heart that had subsided had came back in full force. She looked over at her boyfriend, wondering just how deep he was in the street life and what she'd gotten herself into by being with him?

"I think so."

"I hope you don't leave me when I tell you, but I understand if you do."

Christian looked over at her man, shock reverberating her at his words. Did he think that she could ever leave him? She wasn't sure whether she felt insulted at his suggestion or not. She then saw the fear in his eyes and the toll sharing himself would take on him. Still, Christian remembered the grace he extended her when she shared the worst parts of herself to him. He hadn't even judged her harshly. She knew whatever it was she couldn't do the same to him. Even past that she knew in her heart she could never leave Evander. That was hardly in her plans.

"I love you, Evander King." She said, "This is scaring me but I'm not going to just pick up and leave. Have more faith in me than that."

The determination in her voice as she made her plea warmed his heart and made him chuckle lightly. He reached for the ignition and started the car again. Before he pulled off, he looked his woman directly in her eyes and said his piece.

"I have more faith in you-in us-than you can imagine. If you don't believe anything else, believe that."

With that said, he pulled off towards his own stomping grounds to reveal a part of his life that could change the charter of their relationship irrevocably.

"You didn't kill anybody, did you?"

The twosome pulled up to the same dilapidated house from years ago. Evander glanced over at Christian, smirking at the worried gaze on her face. He toyed with how much of the truth he wanted to tell her and decided full-on truth was best.

"Nah. I had people punished, rarely killed." He said, "But before you get up in arms about that part…"

Christian sucked her teeth, "You was really out here putting hits out on people?"

"These weren't regular people, baby. These were dirty, filthy niggas, just like I was. There're rules in this business, just like in our world. Only difference is you pay with your life in the worst-case scenario. Hmm, maybe it's not that different."

Christian raised an eyebrow at the devil-may-care attitude that her boyfriend was displaying in that moment but decided to hear him out. In a sense, she could see where he was coming from but never had she gone as far as to put a hit out on someone. In her world, that was unheard of.

Still, had Jupiter bypassed jail-even keeping her license-going through the lengths of blacklisting her from every reputable company would have been her next move. Destroying someone by means of hitting their pockets was another kind of death. Just because the wounds didn't show didn't mean it wasn't a hurtful option.

Perhaps Evander had a point.

"Are we going inside?"

"No." he said, "I toyed with the idea but you don't belong in a place like that. And on the off chance that it gets hit by the police you can't be seen being dragged out of it after all your hard work…

Christian nodded somberly, thankful for his foresight. Not to mention it wouldn't look good for him to come out of the trap house either.

I'm waiting for an old partner of mine to pull up. He might have some info that I need."

A man emerged from the house in that moment and Christian took him in. He was a caramel skinned man, who appeared to be the same age they were. He came across with a different kind of charm than Evander. His smile was crooked but endearing and for some reason Christian found him adorable. She knew that looks were deceiving however and it wouldn't surprise her if he came with his own bag of secrets.

"Clint."

Evander had rolled down his window as he made the greeting and Clint held out his hand to give him a pound. Clint had almond shaped eyes that shone a beautiful brown hue when the sun hit and they twinkled when he laid eyes on his friend.

"Vill. It's been a long time."

"It has. How're things?"

Clint smirked, "You know I'm good. You don't worry your pretty head about it, nigga."

Evander laughed and then turned to Christian, motioning to her, "Clint, my lady, Christian. Christian, my man Clint."

"Nice to meet you, Christian." Clint said, "Any reason you'd bring your lady out here, Vill? I hope it's not on a date."

"Nah. We're passing through. I just wanted to know though, that girl they just put up in the hospital. You know who might've done that?"

Clint went silent for a few seconds.

"Only person I can think did that was Neely. I can't think of a bolder nigga who'd make a hit in broad daylight like that."

Evander went quiet. Neely was one of the most notorious hitmen in Atlanta. In all of Georgia if he were honest. There was almost no job that Neely wouldn't take so long as the price was right. Evander wasn't sure how he slipped away from most hits because like Clint mentioned, Neely was bold. He was so bold it was a miracle the police hadn't booked him not one time. Then again, considering he hadn't killed anyone of importance, the police weren't looking for him.

Still, he was more thorough than to let a mark end up at the hospital, so he wasn't sure it was his work. Normally if Neely was sent after you, it was an ironclad guarantee that the person would never see daylight again.

"I don't know about that, Clint."

"I don't know who else might've done it. I can't think of another dude who'd have the balls. Anybody else might've caught the lady at night if it was hat pressing…Why?"

"I was just wondering about something. She's not the usual mark so I wondered."

Clint looked closely and noted that Christian's face was familiar to him. When he remembered her as the lady who was accused of stealing from his friend, he rose a brow but decided to leave well enough alone. He knew his friend to always have a handle on things, so he'd trust that Evander knew what he'd gotten himself into. Also, as he didn't deal in the world his friend was in, he crossed it off as not his lane to figure out.

"But yeah, homie, I can't see it being nobody else. Who knows what the contract had on it? Maybe he wasn't supposed to kill shawty."

"That makes sense, too." Evander said, rubbing his chin, "I think it's out of character for him but not out of the realm of possibility."

"You not making this dropping by shit a regular habit, are you? Not that I'm mad at you or anything but…"

"Nah. I had a purpose for swinging by. I figured you might know something, but you know I'm not about stepping on your toes, homie."

"Not even that."

Clint motioned toward Christian who sat pensive next to him. No matter his thoughts on the woman, Clint still saw she wasn't built for the surroundings his friend had drawn her into. Deciding to be ambivalent to whatever situation his friend had going on, it was only right that he got her out of the area as fast as possible.

"She shouldn't be here and I'm shocked you'd bring her here."

"Easy on me, Clint."

Clint nodded but still smiled at Christian.

"Nice to meet you, even briefly. I won't promise to see you again because sincerely, I hope I don't."

Clint eyed Evander as he gave him one last pound, making the latter chuckle a little bit.

"I heard you." He said, slowly pulling off, "Stay up, homie."

"No doubt."

Clint watched his friend drive away with a smirk. He watched until his friend drove well beyond the point at which he could see him and nodding, turned back to the entrance of the house they'd supervised their product in once upon a time.

Clint knew it'd be some years before he saw him again but that was the agreement they both made years ago. It was an agreement he took very seriously and far as he was concerned, Evander had no room to go back on his promise.

Life on the other side suited him much better, anyway.

Christian watched pensively as Evander drove quietly. She wanted to burst with questions but waited, figuring at some point he'd fill her in. Evander didn't disappoint.

"The name Buddy King ring any bells for you?"

He'd broken the silence and Christian took her time to think. She remembered while she was still in junior high there'd been a highly publicized and notarized case going on with a man of the same name. The case had been her father's entertainment more than reality TV for most people. His opinion that he deserved jail time for his reign of terror over Georgia was never lost on anyone who had time to listen or were unlucky enough to have to bear it. She used to listen to her father's groanings with half an ear, wishing that he'd turn the television to something more entertaining for her to watch. She hadn't been allowed to watch certain shows growing up until she'd reached high school. Even then, she still had to bear her father's nightly rituals of watching the news. Buddy had become an integral part of her life until he was finally convicted.

"Buddy King?" she asked, "I remember he was supposed to have gone to jail but died…"

Christian gasped, looking at her man as she pieced it all together. She felt her heart race, as she tried to swallow the surprise and the horror of all he was implying. She watched as Evander's face took on the appearance of shame.

"That was your father?"

Evander nodded, forcing Christian to bite her lip. She prodded her boyfriend on, wondering how come they couldn't have had this conversation at her place or his. Surely she hadn't needed to see Adair Park in all its glory to have to hear this tale.

"Yes. He died pretty much when he was convicted of every single charge on the ticket. He passed the operation off to me before he'd done so. It was already decided a while back that I would before he'd gotten sick. He was ready to kick back and let his money start working for him."

"That's why you said it wasn't a good idea that we never hooked up back then."

"Yeah. I thought I had things under control but they weren't. I had too much going on and it wasn't safe. I was Buddy's son but the streets didn't respect me as Vill until I proved myself. I had enterprising ways."

Evander chuckled as his last thought, but it held no mirth. Christian was still in shock that she was dating a man who had dealings in the streets. Her mind started to race thinking about the monies under his name at her place of business. She looked at Evander, opening and closing her mouth several times before forming the thought she needed.

"So let me get this right for my edification." Christian said, "You're a drug lord? Like, I thought you ran a tire company?"

"I'm *not* a drug lord." Evander replied, "I'm…I'm not my father. I took over his dealings when he died and then I switched them over to what I envisioned later on."

Christian nodded, her sighs coated with relief.

"So what's the story on taking over your father's business, then?"

"He expected me to deal in drugs. I decided that I wouldn't. I'm not going to lie and say that I hadn't done things or had things done. That's the nature of that beast. I had things going in a transitive motion. I still had people to take care of that'd been working for my father for years. I couldn't leave them high and dry. I had to figure out how to keep payroll happy without totally alienating them once I switched things up."

Christian tossed his thoughts around her mind and figured they were sound. Although their business was illegal, there were still people who made the business what it was. It would have been evil to leave them without a dime to their name.

"I can't complain, I got the best of everything. I dressed well, went to excellent schools so in a sense I was already a different breed. During the day I was in the books and at night I was in the streets. I knew overall that I wanted what a good education could afford me, not the streets."

They cruised through different neighborhoods, each one just as horrible as the first one they rode through. Every now and again, someone spotted Evander and nodded to him, knowing his face. She watched as he acknowledged the people who greeted him but noted that he kept driving. Christian hoped that people wouldn't keep noticing him in light of all she was hearing. Thankfully as night fell over the city, that became less of a problem.

Evander had pointed out some of the houses they'd done business in. She noted that there were many of them and wondered at how his father had kept up with it all when he was living. Alternatively, she wondered how he had after his father's passing.

She questioned him on her thoughts and Evander shrugged.

"I had to keep things moving while he was alive. When he died, Clint and I shared that responsibility. Once I got things under control, I passed them off to Clint. He was always a street dude and the closest thing I had to a brother out here. It only made sense."

"Hm. So long story short you inherited a business you didn't even want?"

"Yes. I ran it for a while out of respect for my father. It wasn't out of love but more of duty. If I'm honest, I hated my father from the moment he pulled the wool from over my eyes and demanded that I started taking an interest in what he was doing. My mother was hurt by him. He was a rough teacher, but he also didn't tolerate the thought of her taking me away and starting over. I was his only child and on top of that his legacy. He wasn't hearing me not taking over in his stead."

"How was she hurt?"

"He didn't love her. He cared about her. He took care of her but his heart was with somebody else. I think in his own way he loved her. It just wasn't the way she wanted. She was a last ditch effort to get over the chick he was so fond of. He treated her like shit too, so I don't entirely understand his aim as far as it came to women. I give him that he taught me not to treat any women horribly. Far as him though, he was the worst. All that to say, I don't want the same fate for us."

Evander had taken a moment to finally merge back on the highway and get out of the neighborhood they'd been driving through.

"So, he didn't clue her in on his...dealings."

"No. Only when he had to, which wasn't often. Even then it was out of the question for her to speak on it. He gave her notice when he had to...I'll be honest when I say that watching him treat her a certain way was a bitter pill to swallow. My mother was a beautiful, patient woman and while he did take care of her monetarily, the emotional part was missing. She might as well had been roommate to him."

Christian's heart ached for his mother in that moment. Though the severity varied, something about his father reminded her of Jerrell. Every part of that relationship must've been orchestrated to his liking and being that she had no say so it had to feel like a prison.

"I know this is a lot, baby, but I had to tell you. I can't say I love you and not share every part of myself with you, especially with everything going on. If I was to catch wind of who stole from me? I'd need you to be aware of and not be surprised if that person turned up missing."

A cold chill ran down Christian's body at his words. Of course, she understood the insult of what happened to him. She had felt the same insult while the scandal that had marred her good company's name prevailed. If she could have squeezed the life out of Jupiter's neck, she would have for what she'd done. There were times she ached to slap Jamie around for allowing things to escalate. She could have put a stop to it long ago. Still, to kill or have someone killed

"Baby, I don't understand though. Jupiter is already in jail. The money is being repaid to you. Why contemplate something like this?"

"If I'm honest, I don't believe it was only her in on it. Sure the other girl got forced to change up the paperwork but when I think about it, what did she gain other than keeping her job? Nothing. Somebody still got away with stealing from me and the thought doesn't sit well, baby, I'll be honest. I grew up under different rules and one thing I never tolerated was thievery. If you could steal, you could kill. Far as I'm concerned, a nigga definitely tried to take me out and I take that *very* personally."

Christian was silent.

"You were failed, I get that, but you were-"

"-this isn't a slight against you, Christian. We handled our business in that arena. This shit is street justice as far as I'm concerned."

"You just told me you weren't for that street shit anymore. Why are you thirsty to punish someone? Or am I wrong in thinking that part of your life is over?"

Evander sighed, reaching over to grab Christian's hand as he merged back into Buckhead. He stewed in silence for a moment, thinking that she was right.

Although the street life wasn't at the forefront of his life any longer, he still had the taste for vengeance in his blood.

"Vann…I can't sleep at night knowing something like that happened."

"You want due justice and so do I. All things considered you're right. That's not my life anymore. We could both agree however that they'd deserve it."

Christian nodded. She didn't fault his anger, only his tactics.

"So to summarize. Buddy died, you took over for a time and then gave the reigns to Clint. Then you stepped away?"

"Finagled a cut of the money and started King Tires. Helped Mama sell her house and get her a new one. Stayed with her awhile until King took off and then got my own. She met a nice man so I'm happy for her. I keep tabs on him every now and again but he's a regular joe who's just happy to have my mama for a wife. She's happy so I'm happy."

Christian smiled at the thought of the end game for his mother. It didn't make sense how some men wasted a woman's time and did so unashamedly. That was crime enough for her past his ultimate wrongs in the eyes of the nation.

"I'm glad." She said, sighing, "I love that for her."

Evander smirked at her response but rubbed the top of her hand with his thumb. The silence had become comfortable until Christian spoke up again.

"So there's no chance the police can take you away?"

"No. That's something you never have to worry about. You're stuck with me…if you still want to be."

Christian giggled as he pulled up to her house for the second time that day.

"I said to give me more credit, Vann. This conversation could've been had at either of our houses, though."

"No. I needed you to know that this wasn't a fairytale or a bedtime story to tell you after we finished making love. This is…this was my life, baby."

Evander had caught Christian's gaze as he made his point. Looking deep into them, he caressed her face, grateful that for all intents and purposes she hadn't run the other way yet. He would have understood if she had because it wasn't an easy pill to swallow. Evander's fear was that he would look less than worthy in her eyes.

"As long as it's behind you. I want it all with you, Vann. Like you said, marriage, the kids, the house…I'm going to drive you up the wall customizing that house, just so you know."

Evander grinned, and it melted Christian's heart. Normally she would have felt embarrassed to bring up children, but she knew in her heart she wanted children with him. Despite her misgivings she decided she wasn't going to run from any of it. He'd given her his truth which was more than most men ever would to their significant other. She was sure if she hadn't already fallen in love with him, the moment they were sharing might have cemented it.

"That's part and parcel with you. Plus watching you dedicated to something other than Adams' might be refreshing for me," Evander chuckled. "We could get an acre and start from there. I always did like space."

"That's not a bit much?"

"Nah. I lived in a big house but didn't have much room…to just be. Our kids will have better than we had. They'll have freedom."

Freedom. It was something to be envied amongst other children whose parents didn't have a set schedule for their day or future plans for their lives. It seemed in different ways they both were stripped of that in their former years. She wasn't sure whether it did them much good or not but she knew in the coming years they'll preserve that gift for their children.

"Let's get you upstairs. Look at you, past your bedtime."

"More like past my wine time." Christian quipped, laughter in her tone,

"Oh, how could I forget my favorite wino is on a schedule?"

They both laughed companionably as Evander opened the door for his love. Taking her hand, he watched as she daintily stepped out, one foot after the other and walked with him as he closed her door. They'd stepped into her building and went through the motions to get to her floor. Evander still clung to her hand until they approached her door.

"Pick you up early tomorrow for breakfast? Give me the day. Tomorrow's Friday.""

He slid an arm around her waist and pulled her close.

Christian smiled, "Let me think about it. I'll let you know before I go to sleep."

Evander nodded and leaned in to kiss her lips once more.

"Let me know. I love you."

Christian smirked, "Let me find out…"

Evander chuckled as he pulled away. His love blew him a kiss after she opened the door and then disappeared behind it.

He left soundly with visions of what their future together might look like. It put a smile on his face that he didn't realize was there.

Chapter

Nineteen

Sharin breathed out slowly, holding onto her fiancé's hand as they pulled up to the Reynold's estate. Dinner was held there every other Sunday and it was an obligation she'd rather avoid. As a child the custom was commonplace when her grandfather was still alive and though she knew she'd been the apple of his eye, she hated having to attend knowing that her wayward cousin would be in attendance.

"Calm down, love. It's only dinner."

"It's a pain in the ass is what it is." Sharin commented, looking forlornly out of the window, "I don't want to stay long, Maddox. An hour from start to dinner. I'm not in the mood to play nice with my family today."

"You're normally happy to see your mother." Maddox chuckled, "What would she think if her baby girl just upped and left dinner?"

"My aunt and cousin will be there. She'll understand in light of *recent* events." Sharin replied,

They were met at the front door by a valet, who was all too happy to park the silver Mercedes E-class. Maddox tipped the gentleman and then turned to Sharin. He lifted up her face and leaned in, sealing his lips with hers. The gesture made her smile and calmed her heart slightly from the impending evening.

"An hour, you said?"

Sharin nodded, resolutely, "An hour."

Sharin reached in and rang the bell. Not even a second later the door opened and Sienna, the head maid welcomed them in.

"Miss Sharin. Master Maddox." She greeted them, "Your family is settling in the main dining room now."

"Thank you, Sienna. I hope all is well with you?"

"It is, thanks for inquiring. Enjoy your evening."

Sharin smiled what may have been her final genuine smile for the night. She fought an eyeroll as she walked in tandem with Maddox to the formal dining room. A happy squeal erupted from her mother who leapt out of her seat and lightly jogged to her daughter to enfold her into a hug. Sharin backtracked on her earlier thoughts as her smile broke despite what she knew would be a train wreck of an evening. Like Maddox mentioned, she loved to see her mother.

"Mona, if you would let her go. You still react to her like she's the same baby girl from years ago."

Sharin stiffened, hearing her Aunt Mila speak. She decided to act as if she hadn't heard her as Mona released her and returned to her seat at the end of the table. Sharin's father Andrew sat at the head of the table and he himself stood up to receive a hug from his daughter as well. Maddox and Sharin took their seats on the right side of the table and greeted the McCain family. All but Samuel was present and Sharin had asked why.

"Oh, he's at the hospital with that wretched girl." Mila answered, rolling her eyes, "We keep trying to get him to see reason but he's besotted with her at this point. So, I have nothing for him."

"That's harsh isn't it, Mila?" Andrew questioned, "The girl was found innocent…"

"She was but I don't really care for her, anyway. Samuel could do so much better and all he settles for is a woman who has to sweat to make it through life? What good is she for him?"

"I don't know, giving you grandchildren in the future?"

"I won't be claiming any children that come from her womb. Please, Mona." She said, "I'm certain if Sharin bought anyone other than Maddox home, you'd be displeased."

"That's foolishness, Mila. As long as he has viable employment and loves my daughter I could care less. I'm ready for grandchildren."

Sharin fought to keep her hands under the table, awaiting someone to approach with a hot towel so that she had something to do with her hands. Her nerves were already starting to close in on her and she was doing her best not to listen to the ridiculous things her aunt was saying.

When a maid appeared with a towel she uttered her grateful thanks and concentrated on wiping her hands in preparation for the appetizer. She was again thankful when the maids started to serve the aperitifs to everyone seated. She took a dainty sip, though she wanted to down the glass.

"I'm sure you are."

William McCain answered Mona, a grin on his features. He was silently praying that they'd make it through dinner without incident himself. Thankfully things were going smoothly so far despite his wife's outrageous remarks. Although he agreed to a certain extent, he didn't understand why she had to broadcast to the family that the woman his son chose was not their ideal. Still in all, he loved his son and if Jamie Smith was who he wanted, he wouldn't object.

"So how about you, Chastity?" Andrew questioned, "You have anyone special in mind?"

Chastity had been deep in thought the entire time, her thoughts far away from the conversation at hand. She was reeling and annoyed at the fact that Jamie Smith survived the attack in the first place. She was stuck between demanding her money back from Neely and letting the matter go. Still, she was angry that the best assassin in all of Georgia failed the assignment and didn't deign to even send her back the money she was owed. If she knew she could get away with outing him, she would have but knew she'd have to abandon her plans.

"Chastity? Your uncle's speaking to you."

Chastity looked up at her step-father and almost rolled her eyes at the tone of voice. She barely recognized her aunt as her aunt so Andrew's presence meant little to nothing to her. In her eyes he was just the body her aunt settled for. The true prize had died a long time ago.

"Okay?"

Sharin's face furrowed at the blatant disrespect shown to her father in his own home but held her tongue. Her leg bounced up and down without her realizing it.

What had been even more damning was that Mila hadn't corrected her daughter either. William eyed Chastity, embarrassment the root of his anger.

"Let's call a spade a spade." Chastity said. "I don't really care about anything y'all are talking about at this table. This family is fake and it's about high time we all stopped acting like we care about each other."

"Chastity," William warned.

"No, you're so thirsty to get me to respect this man when first of all, both of you are consolation prizes. Neither one of them wanted to be with y'all."

"That's enough, young lady." Mona cut her off, "You need to watch your mouth in our house…"

"Oh, that should have been my mother's?" Chastity said, "Play all you want to, Auntie, but this should have been *her* house. Grandad didn't want to stop at the majority of the money but the houses, too? And you didn't even find it in your heart to share with us. You're nothing but a greedy *bitch* and you and your family deserve *nothing*."

"That's enough." Sharin said, "You're not going to keep disrespecting my mother in front of me. That's out."

Chastity turned her attention to Sharin, and her expression changed into a sultry smile.

"And you're still upset that I tried to get Maddox to see reason." Chastity chuckled, "I thought you'd get over it. He obviously doesn't care that you're subpar amongst women."

Sharin found her teeth gritting as she swallowed her anger. The words she wanted to hurl back at Chastity were hardly appropriate to say in front of her parents. Even her fiancé didn't deserve the barrage of profanity she wanted to release.

"Am I really subpar, Chastity or is that what you keep telling yourself? You've been trying to get me to see this so-called truth for years. Aren't you tired?"

"I'll never get tired, Sharin. You really think you're somebody, walking around as an heiress but *choosing to work*? It's disgusting and you're an embarrassment to this family for ever clocking in and out at a godforsaken job. And you think it's a benevolent thing. Please."

"Baby, let's go."

Maddox made to move when Andrew raised his hand, making him halt his movement.

"No. I think it best for William to see his family home."

Andrew's tone left no room for argument and with a nod, William motioned for his family to vacate the table but Chastity stood up, walking toward Sharin with a twisted smile on her face.

"Just another reminder that nobody thinks you're worth pissing on, cousin. No matter what you do, you'll *always* be subpar."

"Whatever helps you sleep at night, Chastity." Sharin rolled her eyes, "And you're horrible for letting her talk to me like that, auntie!"

Mila walked past as Chastity was talking but stopped when she was addressed. She turned to Sharin and let a giggle of her own slip.

"Am I? I don't contradict my daughter, especially when she's right. Do have a good night, niece."

William shuffled both women out of the dining room just as appetizers arrived. Andrew instructed the maids to alert the chef that the McCain's had to leave early.

Dinner had resumed quietly without so much as a word passing between the remaining people present.

"Chastity's right." Sharin said, with a sigh, "There's no use in acting like we like each other."

"Sharin…" Mona started, "They're still family…"

"Mom. I love you but what happened earlier was inexcusable. She's harassed me for years. She's the reason most of my life has been *hell*. They hate us, Mom. They literally cannot stand us and they don't even hide it. My enemies have more class than that."

Sharin thought of Jupiter often and though she knew it was because she was her superior for the most part, it still went without saying that Jupiter did have more class.

"She's right, you know."

Andrew sighed.

"I've seen you two struggle for years even after we met. All that animosity has done was fall down to the next generation. Are we to keep letting it foster down to the grandchildren you both so desperately want?"

Mona was silent in the wake of her husband's question. She sighed.

"My father would have wanted…"

"Your father would have wanted you two to figure it out, yes. But not at the cost of peace in our house. Our child. I suppose it's too little too late but I had no knowledge that Chastity was this bad off. To speak to our daughter like that is horrific."

Sharin swallowed the ball of tears that rose in her throat at her father's words. He wouldn't have known because he was always working. His running different businesses and several holdings wouldn't have left him enough time to figure out that his niece was a terror. It was entirely on Mona that things had progressed the way they had. Still, she didn't hold it against her mother either. Sharin learned she had to stand on her own two feet as it stood to Chastity.

Besides, the customs in her family were a thing. The sisters threw balls together, despite the issues between them. They hosted dinners. They put together fundraisers. They were perfect socialites, raising awareness for the issues of the less fortunate. It was something ingrained in them by their father.

Mona sighed, eating her dinner on auto pilot as she chewed on the words her daughter told her. She wasn't wrong but it was always her hope that her sister and she could put behind their bitter past and move forward. There was no real reason they couldn't but the dinner that unfolded before her showed her otherwise. Her sister was not willing to let bygones be bygones and the legacy of hate was passed down to her niece. It was a recipe for disaster that would affect their home should they still be allowed to visit.

"I have to talk to you after dinner." Sharin said, pointing her gaze at her mother, "There's some things I need to know."

Mona nodded. She wasn't surprised because of some of the comments Chastity made. There were things that she hadn't made known to her daughter, simply because it was a private matter. She wasn't sure why her sister would make certain things known to Chastity.

Still, it was all a moot point.

It was about time Sharin understood the entire history between herself and her sister. It'd been a long time coming.

Mona and Sharin settled in the living area, two glasses of Port between them. Sharin sipped slowly, settling into the couch as her mom did the same.

"So. Dad and Uncle are...consolation prizes?"

Mona's laughter was mirthless. Sharin was saddened by the sound, wondering what it meant. She sat quietly as her mother sipped from her own cup and turned to her, with a light shake of her head.

"I guess we'll start there. Your cousin is referring to my ex-boyfriend before your father...Buddy."

She hadn't said his name reverently, but with quiet resignation. Still, the name was familiar to Sharin's ears. It took her a few moments to remember when her teen years came flashing back to her.

"Buddy...Buddy *King*?"

Mona nodded, "One and the same. I met him so many years ago. Way before your father was thought of. Your aunt and I went to Spelman but attended parties at Clark. Buddy would be there just to be seen. Everybody wanted Buddy...but he chose me."

The memory was dear to her mother, she could tell. A soft smile played on her face as she took another sip of her wine.

"Long story short, we fell in love. I...I loved that man. I love your father, let that be known. But Buddy, he'll always be my first. He was also my worst. Your aunt came onto him one night. She let me know she had, hoping we'd break up. We didn't. I refused to let him go but after a while the cheating was wearing on me. Plus the competition aspect had gotten tired. Neither of us were raised like that but here we were, really battling for the affections of one man..."

Mona's hands started to shake but she caught herself, sighing. She placed down her wine glass and took another steadying breath.

"She knew Buddy loved me. She also knew he wasn't going to leave me. Instead of finding her own she decided she'd keep trying to take him away from me. After a while, I left him. He eventually stopped dealing with your aunt and met another woman. Years later, I met your father."

Sharin smiled at the change of tone in her mother's voice upon mentioning her father. Buddy had been a lot of things to her mother but it was evident that her father was more.

"So yes, that's pretty much the gist of why I don't care for your aunt but let it be known, your father is *not* a consolation prize."

"So, what's her beef with you, then?" Sharin questioned,

"You heard Chastity. Her issue isn't totally with me but with your grandfather. She's upset that the terms of the will named me as majority owner of everything he left. She felt it should have gone to her even though I'm the oldest and more responsible party. Your aunt has always been spoiled in thinking she should have whatever she wanted from Pop. He obliged her while he was alive and even in death, still gave her a sizable amount."

"So...she just feels entitled to what belongs to you? After all this time. I have to ask Mom, if Buddy were alive today and Dad came along, do you think you would still be with him?"

"Yes. Buddy would've already broken me long before your father came along. Either way, things happened the way they were destined to happen. If I were meant to be with Buddy it would have worked out. If he had loved me worth anything, he would've rethought a lot of things he'd done. As it were, I'm sorry for my many decisions concerning him. I'm grateful I had enough backbone to walk away."

"So...why is Chastity so upset with Uncle Will?" Sharin asked, "He's always taken care of her."

Mona looked at Sharin, getting ready to open her mouth to answer and then closed it. She picked up her wine and began to sip on it, going into deep contemplation. She'd been thinking so hard that she jumped when Sharin's voice broke through her conscience again.

"I'm sorry, love. I was wondering why myself." Mona smiled, thinly, "It's getting late. Are you and Maddox going home or staying here tonight?"

Sharin sighed, balancing her options. They weren't married yet and though her parents weren't super strict she knew it'd be better if they slept separately in their house. She was pretty sure Maddox was drinking with her father and discussing entirely different issues. If that hadn't been the case she would have opted to go home. Before she could answer, Mona called for a maid.

"Laura, see to it that two of the rooms are prepared for Sharin and Maddox. They'll be staying with us tonight. Also, alert Jasper that they'll be in for the morning."

"Yes ma'am."

Sharin looked at her mother with a grin.

"It's only so often I see you anymore. Cut me some slack. Also, I didn't get to congratulate Christian for an excellent interview the other night. Do send my regards…"

"I will."

"Is she dating again? She looks…different."

Sharin giggled as the twosome rose from the couch to vacate the living room and search out their men. One thing was for sure, two things for certain; the more things changed, the more they stayed the same.

The following Monday, Christian, Sharin and Monica met up in Sharin's office. Neither Christian nor Monica knew why Sharin wanted an informal meeting without Tiffany's presence included but once she started sharing the shenanigans, it started to become very clear what was going on.

Christian was especially concerned once she heard Buddy King's name for the second time in two weeks, however close the days were together.

"Wait, wait, wait."

Sharin had been pacing and telling the story. She'd stopped in her tracks behind her desk and turned to her friend. Monica lightly chuckled.

"Shay, you have to calm down."

"I…admit to being a little excited about how messy this is. Also, it makes me nervous."

"Why?"

"Because it's even more motive for Chastity to have actually been a driving force behind all of this. Except for a pop-up at Sharin's house we had nothing." Christian explained.

"This is better than daytime TV." Monica said, laughter in her tone. "Not trying to make too much light of it or anything but…come on. A love triangle? Bitter relatives still upset to this day? Rivalry? It's enough to sell!"

Christian laughed, "So…me dating Buddy's son would just top it all off, huh?"

Christian's tone had been so carefree and breezy, Monica almost missed it. That was until moments later it clicked for her, and she slowly turned to her friend with a wide grin.

"Buddy's *son*? Now *this* you have to spill."

Christian divulged, as the blush rose in her face. Both Sharin and Monica watched, entranced as they listened. When Christian finished, she turned to her colleagues and threw up her hands.

"So you were dating Vill, all this time?" Sharin questioned, "He thought he was so cool and you thought his ass was cool, too."

Christian flushed, "Mind your business, Shay."

Sharin giggled, "Monica, I wish you would've seen it. He was playing in her hair and all types of business. She forgot she had to get home the whole time."

Monica smirked, "Now he's back in all his businessman glory, getting his money back *plus* his woman. It's all very full circle."

"Isn't it?" Christian gushed, "I'm still floating but that's beside the point…

we've already squared this money thing away for the most part. Jupiter is actually the one who took the money and put it away."

"Still, if they were acting as partners, the original plan would have been a fifty-fifty split. Just because she threw rocks and hid her hands doesn't make her less culpable. Me knowing Chastity, she probably was the one who cooked the whole scheme up. All three of us know she's good for it."

Sharin said that much to Christian, who nodded her head solemnly. The fake scenario where Elijah had been in love with Sharin hadn't been the only scheme Chastity concocted. There'd been a few more that hadn't gone noticed until it was too late.

That was back in high school.

Monica added, "Also, you might be able to sidestep this piece of information as like you've said on the surface it's legit. King gets his money back and the actual thief in jail. Still…this is your man now, Christian. It won't bode well for you to keep that much from him."

"Even the police…" Sharin mentioned,

"The police might do little to nothing without her name popping up during a hearing at this point. I'm sure she's gotten to Jupiter already and until Jamie is back on her feet there's nothing to do done about it."

"That's the missing piece though." Christian said, "I wish we'd thought about holding off her return."

The three were quiet, each stewing on the misstep they'd taken in trying to rush things back to normal. Had they waited, perhaps Jamie wouldn't have had to go through the horror she had. Alternatively, she might have died had it been a different scenario. The problem was that the variables didn't promise a stable end to the situation no matter how the story lines were flipped.

"What happens when she comes out?" Sharin questioned, "If indeed Chastity has part of this, I'm sure she knows Jamie is still alive and well and might confess to her being a part of the scandal."

"She might end up going under." Monica said, "Especially if the people on the case think it necessary. After this if they haven't already put the pieces together, they will shortly."

"She might decide to not speak with the police at all." Sharin countered, "After a near death experience, she might decide that her life is too much to gamble with."

Christian thought of her boyfriend's words from days prior and her breath started to quicken. He hadn't lied about not being beneath putting a hit out on someone. Jamie was a part of the scandal but indirectly. Still, her having part and his knowledge of it gives him a motive for putting the young woman in the hospital. The thought didn't sit well, and it made her nervous.

"I'm unsure she'll go underground, y'all." Christian said, "Her charges being dropped was on the condition that she was willing to talk. It'd be a great disservice to Christopher for her *not* to say anything, including now."

The door peaked open and Farrah poked her head in, smiling apologetically.

"Christopher wants to meet with you guys." She said, "Should I direct him to one of the conference rooms?"

Sharin nodded her approval. "Tell him to give us five."

Farrah exited quietly. Sharin looked at her two associates with a worried look on her face.

"I hope all is well...it's not like Christopher to want to sit with us."

"No, it's not." Christian said, "Let's see what's up."

They met in conference room B. Each Partner was shocked to see that Christopher looked pretty down. The horror fell on Christian like a wet dog when she laid eyes on him.

"Christopher...is Jamie..."

"She's fine. I'm just exhausted." He said, "She's due home next week so she's healing well. They have a police officer standing guard at her door right now. They're looking seriously into who might've attacked her but it's deeper than it's looking."

Christopher ran a hand down his face and then looked up at Sharin.

"Sharin...you'll forgive me for my disrespect toward your family but respectfully Ms. Reynolds, they ain't shit."

Sharin chuckled dryly, "I'm just now finding out, so I don't take any offense."

Christopher nodded. "Long story short, Tiffany and I are leaving the hospital and we bump into Jamie's boyfriend. I had no clue he was your cousin. All that aside, good kid. I'm not mad at him or anything. But I pulled him aside to talk and come to find out...Chastity has a hand in this shit."

The three looked back at Christopher with knowing looks on their faces. He looked back, his features suddenly marring.

"Oh, so y'all *knew*?" Christopher questioned, "I've been killing myself trying to figure some shit out and y'all *knew*? Are y'all fucking kidding me?"

"No Chris, it isn't like that-"

"-so what's it like, Christian?" Christopher snapped, "Because that'd be some unforgivable shit if y'all *knew* and said *nothing*."

"We didn't know." Monica said, "We're just now putting all these pieces together, Christopher. You know if we knew early on, we'd have done something about it."

Christopher looked between the three women, taking their word as gold. Still, he took a moment to breathe in and out. The anger washed over him so quickly that he was becoming the person he left behind.

"Excuse me, ladies. I'm exhausted of this whole thing. I know this been tiring for y'all too but seeing my niece laid up in the hospital like that isn't sitting well. I almost preferred her in prison. At least she was still well."

Silence was their response, mostly because there was nothing to add to it. It was a heinous thing that happened to Jamie and none of the parties present would have dreamed for it to happen to her.

"So yeah, it's looking like Chastity has her hands in it but there's no way to prove it." Christopher said, "I can't be upset if Jamie doesn't want to testify any longer but I hope she does. With Jupiter already in custody and the one who was pretty much the star of the show, there's no need for the police to even look at her."

"Not really." Christian said, "And knowing how the police operate with the rich versus the everyday guy, it's infuriating. I dearly want her to pay for all of it. As it were, I think we need to brief you on some things."

Then Sharin and Christian each took turns telling him what they knew. By the end of the conversation, Christopher was almost as flabbergasted as Monica had been earlier. The overload was a bit much to bear.

"So…a love triangle gone bad. That's what all this is stemming from?" Christopher asked, "And you dating the man's son after all this time?"

Christopher had looked between Sharin and Christian who both could offer him nothing but embarrassed shoulder shrugs. He laughed, dryly.

"To be fair, my mother and aunt always had that push and pull between them. I think when Buddy became a thing, it became worse. And my aunt basically raised my cousin to hate me. So she made it her duty to make my life a living hell. My mom didn't understand how deeply that hate ran until the past weekend. I was never taught to hate her but I'll be honest…I've learned to over time."

"Just because." Christopher said, "This is bullshit."

"It is."

"So the other question…you telling King about any of this?" Christopher questioned, "I knew about his earlier life but I didn't truly run with him. I know what kind of man you're dealing with here."

Christian gulped and it was her turn to run a tired hand down her face.

"If I'm honest, I'm afraid. Even if I wanted to keep this from him, however, the truth is I can't. He's pretty much the star of the show."

"Indeed. Rather the dearly departed Buddy is. I'm shocked he never came up in conversation for as long as I've been growing up. My father was the only one who had something to say when he came on the news. He'd been mostly amused though and *now* that part makes sense."

Sharin giggled, slightly while shaking her head at the irony that'd been lost on her for years. Christian joined in a little bit seeing where her friend was coming from. She sobered up quickly however.

"I had to think really hard when Vann bought him up. I didn't even care back then. Now the man is still screwing things up and he's dead."

Christian stood up, releasing a huge sigh and began pacing the length of the room slowly.

"I love Evander. I don't care about Chastity but I can't have her death hanging over my head or over this company. I…made the mistake of withholding information before and it's cost me a friend. I can't lose the best thing that's ever happened to me in the same damn year."

"You trust him?"

That question came from Monica who'd been sitting idly by, taking in everyone's body language and noting that the air was becoming stressed with all the revealing knowledge being shared. She kept her eyes on Christian, awaiting her friend's reply.

Christian paused her pacing and turned to Monica, thinking on the question that was posed. Days ago she would've answered in the positive without hesitation. Presently she wasn't sure. She wasn't sure if he'd go against her wishes to let the proper authorities handle the situation or go the alternate route. She wasn't sure if the former drug lord and the businessman were separate entities of himself or rather the same person. Nothing about the situation was certain but she knew from her end she had to see. Christian had already honored their end of the deal as his client but wasn't so sure about how her man would feel.

"At this point, I'm not sure. I'll just have to see if he was telling the truth about not being about that life any longer."

"For both of your sakes, I hope it ends well."

Christian looked at Sharin who responded to her and remembered that it was her family member's life they were talking about. Though the woman put her through hells unmentionable, they were still blood. It was the reason above all else that Christian didn't want Chastity harmed. It wouldn't sit well with the Reynolds' family if any of their own ended up murdered over the missing money. It wouldn't bode well with Adams' Accounting if the reason was tied to their business. All in all, there were more reasons Chastity McCain had to stay alive rather than for her to die.

"For all our sakes, Shay."

The group closed out their conversation and parted ways for the day. It laid heavy on her heart that at some point she would have to face her man sooner rather than later. For the first time in their relationship she hoped it would be the latter.

Chapter
Twenty

Christian breathed a sigh of relief once it was announced by the law office that the last payment to King's Tires was made. She barely heard McGinnis state that they'll email her the receipt of payment and consider the matter closed. The good news put her in a mood to celebrate and she thought about doing so except she remembered the long list of things that still needed to be done.

Christian received a call that the other partners were ready to meet in conference room A. She made her way down to see all parties present, including Mia Lanston.

The list had been short in her mind for who would be Sonya's successor as many of the other accountants were newer, but Mia had been one of their senior accountants from the opening of Adams' Accounting. She'd been hard working, loyal and her clients never had a bad thing to say about her. Many of her peers moved on to Big 4 companies or started their own small businesses but Mia held on and that much was noticed by Christian.

Sonya also never had a bad word to say about the woman as well so that went much further as Sonya ran just as tight a ship as Sharin did. If the person wasn't fitting the bill for the company, Sonya had no problem sending them on their way.

Christian entered the room to see her Partners seated across from Mia. Mia smiled upon seeing her and flushed a little when Christian smiled back. She took her seat after greeting Sharin and Monica and took a deep breath, spreading her hands across the table.

"Mia." She said, "This isn't so much an interview as it is an offer for promotion. Unfortunately, Sonya Powers is no longer apart of the company and in her exit we now have an opening for a new Partner. Your loyalty to the company hasn't gone unnoticed as we've known you to be with Sonya and more importantly Adams' from the beginning. Your work has been exemplary and I can proudly say that I haven't heard a bad word about you from any client you've been the lead over."

Mia smiled, "Thank you, Ms. Adams, I appreciate hearing that."

"So with that being said we hope you're interested in filling the role and becoming a Partner with us here…"

Christian then walked Mia through all the particulars of what the job entailed as well as the salary and perks. She held in her laughter as Mia's eyes started to glaze over and knew that the young lady was becoming both excited and nervous at the prospect of taking on the role. Christian was happy that the woman had respect to what the role entailed because she was certain Jupiter had none at all.

It had gone around for months before the scandal broke that Jupiter was starting to boldly make claims about Sharin. She didn't understand the extra hours Sharin spent making sure that her employee's lives were easy every day that they came into work. She didn't understand that as much as she saw Sharin dining out with potential clients, that the energy she had to expend to bring in clients wasn't as easy as it looked.

Jupiter had gone about things the wrong way. Their being lenient with the woman cost them Adams' picture perfect image. It was a thought that made Christian's teeth grit whenever the woman's name came up. Had Jupiter waited or even made her concerns known professionally, something might have come of it.

Christian often wondered if they'd been slow to jump on promoting Jupiter. Every time she pushed the thought aside. A normal person would at least try for the position. A normal person might have even left the company quietly if their demands weren't being met. Helping a strange woman to ruin not only the company she was employed at but steal from another company was inexcusable.

Christian was more grateful for Mia than the woman knew. Mia was the picture-perfect example of what hard work got you. She might have had the same feelings toward Sonya, but nobody knew it. She'd demonstrated her loyalty and kept her head down, producing excellent results each and every time. It was obvious that Mia loved her job and working for Adams' was a dream for her. So while the woman felt like it might've been a shock that she was chosen, to Christian it was no mistake.

"...so that's the end of the long list. Do we have any questions or concerns?"

Mia blew a raspberry and caused everyone in the room to laugh. She apologized but they all waved her off.

"Get comfortable, girl. You're at the top now...should you accept the offer." Monica said, "Christian is a hard ass but it's pretty much the same as it's always been. You produce the results, you'll be paid well. It's as simple as that. Plus, we'll hold your hand for a little while so you get accustomed to things. This will be a little different from what you're already doing so you'll have to get used to transitioning from an employee to a boss."

"I see that." Mia said, "It's a little daunting but as long as you'll help me adapt, I accept."

"Good!" Christian said, "Don't worry about it. Monica will mostly be helping you get comfortable but if you need anything from any of us, don't hesitate to visit. I have every confidence you'll do well."

Mia nodded and stood as Christian held out her hand for Mia's to shake. In a blink, a flash of her shaking Sonya's hand was the image that flooded her mind and just that quickly, it was gone.

"Thank you for the opportunity, Ms. Adams." Mia said, "This is the beginning of a new era, and I won't disappoint."

SHAREEKA ELLIOTT

Christian smiled and watched as Monica led Mia out of the door to begin to settle her in as a new Partner. Her heart felt like it could burst as she finally released the insult of her former friend and embraced the new promise of a new era, just as Mia said to her. It was a freedom that demonstrated to her just how good it feels to let dead things go.

Jamie grimaced as she tried to get comfortable in her bed. She rolled her eyes inwardly as Tiffany rummaged through her room, searching for fresh underwear for her to put on in a few hours when she showered.

For the interim she was adorned in a sleep shirt that she tossed on when she first got home. The only thing she wanted to do was fall asleep as it was hard to do in the hospital. Between the many tests, moments when she had to wait minutes too long for pain medication. Questioning between the doctor, nurses and even the police kept her awake for more hours than she would have liked wore her down. Not to mention her family and Samuel coming to visit.

They were making plans for her to move in with him once she was released from the hospital. At first, she was against the idea but the energy that Tiffany was serving her already dictated her answer. She couldn't bear to live with having to put up with her curtness and passive aggressive behavior. It had only been less than an hour and though she was going out of her way to make sure she was comfortable, it was obvious that she didn't want to be there.

"Thanks for being here." Jamie said, "I know this wasn't what you had planned."

Tiffany had been folding up clothes and putting it away when she paused. Turning around she glared at Jamie, her lip trembling. Her eyes formed into slits as she tossed the article of clothing she held in her hands aside.

"You're right. It wasn't what I had planned. None of this. When I ended up dating your uncle, you were supposed to be a non-factor. Now, every day, you are *the* factor. I walk on eggshells because you're a raging idiot."

Jamie sat quiet but felt herself gritting her own teeth. That was not the reply she was expecting by a long shot. She also wasn't too keen in cursing Tiffany out as she was still at her mercy in the given moment. Also, she knew Christopher wouldn't take too well to the situation if he got wind of it.

I tried to reason with myself and your uncle. I try to understand daily why a *grown ass woman* would let another grown ass woman infringe on her entire life. You were blessed beyond what some girls should hope to be in this lifetime, and you blew it. All of this devotion from Christopher and you'd flush it down the toilet for what?"

"I was coerced. You do know what that means, right?"

Tiffany rolled her eyes, "I wouldn't give a damn if they held a knife to your throat. You had more than enough time to discreetly go to Sharin. To Christian. Hell, even to me! You did none of that and now, over and over again we have to clean up your mess! You should have been left for dead."

215

GREEN

Jamie's face furrowed.

"You're out of your mind. You're so mad at our relationship that you feel like you can just say anything and that's not fair. This whole time y'all been dating I haven't had much to say except a polite *I don't like her, unc.* You've been waiting for a moment to honestly get all that off your chest and now you have one and now you feel justified but just own up to the fact that you don't want me around and we'll be cool, okay?"

Tiffany opened her mouth and Jamie shook her head furiously.

"No, because it's only obvious that you're only here to stay on my uncle's good side. I can't say that you don't love him but it's crazy for you to even utter those words based on all that's going on. I already knew you didn't like me. How would I have felt safe going to *you*? On top of that you're obnoxious and probably would have made things worse in the grand scheme. Make it make sense!"

"I don't have to make sense of anything but what I've seen. You had ample chances to be a whistleblower and call foul. You did not. Now you're living with the consequences of those decisions. That's what's going on here. Besides, I don't get how Jupiter Classon could make you fear for you losing your job. It's not making sense."

"Because it wasn't Jupiter Classon making me fear for my job. It was Ms. Reynolds cousin making me fear for my life!" Jamie yelled, "And not only my life, but my uncle. I don't care what you feel about me but if I have any power in the situation, nobody is laying a finger on my uncle. *Nobody.*"

Tiffany was silent for the longest while as she digested the information that Jamie screamed at her. One minute turned into five and then five, ten. Tiffany had held her peace for the longest time as she turned the words around in her head repeatedly.

Jamie decided to turn on her side and begin to sleep. Before she had she decided she would break the ice after her confession.

"You won't have to worry about me after I'm healed. I'll be moving."

Tiffany turned around to see the young lady laying on her side, her face staring blankly at the wall.

"You feel like you should be the only one who gets my uncle's attention and it's sick, Tiffany. He loves you as his woman. He loves me as his niece…you wanted a good man but don't want all that comes with him and that's nuts. But like I said, I'll be out of your way in a short while. I did the best I could in a bad situation and even the one person who should be the most upset with me isn't even nailing me to the cross. Just you."

"I know you're not mentioning, Christian, sis…because…"

Tiffany was about to repeat a few things Christian said in private meetings. Jamie laughed lightly.

"Don't do that. I'm talking about Ms. Reynolds. Even if Ms. Adams had anything to say about me, this is her business, and I can't be upset with however she feels. Still…those women decided however bad my involvement was, they understood what went wrong. They also decided to reach out an olive branch toward me which is more than what you're doing right now."

216

Tiffany suddenly felt shame wash over her for her words. She sighed, the tears starting to stream down her face. Jamie could hear her sniffling but wasn't moved, the damage already being done.

"You had your uncle worried sick."

"Nobody knows that better than me, Tiffany. Please leave me alone. If I need help, I'll let you know."

Tiffany sighed and exited the room. It'd be the last time they ever had a conversation until the holidays every year afterward.

A few weeks later, Evander took the day off to watch the trial concerning his missing money in the privacy of his home. It'd been all he'd been thinking about day after day since he learned it would be televised.

Evander watched as the bailiff marched Jupiter in and he felt his heart start to race. Picking up a beer he sipped, wondering what connect he could find to end her right in prison. He slowly went through his choices but as he did, he felt his stomach start to turn in a way it never had years prior. The reaction bothered him because all in all, he was a man who repaid the thief back in kind. In his mind when Jupiter decided to steal from him she was better off killing him. He worked hard, long nights for his company and the audacity it took for her to steal from him while she smiled in his face was an egregious move on her end.

Still, the picture of Christian's face as she pleaded with him not to turn to his prior ways flashed in his mind. Her questions cut him to quick and though he pushed back every time the thought entered, the picture of his girlfriend kept flashing back in his mind again.

In his mind, Jupiter should pay for what she'd done. Even in his prior life, thievery was taken very seriously. No matter what side of the tracks you came from, business was business. That was something Christian understood better than anyone he knew and it was why he wondered that she was so against him taking revenge.

He sat quietly as Jupiter's voice filled the speakers in his living room. Watching her he shook his head. Evander sent countless compliments to the team for Jupiter's good work. He made sure that she received extra in her lengths to go out of her way to make sure his money was situated correctly. For a time they had been and there was no issue. Not until things started to look off and he had to call an outside auditor to check her work.

When the auditor called foul for his accounts going back a couple years, livid was amongst the many adjectives he could use to describe what he was feeling. What he had craved however was simple and to the point: blood.

Jupiter Classon was on his hit list but after revealing his past to Christian, he was no longer sure that he had a hit list.

His eyes rose as he saw another woman go to the stand. He recognized her as the young lady from the hospital who'd been assaulted. Taking another sip of beer, he wondered at the woman's presence at the hearing.

Still, as she corroborated the story that Jupiter had told, he started to feel compassion for the younger woman as Christian mentioned. Coercion was not a cakewalk to deal with. Being that she wasn't directly responsible for his money going missing, he found forgiveness much easier for the other woman.

Evander studied Jupiter's face as she sat next to her lawyer. He read the shame and the worry on her face as the trial dragged on. Another sip of beer and he again contemplated who he could call to make a hit. His stomach turned again when his mother's face came into his mind's view. She'd raised him not to harm women, no matter how evil. His father even made an appearance and though it annoyed him greatly, he knew his father didn't condone violence against women either.

"Still, I could get someone to do it." Evander thought, *"She can't go unpunished for that shit."*

His reverie was interrupted when the judge adjourned the court and mentioned that sentencing would happen when they came back.

In that hour and a half, Evander sat on his couch, contemplating every move almost obsessively. Still, it made his stomach hurt. The constant thoughts were making him physically ill until he tossed away his beer. He'd been ready to throw up and wondered exactly why he was going through the motions and again, Christian's face flashed in his mind's eye.

"You just told me you weren't for that street shit anymore. Why are you thirsty to punish someone? Or am I wrong in thinking that part of your life is over?"

Evander sighed. That same question circled his head the whole time. Running a hand down his face, he came to grips with what the next move would be. Harming Jupiter wasn't the move as it would bring unrest to not only himself but his woman.

"Guess I'm truly a changed man these days…" Evander mumbled, "She's lucky I love her."

As Christian's face passed his mind again his stomach churned for a new reason. He hadn't seen her in days since he told her about his past life. He wanted to chalk it up to her being busy but wasn't entirely sure that was the case. He wondered why it seemed she was distant but decided to push those thoughts aside for the interim. Evander knew where to find her when he wanted her, that was no issue.

The only thing that he wanted to do truthfully was speak to his assaulter face-to-face. There were some questions burning his mind that needed answers. It was obvious that the young lady hadn't acted alone and there was a piece of the puzzle neither party was telling the public.

The young lady hadn't been afraid to take the stand, but a part of the story was missing. If she had been coerced in keeping silent there was no need for her to be assailed upon her release from prison. There was someone else that knew what she knew and wanted to silence her. It couldn't have been Jupiter as she was already locked up. The question was who?

It was why he questioned Clint about who he thought the hitman was. Most people in Atlanta were fueled by money and there were some who weren't beneath taking another's life. It was a horrible exchange, but assassins weren't moved much by their morality.

Evander made note to visit Jupiter and get to the bottom of everything. He wouldn't rest until he knew the truth.

Jupiter laid in her twin bed in her new cell, Chastity circling her mind. She thought about the day that she approached her. Thought about the singular moment that the twosome became partners in a crime that would've paid off in spades had things gone the way she wanted.

Jupiter sighed heavily, remembering catching the eye of her parents in the courtroom. She could see the shame and the hurt radiating off them in waves until she couldn't bare to look at them. Neither of her parents visited her from the time she'd gotten locked up and for some reason, their blatant disregard for her hurt. She'd seen worse offenders get visits from their families. The only person who'd came to see her at all during her entire stint was Chastity. That was only for her to tell her she was running off with the funds and that she could rot in jail.

Sharin was another person who stayed rooted in Jupiter's mind and these days, shame would make her wallow in her thoughts. Jupiter hated that Sharin was an heiress and didn't believe that she made it as a Partner based on hard work and merit. She couldn't understand why someone living in the lap of luxury would deign to spend forty hours a week slaving away for someone else's dream. Then again, in her mind Sharin didn't have to slave that much in her position. From the outside looking in, Sharin had it made.

She'd begrudged the heiress, mostly because she felt as if she were wasted space. None of the other Partners came from wealth. Most of them knew and understood what hard work and grit had come from. Still, many a time it was pointed out to her that Sharin still had to deal with a strict upbringing. Every now and again her coworkers would point out that Sharin helped people whenever she could. There were a few young ladies that she mentored who moved onto bigger companies and blazing a trail in the accounting world.

Her fixation on wanting what Sharin had should have embarrassed her. It did now that she looked back. She didn't appreciate the dream that most Black professionals would have hoped for, especially those who attended HBCU's and wished there was an environment in which they can thrive. Thriving without heed to the color of one's skin was more than rare in these times, it was a myth. Instead of her being happy that a Black woman was her superior, she worried about her socioeconomic background and deemed her ineligible to be a person of importance.

Taking a hard look at herself, Jupiter came into the realization that she let someone else's hatred of their own family fuel her own envy of her boss. It evolved into jealousy and now, sitting in a jail cell, she realized she never once questioned why this woman was on her own mission to ruin her cousin's life.

Jupiter had only wanted Sharin out of the building. She had wanted her wealth and lifestyle and was upset that the heiress didn't have to work to get it. Her existence was a slap in the face of someone who came from humbler beginnings.

Bitter tears flowed down her face at the five long years she had to look forward to. Sitting with those truths for that time made her swipe her face clean. Jupiter made a promise to herself that however she had to get rid of the other heiress, she would.

Of course, she accepted that she'd ran a risk in what she was doing. Still, she felt there should have been some honor amongst thieves.

Jupiter closed her eyes, trying to get some sleep. Perhaps some measure of peace would calm her troubled mind.

"Jupiter Classon? Wake up, you have a visitor."

Jupiter's eyes flipped open. They made eye-contact with the correctional officer. She stood up, eager to see who would come visit her. She hoped it was her parents. However she could apologize to them, she would.

She followed the officer to the visiting area for the first time in years, feeling hopeful.

Her hopes were dashed in the sand when she saw Evander King awaiting her in the flesh. She started shaking her head and asking the officer if they would take her back upstairs. The officer chuckled, shaking his head in the negative.

"It's only about twenty minutes. If something happens, I'll step in."

Jupiter sighed and took her seat. Staring into Evander's eyes she saw his overall disgust of her. She opened her mouth, uttering the same words she wanted to say to her parents.

"Look…I apologize for all of this. All of it."

Evander snarled, "Save your apology. I don't need it."

"Then why come up here?" she questioned, "Surely you didn't just come up here to look at me in vain disgust."

Evander stared at Jupiter and smirked. Before Christian became a thing in his life, he had to admit enjoying Jupiter's presence. Nothing ever happened between them but every now and again he toyed with the idea. She didn't inspire the same fire in him that Christian did, however. No other woman could. Still, her wit was always entertaining to him.

"No, that's not the only reason. I will admit I was very upset and deeply hurt that you would pull what you did against me. If you'd been a man, your family would already be making funeral arrangements for what you've done."

Jupiter looked down, "Listen…I'm not going to act like I don't deserve your anger. Still…if there's no real reason for this visit, I'm going to head back to my cell."

"Well." Evander said, "There's one way you can redeem yourself. At least in my eyes."

Jupiter looked at her old client with a raised brow as he leaned in and dropped his voice low.

"Tell me who else was apart of this scheme." He said, "I know it wasn't just you siphoning my money just for shits and giggles. There was a purpose."

"There was." Jupiter said, "Chastity McCain."

Evander suddenly had a vision of a woman standing at the door to the family home more than a few years ago. He'd been but a few years old, but he distinctly remembered his father telling the wayward woman to leave his house and to never show her face again. The name of the woman sat at the tip of his tongue, but he couldn't clearly remember. Still, something about this woman's name was familiar.

His father shoo'd him away the moment he closed the door on the woman. Days later Buddy had sworn him to secrecy. Evander would forget about the incident as days gone by.

"Chastity. McCain." He said, "I know of the McCain family, but I only remember them having a son."

"They have a daughter as well. She'd be about my age. Her cousin is Sharin Reynolds who was my former boss. She approached me at a bar two years ago. I'd been slightly tipsy and feeling sorry for myself when I met her. Then…the plan itself came to fruition."

Jupiter was shocked that she would easily start to give the man details about the entire operation. Still, any redemption was better than none at all.

Evander listened as every piece fell together before his very eyes. The more he listened the more he saw that Jupiter had been a pawn more than anything the whole time. He started to pity her but turned away from those feelings fast. She still set out to help the woman undo him and his company and would have ridden off into the sunset if she hadn't been double crossed. Still and all, he saw that his anger would be wasted on Jupiter. She'd do her time and she'd learn her lesson. He hoped that after her time she'd pick up the pieces and start over.

"So, you bit off more than you could chew, then?" Evander questioned, "All because you thought it should be you?"

Jupiter nodded, looking down at her hands like a petulant child. Evander scoffed.

"I bet you'll think twice before making foolish schemes with hateful strangers again, hmm?"

Evander stood up, not deigning to hear her response. Now that she was a non-factor, his sights were set on Chastity McCain. He'd get her story and then settle the score.

Christian read over the final reports of the day with a smile on her face. She'd just finished a call with Jasmine, reporting that their summer was closing on an upswing. Since the interview, their clientele had begun to increase again, and it was giving her material hope that things were coming back together after a rough season. She sighed, feeling lighter than she'd been in a long time and wondered if it was how it felt to be free.

The scandal taught her quite a bit about who was in her corner when things got rough and who were only as loyal as a wet loose-leaf paper. Thinking of Sonya for a fleeting moment made her heart ache only slightly but she turned away from the negative feeling, reminding her that her friend chose violence and not the other way around.

It'd been a few days since Mia took over her post and though she was clearly nervous to wreck everything, she was slowly befitting the role and Christian was pleased to see the maturity in her former senior accountant. While it was on her mind, she blocked off time to meet with her next Monday to get a feel for how things were going overall. She hadn't realized how much she appreciated her loyalty until it was time for Sonya to exit. Some things often get overlooked in the background and Christian made note to pay better attention to her staff. Also, it wouldn't hurt to tell her Partners to do the same thing. Jupiter's upset with the company led to its growing pains and overall, it was a hard lesson learned.

Sharin's bachelorette party was another thing on her mind. Christian was still agonizing over a gift for her friend's shindig but would find the time to search when she got home. Tiffany's engagement party was the weekend after Sharin's party so she'd also have to figure out what dress she would wear to that.

Christian was wary of repeating a dress that she'd worn out on a date with Evander not too long ago. She smiled at the thought of her boyfriend, but the smile fell when she realized she hadn't seen or heard from him in a few weeks' time. It caused her heart to beat faster and then harder the more the realization set in for her. She wondered why he would go missing without so much as a peep and decided she was going to call him.

She grabbed her iPhone and commanded Siri to call his number. Once, twice, three times the phone rang. She knew on the fourth he wouldn't pick up but still waited it out for the fifth, sixth and seventh ring. Hanging up she tried again to no avail. Christian felt her breaths come in shallower as the worst thoughts started to cloud her brain.

"What if he found out and is making arrangements behind my back?" was the thought that was most harrowing. She wanted to believe that he would take the higher road since he was so-called changed from his past life. She hoped that he didn't believe in street justice since he preached about not wanting any parts of it.

Christian decided to close up for the day and head home. There was no point in trying to worrying about what he had done or hadn't done. Perhaps he was busy as well, being that he was CEO of his own company as well. He didn't have to be up under her every single day.

It wasn't the case but overall it didn't sit well with her that she hadn't heard from her man in so long.

Something wasn't right.

Christian called him once more and was annoyed when she got sent to voicemail.

"If you're busy you could at least pick up the phone to say so, Vann. Call me later."

She hung up the phone and decided to go about her day.

Evander was at Christian's door a few hours later, pounding on it. He stood back waiting and was slightly amused when she snatched it open. Her face was flushed, and she was wrapped in a plush white towel. Her hair was soaking wet indicating she ran out of the shower to see what the noise had been about. Evander fought against his natural response to her. If he hadn't been so upset with her, his first instinct would have been to show her just how sexy of a picture she made standing at the door.

"Evander, what the hell?"

"I need to talk to you."

"Now? You need to talk, now?"

Christian pulled back the door, allowing him to enter. She shut the door gingerly and turned around to look at her man with all the displeasure in her expression.

"I called you earlier, a few times and you didn't pick up. What do we need to talk about now?"

"The fact that you knew that Chastity McCain had part in taking my money and you said *nil* about it to me!"

Evander's voice filled the apartment with his anger, and it made Christian slightly jump. She couldn't find the words at first to contradict him.

"First of all, I just found out." Christian said, "I had no clue. Besides, why did you need to know, Vann? It's like I've already said, your money has been returned to you. Every. Red. Cent. The perpetrator has been caught. Why must you have blood?"

"Because she STOLE FROM ME!" Evander yelled, "You must not understand the gravity of what this woman pulled, Christian. I was *very* lenient with you."

"Lenient, Mr. King?"

"Oh, very. We already know how lenient I've been. Don't play with me."

"Who's playing, Evander? You're the one who went missing for weeks. I haven't even begun to blow up your phone until *today*."

"Oh? So the guilt wouldn't rest on your shoulders from the *truth* you kept from me? Baby. Please spare me the theatrics. You knew this woman had part in this and you could have said *something*."

"How, Evander? So you can do whatever you wanted to do? So you can come back in my house after you've *had her killed*? That woman-as much of a pain as she is-is somebody's daughter! She's somebody's cousin and you forget that I have a full-scale business that will get EVEN MORE FLACK IF YOU HAVE THIS WOMAN KILLED!"

Christian's chest started to heave up and down and tears started to run down her face. She furiously wiped them away and pulled her towel closer in so it wouldn't fall to the floor.

"See, this is where you fuck up every time, baby."

"Don't call me baby."

"Don't pull semantics into this. Between all the dating and the kissing and fucking and oh, let's not forget loving, you don't tell me *exactly* when you found out. You're waiting around just because I told you the truth about myself and you didn't have the presence of mind to let me know until weeks later? You're worried about how I'll react when you haven't even given me the benefit of the doubt."

"You *told* me you'd retaliate if you knew. That wasn't smart on your part. I'm still *me* at the end of the day. With you here or *not,* Adams' Accounting is *mine*. You want me to be ashamed of who I am? When you walked through that door to rail me you knew who I was. You can't expect me to suddenly *not* be me and fall at your whim because I'm your woman. I can't have this woman's death on my shoulders, and I can't have it marring the name of my business. I worked hard! I sweated! I prayed! I don't care what you think of me for it, Evander but I have people's lives in mind, and I have people dependent upon us to do what's right as well. I can't take your emotionalism into account in every single *fucking* move!"

Evander crossed his arms, taking a full sweep of his woman as he looked her up and down. He found himself stunned by her thought process and swallowed the ball of anger that formed at his throat. It wasn't that she was totally wrong in her thought process but he wished she'd had a little more faith in him. He wasn't a total animal that didn't think things through. He deserved the benefit of the doubt just as he'd given him plenty of times.

"So it's like that, shawty?"

He asked the question and watched her raise her right eyebrow. His heart sank at the action.

"You should've considered it grace that I would even turn a blind eye to any of this. If you decide to do something rash I'm tied with you for conspiracy to murder and damn near accessory. Like, what the *fuck* do you want from me, Vann?!"

"Trust! I wanted trust from you. You asked me to chill and I said I'd consider it. What home girl did was still messed up on several fronts. In my former days I been would've put the hit out instead of entertaining this conversation."

Christian felt her heart palpitating. There was fear. The fear was so heavy she almost couldn't breathe. She took steady breaths as it was as she fought through the undertows of Evander's anger. She fought biting her lip as she saw the hurt in his eyes. The last person she ever wanted to hurt was her beloved. Still, she felt he asked way too much of her to accept what he was considering.

"My grandmother always said, if you steal, you'll kill. Far as I'm concerned, shawty already came for my head several hundred times over. Fifteen million times over, Christian. My Pops been dead way too long for her mama to still have an issue. Especially when her mama was the whore of the story."

Christian opened her mouth, shock registering through her system that he had knowledge.

"Yeah. I knew. You won't make it too far in the streets or higher society without that story being whispered about. It was all everybody talked about until he got locked up. There was still a picture of the lady in his wallet before he died."

Christian sighed, shaking her head. She ran her hands down her face. Evander sucked his teeth.

"So what do you want from me?"

Evander sucked his teeth in response.

"I don't know what I want from you, now. The one thing I wanted from you, I don't have. I…I gave you my *life*. I showed you who I was and what I became. I felt like you could've clued me in instead of pussyfooting around. For all the boss lady shit you be on, the moment you're supposed to go to war, you silent."

Christian felt hot tears leave her face. Before she knew it, she was marching towards the door. Evander looked on, despite himself alarmed at her tears. He moved to walk closer to her as she snatched the door open. Before he could reach her she shook her head vehemently, denying his touch.

"Get out."

Evander looked at his woman closely and wondered if he meant her house or away from her as well.

"You can't be serious."

"You're not going to spit on me, after everything and think what you said was okay. You claim you're finished with the street life but you're sitting here, expecting me to react as if I'm supposed to be a ride or die instead of a CEO. I love you but I won't accept that bullshit from *anybody*. Not even my parents. So yes, I'm *very* serious and I won't change my mind on that. I've done due service to you and delivered. With that much said, have a good night, Mr. King."

Evander's lips tightened as he held in all the words he wanted to say but knew none of them were worth saying. He loved her so until he knew he wouldn't say anything he'd regret, he found leaving was the best option for him.

Evander turned his face away from her and walked out of her house without another word. When the door clicked behind him, Christian wiped her face and then walked toward her kitchen. She grabbed a bottle of unopened Pinot Noir and went through the motions of making herself a glass.

She sipped, thinking of the first time she toured the building that would become Adams' Accounting. She reveled in the memory, remembering it as a proud moment. The work to secure the millions to procure the building had been a tedious journey but it'd been a privilege to her that many people had believed in her vision. It'd been wonderful to realize her dreams when so many were still searching in the world for their own.

She padded to her room as she sipped and stopped short as she entered, the picture of herself and Evander staring back at her as if it mocked her. More hot tears sprang out of her eyes as she marched toward the picture that stood there, picked it up and flung it at the far side of her room. Deeply saddened, she sat her wine down and proceeded to continue her self-care routine for the night.

Laziness and frustration joined in her misery as she decided to pull her hair back in a ponytail and decided to fix it up later. When she was satisfied for the interim with her hair, she grabbed her glass and nursed the cup as she walked back into the living room and found her mind racing back to the first moment she'd met Evander.

She'd been all but happy to set him straight. The risk of talking with him without representation had been high but once they saw common ground, things sailed smoothly. Against her better wishes, she started a courtship and then entered a relationship with him. It'd been dreamy the whole time until he decided to share what his past life had been. Christian sighed, wondering why he couldn't see reason that his past life would cause her to be hesitant to share any information with him.

Still, after she calmed down, she understood that it was her trust that he was looking for. She'd been wary to get it as he also hadn't been forthcoming in his movements with her either. That was what she failed to get across from him. Now her man was convinced all she cared about was her business.

"Still. He had to understand that it's not just me he'd affect." She thought, sipping from her glass once more, *"It's like he's only thinking of himself and that's not fair."*

Christian walked back out to her balcony to get some air. She stared back out into the city of Atlanta, admiring the city line. She again thought of all her successes, back from middle school and into high school. She often detested the way her parents raised her, but they'd taught her discipline. They taught her focus. Out of that was born grit and the ability to lead. Christian became a person she could be proud of even in failure.

There'd been many after they set her free to move onto college. There'd been moments when she wanted to beg her parents to come home but they'd made it clear that once she left there was no coming back. That had made her a tactician. When things went left she had to figure out a way on her feet. Thankfully she had the support of her friends to guide her even during dark days. Good advice or bad, they'd been there. It made her see that she was always loved.

She knew in her heart that she didn't need Evander. While she loved him, his brand of drama wasn't for her and she didn't need to tolerate it.

Still, she understood his upset. That was enough to destroy the house of cards that she built in her mind. Her thought processes were destroyed as well as her ego.

That much forced her to walk back to her couch and flip the TV on. Hard as she tried to get her mind off of the argument. The insult and hurt in his eyes haunted her and so she finished her wine and succumbed to tears until the pain faded away.

Christian didn't remember when she stretched out across her couch and cried into her pillow but before long, her tears followed her into sleep.

Chapter
Twenty-One

Chastity walked into her private condo after a long day of arrangements with a smile on her face. She'd thought of the money that she finessed from both Evander King and Jupiter Classon that sat in an offshore account in Europe. She was surprised that the police hadn't found it but was still all the more grateful for the turn of good luck on her side.

Thinking of Jupiter, she finally felt a slight tinge of guilt that the lady was serving time but didn't let it overtake her. She had served her purpose. It was never a part of the plan to leave her to rot in jail but the opportunity served as a sign that she was meant to part ways with the woman earlier than planned.

Chastity's mind then turned to Neely and the thought of him both excited and angered her. He'd failed the assignment, but he didn't demand the other half of his payment as promised. Still, she'd wanted to give him a piece of her mind. She had heard he was the best hitman in all of Georgia and the fact that Jamie had lived to testify didn't sit well with her. Jamie hadn't put her name in the mix of the testimony which had shocked her. Then again, after the assault she wasn't feeling as bold as she once had in the first place. That much put a smile on her face.

Chastity grew annoyed however, knowing that her brother was still going to marry the woman. Even if she didn't plan on building a relationship with her it was still a pain that Samuel was going against the family by making her a part of it. She offered nothing in her mind's view except being the kind of woman she hated. In her mind any woman who decided to work for what she wanted when she didn't have the need to was an abomination. It was one of the very reasons she hated Sharin with every fiber of her being.

Then again, if she were honest with herself, Sharin just got everything out of life that she did not. Her grandfather already favored her before she was born. That much had been apparent when he deigned Mona to have the lion's share of the will. She had both of her parents in her life. Sharin never had to respect a man that she never cared about.

Chastity's arms were starting to shake, thinking about her subpar cousin and family. She decided she would focus on the fact that she and her mother were about to vacation in the Maldives. It served as a nice middle finger to the seed of the man who'd broken her mother's heart. Knowing that she also caused her cousin more pain and discord in her life was the icing on the cake.

The thought of all the hurt and pain she caused everybody was enough to cause her insides to tingle. Her smile spread wide in excitement.

Those thoughts had put a spring in her step, and she decided to celebrate with a nice glass of Merlot. She'd happily poured it thinking gleefully of the last time she spat words of venom in her cousin's face. She was humming a tune to herself that she didn't remember but it fit her mood, so she kept humming.

Once she'd dutifully put everything back in its place, she made to walk into the living area. She paused, her feet firmly in their spot as she looked upon Evander King sitting on her couch. He was seated in a lounged position, staring at her casually. The drink she'd been holding fell to the floor.

Merlot stained her carpet as she eyed the golden desert eagle sitting on his lap. Chastity forgot to be insulted that this man even broke into her house and wondered how he had. She swallowed as the silence thickened.

"Evenin', Ms. McCain. Glad to meet your acquaintance. I know you didn't invite me over, but I felt I should take the liberty as we have some things to discuss."

Chastity opened her mouth to respond when he lifted up his hand, signaling her to keep her silence. Affronted, she crossed her arms at the chest, blinking her eyes rapidly.

"Who are you to break into my home and demand to discuss anything? We have-"

"Don't tempt me to shoot you in the foot, now. Like I said, we have some things to discuss." Evander said.

His tone was still mild, and it shook Chastity up even more. She kept her arms crossed, unsure if it was a good idea for her to relax them at her sides.

"See, I've heard about you. I heard about your mama and your aunt. I'm very ashamed Black women just can't get along."

"What does that have to do with me?"

"A foolish question to ask since you're about ten seconds away from going under."

"*Fuck you.*" She spat, "Feel how you want to. You should consider it mercy-"

"-I don't have to consider *shit* from you! You're lucky I didn't have your brains blown out for what you've done. I'm shocked in all this time, nobody has ever truly put you in your place. *Nobody*. You have a chip on your shoulder that's not even really your chip but you're just running with it like a dumbass."

"You know nothing about-"

"-your mother is still pissed with our dearly departed. Your mother wanted very badly to be the one that took Buddy from your aunt and she *succeeded*. I was a lil' shawty that night your mama came to the door and demanded for Pop to take responsibility for you. I ain't get the whole conversation but I do remember him telling your mama not to ever show up at his house again or that would be her *ass*."

Chastity started shaking and she clenched her fists.

"Oh…I see I *do* know something." Evander grinned, "So basically, you're upset because *our dear old dad* never claimed you and sent your mother on her merry way. You mad at me because I got claimed? I don't get it. Why steal from me, Sister?"

"Get out my house."

"You stole my money. I'm not going anywhere until I get a proper explanation."

"I don't owe you shit. Far as I'm concerned, you owed me every dollar plus interest for what *your* father did to us."

Evander looked into her eyes and saw that she truly believed whatever vitriol her mother fed her. It was obvious that there was no changing her mind so on that front, he decided to end the conversation there and then.

He stood deliberately, and Chastity felt her heart beat against her rib cage like a speedbag. Her eyes never left the gun that was now in his right hand. It left her notice that Evander had been advancing on her until she felt the cold metal pressed against her heart.

"I wonder if shooting you in the heart is just because you don't have one." Evander said, "Somebody mentioned that gold is for righteousness, and I do feel righteous enough to kill you. My father would've *been* had you offed."

"What a pity. All he left behind was a pussy."

Chastity's voice wavered as she delivered the reply. Evander looked her in the eye and chuckled, deciding to move the gun to her right temple instead. He pressed against it, answering her sarcasm with a smile.

"Sister, you don't know me. I suggest you shut the fuck up while you're ahead. I'm sorry your mother didn't school you on who you was fuckin' with. Well, almost. Like I said, somebody had to teach you."

Chastity barely heard his words, but the metal pressed against her temple and the fact that she would very well die in this position caused her to let go of her urine. Tears started to leak out of her eyes and she was unsure whether it was in fear or anger. She never in her life had a man encroach upon her space in a way that was other than sensual. Evander King wasn't playing any games and she knew she couldn't charm her way out of the trouble she'd gotten herself in.

"I have a proposition for you, Sister. You're going to turn yourself in. You're going to plead guilty for all the shit you've done. If by some miracle you've ditched jail time, you're going to sell this place, pack your bags and not return to Atlanta ever again. Matter of fact, you're going to find a nice lofty place outside of Georgia and not pass the line. If you do, Chastity McCain I promise I'll end your life, personally."

Chastity felt more hot tears run down her face. She would've threatened to have her stepfather go after Evander for his deed but she'd burned that bridge when she'd embarrassed him at the Reynold's residence. It would've been laughable for her to go to him for any retaliation. She knew her mother wouldn't help her especially when she turned herself in. The news that would break would cause huge embarrassment for her family and that above all else was paramount in their household. To do anything else was fine, so long as it didn't make the news. Over the years she excelled at keeping herself out of the news but this time she would fail in spades.

There was nowhere to turn. It was either Evander's out or imminent death.

"Do we have a deal, Sister?"

Chastity blubbered out a yes. Evander then left the apartment as quietly as she entered it.

The sharp knocking bought Christian back to the land of the living, along with an aching headache and light sensitivity to match. She cursed savagely as she stood up, trying to gather her balance and grabbed her head, willing the noise to stop. When she realized the knocking was coming from her door, she walked over to it, ready to lay into the individual on the other side.

Jasmine stood on the other side, her face furrowed in concern as she took Christian in. The former pushed the latter aside and closed the door behind her.

"What the hell is wrong with you?"

"What the hell are you doing at my house?" Christian asked, rubbing her eyes, "You didn't call or nothing."

"Apparently I'm coming to your pitiful ass rescue. You need to wash your ass, drink some water and put something in your system."

"What the fuck are you talking about?"

"Christian…Chastity turned herself in this morning."

Christian's world stopped turning for a second. Physically and literally.

"What?"

"Chastity McCain turned herself in this morning. My contact called me."

"How do you have contacts and I don't?"

"I'm your most viable one, so you don't need to worry your hungover self about that. Worry about the fact that you've looked better on most occasions."

Jasmine picked up the smell of wine and saw the almost empty bottle on the floor. She sighed, thankful that Sharin suggested that she just go directly to Christian's house in case anything was wrong. Thankfully there was nothing wrong except Christian drowning in her feelings for whatever reason she had for that day.

"Stop pointing out the obvious Jasmine. I don't need you here for that."

"Obviously, you need me here. Your stankin' ass ain't washed your ass since last night and you out here cuddling with a wine bottle. You and Evander got into it?"

At the mention of his name, Christian's eyes watered up and Jasmine inwardly cursed. Suddenly she wished that Sharin was there because she wasn't good at being sympathetic. All she knew was tough love and at the same time, in her position, she'd want somebody to pamper her feelings if her and any partner she had got into it.

However, that wasn't her mission statement so Plan B it was.

"Look, wipe your eyes and cut that crying out. You and he fought and y'all will work it out. We have business to attend to, Red."

Christian smirked at Jasmine's tone but wiped her face anyway. The thought that she pushed away the best thing to ever happen to her in a long time was still crashing down on her. It felt as if it were happening over and over again and it only happened once.

"I know it's just…you ever pushed away the best thing to happen to you?"

Jasmine sighed, "The best thing to ever happen to me hasn't happened yet. So far my firm is the best thing and it hasn't betrayed me yet. So, I'm good."

Christian rolled her eyes at Jasmine. Jasmine giggled and shrugged her shoulders.

"Obviously something's tearing you up so go wash up and I'll cook and you can talk to me about it."

"But…"

"In case you wanted to understand why I came over here, for context? Again, Chastity McCain turned herself in this morning. There's a huge chance the news will want to get some sound bytes of your opinion on it. So, in the mix of me visiting the office to figure out if you were down, Monica tells me you're not in. We tried to reach you, so somebody had to make sure you were okay in the mix of this."

"How could I not be okay?"

"One of your employees got folded up and you're really questioning me?" Jasmine said, "Like I said, freshen up Red, before I change my mind."

Christian rolled her eyes dramatically and then took her leave. She smirked as Jasmine's grumbling reached her ears as she trailed up the stairs. Jasmine was rough around the edges but she was full of love. Her brand of tough love was what she needed to get out of her funk.

When she returned from her shower about an hour later, Christian was greeted with a heavy breakfast consisting of grits, eggs, bacon, and pancakes. Jasmine had been on the phone with Sharin, relaying how they would handle any reporters that might approach Adams'. She's been wrapping up the call when Christian settled down at the bar facing her kitchen.

"I'll hit you later when I figure out what's wrong with Boss Lady."

A moment later the phone call was a thing of the past and Jasmine turned her attention to Christian, who had already begun eating.

"Alright, so what's wrong with you?"

Christian groaned as she took the first bite of egg. She ignored Jasmine's question and continued to eat. Jasmine sucked her teeth and began following up on her other projects on the phone. Thirty minutes later, Christian finished her food.

"Thanks. I still feel like shit."

"Well, you don't look much like shit anymore so now we can talk."

Christian eyed her friend and rolled her eyes but pressed forward nevertheless. "Before I tell you anything all of this is off record." Christian eyed her, "Most of this is sensitive information."

Jasmine nodded, though she hadn't understood until Christian regaled her of the story of her boyfriend's past. Upon hearing it the context had become clearer.

"So what does this have to do with you being out of it?" Jasmine asked.

"Me and Evander fought last night. He found out Chastity was in the mix of the and he was upset about the fact that I didn't tell him about it. I pretty much told him to go his merry way since he didn't want to see things from my point of view."

"Mhm. You know that man isn't hearing you though."

"What you mean? I told him I'm over him."

"Yeah, okay. Like he's going to let a stupid fight y'all had keep him from being with you?" Jasmine said, "I know you haven't been in a relationship in quite a while but...serious fight, little fight or other fight if a man loves you there's no keeping him away. You might have to apologize to his ass but it can't keep him away."

"I will absolutely *not* apologize to him...yet."

Jasmine barked out laughter that made Christian bristle.

"I mean...let's cut out the bullshit while we're ahead, Red. It's obvious that you're happy with him and I don't know him but the little bit I do know of him he's happy with you too. Sometimes love is pain but when it's real and when it makes you smile? You don't just drop it. You have to finally understand that he's not Jerrell."

Christian's face turned up at the mention of her ex's name, ready to defend herself but stopped short. She tossed the idea around her head a couple of times but to no avail. Perhaps the fear wasn't present, but she had to admit she was afraid of Evander turning his back on her if he figured out that she had knowledge of Chastity's involvement. So, in her typical style, Christian decided she would make the power play to shove him out the door first.

"Don't contradict me because I'm right. You've been scared ever since that another man would leave you when it's only Jerrell that's stupid."

"Not actively afraid." Christian said, "This thing with Evander though...it's different."

"Of course, it is. Y'all will figure it out." I said, "For now, you have a pretty little lawsuit that will do well for Adams' if you decide to see it through."

"Lawsuit?" Christian questioned, "Please expound."

"Chastity turned herself in as the conspirator of the whole thing. Long story short you're able to sue her and her family for damages against the company."

"That's good news. I like that!"

Christian began to get excited. She wanted to sue for the exact amount that she had to pay Evander's company back and that would put her ahead again. The only concern that she had was that she was certain that Chastity wouldn't stay in police custody very long. She already knew that her stepfather was in the background, pulling strings to get her released, more than likely on the strength of her mother. It would prove very hard for a lawsuit to stick to the McCain family.

Christian relayed these concerns to Jasmine who waved them all off.

"She's not getting out. I don't know what happened, but she's stuck in there." Jasmine said, "My contact told me nobody has been to visit or anything. He found it odd because usually rich families always make an appearance to avoid embarrassment. She probably fouled out bad with stepdad. Besides that, the bail is too high."

Christian wondered. She remembered Sharin detailing the last dinner they had. Chastity did say some untoward things about both of their male parental figures. It couldn't have been a savory moment to hear your stepdaughter all but spit in your face in front of the rest of the family.

"It might be the case." Christian shrugged, "I'll explore it. If we get that money back, I can start expansion again."

"Good." Jasmine said, "I'm not that kind of lawyer but I can poke around and see who I find."

Christian knew Jasmine already had someone in mind before she bought up the possibility of a suit. One thing Jasmine Brown never did was half step. Still, she wasn't in the mind state to fully talk about the lawsuit, that was for sure.

"So, what's the move, Christian? You heading in today or staying home?"

Christian sighed, "I think I'll stay home. I want the staff to decline comment on Chastity's arrest. Adams' wants nothing more to do with that sideshow."

"So noted. I just wanted you prepared just in case. Now that that's out of the way. You shopped for this party?"

Christian rolled her eyes, "I did but I don't feel like going. As it is I'm going to have to show my face just to direct the staff on the next move if the press starts to show up again."

"I've already told Monica to take a no comment approach for the interim." Jasmine said, "I wanted to know if you wanted to add your two cents for a little razzle dazzle, but it isn't necessary. I was thinking your face on television after the case was closed might put you back on people's minds but in a better light."

Christian nodded.

"Let's go over some things for you to say just in case." Jasmine said,

They worked on her statements for the rest of the morning, still, Evander sat in the back of her mind. She was still on the fence about reaching out to him. Though she understood his upset, she was still adamant about her stand as a citizen and even more as a businesswoman. She knew inwardly that as much as it would pain to her to never speak to him again, she'd give him up on the basis of integrity. It was very possible that he hadn't left that life behind.

"Cousin."

Sharin walked up to the cell Chastity was currently sitting in, with tears running down her face. She'd been able to control them since the news broke about her arrest. It was one thing to have an inkling but once again, her cousin disappointed her. Sharin supposed she should have been used to it but this particular move on her part was the icing on the cake.

"What, Chastity?"

"Bail me out." She said, "Please. I can't stay in here."

Sharin felt her arms cross as she eyed Chastity, wondering why she was shaking like a leaf.

"Chastity. Do you really think I'm going to put up a hundred thousand dollars to bail you out? For what? You to skip town and leave me in debt? Are you crazy?"

Chastity's eyes started tearing up at her cousin's denial.

"Look. I know we haven't gotten along over the years, but I love you, cous. I don't hate you. I can't even explain why I did what I did."

Sharin's eyes leaked faster at the desperate admission. She shook her head, stepping back two paces from Chastity's cell. She wiped her face.

"Chastity. If you love me, you have a funny way of showing it. Why do all of this? Why steal from this man and pin it on us? What sense did that make?"

Suddenly Chastity was glaring at her again. The same woman she knew came back to life and the desperate version of her disappeared. Sharin was glad she hadn't bought into the hype of the past few seconds, as tempting as it would have been to believe in it.

"I did what I had to do. You needed to be knocked down off your high horse and Mr. King already knows why I hit his pockets. The sire couldn't be reached as he's dead so unfortunately the sins of the father fell on his shoulders."

Sharin's eyes furrowed at the random testimony she'd heard from Chastity's lips.

"*Sins of the father*?" she thought. Sharin repeated her thoughts out loud before it hit her. "Buddy...was your father?"

"Ding, ding, ding," Chastity said. "You're not so stupid after all. Now get me out."

Sharin stared in her cousin's eyes and wondered why it was, after all this time that she could never be humble for a moment in her life. During childhood, she believed whatever Sharin had to be hers. During their teenage years the same belief rang as true. Chastity felt as if her mother was the judge, and she was the juror. Sharin decided in this case it would be she that would be the executioner. There was no way after all the trauma she caused-not to mention her friend-that she would give Chastity one cent towards bail.

"Get you out? What made you even turn yourself in?"

"Big brother found me out," Chastity rolled her eyes. "Look, are you going to help me or not? I don't have time to have long drawn-out conversations with you about any of this. What's your next move?"

Sharin looked upon her cousin, still surprised that she would always find the audacity to utter inane things. If she had any compassion in her heart for her cousin at all, it was quickly diminished by every sin of hers, past and present. If she got any help, she knew it wouldn't be from her. It was also common knowledge that William and Mila weren't coming to the rescue.

Sharin Reynolds turned her back on her cousin for what she knew would be the last time.

Christian decided days later to stay at home and work her hours instead of heading into the office. She realized her exhaustion had more to do with mitigating the ins and outs of the scandal and now that things were calming down, she needed a well-deserved break.   She would take a full one in the days to come but the thought of picking out an outfit, plus doing her hair and makeup made her more tired. The interactions with people she normally didn't mind started to make her tired. She thought it best to take a day or two and work from home. Adams' wouldn't fall in two days and being in the comfort of her home was much more attractive.

Netflix and order in had called her name so episodes of NCIS played in the background. Once she ordered her food, she decided to call Christopher and let him know she wouldn't be making his engagement party later that night. He graciously told her he understood her plight and still thanked her for her involvement for covering Jamie's hospital bill.

Since Samuel covered her bills, the money that Christian and the others put in was given back but Christopher still acknowledged their kindness. Being that he was a huge part of Adams', Christian couldn't imagine not helping him in his time of need.

The two talked back and forth about the plans Jamie had for her return and Christopher had gone silent.

"I take it that means she won't be coming back," Christian said. "I understand."

"Yeah. She told me she wanted to take a break. She's supposed to move in with Samuel. I have a feeling she might not get back into accounting but it's her life, you know?"

"If it works for her. I just wanted to tell you from my heart Christopher, I'm sorry for all that's happened. If I had been thinking more clearly..."

"Nah, Christian. I appreciate your apology, but Chastity was going to get at her one way or the other. That's how she is. If you would have waited, she would have waited. Either way it would've been the same. I'm just grateful she's alive and she'll be around to figure out what she wants to do. I think homeboy trying to marry her soon...I'm okay with it."

"I'm shocked to hear you say that."

"Well...she's grown, now. Been grown for a while. I'm ready to get married and start my own family. Jamie will always be my baby but...it's time."

Christian agreed with him. She thought of Tiffany who had given her resignation notice. They came to an agreement that she would stay until she onboarded the next secretary. So far there wasn't a new lady yet but the job notice had been put out so there was no doubt that someone would take Tiffany's place soon. On one end, Christian was saddened since Tiffany had been her first and only secretary. On the other end, she was glad to see her go. Once Jasmine stepped in and opened her eyes to her unprofessionalism, Tiffany had been less agreeable to work with. It hadn't been in her heart to fire her, but it was clear that being with Christopher was becoming more paramount than working her job. It just saddened her that both of those things couldn't be important.

Still, she wished her well in her next chapter. Sometimes your new blessings couldn't come until others walked out of your life.

"I'm grateful for your loyalty, Christopher." Christian said, "It's been a ride but I'm grateful you're still here."

"You gave me a shot and I knew I couldn't blow it. So it goes without saying. I'm down with you until the end. Don't miss my wedding, though."

Christian laughed and assured him that she wouldn't. The two ended the conversation on that note and she felt her heart get a little lighter.

Evander clouded her thoughts as she worked. She sighed, remembering the hurt she read in his eyes as they argued back and forth. It bothered her although the hill she stood on she was prepared to die on it. She couldn't have been too sure about his plans and the fact was all he'd spoken on was getting even. There had been little to no leeway on his end so what should she had done?

She'd never been raised in the streets and the first time she met him as *Vill* was her closest encounter. That one time event was something both she and Sharin silently agreed they would never repeat. It was obvious that world wasn't for them and going against their parents wishes wasn't something they wanted to test the waters on time and again just for a thrill or two.

However, she realized that she hadn't even given him the benefit of the doubt. Had he not revealed that part of his life to her, she would have told him about Chastity's involvement without question. It was obvious that was the part that hurt. It was the part she wanted to apologize to him for.

They hadn't spoken in about a week's time after that and wondered if they ever would again. She unceremoniously kicked him out of her house and both parties knew that wasn't a moment to be taken lightly. At the very least she hadn't.

The sun had started to go down hours later and Christian had moved on to watching Bridgerton. She binged the next few episodes, content in her loungewear and more takeout. She started to think to herself what wine she would pair with the pasta dish she purchased from Pappadeux's and got sad again. Their first unofficial date crept in as a sweet memory, causing her eyes to well up with tears.

Christian reached over to her console table and picked up her phone, flipping up the home screen and going through the motions to find Evander's number in her favorites. Her finger hovered over his name but she couldn't bring herself to call. Sighing she tossed the phone down and wiped her tears away. Settling in, she decided to focus on watching the rest of Bridgerton. Her heart ached more as the Duke and Duchess seemed to be fighting over the same issues she and her beloved were.

Deciding to just wash up and tend to herself, she exited Netflix and turned off her TV set. Christian made to walk away from the living room when her phone rang. Noticing it was Evander's ringtone she turned around and watched as a picture of his smirking face looked back at her, forcing her to suck her teeth. She picked up against the rising annoyance in her chest.

"Come outside."

The command was delivered before she could even say hello. That had annoyed her more and in response she sucked her teeth again. Evander's chuckle was dry, lacking amusement.

"Christian, so help me, I'll walk in that motherfucka and drag you out myself."

She sucked her teeth once more and hung up the phone. Deciding not to test him however, she walked over to her closet, grabbed her jacket and keys. She took the elevator down, wondering what it was that Evander wanted to talk about. She started to get anxious but decided not to dwell in fear. She'd been through worse in her life than the born again CEO and she would survive him too if he wanted to leave well enough alone.

She walked past the concierge and the doorman, greeting both politely on the way out of the building. Once outside, she caught sight of Evander parked across the street, leaning against his car. The sight of him made Christian's heart ache again. Overcome by the emotion, she stood rooted in her spot, feeling as if she should turn around and act as if she'd never seen him.

The time seemed to have stood still as she took him in as if it'd weeks instead of days. A thousand apologies came alive and died in her mind. Each one didn't seem good enough.

Evander took in his woman from across the street and sighed, wondering how strength and vulnerability could both become her. He wondered about her very complexities and marveled that none of it mattered to him. Christian Adams was a handful but he loved her. He wondered just how much he loved her.

That much was crossing his mind over and over again as he crossed the street, seeing as how Christian wouldn't move from her station in front of the hotel. He found himself grinning, even as he saw the contriteness in her eyes. His heart melted when he saw the tears gathering in the corners of them.

When he reached her, he stopped short a couple of inches and took her in. He watched as she did the same to him.

"Baby," he said, opening his arms. "Come here."

Quietly she closed the distance between them and gave a watery sigh as he closed his arms around her. She had no clue how long they stood in front of the doors of her building but found it amazing the way her world righted itself again.

"I don't deserve you."

Christian hadn't known she said that much until Evander started chuckling. He pulled back to look down at her and reached up, wiping away the lone tear that escaped her right eye with his corresponding thumb. He leaned in and kissed her lips softly. Pulling back, he sighed.

"I wouldn't go that far. This wasn't something that couldn't be easily fixed with a couple rounds of makeup sex and some good cooking. Possibly a foot rub."

"I'll never mess up enough to have to touch your feet," Christian laughed, despite herself.

"So you forgot about kicking me out of your house the other night like I wasn't shit?"

Christian's face fell again. She looked up into Evander's eyes and reached up to touch his hand that still laid on her cheek.

"Well, that's because I wasn't shit. So let me apologize."

"I'm listening."

Christian sucked her teeth softly.

"You trusted me enough to show me your life and I used it against you. It's true that I stand on the integrity of my business but I didn't have to move the way I had. My fear was that you hadn't changed and I'm sorry that I let it dictate how I handled things. I'm sorry that I hurt you. I should've just asked you not to go after her. I didn't want you to leave me so I kicked you out. Please forgive me."

Evander sighed, deeply. It made Christian nervous until he leaned in so close that their foreheads touched. His left hand that'd been on her waist pulled her in closer until there was no detectable space betwixt them. He shuddered lightly at their contact and sighed again.

"Christian...I fell in love with you when I saw you. I don't think you knew that. I don't even think I knew it completely but you fell right into my life and disappeared just as quick. You ran from me."

"I had to. My father would've killed us both."

"He would've been right to. I wasn't ready for you." Evander pulled away again, but only enough to look into her eyes. "I never wanted the life my father chose for me. He loved the streets. Until he died they'd been good to him, even when he was still in jail. I respected my old man but I wasn't into the stuff he was into. I was always about education and running my business. I always wanted to get right and meet somebody worth it. I got right and coincidentally, I met you again. The second time was almost as good as the first."

"Almost?"

"You were nicer to me the first time, baby. Let's not mince words here."

"You were also nicer to me the first time, *baby*."

"Suffice it to say, I admired you. I fell in love with you again because you're everything I've ever wanted and more. Even the less desirable parts of you I'm here for. So don't ever feel like you need to hide from me. Even if I get angry Christian, I want you. Over and over again."

Christian tried to blink away more tears but they fell. Evander wiped them up as they did. Leaning in, he kissed her again.

"What I'm saying, baby, is you can trust me. I know how much you love your business. I know how much love you have for everybody that's a part of it. I'd almost be confident enough to say I know you...and I'm sorry I didn't say that before. Maybe you wouldn't have been defensive in the first place."

"Maybe." Christian sighed, "Maybe just a little bit."

"Anyway, I accept your apology. I still demand copious amounts of makeup sex and good cooking."

"I actually have some Pappadeux on the way..." Christian said. "So we can share that."

"You would try to slither out of an apology with take out."

"I was in the middle of being sad so Pap it was. Take it or leave it."

Evander loosened his grip on her but kept his arm around her waist as they finally moved from their position in front of the doors. It hadn't hit them how many people witnessed their embrace for the past few minutes. After both of them quietly thought about the fact that they'd made a spectacle, they decided they didn't care much.

"I guess I have to take you home and take what I can get. I like how my woman does me wrong and picks and chooses how she'll make it up to me."

Christian laughed as she watched the delivery boy pull up. She waved him down as she saw the tell-tale bag that held her dinner inside. Evander tipped him and told him to keep the bag. Confused, the delivery man gave his thanks and rushed back to his car before Evander could change his mind. Christian looked up at him with an angry face.

"How you send the man away with *my* dinner?"

"Because we gonna head out and get dinner. Unless you want your half cold food back, Ms. Adams?"

Christian didn't contradict him as they walked to his car. He opened the door and waited for her to slide in before jogging to the other side.

Christian looked at Evander as he reached to turn on the ignition and stilled his hand. He looked up at her in silent question. The readiness in his eyes made her want to cry again. How could she have gotten it so wrong?

"Evander…I love you."

"I love you too, Christian. Let's move on."

She smiled softly and watched as he turned on the ignition. Years ago, she waited for the day when her life was her own. Suddenly she wished for nothing more than to share it with the man she rode shotgun with.

Christian Adams sighed contentedly as she felt her man reach from his side, pick up her hand and intertwine them with his own.

Chastity McCain was in jail. Christopher's niece would recover and move on with her life. She'd go through some punishing days, but she'd recover. Her closest friend would marry and walk into a new chapter of her life. More importantly, she was finally free of the evil that was her cousin. Her business was showing signs of a comeback and the hope that came from that was almost overwhelming. Lastly, she finally came into the fullness of knowing that her partner was in it for the long haul. It amazed her how life twisted and turned and at times bought good even when evil threatened to destroy her.

Smiling softly, she felt the weight lift off her shoulders. Evander suggested they move on and it bought her joy. The all-encompassing joy that they'd be doing so, together.